Malatesta
d. 1437

Ridolfo M. *Francesca*
b. 1430 *di Castel*
d. 1501 *San Pietro*

Carlo

Adriano
(Morgante)
d. 1502

Gismondo
d. 1500

Marcantonio
d. 1500

Troilo
d. 1526

GIANPAOLO
b. 1471
d. 1520
M. Ippolita
da Conti

Simonetto
d. 1500

Panthasilea
M. *Bartolomeo*
d'Alviano

Oddo
d. 1478

Malatesta
b. 1491, d. 1531
M. Maddalena
dei Monaldeschi

Orazio
b. 1494, d. 1528
M. *Francesca Petrucci*

Carlo
d. 1518

THE
MERCENARY

THE
MERCENARY

THE FORTUNES OF
GIANPAOLO BAGLIONI
OF PERUGIA

CHARLES DURBIN

HOUGHTON MIFFLIN COMPANY · BOSTON

The Riverside Press Cambridge

1963

TO MY WIFE

I should like to take this means of expressing appreciation and acknowledging the unstinted cooperation which I received from Mrs. Joyce Hartman, New York Editor of Houghton Mifflin Company.

CONTENTS

BOOK I

THE GREAT WEDDING MASSACRE
1500

BOOK II

THE HOUSE OF BORGIA
1500–1503

BOOK III

THE HOUSE OF DELLA ROVERE
1503–1513

BOOK IV

THE HOUSE OF MEDICI
1513–1520

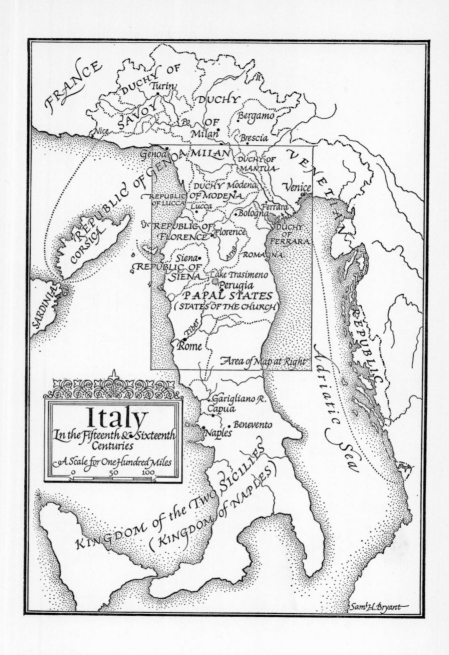

FRANCE

DUCHY OF SAVOY
Turin

DUCHY OF MILAN
Nice
Po
Milan
Bergamo
Brescia

Genoa
MILAN
DUCHY OF MANTUA

REPUBLIC OF GENOA

DUCHY OF MODENA
Modena
REPUBLIC OF LUCCA
Lucca
Venice
VENETIAN

CORSICA
REPUBLIC OF FLORENCE
Florence
Ferrara
Bologna
DUCHY OF FERRARA

SARDINIA
Siena
REPUBLIC OF SIENA
Arno
ROMAGNA

Lake Trasimeno
Perugia
PAPAL STATES
(STATES OF THE CHURCH)
REPUBLIC

Tiber
Rome

Area of Map at Right

Adriatic Sea

Italy
In the Fifteenth & Sixteenth Centuries
A Scale for One Hundred Miles
0   50   100

Garigliano R.
Capua
Benevento
Naples

KINGDOM of the TWO SICILIES
(KINGDOM of NAPLES)

Sam¹ H. Bryant

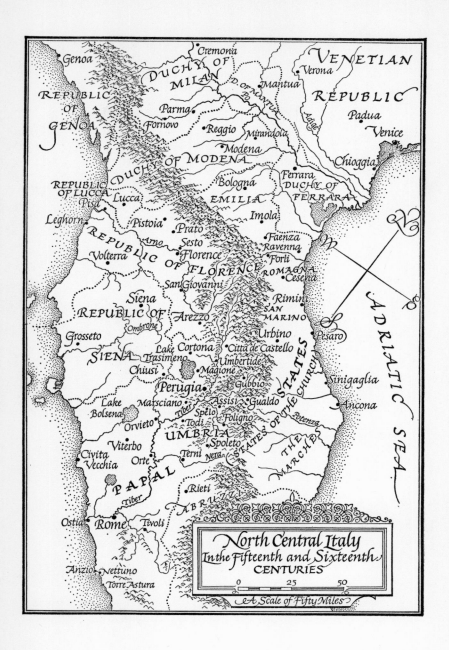

North Central Italy
In the Fifteenth and Sixteenth
CENTURIES

0 · 25 · 50

A Scale of Fifty Miles

BOOK I

THE GREAT WEDDING MASSACRE

1500

1.

THE FLY

GIVE a condemned prisoner writing materials and it is certain that he will use them. The silent cell encourages such activity. There is leisure in which to reflect. The shadow of death rouses a creative ferment — a false one, no doubt, as patients look healthiest just before they expire. But men are limited by what they have been in life, and the Angel of Death is no miracle worker. Some condemned men will compose prayers, some appeals, sonnets, protests or jokes. The literary-minded may attempt to write their memoirs. Impending annihilation often pushes the most unlikely individuals into a confused writing orgy. They deck their drabness in the color of their unique predicament, as witness the thief who once told me: "It is my distinction in life that I am being hanged." And so, by such illogical levers, they achieve a self-esteem adequate to consummate a literary labor of sorts. Even a fly will abandon itself to a flurried instant of divine frenzy before the mystery of approaching death. The fly is writing its memoirs.

Since my arrest on March 12, 1520, I too have become a fly of letters. The task has helped to pass the time satisfactorily, for there is a certain pleasure in the discipline, if one is so inclined. It is not a duty, but the deed invests one's departure from this world with a new and pleasing texture. One has performed an act of purposeful punctuation. One has sounded a fanfare on silver trumpets while all the world lies snoring at dawn.

I am trying to tell about myself without gloss or concealment — a somewhat difficult feat. We insensibly avoid those episodes which reflect no credit on ourselves. Our intentions are good, but our memories are tactful and fail us at convenient moments. Then, there are some men who reverse the error and overzealously charge themselves with sins and crimes of which they are innocent, like those strange old women who admit to witchcraft when they are merely mad.

I have passed lightly over many details of my early life, for I do not know when Count Annibale Rangone will come knocking at my door and call me to die. It is only right that the important facts should be given priority. If I have additional time, I shall tell you about my childhood. As it is — I am writing against an uncertain schedule. Which invites a reflection: the condemned state might be a useful device for training poets. Men writing in the headsman's shadow will avoid flourishes and strive for that precision of thought which is the essence of good poetry.

My life has been bisected by the edge of the Great Wedding Massacre, which occurred twenty years ago in July of 1500. I was then twenty-nine years of age, and prior to that event my pattern of living was the ordinary one for a man of my birth and circumstances. The bloodshed of that summer wrenched me from my accustomed channels and flung me into a turbulent river of great affairs.

I am thinking back for a moment to another year, that of 1492, when I was twenty-one and had been Ippolita da Conti's husband for eight months. Our family was still fighting the House of Oddi in those days, as we had been doing intermittently since '88. In that summer twenty-eight years ago, Italy was already unwholesome and the juice of trouble to come oozed out everywhere as from rotten fruit. The land swarmed with my ambitious fellow condottieri, with sullen peasants, contentious scholars, avaricious merchants, doubting priests and puffed-up princes. The princes bickered, played, snarled, smiled and battled one another by means of our services. It is true that we condottieri, more often than not, laughed at our employers and mutually agreed to leave well enough alone. We have been severely condemned for it but there was some justification on our side and I shall discuss these matters presently.

Who shall say whether Holy Mother Church ripened or rotted in that year — but she did so with a sedate majesty under a new pastor, who had been Cardinal Roderigo Borgia and who took the name of Pope Alexander VI. During the same year, Lorenzo de' Medici, that magnificent prince, closed his eyes and expired, I truly believe with a sigh of profound relief, for many troubles broke over Italy in the years which followed his death and many accounts were settled.

As to the significance of my life and the worth of the things I did or omitted to do, I cannot judge. Those who come after me will evaluate it, if they are interested. In the final analysis, I view myself as an unimportant man. If there is some God above us, I shall address myself to Him directly, without intercession of Mother Church and the pope.

It has been said that God's all-embracing vision ranges from Earth to Infinity, that He has the inclination and the ability to observe all living things at any instant of time. It is conceivable that His eyes have at some time brushed over the land-mass of Italy, narrowed on the province of Umbria, squinted at our city of Perugia and finally mused on myself and taken note of me. The priests tell me that God has encompassed my life and is aware of me, that no man is unimportant and wholly unacceptable. Be that as it may, I have set down the facts for men to read. God maintains his own records and has no need of mine.

Let me say here that I am Gianpaolo Baglioni, who until this time of arrest and imprisonment in the Castle of Sant' Angelo by Pope Leo X, was master of Perugia. My father was Ridolfo Baglioni and my mother was Madonna Francesca, the daughter of Simonetto, Count of Castel San Pietro. I am also the nephew of Braccio, who was in his time the greatest man of our House. If my life has been pointless — but what man can appraise himself accurately? It has been a strenuous life, but let the chroniclers read meaning into movement. What, if anything, they will say I have no idea, and I have been too busy keeping afloat to court their attentions. The only man of letters I have known with any intimacy is Niccolò Machiavelli, whom I last saw seven years ago. Should he write something about me, I suspect it will not be complimentary. But if he does so I will not hold it against him.

I am a citizen of Perugia and have been a professional soldier all my life. I have always been among those who sat at the chessboard and moved the pieces. I have been a piece as well as a player and the roles are more interchangeable than we realize. I was born in 1471 and it is a foregone conclusion that I shall die here in Sant' Angelo in my forty-ninth year, by order of the pope who was once Giovanni de' Medici and the friend of our House.

I have served the principal states of Italy in my time, and the popes Alexander VI and Julius II, who preceded this present Holy Father. My tenure of life and fortune has always been precarious, whether from the enemy of the moment, from my employers or from my own kinsmen. I have managed to outlive the sagacious Alexander, that pope's formidable son Cesare Borgia, and that violent old man, Julius II. I have fallen finally into the trap of Pope Leo X, a mild and pleasure-loving man, the prince least likely to have snared me.

I leave behind me two lawful sons, Malatesta and Orazio, to

continue the rule of our House if they can. I hope and believe that they will kill my cousin, Gentile, who betrayed me to Pope Leo.

Perhaps I was born too late, or have lived too long, but the times are out of joint with me. Let me tell you something about our family. The Baglioni have been intertwined with the fortunes of the city of Perugia for generations. Our enemies say that we have plagued, oppressed and subverted the republican institutions of Perugia. This is substantially true, although we also made Perugia a considerable factor in Italian politics. Our family has always had its share of dedicated enemies — an inevitability, when you consider our readiness to encroach on others. Our men have always held abrasively resolute views and have not hesitated to put them into practice. We have had also our unfortunate weaknesses. Whenever external enemies failed, we invariably obliged by killing one another. There was seldom a season when we were not at war. On those rare occasions when the country was at peace, we usually turned and bit ourselves.

There are legends in our family that one of our ancestors officered troops under the Emperor Gratianus. I doubt it and will not press the point — nor that other legend that one of our forefathers came down into Italy with Charlemagne. Had Charlemagne brought down as many noble ancestors as my princely contemporaries claim, there would have been no room on the peninsula for the enemy. The records do attest that an Oddo Baglioni received the guardianship of Perugia from Frederick Barbarossa more than three hundred years ago. Perhaps this is so — although the monks of those days were notoriously untidy recorders.

Although I might like to do so, I have little time to lead you by the hand through the tangled forests of Perugia's history. There is no purpose in traversing these murky places. I gather from my own reading that those decades staggered along in the

usual stormy succession of warfare and hatreds, interspersed
with infrequent high points of honor and devotion arising from
absurdly trivial — or fanatical — considerations. But it was
nonetheless politics — though one man's politics may be another's idiocies. Politics has always been a serious business with
us — the only one. The Baglioni were endlessly committed in
these struggles, now on one side, now on the other, as our real or
fancied family advantage dictated. Ours was the enterprise of
energetic, not overly intelligent children. In truth, I see no improvement in the present prospect. In addition to fighting with
our neighbors, we undertook condottas for various states and
embassies for the Perugian Commune, and we officiated as podes-
tàs in foreign cities. Perugia, like every other commune, suspected its nobles and refused to entrust them with internal offi-
ces. There was justification for this. Nobles are good for fighting. Beyond that they are as incompetent as they are arrogant,
and the old Florentines wrought well in condemning nobility
within their borders.

In Perugia, our struggles with our neighbors were tedious and
endless. The victors drove the vanquished into exile. The
exiles nursed their grudges, gathered their strength, regained
power and the cycle repeated itself. More recently, less than
two hundred years ago, my ancestor Pandolfo was expelled from
Perugia after a long struggle with the Michelotti family, and his
followers were exterminated. My grandfather, Malatesta, was
an exile and a condottiero under Braccio Fortebracci da Montone, who was a captain of considerable ability before he went
mad and had himself slain at the Siege of Aquila. It was only
one hundred and four years ago that Fortebracci and my grandfather defeated the party of the Raspanti and finally regained
Perugia after a tiresome exile.

It was under my clever uncle, Braccio, that the Baglioni really
came to prominence. Like all the men of our House, Braccio

was tall, strong and of pleasing features. For a change, he was highly intelligent. He had no right to rule Perugia but he did so nevertheless. Braccio was also captain-general of the papal army and he utilized his position to deflect the covetous popes from Perugia. Yet even he was unable to satisfy everyone. There were enough zealous republicans in our city who agitated for even more independence from the popes. Braccio could not accomplish everything, but he managed to remain a crafty buffer between greedy pontiffs and fanatical republican patriots. He kept the rival nobles of Perugia in check and dug the first grave for the aspiring House of Oddi, which we have finally destroyed. He led Perugia out of her untidy past into the dubious amenities of this modern and enlightened age.

When Braccio died forty-one years ago, his brothers — my uncle Guido and my father Ridolfo — assumed the joint rulership of Perugia. I was eight years old at that time. There was no one, of course, who conceded our legal right to rule Perugia. The city's constitution never made formal acknowledgment of any hereditary or princely authority on our part. We have always been *de facto* rulers and Umbria is filled with candidates waiting patiently to improve on our performance. The foremost among these claimants have always been the pontiffs in Rome. They insist that they derive their perennial candidacy from a succession of shadowy emperors, from God the Father, no less. It is a majestic precedent which the popes cite, but as you doubtless know, the weightier the argument, the higher Italians tend to raise their eyebrows.

There you have it, and now I shall begin by telling you about the Great Wedding Massacre (or the Great Betrayal, as it has come to be known), which marked a break with this past history. The affair caught Italy's attention for a while. It provided our friends and enemies alike with an abundance of after-dinner conversation, and it almost destroyed the House of Baglioni.

From that time forward, our family fell under the thoughtful and malignant eye of Fortune. To the superstitious, we were accursed. We were cut out, fixed in the fierce light of some heavenly hunter, and never again permitted to melt into the comfortable anonymity of the pack.

2.

THE WEDDING FEAST

THE GREAT BETRAYAL occurred during the wedding of my cousin, Astorre, to Lavinia Colonna Orsini. I recall how my wife, Ippolita, and I escorted some of the foreign envoys through our sunny palace gardens during the festivities. Ippolita pointed out the greenhouses with pride, saying, "I had them built three years ago to house my oriental shrubs and to protect them against the dreary Perugian winter. I have rare plants here which were brought to me by Venetian shipmasters from as far away as Constantinople."

Lovers tend to be as elusive as wild goats, but we finally found Astorre and Lavinia escaping from the world and the July heat on the far side of a miniature lake. Ippolita had laid out this lake to her own designs to give herself the illusion that she was in the Conti gardens in Rome. Although we had been married eight years she saw herself inwardly as an exile, and this was but one manifestation of her great discontent.

The Venetian envoy, being senior among the guests, took precedence and kissed Lavinia's hand ceremoniously. Then he complimented Astorre most fulsomely, saying: "I scarcely recognized you without armor."

With these words he presented to Astorre a massive golden chain with a pendant jeweled seal bearing the likeness of the

Lion of Saint Mark, adding that the Most Serene Republic most lovingly felicitated her distinguished captain on his wedding day.

After more compliments, we parted from the bridal pair and strolled back to the palace. When the Venetian observed that it would be a good marriage for the Baglioni, I pointed out that it would benefit the Orsini also, to which, in the subtle way Venetians have of minimizing the state of others, he replied, "All marriages are good when they are carefully negotiated. With Cesare Borgia stirring such a dust cloud and the future so uncertain, you Baglioni are wise in strengthening your hand."

I interpreted his fine-spun attitude of deprecation as a defense of the chronically successful against the aspirations of lesser men and reminded myself that his primary business at the wedding was to impede Borgian plans wherever possible.

We showed Lavinia's dowry to the envoys, a fine display of teak and rosewood chests standing open on marble tables and brimming over with jewels and gold coin. The Venetian and the Florentine were unimpressed, which was to be expected as they were richer than everyone else, but they had the tact to admire what they saw. When my younger brother, Simonetto, entered the room the guests made much of him, particularly the Venetian with his great skill in turning compliments. "All Venice has heard how you welcomed the Oddi home in '95," he said. "You are young for such a weighty reputation."

Simonetto's scar-battered face cracked into a smile. "Without the help of Astorre and Gianpaolo, I would have been carrion seven times over," he replied.

Simonetto's speech was marred by two missing front teeth which the Oddi had knocked out of his close-cropped soldier's head. In spite of his eighteen years, his muscular body was inured to angry blows. He stood with smiling lips but restless eyes, impatient to get away.

I finally excused Simonetto, explaining that he was involved in arrangements for the guild banquets. "He has just had the Great Piazza decorated with hangings," I said. "The floral decorations along the processional route, the triumphal arches, the tableaux and the pageants — all of these are the work of my younger brother." The guests acknowledged that Simonetto was indeed versatile. "Even my wife, who considers us nothing more than uncultivated soldiers, admits that Simonetto would have made a good artist. He paid from his own purse to repaint and landscape the façades of even the poorest homes."

"Simonetto has a feeling for design and color," said Ippolita with that patrician omniscience which lay like a worm between us, "but his artistic talent is an unknown quantity. We Romans have exacting criteria in such matters, of which the provinces are innocent."

While I was savoring my irritation, a page entered to announce that they were awaiting us to begin the banquet. We were seated at the bridal table among the notables and the feasting began. This banquet was the end result of months of effort during which the servingmen labored cleansing the dusty rubbish of years. It took place out-of-doors in the fine weather, but the palace, under Simonetto's direction, had also been renovated. Tapestries were dragged down from the tower storerooms and hung to conceal the stark and stony walls. In the weeks before, a procession of cattle had been driven into the city to be slaughtered and dressed by butchers in the palace kitchens and courtyards. The fowlers came with wagonloads of game birds, and there were special cooks to dress the peacocks. They did not shame us, nor did the fish-cooks, whose offerings appeared on great golden platters so cunningly dressed that all present applauded. And when the peacocks were borne in, silly-eyed, triumphant and looking very much alive, the applause broke forth anew and my uncle, Guido, the bridegroom's father, was much gratified.

Lavinia looked correctly radiant in a gown of dark green watered silk with wide sleeves of a lighter green satin. She wore several ropes of choice Persian pearls and on her black hair a golden cap set with rubies. The banquet ended with heavy Sicilian wines, confections and cakes in the shapes of temples, animals and Grecian statues and, finally, heavily perfumed sweetmeats.

Now Guido rose, holding high a wine-filled crystal goblet. "It is our custom," he said, "to remember sinners and malefactors in a time of great joy. In honor of my son's wedding, I declare an amnesty. I pardon all prisoners in the keeps of Perugia save those charged with murder. Let the prisoners be unchained!"

There was further applause.

It was well that no one questioned the absence of my father, Ridolfo, from the wedding. He was gravely ill of the mal francese, that royal and sacred disease which is named after five saints and hell-fire also, and he would have made poor company at an outdoor summer wedding. I shall have more to say regarding this formidable malady which resisted the best efforts of the physician, Nicolò Leoniceno, who came from Padua to treat my father with the latest remedies, including guaiacum wood. He held with the virtues of the diaphoretic regime, saying that when the patient perspired the corruption would depart from the body together with the sweat, and for my father he ordered mercurial friction, inunction, purgation and bleeding. But I fear that Messer Leoniceno was a better compiler of medical curiosa than a physician. My father did not improve and excused himself from attending his nephew's wedding, saying that he had no desire to appear as a churlish specter at the feast, that he did not hold with the custom of thrusting coffins and morals into the midst of joyous occasions.

My crack cavalry squadrons paraded before the guests between courses. They trotted by with their lances at rest, wearing the blue and gold of the House of Baglioni, some blazoned with the Perugian griffin, others with the falcon and the golden Baglioni chevron on an azure background. Then followed the companies of mounted trumpeters and drummers and still other squadrons of lancers in silver armor on Arabian horses from Astorre's own stables.

Astorre pleased the guests by rising from the table for a time to lead the parade. He sprang on a silver-saddled black charger which trailed blue-and-gold housings. The cathedral bells began to peal and the signal guns on the campanile boomed at measured intervals.

The Mantuans at table nodded grudgingly as they watched, saying that Astorre's horses were as fine as any ever seen in the Gonzaga stables — a notable admission, for the horse breeds of Francesco Gonzaga have always been the choicest in all Italy.

Our guests applauded the tableaux and the entertainments after the feast out of more than mere politeness. We were experienced hosts, accustomed to serving princes and the representatives of states and rulers. Yet, if I have spent excessive time in describing these amenities, it is not out of vainglory and to vaunt our House, but to prepare a contrast for what followed.

On that evening, Ippolita and I presented our sons to the guests. We summoned nine-year-old Malatesta and seven-year-old Orazio to the marble terrace and they bowed before the foreigners with a composure which pleased me. Some of Ippolita's Roman kinsmen, who had escorted Lavinia on her bridal journey, now complimented us on the bearing of our sons, to which Ippolita could not forbear replying: "You are courteous, signori, but this is a far cry from what I have known in my own youth. The House of Conti expected and received more from children at the ages of my sons."

The Romans replied that the House of Conti was a criterion of excellence toward which the rest of Italy could strive without achieving. Ippolita nodded her acceptance, saying her family had always been cognizant of their duty to set a sound example.

"Madam," I said with an irritation that had become habitual, "we have done well enough until now without the self-appointed standards of the House of Conti. We shall continue to strive in our own simple way with which you must bear, for you are now one of us, if you will only deign to remember it."

Ippolita smiled with the assurance of the heaven-born and said, "I defer to my husband."

"And I defer to the bridegroom," I said briskly. "Since we are in a mood to admire, let us admire Astorre Baglioni, a man of taste and so tactful and gracious that he has never been known to offend anyone knowingly. Let me recite all his virtues. My cousin is, above all, a well-rounded man. I need not speak of his soldierly attainments. He has a decent respect for learning. He has composed sonnets which have been commended by connoisseurs. He is even a collector who rejoices in a few choice though modest pieces of antique art."

"A collector of art?" smiled Ippolita. "The Riario and the Conti ——"

"We do not presume to compete with the Riario and the Conti," I said. "We are still too poor for that."

The Romans smiled with light malice and one among them would have spoken but in that instant my cousin Gismondo, the brother of Astorre, wearing black and a squarecut chin beard, joined our group. Lithe and silent as a cat, his sudden materializations were often disconcerting. He was feline in physique and temperament and could vault over a horse in full armor. He could make a running jump, turn a somersault on the ground and land upright in the saddle. He improved on the feats of the Albanian stradiotti by standing on a galloping horse while controlling two additional horses on each side. Gismondo listened to our conversation with a half-smile on his traplike lips and said little except to praise Simonetto's good management of the wedding.

Lavinia Colonna Orsini had entered Perugia a week before with a train of Roman gentlemen and servants and a treasure of gifts. My cousin, Grifonetto, welcomed her at the San Antonio Gate and escorted her to his palace, where his lions, chained in the courtyard, greeted her with welcoming roars. Perugia's five wards exerted themselves to entertain the bridal pair. In the days which followed, the competition grew warmer. The Sole Ward entertained them on the second day after her arrival, the San Susanna Ward carried them off for the third day, and thus it went. The San Susanna people were celebrated for their cunning confections and even our sophisticated Florentine guests were impressed to see what could be done with dough, gilt and spun sugar.

But there were also clouds on the horizon, and guests superstitious, perceptive or both. There were those who hunted for omens and found them. It was regarded as a sign that Lavinia was almost drowned while crossing a river on her way to Perugia. On the night following Porta Sole's reception, a savage thunderstorm battered down their arches and pavilions. The Sole people loved Astorre, and following the storm they labored swiftly to repair the damage. But this was also a dark messenger.

There was gossip for the sake of gossip. Astorre's mother, dying at Spello, became an omen, together with the fiery comets that flared over Fossato. Why had not Marcantonio, Astorre's brother, quit Naples and appeared at the wedding? It was generally known that Marcantonio was living a life of pleasant semi-invalidism at Naples. Nevertheless, his absence was given an ominous construction.

If my kinsmen noticed anything, they did not care or did not show it. My father was too ill to be concerned. He had appeared but once at a joint reception tendered by Porta San Pietro and Porta Eburnea. He was carried in a chair and came only for the pleasure of seeing Simonetto. At this feast Simonetto, in ancient Roman costume, bestrode a gilded chariot, shoveling confections from a silver cornucopia and scattering them to the people. My uncle Guido buried himself impassively in the role of official host. Astorre had eyes only for his tall Roman brunette. Gismondo stalked like a leopard, caring nothing for shadows. Simonetto said: "Better to be dead than to start at signs and ghosts." As for me, I watched and waited.

During the fourth and fifth days of the festivities came the tournaments and the first discords. On the occasion of a single combat between Girolamo della Penna of Perugia and myself, the crust of harmony cracked and a pus of hatred oozed from the secret wound. Simonetto, for all his youth, was knowledgeable in such matters and officiated as referee. We lowered our blunted lances at his signal, drove in spurs and thundered toward one another to meet in a bone-jarring shock. Girolamo was lifted from his saddle and flung to the ground. His saddle-girths broke loose; his horse reared, shook off the saddle and galloped away to the far end of the field. Two arbalasters ran into the field and raised Girolamo, dazed and unhelmed, from the dust. I swung about, lifted my visor and rode back. As I trotted up, Girolamo drew his sword and aimed a wild slash, cutting through my bridle-reins. Simonetto cantered over and struck down Girolamo's sword with his own, saying: "What have you in mind? The combat is over."

"My saddle straps were tampered with," snarled Girolamo. "I refuse to accept your decision."

"I have not given it yet," said Simonetto.

I stared down at Girolamo at that moment, not only from the height of my saddle but from the height of secure position. For what was della Penna in those days? A fire-eating upstart, a petty dissolute noble with pretensions, a rake with vaunting tastes and a flat purse.

A crowd of spectators had drifted out from the stands by this time and Girolamo cut a poor figure as he glared up from the dust.

"Make good your charge," said Simonetto.

"The horse I rode is not mine," said della Penna. "He is unused to my handling."

"To a horseman as perfect as yourself, a strange horse should make little difference," said Simonetto.

"This horse is from Gismondo's stable!" shouted della Penna. "The saddle girths were tampered with, I say. Otherwise, I'd never have been thrown."

Gismondo joined the dispute at this moment, saying, "Perhaps you should have selected a charger from your own stalls."

All present savored this jab at della Penna's well-known poverty with a scatter of uneasy laughter. Then an expectant disquiet fell upon the spectators. There was a blood feud between Gismondo and Girolamo della Penna. By this time, the dark and tangled dispute between them was two years old and the blood on it had dried to a festering crust. How it had arisen no longer matters. To criticize the childish origins of other men's quarrels is a pleasant way of flattering our own defects. Suffice it that Gismondo and della Penna had patched a truce through Cardinal Borgia on two separate occasions, though without coming to a true reconciliation. From that day forth, della Penna never slept in the same bed twice and he kept his sword within easy reach. Moreover, Gismondo had grown his beard, saying: "I shall not shave it until I have slain Girolamo della Penna." Thus the matter stood and all men in Perugia had wagers on its outcome.

Gismondo now stroked his beard. "You must not accuse me of playing jokes on you, Girolamo," he said. "I would not do so after we had been so solemnly reconciled by Holy Mother Church. If I meant to do an enemy harm, I would kill him at one time or another without practicing tailor's tricks. In the meantime, let us examine the saddle and set your suspicions at rest."

No evidence of tampering was discovered. Della Penna, conscious of his weak case, was uninterested in pressing it. He bowed impassively. "It is evident that I was wrong. I agree with Simonetto's decision in advance. Gianpaolo is the winner." With these words, dusty and forlorn, he limped off the field.

As we rode back to the barrier, Simonetto said: "I have begged my uncle and father on three distinct occasions for permission to kill that serpent. They have refused me each time."

"You must not annoy them with such trivia, for they are beyond it," said Gismondo. "Moreover, della Penna belongs to me and you must not interfere. When the time is ripe, I shall kill him and not before."

But the matter turned out quite otherwise.

3.

THE CONSPIRACY

ALTHOUGH the admirable concept of the Great Wedding Massacre originated in the minds of men older, wiser and more timid, it was Carlo Baglioni who executed it. Soldiers can best breathe life into the pleasant theories of philosophers, and Carlo was a good soldier. He was twenty-seven years old in the year 1500, a tall broad-shouldered man with a sallow complexion and a gloomy scowl, as ill-favored as Astorre was comely, not because his features were irregular, but because his soul was dark. The citizens of Perugia said of Carlo that he was an evil-liver, a man who delighted in the company of bravos as idle and dissolute as himself. Yet he was as brave as he was bitterly envious and ferociously ambitious.

Carlo Baglioni was my second cousin. He had been left fatherless and unprotected in his childhood. For this reason Guido and Ridolfo Baglioni neglected the orphaned Carlo and pushed the fortunes of their own sons, from which you may see how men raise up future evils by indulging their human weaknesses. Guido and Ridolfo never permitted Carlo Baglioni to prove his ability in governmental affairs. Such neglect compounded my cousin's resentment and gave it the color of justification. All of us ignored the brewing storm in the heart of this man, the poorest of our clan and the greatest spendthrift.

Through our common selfishness, it was I who inherited Carlo
Baglioni's enmity and he proved a tough and able enemy until
his death in Milan eighteen years later. The marvel of it is that
Carlo died in his bed. Had Carlo been my ally during these
past years in place of my cousin Gentile, I am certain I would
not be a prisoner today, awaiting execution.

We had another cousin to be reckoned with — that Grifonetto
whom I have briefly mentioned. The ramifications of our family tree may be confusing, but bear with me a little longer. Grifonetto was great Braccio's grandson, by direct descent, the
youngest, the comeliest and the wealthiest of all the Baglioni.
He lived with his handsome widowed mother, Atalanta, in
Perugia's finest palace. He lived as a prince, rattlebrained, pampered, but a veritable prince, surrounded by hounds, horses,
lions, falcons, dwarfs and clowns, by an adoring wife, Zenobia
Sforza, and by his loving mother. I can speak only good of Atalanta. Her husband was slain at the Battle of Ponte Ricciole and
out of regard for his memory she remained a widow from her
youth, devoting herself to her son. Atalanta rescued my sons at
the height of the massacre and she was not implicated in Grifonetto's treachery. She was my second cousin, the great-grand-
daughter of Pandolfo Baglioni, a geniune Baglioni on both sides,
by direct descent.

Now, in order to tell you of still another principal conspirator,
I must impose some further intricacies of our family relation-
ships upon you, and then it will be over. It may be that our
family tree needed pruning at this time, for it was becoming
tangled. I shall tell you now of Filippo di Braccio Baglioni, my
uncle Braccio's bastard. Like my cousin Carlo, he was landless,
a poor relation and barely recognized as a gentleman, for all
that he was the love-child of such an illustrious father. Filippo
had ripe years — forty of them — and a reputation for baleful
wisdom. He was Grifonetto's tutor in fact and in folly and,
through Filippo, that young fool came to a bad end.

These men had understandable motives for seeking to slay us. They were driven by the simple humanities of ambition, greed, envy and the lust for power. I would not put it past any man. Filippo persuaded Grifonetto that the young man's wife lay with me adulterously. Grifonetto, all on fire, rose to the bait and joined the plot. Jealousy aside, he had other discontents. He was Braccio's legitimate heir and had been superseded by his able uncles, Guido and my father. Grifonetto truly believed that I was playing at love with his wife, an insipid creature who could never have contented a man of my humor. But the usurpation of his power was a graver matter. Grifonetto was indeed Braccio's grandson and, consequently, more honorably descended than any of us. But he lacked the dual quality which men require if they would wield power — judgment and maturity, which I will sum up in the word "virtù." We Baglioni have never taken a narrow view of legitimacy, for we have never been able to afford it. A man's right to the succession is not guaranteed by the simple fact of birth. There is no magic in birth of itself and no God-given right to power. I have often seen the able bastard chosen at the true son's expense, and quite rightly. Men have sufficient difficulty in managing their affairs and ought not to rely on the haphazard selections of a preoccupied and disinterested Deity. Men have risen among us as often by virtù as by birth and some of our most celebrated condottieri were born in huts and suckled in pig-pens. I give you the great Muzio Attendolo Sforza, for example, whose son, Francesco, rose to become a magnificent Duke of Milan. I have no personal bias against bastardy and have begotten several of my own as did my father in his day. "Bastard" is not a dishonorable state when borne by an able man, as we have seen with the love-children of certain kings who were distinguished captains of war. As for myself, the peasant who performs ably shall be my captain, for I have always looked to the talent of men rather than to their birth. Nor did the Baglioni themselves rise by the accident of good birth but by the salt in their brains; and of all our men, Guido was the saltiest and the wisest, after great Braccio himself. The simple arithmetic of it was that milk-cheeked Grifonetto proved incapable of ruling; he was a mere idle boy.

If I have spent excessive time in recounting these preliminaries, you might remember that a conspiracy to murder a man and his family is a subject of abiding interest to that man. These three conspirators, together with Girolamo della Penna, wasted no time in recruiting qualified lieutenants. They engaged several young men of the junior branch of the House of Corgna, a fact which I would stress, for our relations with the senior branch were excellent. These youthful Corgna were cadets, discontented outsiders, without possessions and without power. The same situation obtained not only among the Corgna and Baglioni, but among all the great houses of Perugia. Outsiders are not an evil of themselves, they are merely the hungry opposition. Here, in miniature, you have the history of Perugia, or a considerable aspect of it.

These Corgna were all of an age, no more than twenty-two or -three, all alike in appearance and outlook. I knew them all from childhood. They were tall youths, athletes and horsemen, well-muscled, expert in arms, reckless fighters and passionate hunters. However, they differed from the young Frenchmen who had recently come down into Italy. Despite their youth, these Corgna scoffed with the bitterness of grizzled age at the honor which the fiery French cockerels sought on the battlefield. What indeed is this quality called "Honor"? Ask an Italian and he will smile, for having lived beyond it, he sees through it. The Corgna are all dead now, feeble dusty ghosts toward whom I feel no hatred. I wish they were all alive again so that we could play it over. Death, shadowed in his wings, rustles closer each day, and I shed the world as a swimmer on the far shore sheds his armor. But back to my tale.

Girolamo della Penna promised Lavinia's dowry to the re-
cruits. Her jewels alone were worth seventy thousand ducats on
the Florence exchange. The Corgna refused mere pay, saying
they were not bravos. They demanded the rule of the San Susanna Ward, which was held by their senior kinsmen. These
ambitious outsiders were willing to slay their kinsmen in order
to gain power. The chiefs admired their lieutenants, congratulated them and acceded. The victims were assigned without
further discussion. Della Penna reserved Gismondo for himself,
declaring that once and for all he would shave off his enemy's
beard.

A wedding is an ideal occasion to take a family at one blow.
Only an interruption delayed the immediate execution of the
plot. Simonetto and I were ordered away to quell an outbreak
of cattle thieving in the Todinese contado, and the conspirators
postponed action. We returned on July 13, one day before the
planned stroke. Guido summoned us to his apartments as soon
as we dismounted. We went to report to him, still in armor, hot
and dusty.

"We broke them thoroughly," said Simonetto. "Their black
heads will not be raised for a while. We lost twenty-four men
and they, two hundred and fifty. We burned them out completely."

But uncle Guido had weightier matters in mind. "The nun,
Colomba, has been speaking with me again. She is having more
dreams, a whole black bagful of them this time. She dreamed
last night that as she walked alone in a dark wood near Gubbio,
she saw suddenly a golden falcon hopping along the ground because it had been lamed in one wing."

"Our family?" asked Simonetto.

"Perhaps," replied Guido. "As Colomba watched, a serpent
fell on the falcon from an overhanging branch and coiled about

the bird. The falcon struggled and slashed. The serpent tightened its coils and choked the life from the falcon. Then it
writhed into the underbrush. At that, Sister Colomba was seized
with a great fear. A fiery storm broke and lightning bolts
flashed lividly across the sky. One bolt plunged downward,
blasting the tree from which the serpent had hung. Sister
Colomba begged me to be watchful. I thanked her and said
that I had no belief in omens. I do not fear for myself but,
nevertheless, I feel it important enough to relate to you."

"The serpent is Girolamo della Penna," said Simonetto. "Kill
him, I say, dream or no dream! You well know what happened
at the tournament."

"Yes," said Guido, "but I have also a low opinion of young
Girolamo's ability. He may have the hatred but he has not the
courage to realize his ambitions. In any case, I hold that our fate
is set from the moment of birth, that each man's fate is branded
upon his forehead, yes, even in his mother's womb. No human
agency can alter that destiny. What need, therefore, to worry
about the Unknown?"

"Why, then, listen to Colomba?" I asked.

"For myself, I pay no attention to it," said Guido. "But I
would be remiss if I did not pass the warning on to you."

With these words, he dismissed us. Simonetto and I thought
we were going to our rest and we were both wrong. I survived
only by flight and Simonetto went headlong into that limbo of
darkness which is inhabited by the sleepless ghosts of murdered
men.

4.

THE MASSACRE

THE NIGHT of the massacre was serene and mellow as that of the Nativity. There was no moon, but the stars glittered down on the silent hilly streets, on the palaces and on the sleeping Baglioni within. The conspirators dined together that night and rehearsed their plans. Considering the conspiracy from the prospect of twenty years, there was a quality of virginal simplicity about it, a wholesome exuberance, that absurd comicality with which one mourns one's lost youth. Had the target been someone other than ourselves, I would have judged Carlo Baglioni's military impetuosity admirable. A hundred-man reserve awaited the attack signal in Carlo's house. Twenty additional arbalasters were detailed to Porta Marzia and Porta Savino to pick off any of us who got away. The general assault signal was to be a heavy boulder dropped from my uncle Guido's balcony into the courtyard. A noisy, bustling innocent summons, would you not say? In addition, Carlo thoughtfully prepared timber rams so that a fifteen-man detail could batter in through each of our locked chamber doors. Even today, I am impressed by the open-handed quality of their preparations. Having made their final decision, did the conspirators feel uncomfortable? Did they proceed by mere momentum because it was too late to withdraw? It is an interesting question to which

I have no answer. What matters is that they did execute the plan. The timid shy away from murder plots, ever finding a wealth of proof to demonstrate the inevitability of failure. But Carlo was a soldier, a good one, and what he consummated in fact was a military operation. These things are a challenge which the brave and the stupid accept, and more often than not they succeed. Were Carlo and his friends stupid? It is not important, for courage which conceals and forgives a bagful of defects is the supreme virtue. If one is willing to risk the penalty of failure, it is always best to act and strike.

Carlo and his friends struck.

I am of two minds about assassination. In self-defense, I have killed men in battle. I have condemned men after careful legal process and have seen them die under the Question. I was compelled on several different occasions to silence certain individuals, but I never did so secretly. Perhaps a distinction ought to be made between murder, openly committed, and the private aspect of assassination. I will not point a pious finger at the practice of others, but I have always found such furtive procedures repugnant. Assassins move in the black of night, they start at every noise, they carry fear in their hearts, or at least anxiety; and they limit the deed to as few accomplices as possible — altogether a shabby mode of behavior. Herein, I will concede that Carlo and his associates were exceptions to the rule. They did not behave as true assassins and moved boldly, which was to their credit.

Ippolita and I were the last to retire on that night. The Todi fighting had overtired me and I sat wakeful on the balcony with Ippolita beside me. We looked down on the sleeping city and drank in the cool wind from the hills.

The city of Perugia has a soul of sorts and, no doubt, sensed the impending blow. Only those born and reared within

Perugia's walls may accept this without question. All cities can communicate with those who are the bone of their bone. Every city sings a song and whispers a message, but Perugia's has never been one of love. She is too crabbed, ancient and malicious for that. Yet, she knew, I say. The mossed Etruscan walls listened with treacherous amusement and waited for the boulder to drop.

Our sons slept soundly in the chamber behind us. Through the black alleys between the stark and towering fortress-walls, a vagrant wind howled in from the hills and swept the rubbish before it. The cats, by right of ancient tenancy, were making love in the Via della Gabbia. There rose their favored resort, the squat bulk of the Podestà's palace where the cage of justice, high on the corner wall, was always occupied by a dead or dying malefactor. The feline snarling and caterwauling drew closer and grew louder.

"What is it?" asked Ippolita.

"The mongrels are driving the cats away," I said.

Ippolita shuddered, saying, "Even after eight years, I am unaccustomed to your barbarous ways. At least, we refrain from the use of cages in Rome. This place, with its battered towers and pitted walls, is like a brutal warcamp. Perugia has no heart."

"A better heart than your Rome," I said, "with no fat around it, even though it's worn down and cool after so many centuries of warfare. Perugia, like all ancients, is remote and disinterested. But even if she did speak to you, you would lack the ears to listen."

At this instant, we heard a dull and sullen crash. I seized a sword, ran through the bedchamber and unbolted the door. Simonetto's voice came roaring through the blackness of the corridor:

"Baglioni! To arms! Hold them off, Gismondo!"

My squire, Maraglia, rolled from his pallet before the chamber door and seized an axe from the wall. Ippolita and my sons peered through the open door. Carlo and Grifonetto came charging up the staircase with a mob of armored men behind them. And now we saw Simonetto at the head of the stairs, laying a two-handed Swiss sword about him in whistling slashes. He was stark naked, bloodstained and frothing rabidly. A soldier thrust forward rashly. Simonetto caught him in the neck joint and split him down to the waist. He howled like a wolf all dripping red, slashed a man's leg off and roared: "There! Carlo, son of a whore! Come and have some."

Then Simonetto slipped on the bloody stairs. Carlo's faithful partisan, Baldo Fioravanti, drove his sword through Simonetto's chest.

In spite of Maraglia's axe and my swordplay, the attackers forced us back.

"Remove Madonna and the children!" shouted Maraglia. "I can hold them with the axe."

I retreated to the chamber door, thrusting Ippolita and the boys out into the black corridor. "Make for Atalanta's room on the upper floor," I told them. They began running.

Maraglia and I each killed a man, thrusting them back down into the howling confusion on the stairs.

"Go!" roared Maraglia. "I can hold them."

As I leaped up the stairs toward the next landing, Maraglia's shouts grew fainter. Two soldiers broke through his guard and followed. I reached the landing, up-ended a massive marble bench against the wall and sent it crashing downward. It struck them fairly. Groping along the corridor, I caught up with Ippolita and the boys.

"Atalanta will not hide us," said Ippolita in a low voice, "for that was Grifonetto down below."

"Peace and move on," I said. "We'll find out soon enough if Grifonetto has the spirit to slaughter his own mother."

I hammered my sword hilt against the door. There was no response and I hurled my weight against it. It opened suddenly and I went flying into the room. The boys ran in and Ippolita after them. She slammed the door, threw the bolts and leaned back, panting.

Atalanta materialized from the shadows, holding up a flickering lamp. She was a tall and slender woman in black, and of her celebrated beauty I could see little enough at that moment. Only her dark somber eyes were visible, and a part of her pale face swathed in a black scarf. She nodded at me stonily and said, "Is he down there with them?"

"Very much so," I said. "Your little son is ramping around like a dragon-slayer."

"I found out too late to give warning," she said. "Will you believe that?"

"Since you say it," I answered. "Hide the boys. I must leave."

But Atalanta was not listening and continued half to herself, "He accused his wife of lying with you." She spat on the floor. "His father should have died at the Battle of Ponte Ricciole before he got me with such a devil's abortion."

"With such a gullible ass," I retorted, "and do not charge his father with more than half the credit."

"I no longer have a son," said Atalanta, wringing her hands.

"You have," I said. "Do you hear him down there?"

Atalanta put her hands to her ears.

"Beautiful cousin," I said, "we will talk about it later."

Ippolita shuddered away from me when I approached her, but I embraced Malatesta and Orazio and said: "Should I not return, revenge me. You will soon be men." Then I slipped out and ran for the attic stairs. Once on the attic landing, I began testing doors. One swung open and I found myself in a disused storage chamber. As my eyes grew accustomed to the gloom I made out a small square window giving on the roof. I shattered the glass with my sword hilt, squeezed through, crept carefully along the sloping metal roof and finally crouched in the shadow of a chimney pot to catch my breath.

The rooftops of Perugia have always been a traditional battleground. Across those roofs, we Baglioni have pursued and been pursued by the Oddi and other enemies, slithering, stabbing and ambushing in endless feuds. The losers were thrust off, to be found in the streets at dawn. One's life depended on a knowledge of such topography. The feudists fought at night, in the black alleys, in the shadows of the walls, and always over the roofs. Death was not the only fate to befall the defeated; exile was often worse. The fugitives sank into outlawry, skulking in damp cavernous fortresses in the contado. Their life was reduced to hunting and brigandage, varied with swift raids into the city, across the walls and over the roofs to reach the storerooms for supplies to further their warfare.

Since the stakes were not inconsiderable, this strife was pursued earnestly, and the friars preached in vain of Christian charity. If beaten back, the exiles resumed their vigil, never surrendering hope of regaining power. If victorious, they gave no quarter. The newly vanquished were driven forth to taste the joys of foreign travel. Behold with what an abiding tenderness our people loved their hearths!

I moved nimbly among the slates and chimney pots until I reached the San Biagio district in the vicinity of the New University, where the scholar Amico Graziani had his house. The New University, which had been erected a quarter century before, rose on the hill which dominated the Church of Sant' Ercolano.

By now, as I continued across the roofs, I recognized that I was approaching the piazza which lay before the New University. At this point, I was compelled to clamber down to the streets by way of ladders through abandoned warehouses and empty shops. I finally reached the ground and found myself in a labyrinth of alleys so dark that I felt my way. When I came to the students' ancient church of Santa Maria del Mercato, I recognized where I was. This was the church where those New University students of a devout bent were wont to worship and where they assembled annually to elect their rectors.

I had good reason for seeking out Amico Graziani and the university district. The collegiate community of Perugia possessed as much autonomy from municipal law as any in the entire peninsula of Italy. In order to attract scholars from every land in Europe, the House of Baglioni had encouraged special statutes placing students beyond the jurisdiction of the communal courts and constables. Soldiers seldom roamed there and I had an improved chance of evading Carlo Baglioni's bravos in this privileged enclave. Moreover, since I was in my nightshirt, the best garment I could hope to obtain was a scholar's gown. This costume, the cappa, was an effective protective coloration; it served notice alike on soldier and sheriff — the bargello — that the wearer enjoyed an immune status.

From Santa Maria del Mercato, I ran off into a narrow alley known as the Malacucina. In this area were located the brothels of Perugia — a convenient circumstance, for those who break their heads over Aristotle by day are notable wenchers by night. I avoided the piazzas, for on warm summer nights it was certain that they would be swarming with citizens and soldiers. Whenever I spied drunken revelers emerging from the brothels, I waited in a doorway with my sword ready until they passed. Thus I proceeded until I came out of the Malacucina near the Piazza de' Servi in which was located the New University. Not far distant from the School of Law stood the house of my erudite friend.

Amico Graziani was a professor of the law at this time and had proven his devotion to the Baglioni on many past occasions. He had a distinguished reputation as a jurist and was a notable diplomat as well as one of Perugia's most persuasive orators. The University of Perugia always sought the best teachers and our family did not stint money to tempt able men from the law faculties of Bologna and Padua. In all the years that I held power subsequent to these events, Amico Graziani served as my principal minister.

I finally recognized the tall narrow silhouette of his residence; lit up by a cloud-torn moon, it leaned crazily across the black street. I hammered on the door until an old servingman opened it. As I limped into an inner chamber, Amico Graziani himself started up from a book-scattered table. He was still in his middle thirties but already sleek and portly as befitted a learned *jurisconsult*.

"Peace to all in this house," I spat out, stumbling forward. "Peace and murder! We were surprised like a flock of damned chickens."

Then I felt Amico's fingers on my wrist and heard his voice shouting to his servant to bring hot water. He loosened my grip from the sword and helped me to a couch while his man came running. Together they cut away the filthy nightshirt and bound my gashed feet.

Amico made a quick examination, saying, "A little lost blood and no broken bones. You will have to take my word for it though; my work is patching briefs, not bodies." He leaned closer to me. "What has happened, Gianpaolo?"

I groaned into a sitting position and gulped a cup of wine the servant had brought me, spilling half of it on my beard. "A small matter of murder, no more," I replied. "We were surprised in our beds. I cannot tell how many are dead. I recognized my cousin Carlo and Grifonetto also. Possibly Girolamo della Penna and Filippo di Braccio, but I cannot be sure now. I know only that I must leave the city quickly."

Amico nodded and measured me with a cool eye. He went off and returned with linens and a scholar's black gown. "If you

were a respectably plump man of the robe," he said, "these garments would fit you perfectly. But since you are only a lean soldier —" He sighed and patted his generous bulk gingerly.
"Put them on, Gianpaolo, and let us see if you can pass for a
peaceful scholar."

The wine warmed me and I pulled the gown over my head.
"Well, what kind of magister do I make?" I asked.

"An unconvincing one, to be sure," replied Amico. "It would
be advisable to shave off your beard."

"I have no time for that," I said. "Send your man below to
see if there are loiterers about."

"Bring up the hood over your head, at least," suggested
Amico. "Your face is too grim for a civilian and a man of the
faculty."

The servant soon returned to report that a mob of soldiers
was gathering in the portico of the School of Law.

"They must be waiting to welcome our guest," said Amico.

"No doubt," I said, "and by dawn they will begin searching
the surrounding houses."

I chewed on some bread and dried meat and drank more
wine. With the return of strength came feeling, and as I belted
the naked sword around my scholars gown I said to Amico, "I
shall be an earnest and industrious student. I shall teach the
plotters rhetoric and eloquence. I shall probe their secret
places with hot irons."

Amico shook his head ruefully. "We have one of the best legal faculties in Italy," he said. "Yet what can we tell the
foreigners who flock to our lectures when the rulers of the city
set an example of violence? They see with their own eyes that
all our young men are bravos who make their own rules and
defy the podestà. Assassins with prices on their heads swagger
openly in the streets, and if they are friends of the Baglioni
the podestà shrugs and pretends not to see them. He knows
from past experience that they will escape punishment. Honest

citizens are robbed and murdered with impunity and the House of Baglioni, for all its good words, does not support the officers of justice. Not only that, but all public honors are put up for sale and —"

"What of *this* violence?" I asked angrily. "I did not kindle it. I am the injured party."

"There is always an injured party," said Amico in a melancholy voice, "but since those who make the laws are the first to forget them, they should not complain if their subjects and kinsmen follow their bad example. If Perugia, for all her university, also enjoys an unparalleled reputation for lawlessness throughout Italy, the fault can only lie with the House of Baglioni."

"Spare me your lectures," I said hotly. "You are not on a forum and I am not one of your students."

"You could learn something to your profit in my lecture hall," said Amico. "Although I serve the Baglioni, I cannot close my eyes to the fact that rapine and murder arise among you from every slight difference, that nothing is settled with reason."

"Peace," I said. "I will cure this disease when I return."

"If you return," said Amico. "Let me leave one thought with you: Perugia is a poor city by the standards of Italy, and the Baglioni have been among the most flagrant in maintaining a magnificence far beyond the city's means. From this alone, if from no other cause, arise many of our woes. If, in order to satisfy your vanities, you are the first to flout the statutes, what can you expect from those beneath you and from envious kinsmen who are kept from the bowl?"

"You are going far afield, Amico," I said.

"I speak more pertinently than you realize," he replied. "If you should win back, proceed against the plotters, not for private vengeance, but in the spirit of justice."

"Amico," I said, "do not ask fugitives to reason like judges.

They are waiting out there to carve me into catmeat and you prate of the law."

"No torture without trial," said Amico.

"I reserve reply," I said.

Amico's servant re-entered the house for the second time and reported that the street was clear. We crept out silently, the servant going before, Amico and I hanging back in the shadows. We moved carefully through the gloomy alleys and the arcades built under the houses. Occasionally we picked out a lantern or a torch in the darkness but no passerby crossed our path. The moon rose clear in the heavens and we saw the old walls looming up before us. We sidled past a gibbet, bare of fruit for the moment, and finally reached the open postern of the towering Borgnia Gate.

Amico turned to me.

"Go with God," he said. "Return to us safely."

"I shall return," I said, "and, when I do, I shall thank you properly."

Slipping through the postern, I began running.

I kept that promise — and the others also.

5.

THE FLIGHT

DURING these years of which I write, the mal francese (that Lues Venera which some called Saint Anthony's Fire and others, the sickness of Saint Job) was scourging not only Perugia but many other places in Italy. My father was its longtime victim, which enabled me to observe the disease in him and in others. Those taken with it found their first intimation a small enough matter, a hoarseness and tenderness of the throat. Others noted skin pustules and the like, which occasioned them no great discomfort. With others, it was notable that their hair and beards fell out and they lamented with a soreness in their joints and bones. Still others became grossly fat in a brief span and wholly or partially lost their sight, babbling the while like madmen. The disease fed also on the tendons of their limbs so that they walked drunkenly and, still breathing, were already dead, sepulchers of leprous flesh, each man an *ulcus putridum* who ran to hide from the sun. What with fevers and grievous pains, many in our city often sought to sell their souls to the Devil for a cure.

I have often noted an assumption in men that the Devil stands constantly willing to strike a bargain with any who offer themselves, as though every soul were a prize of equal value. If this is so and the Devil so careless a buyer, the reaches of Hell must be crammed to bursting. I have often speculated on the number of those who offer to make a pact and are courteously rejected. Even the humblest recruiting sergeant has minimum standards and one should credit the Prince of Darkness with a nicer taste than rascal sergeants.

But these are philosophical, not medical matters.

Many of the afflicted in our city, from desperation and a need to end their sufferings, sought to cast themselves into the Tiber and into Lake Trasimene and so drown themselves. Many did so, being already out of their wits, and among them were undoubtedly many whom the Evil One had disappointed by rejecting. Since it is a mortal sin for a man to take his own life, I pose a question as to how the souls of these sinners fared. Were they accepted uninvited or does the Devil have some suitable place in which to house the unwelcome until he can make some orderly disposition of their cases?

This mal francese smote all classes indifferently but, principally, the well-born who have the means for dissolute living. You may safely assume that gentlefolk were represented among the sufferers in respectable proportion. Indeed, the enemies of princes, ambassadors and cardinals often felled them by presenting them with comely females who had been suitably prepared with the mal francese as cannon are primed with gunpowder. I will also cite the ladies of Naples who assumed the patriotic duty of poisoning the invading French and their idiot king, who still had the wit to name his new acquisition the mal di Napoli. Men sought to flee the curse by passing it to young girls and sickened ladies did the like with youths whom they purchased for that purpose. Since Italy was such a sink of naughtiness, a noble's reputation went unsoiled, seeing that he could share his misery in exalted company. For all that, I had small sympathy with my father, considering his loose commerce with strumpets. He, too, might have died honorably on the night of the massacre. Instead, he corroded and died in his bed like a man of small account.

It is the nature of men to abhor reflection until brute suffering drives them to it. Hang or burn me, I will not think, for that is the greatest of all pains. Yet when we in Perugia had been sufficiently scourged, we began to speculate concerning the nature of this visitation. Some averred it arose from pestilent air, others, from poisoned wells. Luca Guarico, Perugia's paragon of astrological wisdom, a solemn graybeard with the face of a prophet and the soul of a pander, maintained that it was caused by the conjunction of Saturn and Mars as well as by the lunar eclipse. Yet all who played host to this affectionate serpent hugged it with anxious secrecy and knew it behind their faces for the wages of intemperate lust. So it became a pretty conspiracy to ignore the corruption together with the stench. Those theologians with the good fortune to be hale had the bad grace to thunder that the malady was an effect of Divine Wrath, in a way which priests have of turning every matter to good account. A wealth of ingenious remedies were prescribed with indifferent results. The physicians did not know how to attack the disease, and it went on its way until it burned itself out.

We Italians and the French have always mutually reproached one another with having added this condiment to the seething witch-brew of human affairs. But there it was. Men cursed and endured. I recall a Spaniard who came to Perugia with a sackful of sovereign specifics. He treated many citizens with Arabian mercury, commanding that they be covered with the unction from head to foot. Since the unguent was venomous when applied overliberally, many were brought to the point of death. This Spaniard slew others with zealous sweatbaths. Yet he brightened his ignorance with good will and sought to revive his perspiring patients with heroic draughts of fresh goat blood. Aside from that, he identified the ailment indifferently as the French, the Italian, the Turkish, the Devil's Own Darling, so long as it was not known as the Spanish Disease. He enjoyed a thriving practice and wisely departed before his nostrums were put to the ultimate proof. A man of discretion.

Having seen how wretchedly the physicians had managed, I once got a remedy from the witches of Norcia which I used successfully on my troopers during the Venetian wars. As I recall, it contained the essence of crushed bay leaves, oil of scorpions, quicksilver and the lard of a mature sow, all well macerated together with fine-sifted wood ashes. It should be sufficiently plain that I do not believe in witches but, if a remedy serves — and it did in that pest-hole, Venezia — I care nothing for its origin.

I have digressed on the mal francese because, upon fleeing from Perugia, I went to rescue my father. He was in so prostrated a state that I believe he and Saint Job had arrived at some modus vivendi while awaiting the dissolution of nature. I think of Saint Job as a familiar, sitting on my father's shoulder, waiting to receive his soul in the moment of death.

Ridolfo Baglioni had at one time been a splendid athlete. Now, as his frame moved toward a leisurely decay, the decay of his commonplace wits kept parallel time and he sank into a deepening apathy. This lethargy was Death's vanguard and drummer, and Ridolfo was indifferent to everything except the approach of Death. I have mentioned that he barely made an appearance at the wedding and remained secluded in the flower-garden of his villa in Borgo San Pietro. I inherited that villa and lived there briefly when Pope Julius came to Perugia fourteen years ago and expelled me from my palace.

I found my father in the garden. He sat lost and huddled in a great velvet armchair, dozing in the sun, disturbed only by the desultory hum of wandering honey bees, drowsily alive amid perfumed flowers and glittering fountain-sprays. I considered the feasibility of dispatching him with a quick sword thrust, to rid the garden of him, to rid him of himself. Because of haste and preoccupation, I forebore to do so. When I recall him now, resting like a beetle on fresh rose-petals, I consider my coming end a good one.

I shook my father awake and said, "We must leave at once."

He looked up slowly and mumbled, "The wedding. What of the wedding?"

"It is finished," I said. "There is no wedding. They are riding here to kill you."

I said to the servants who came out into the garden, "Call out Timoteo to dress my lord. Prepare fresh horses immediately."

My father gradually roused to full wakefulness. When he finally grasped what had happened, he said, "This garden has a common postern gate with the Church of Santa Maria degli Angeli. I cannot ride a horse. We might escape into the church." He shrugged his shoulders. "Truthfully, I care little how it turns out. I am seventy years of age and my time is well come. It will cause me no displeasure to shrug off this useless body."

When I asked him if Carlo Baglioni would respect the sanctuary of the church, he smiled sardonically and replied, "Hardly. To that extent he is a true Baglioni. We have not depended on sanctuary in these parts for many years — and quite rightly. We might try it, though."

We roused up the old priest of Santa Maria degli Angeli. He found me a priest's habit and, for my father, a dusty black gown belonging to his housekeeper. After dark, we stole away on a pair of bony mules which the priest had also provided.

Three of the late Guido's sons had escaped the massacre because they had not attended the wedding. The first of these was Marcantonio, a semi-invalid and a longtime resident of Naples. He was on intimate terms with the rulers of Naples and had been out of touch with us for many years. The second son was Adriano, whom men called Morgante for his strength and comeliness as well as for his valor and wisdom. Morgante preferred to make his home in Spello and seldom visited Perugia. He maintained friendly relations with his father but took no part in our fierce family rivalries. He had long been in the military employ of the Florentines, and when he was not campaigning he followed the retired life of a country gentleman. I had always held Morgante in high esteem and subsequent events brought us into a more intimate relationship. The third of Guido's sons who had survived was Gentile. He and I fell out in later years and it was Gentile who eventually betrayed me to Pope Leo. But at this time of which I write, we were sufficiently friendly. Gentile's career had not followed the usual military pattern of the Baglioni. Gentile was a soldier, but in his youth he had been inclined toward the church, for which reason the House of Baglioni had purchased the See of Orvieto on his behalf. But the bonds of formal celibacy became irksome in time. In this period of which I tell, Gentile had put off his priestly robes and re-entered the world. He had married Giulia Vitelli and methodically set about the task of producing sons to carry on his name. Like Morgante, he remained at a discreet distance from the turbulence of Perugia and lived as a rustic noble on his estates at Pacciano.

Nothing less than the murder of their father could have brought Morgante and Gentile out of retirement. At the time that my father and I left the villa, I sent servingmen ahead on swift horses to Spello and to Pacciano, with messages for my cousins to meet us at our first halt, the village of Marsciano. My father and I traveled all that night on the mules. By dawn, the old man was near death from exhaustion. We halted at the villa of a friendly landowner, where I was able to obtain and prepare a litter for my father. Here I also exchanged the mules for horses and made for La Fratta by way of the Genna district. At Marsciano, we rested and obtained fresh changes of clothing. Two days after our arrival, Gentile and Morgante rode in with their people.

The Barzi family, which dominated the area, willingly consented to conceal my father in their castle. I was now free to consider some practical plans with my two cousins. I said to Gentile, "Get word to Vitellozzo Vitelli. I have been told that he is in the neighborhood at Pantalla. As he is our kinsman, and yours particularly by marriage, I am confident that he will help us. Since you have been in orders, write the letter and we will have it sent."

We wrote Vitellozzo all that we knew — that Simonetto was dead, that Gismondo's death was suspected, and that Girolamo della Penna was among the assassins. We did not know at the time that Astorre had been murdered. Gentile composed a good clerkly letter summoning Vitellozzo to join us at Marsciano with full speed, by the honor of his House and by the ties of kinship between us.

Vitellozzo Vitelli, Lord of Città di Castello, was a considerable man at this time and a celebrated condottiero. He was cunning in war and displayed a purposeful cruelty for which men admired and feared him. He was far too ready to hang the defenseless over slow fires in order to shake the gold out of their pockets. Since such treatment loosened the tongues and refreshed the memories of the victims, thoughtless people invariably marveled. I suggest that we Italians have an unfortunate tendency to bestow our admiration in the wrong places. As long as Vitellozzo lived, I deplored his unpredictability and the frivolous ease with which he abused the devices of terror. Such methods are the quasi-legitimate working tools of a ruler.

They should be employed discreetly and not for any light end. But Vitellozzo was incapable of higher philosophical levels and never rose beyond a soldier's outlook. Although the mal francese was well into his bones, it was sufficiently quiescent at this time to enable him to sit his horse, dispatch the business of war and perform with the best. But the disease had also dulled and muddied his fierce sharp wits. I do not doubt that it was responsible for the doom which eventually overtook him. Two and a half years after these events, Vitellozzo Vitelli died in the noose of a strangler's cord, by grace of Cesare Borgia.

In the meantime, Vitellozzo rode high and came to our aid, not for the sake of love and kin, but for profit and advantage. He came, he heard, he commiserated. Then he deployed his troops at San Martino-in-Campo and waited while Gentile, Morgante and I spread word throughout the Perugian contado and wherever else we had friends, summoning peasants and landowners to arms in defense of the House of Baglioni. We had wasted little time. The massacre occurred on the night of July 15. I left Perugia at dawn. By July 19 I had set up headquarters with Vitellozzo at San Martino-in-Campo.

The drive to regain Perugia began well. My scouts snared a dozen prisoners at Trebbio di Luciano. With their wrists bound behind them, they came stumbling into the camp, driven forward by whips and lance points. Among them was Baldo Fioravanti, Carlo's faithful partisan. I went to interview the prisoners, who lay chained in a guarded tent, each man hampered by a Turkish yoke about his neck. Placing my sword point against Fioravanti's throat, I asked: "What has happened to my wife and sons?"

Fioravanti shrugged, lay back and stared upward in silence, whereupon I sheathed the sword, saying, "I will do you no favors, but I rejoice to see you again. How fares my good cousin Carlo?"

Fioravanti struggled into a sitting position and said composedly, "Better than you think. It's a hard time you'll have to regain the city."

We fenced back and forth, Fioravanti keeping sullen guard and deflecting each question warily.

"There is a time and place for everything and for loyalty to your master also," I said finally. "Consider now, that no matter how it turns out, you are a dead man. If you are expecting a hard death, you are not mistaken. Even you will not deny that I have a reputation for keeping my word. Speak freely now and tell me all, and in return I promise you a gentlemanly decapitation."

"That would be generous of you," he said with surprise. "I will accept, if you are speaking the truth."

"I am, and you are wise to do so," I said.

In fact, he was, and it proves my point once again that it is unnecessary and even self-defeating to treat men with excessive harshness.

Hoping to escape the tedious flaying of his body, Fioravanti finally spoke. "They are making ready for the worst in Perugia."

"Never mind that," I said. "My wife and children."

"Alive," he said. "They fled with Madonna Atalanta to the Convent of San Giuliano. Signor Carlo wanted them all slain immediately, but Signor Grifonetto countermanded the order and gave them an escort, even as his mother was cursing him. They are safe enough. Signor Grifonetto fears his mother's wrath and Carlo cannot afford to quarrel with that whey-face. Then Madonna Atalanta returned to the city with Grifonetto running after her imploring forgiveness."

"Forgiveness of a kind they shall all have," I said. "Now tell me of my kinsmen."

"You will keep your word?" asked Fioravanti.

"I will keep my word," I answered.

"That isn't enough," he said.

"You're fortunate to be my prisoner," I said. "I can always turn you over to Vitellozzo."

Fioravanti turned sallow behind his grime and said reluctantly, "The Corgna slew Signor Guido with a halberd thrust, though he put up a good fight for an old man and wounded one of them. I was with Ottaviano della Corgna and Filippo di Braccio. We did not have to break down Astorre's door for Filippo had a counterfeit key. We came in softly and found Astorre fast asleep with his arms around his bride. Filippo drove a dagger into Astorre's throat. His eyes opened, the blood gushed from his mouth and he groaned."

"What did he say?" I asked.

"A gurgling cough. 'I die as a coward,' he said. Then he was dead. We did his bride no harm save that Ottaviano struck her head with his dagger hilt, for she was screaming and clawing at him. Her arm was gashed by Filippo's dagger, but not with intent. Then Filippo laid Astorre's chest open, ripped forth the heart and grizzled at it, for which I reproved Filippo, saying that Astorre had always dealt courteously with him."

"Never mind that," I said. "I have already promised you."

"Then Filippo and Ottaviano hurled the body through the glass and out into the street below. But they did the girl no harm and left her lying on the bed in a faint. As for Gismondo, he died almost in his sleep, at the first stroke. Signor della Penna struck very carefully."

"I will not ask about Simonetto," I said. "I saw that with my own eyes."

"He was a good man, Signor," said Fioravanti. "He accounted for six of our men, and if he had not slipped on the steps just then it would have been more."

I summoned the sentries into the tent and pointed out Fioravanti to them.

"Take particular care of Fioravanti and see that no harm reaches him. If he wins the chance to kill himself, I'll give you his punishment. Watch over him, not only with your own eyes, but with the eyes of your mothers and fathers."

Vitellozzo entered the tent and stood listening.

"Our hearts are in our ears," said one of the sentries, rolling his eyes. "No harm shall come to these men save what you measure out to them."

"And I shall add what my friend, Baglioni, omits," said Vitellozzo smilingly.

"You will add nothing to Fioravanti's account," I said. "We have already come to an understanding."

Vitellozzo and I continued probing the defenses of Perugia some days longer. The spies we had successfully introduced now returned and confirmed Fioravanti's story. The scouts drove in additional prisoners, who were questioned patiently and painfully. From the sum total of their unhappiness, the quivering reluctant truth was reassembled.

The prisoners eventually perished before the walls of Perugia in full view of the enemy. A block was set up for Fioravanti and he thanked me as he knelt down before it. He was a good soldier. The stubborn ones who had spoken their hearts reluctantly expired as their limbs were broken with iron bars and the skin was flayed in strips from their backs. On the whole, there were no cowards among the prisoners and they died stoically, even those who had to be carried to the gibbet on litters.

I do not doubt that these melancholy scenes made a profound impression on those watching from the walls, so that when we finally assaulted the fortifications, we encountered proportionately less resistance and thus saved many lives. From which we must draw the conclusion that men, though wayward and fickle, may be instructed, edified and brought to a sober life by earnest correction and example.

Nevertheless, this was a most painful period in my life.

6.

THE RETURN

THE PERUGIAN COMMONERS played no part in our family struggles; few of them loved us sufficiently to take sides. This is traditional; in the fights between nobles, the burghers maintain a
discreetly neutral position and pray for the discomfiture of
both factions. As I learned later, when the citizens found the
mutilated bodies of Guido, Astorre, Gismondo and Simonetto
in the streets at dawn, they were indignant, but merely as a
formal gesture. Such had been their behavior on those past
occasions when we fought the Oddi in the squares of Perugia.
There is no doubt that if they questioned each other concerning
this latest outrage, they also raised secret eyebrows and
shrugged secret shoulders.

One should not take this to heart; those who rule should expect to be loved little or not at all. The Baglioni, in particular,
never exerted themselves to win the love of the populace. But
this is only as it should be; the world belongs to the few, not to
the many. Yet I can also sympathize with the people. In their
souls, and as outraged political animals, they resented their
helpless condition. If they commiserated with one another it
was, doubtless, not for my murdered kinsmen but for themselves and for the unknown evils still to come. Some of them
may have loved us; not all. The men of Borgo San Pietro were
loyal; the majority merely sighed and equivocated. While my

kinsmen lay in the street, naked and bleeding like slaughtered cattle, the students and the townsmen wandered by with dumb impassive faces. They stared and left, saying nothing. All of these things I ascertained after my return to the city.

Following the massacre, the conspirators wasted no time in attacking the Tei Palace in Borgo San Antonio and in firing it. The Tei have been our retainers since the days of Pope Boniface VIII, and even before. They have been the echo, the shadow, the second right arm, a third eye of the Baglioni. It was therefore logical that Carlo should seek their extermination. He was only partially successful. At least one hundred men of the Tei clan had sufficient warning and escaped from the city to join me at San Martino-in-Campo.

We had surely been at fault for keeping such careless watch. My father had been advised on more than one occasion during his active years to post guards about the palace, at least by night. As a reckless soldier, however, he never troubled about the future and the possibility of betrayal and assassination. My uncle Guido was even more indifferent. Yet their viewpoint is understandable; it is better to be dead than afraid.

Carlo Baglioni called meetings to enlist the support of the leading citizens. My friends in the city attended these gatherings and sent me a full report. Most people remained unimpressed and preferred neutrality. During one meeting in the Palace of the Mercanzia, Carlo harangued the crowd, shouting:

"It is incumbent on all of us to remain loyal and faithful to the glorious name of Baglioni. The bearers of this name who are allied to the first families of Italy, should rightfully continue to enjoy the prime honors of our city. Neither Grifonetto nor myself covet power. Our only thought is for your welfare. Yet if you, honorable gentlemen, will have us, we are ready to serve. If you do select us, you will find us vastly different from those late tyrants who would tolerate no peers in the enjoyment of their despotic powers. We have smitten those men, not out of ambition, but to save our beloved and misgoverned city from the oppression of the few. We have cleansed our land of these vile tyrants! Let us not halt now! What we have wrought will be for the greater good of ourselves and of our children. Heaven will smile upon us and posterity will bless us."

I have included this speech as a respectable example of the politician's art. It contained practically every moldy phrase suitable for such occasions. Had the positions been reversed and I in Carlo's place, I doubt whether I could have improved on it, except perhaps in the delivery, for I have always been a reasonably good orator. What Carlo said was at once true and untrue. We were undoubtedly tyrants, but I question whether he could have improved on our performance, even if he had possessed the good will, which he did not. The simple fact is that he lacked the necessary administrative experience and he would certainly have reduced the city's apparatus to a state of slovenly confusion.

Carlo made little headway with the magnates. Those who sympathized with our predicament preferred to hold their tongues. My good friend Amico Graziani was one of these and one of the last to escape from Perugia. When Amico fled to join me, he brought away a stolen letter which Carlo had addressed to Pope Alexander. Carlo's letter included a wealth of ingenious justifications for having murdered his relatives. He closed with a flourish of penitence, entreating the Holy Father's pardon for having shed human blood, no matter how laudable the end in view.

"Carlo has been very industrious," said Amico, rubbing his hands. "He has spread reports that you and your cousins Morgante and Gentile have all been killed. But I fear that it will not help him. The commoners remain unimpressed by the heroics of their self-appointed savior."

"And what is it that the people are saying?" I asked.

"That the fashion of Italy has now become Perugia's. They are singing a song about Carlo, the poor man's tyrannicide. We now have our own little slayer of dragons and of tyrants, they sing. We now have a little Brutus of our very own."

"The voice of the people is the voice of God," I said.

"Very true," nodded Amico, "and like God, the butchers, the bakers, the tanners and the weavers can be sublimely impartial. To hell with the Baglioni, they cry, the bastard Baglioni, the true Baglioni, the dead and the unborn Baglioni. Only when they exterminate one another can our lot improve."

"They are understandably concerned for their future," I said.

"And they have cause for worry. They know that we are not men to lie passive very long. And they also know that Carlo lacks command experience, that he cannot defend them."

"What tolerance! What vision!" said Amico. "Gianpaolo, you should have been a lawyer instead of a soldier. You are always seeing the argument from the other man's viewpoint. That is admirable, of course, but not in your role. To succeed as a ruler, one must enjoy a healthy measure of self-deception. One must be able to rationalize one's faults into virtues. You have been cursed with an inner honesty."

"A grave handicap," I acknowledged. "What have they done with the bodies of my kinsmen?"

"Carlo had them placed on stretchers two days ago, the kind used for the execution of criminals. The bodies were covered with horse blankets, carried off to San Domenico and buried there without rites. It was done at night and in secret."

"And my wife and sons?" I asked.

"Safely in the Convent of San Giuliano with Atalanta," said Amico. "They left none too soon; your sons were next on Carlo's list. It was only Grifonetto who prevented Carlo from killing your sons immediately. But it has not regained Grifonetto his mother's good opinion. She damned him for a traitor and a

murderer. She spat in his face and left his house taking with
her Grifonetto's Zenobia and your wife and sons. The chances
are excellent that we will find them all alive when we regain
the city."

"I have no doubt that we will," I replied.

Carlo erred in not storming the convent and taking my sons
hostage to improve his bargaining position. I suppose he and
his fellow conspirators were distracted by a thousand other
matters. Beached in the place of power like tadpoles in the eye
of the hot sun, it seems they spent their melting hours wran-
gling with one another. More important, they lacked a corps of
citizens trained to arms.

My cousins and I now prepared to march with Vitellozzo, and
the camp stirred into life. The carters harnessed up the baggage wagons. The soldiers moved out to reconnoiter the walls,
and our scouts returned with reports that Carlo was desperately
trying to bar Perugia's main roads with heavy chains against
cavalry incursions. They did report, however, that the Ward of
Sant' Angelo was being strongly defended. The men of this ward
had always been hostile to the Baglioni and had a stubborn
loyalty toward Girolamo della Penna.

The origins of their hostility went back many years. The
ward had always been della Penna territory. Its inhabitants
were hardbitten men with churlish memories. They persisted
in remembering our family when we were only one among
many contending for power. They refused to pay the taxes
which we levied and, when compelled to it, they paid reluctantly. Whenever possible, they murdered our tax collectors.
On the occasion of my wedding to Ippolita da Conti, the Sant'
Angelo people showed their teeth again. My father and I
had escorted Ippolita from Graffignano, her ancestral home, to
our town of Spello in September, 1490, with a very good company of gentlemen behind us. Our marriage was celebrated in

Spello in the presence of all the Conti and the Baglioni and all the nobility of the towns in the Perugian contado. It was on Saint Tomasso's Day, over a year later, in December, 1491, that we entered Perugia with a very great company. Ippolita was honored by visits from all the notables of Perugia and also by those of Todi, Spoleto, Città di Castello and other towns. All the visitors made her gifts of rich cloth stuffs, jewels and valuable silver. There also came all the retainers of our House with appropriate gifts suitable to the dignity and estate of such a highborn bride. The House of Baglioni imposed a wedding tax on each house in Perugia ranging from one half to three florins, according to the means of each household. The Sant' Angelo people refused to pay and even incited the Borgo Sole to follow their example. We would have struck back but we were busy with more importunate enemies at the time. We did not forget. Neither did the Borgo Sant' Angelo, which held its ground warily. Its participation in the wedding festivities of Astorre and Lavinia had been beggarly and grudging. We were preparing a reckoning with these stiff-necked troublemakers, and they were delighted when the reckoning turned out quite otherwise. They backed Girolamo della Penna openly and emboldened him to say that he intended to kill all the people in Borgo San Pietro (a particular Baglioni stronghold) and move his Sant' Angelo men into the ward. Girolamo justifiably did not trust the San Pietro men. When we finally assaulted the walls, it was the San Pietro men who secretly opened a gate for us.

We had assembled eight hundred cavalry and nine hundred foot soldiers for the assault. These we divided into four companies. I led the first, Vitellozzo the second, while Gentile and Morgante disposed of the other two.

Two hours before sunset we struck the Due Porte, that is to

say, the gates of San Costanzo and San Pietro, which lie one behind the other. We lost fifty men in the first attempt and still more the second time. Thereafter we retreated sensibly and waited till our partisans within the walls had successfully fired the inner gate of San Pietro. By the time we battered through San Pietro and into the Old City, the resistance had abated. The strength of the fortifications actually hampered us more than the defenders, for there were few enough of those. I do not wish to inflate this into a major battle; it was never that.

The citizens seemed friendly enough when we rode in. Why not? They had taken no sides to begin with. Carlo had disappeared. Some said that he was already over the walls and riding for Bettona. The citizens began cheering, shouting to us that Grifonetto had fortified himself in the cathedral with his men. "Welcome to Perugia, brothers!" they cried. "Kill the whoresons! They wet their breeches waiting for you."

Morgante rode up with a squad of scouts and said, "I think Girolamo della Penna is also gone. They speak the truth. Only Grifonetto is left at Sant' Ercolano, and most of his men have already come over to us."

With the captains gone, the few active followers cracked. We killed the resisting soldiers where we found them but sent the half-trained peasants home. Vitellozzo also took some peasants. He treated them with unnecessary harshness, as a matter of course, but I had no chance to restrain him at the time.

We finally caught up with Grifonetto before the Church of Sant' Ercolano. Just as we rode into the facing piazza, he emerged from the cathedral, alone and unarmed. He walked up and we stared silently at one another. His fair plump face was now haggard and lined. He seized my stirrup.

"I am surrendering," he said. "Kill me at once and have done."

"I see you are still giving orders," I replied, "even the last one. But then, your mother reared you as a prince and the habit of command persists."

Grifonetto flushed. "You're mocking me. Is it not enough that I am surrendering?"

"It is difficult not to do so," I said. "You will never be a tragic hero, only a pampered child. Unfortunately, you are also my kinsman, so I cannot accommodate you."

"What do you want then?" he suddenly shouted.

"Why, beat your breast a while and reflect on your sins," I said. "It will do you good. Thinking has always been a painful process for you."

Grifonetto sprang at my bridle with a strangled snarl but I reared my horse and kicked him away. Now Filippo Cencio, who had been Astorre's most faithful and favored captain, cantered forward. As he passed, he slashed his sword with light skill, almost playfully, across Grifonetto's back. With a roar, the waiting soldiers charged forward. They began hacking and stabbing and Grifonetto fell on his knees silently. He doubled over, his forehead touching the cobblestones like a Turk at his orisons. Cencio dismounted at Grifonetto's side and began measuring the swing to strike off his head. Someone shouted warning that Grifonetto's mother was coming out of the church. Cencio aimed a kick at Grifonetto's face. He fell over sideways and rolled on his back.

Atalanta stood at the top of the stairs before the portals. She stared down at the soldiers gathered around the body of Grifonetto on the piazza. Then she walked slowly down the steps. She was clothed in a dull black gown with a coarse dark shawl covering her head and hiding her face. Atalanta was an unusually tall and slender woman, and the gloom of her garments as she came forward in the joyous brilliant sun with the bright façade of Sant' Ercolano behind her made her appear preternaturally tall — and ominous also — like a witch that has been summoned from her customary darkness into the busy daylit world of men.

I stood to one side watching as she moved on the slayers of her son. They stumbled back before her, each man melting away as best he could into the anonymous crowd of the townsmen and soldiers, leaving a clear space around the body of her Grifonetto. She knelt down on the cobblestones and eased his head to her lap. A pool of blood spread under both of them and the woman stared down at her son with terrible and beautiful eyes, for Atalanta had the most beautiful eyes in the world. It may be that there was still life in Grifonetto, for as she stroked his blood-clotted hair and seemed to murmur to herself, he seemed to move his hand and she clasped it in hers. So she sat rocking over her son in stony mourning and I said to Cencio: "Have them bring a stretcher out of the Misericordia."

Then I went over to Atalanta and raised her up. The soldiers came with the stretcher and put it down on the stones and dragged Grifonetto onto it. They threw a cloth over him, hove the stretcher to their shoulders and began carrying it toward the yawning cavernous gloom of the Misericordia.

I followed the stretcher beside Atalanta and, thinking of nothing better to say, said: "God be with you, Atalanta."

This admirable woman, well-composed and stern, holding her grief as a jealous private matter, only replied.

"And with you, Gianpaolo." And then she added, looking at me with her Medusa eyes, "Will you forgive my son?"

"Forgiveness is a word," I said. "We are of one blood so let there be no idle words between us. I am neither Grifonetto's judge nor your enemy. The thing is done."

She nodded mournfully and I said: "Give me news of my sons."

"They are with Ippolita and Zenobia," she replied, "safe in

the Convent of San Giuliano. They ask for you daily. I would give my head for them. And there is also Astorre's widow there on the point of death with grief and her mother, poor bereaved women in this accursed city of the Baglioni." She halted before the portals of the Misericordia and said: "Go and take your wife and sons away from this place. Go with God."

"Farewell," I said and so she left me, one of the few good people I have ever known. She was a noble, high-souled woman and it may be that my heart twinged me in that moment that I had not spoken some words of comfort to her.

With Atalanta's disappearance into the hospital, a curtain descended, cutting off my past life.

7.

IPPOLITA DA CONTI

THE FIGHTING did not end with the death of Grifonetto. It flared again and again in many places like isolated witch-fires. The Borgo Sant' Angelo was put to the sword and sacked. Many Sant' Angelo householders crowded into the Cathedral of San Lorenzo hunting sanctuary. It did not save them; the crazed momentum of the soldiers crashed through the portals of the house of God and the people were slain as they knelt in prayer. This was the only ward which we treated as enemy territory. Most of the houses in Sant' Angelo were razed and burned. In the few houses that were spared, Vitellozzo Vitelli quartered his mercenaries and the innocent suffered together with the guilty. Vitellozzo was always over-ready to spoil that which was not his, but I was at least able to restrain him from burning down the entire quarter.

The Sant' Angelo survivors went streaming into the other wards, some babbling with terror, some numb and silent. They went on foot, with mules, some with carts salvaged from the general wreckage of their lives and loaded with miserable broken movables. So they came on, senile graybeards, little children and gaunt women, and after a week the fires burned down fitfully.

A few days after the death of Grifonetto, I prepared to ride out to the Convent of San Giuliano to find Ippolita and my sons.

"Go," said Vitellozzo. "We have secured all the strong places and have everything well under control." But I also spoke to Gentile and Morgante privately. They assured me that they would keep Vitellozzo hemmed in and compel him to hold his hounds in leash. Vitellozzo's assistance was always an uncertain affair and he was over-prone to wanton destruction.

I found my sons in the convent gardens, looking healthy yet sullen, and Orazio struggled bitterly when I tried to embrace him. Malatesta, though more cordial, was also reserved.

"You should be joyful to see your father alive and returned to bring you home," I said to them.

"I wish to go to Rome with my mother and live with the Conti," said Orazio.

When I asked for an explanation, he fell into a dark silence.

"Our mother has told us," said Malatesta, "that this is only the beginning, that it is the natural way of our kinsmen to kill one another. She told us that only by returning with her to Rome will we escape death in the next uprising."

"She told us," broke in Orazio, "that you were as much at fault as those who murdered our grand-uncle Guido. If this is true, I do not wish to live with you."

With these words, Orazio ran away and began to weep so that I saw he still had not conquered his fear.

"And what do you think?" I asked Malatesta.

"If what my mother says is true," said Malatesta, "I will go with her, but I would like to remain here. I am not as afraid as Orazio."

"Patience," I said. "We will make amends and what has happened will never happen again. Will you believe that?"

"If you say it," replied Malatesta.

I left him there with Orazio, and entered the convent to find my wife.

*   *   *

If it may be said that every Baglioni is born under an evil star,
I think that of my sons was the marital discord between their
mother and myself. Matters went badly between us from the
onset. I will not gloss my own faults. As for Ippolita, she was a
coldly imperious woman, a trait which pleased me as her lover
and irked me as her husband. She once ordered a huntsman
flogged for jogging her by chance and causing her to miss a
shot at a prize boar. As a guest of the Conti at the time and
a suitor, I held my tongue. Moreover, the man was one of her
hinds to do with as she pleased. It was another matter when she
tried to introduce these high Roman manners into Perugia. I
warned her, saying, "Our peasants are unaccustomed to such
treatment. For your own safety, act with more restraint." She
did not take my warning kindly. But these are small matters.

Ippolita also clashed with my brothers and cousins and soon
found herself at a disadvantage. The Baglioni, despite their
contentions, were of one mind before foreign wives. I think
that her father, Count Giacomo, had educated her too well for
a woman and she took badly to our garrison world. Ippolita
shocked my father and Guido by refusing to accept my constant absences, a thing unheard of in our city. She offended
them further by preferring the company of artists and scholars
to that of soldiers. Perhaps she had some right — soldiers are
uncommonly dull company for a lady used to men of wit
and learning. But she erred in not troubling to conceal her
disdain for our provincial outlook. Our way of life was no doubt
too simple and crude for a Roman Conti, almost barbarous.

Our life, from the beginning, was a series of recriminations
and, on one memorable occasion, Guido took a hand in Ippolita's reformation. "It is not the business of Baglioni women
to hold opinions," he said at that time. "The true business of
women is to breed males fit for soldiering and it is otherwise
God's pleasure that they should hold their tongues."

I agreed with such honorable views. Ippolita thought otherwise. "I was reared in civilized Rome," she retorted. "I do not intend to pine away in your bandit fortress, bearing sons to an ever-absent husband."

"Madam," said Guido, "you are mistaken in taking this tone with me. I am not to be defied by young women. Were you my daughter-in-law, you would not live out the night."

"Fortunately for both of us, then, I am not," flung back Ippolita. "In the meantime, I am no man's property. The Conti will protect their own."

Guido studied Ippolita in thoughtful silence and turned to me. "Gianpaolo," he said, "this is your mare and I leave her correction in your hands."

Did I thunder at Ippolita in husbandly wrath? Did I abuse her with soldier's oaths? Did I have her chained and starved in a tower till she died of a broken heart? Or, perhaps, I poisoned her with the wasting-sickness?

I did none of these things. Whatever you may have heard to the contrary, I have not deprived others of life lightly, and never from mere anger. If I have been handicapped, it is not with an uncontrollable temper. I have tried to control rather than be controlled by circumstances after an irretrievable act. I have not always been successful, but in this simple domestic situation I tried to act with forbearance. In short, we patched things up and went our separate ways until the next quarrel.

Such scenes, with variations, recurred during the eight years of our marriage. The quarrels were set off by miniscule causes only remotely connected with the fully flowered altercations which followed. The matters concerning which we disputed could not have been the true reason for the uneasy hostility between us. We walked on a capricious domestic ground beneath which burned fires, as they do in certain regions of Sicily, a ground so deceitful that the most trivial speech-tremblor between us disturbed the equilibrium and brought the flames leaping maliciously out of the ground. Joined together, we were both at fault and struck sparks from one another until a resentment burned between us, repelling one from the other. Ippolita sensed from the beginning that I loved her insufficiently, which, as I have observed, is a weighty business with some women, upon which they set all their lives, for they must be reassured daily and forever that they are loved. But how much is enough? Ippolita's proud ways irritated me, though only imperceptibly in the beginning, for being younger I lacked a studious eye in the first years of our marriage. I was not a man to spend too much time dancing tender attention on a woman's heart. I say that Ippolita was cold in love, but was I less so? In order to succeed as a lover, one must possess a bent in that direction. Mine was given up to my profession and I should have married a woman who was content with what scattered leisure the soldier's trade left me. But how could such a thing be expected of a Conti? Even if I had been the most pliable and patient of lovers, I think Ippolita would have remained wholly unreconcilable and querulous. There may have been other reasons, but I will still charge the influence of the religious in her girlhood training. Pride and a cold haughty piety go together and these Conti have always slept in one bed, worn one garment and passed about one eye with the gilded thieves of the Roman Curia.

Of Ippolita's plan to rear Malatesta for the Church, I made short work as a thing unheard of and wholly unacceptable. Nor did she yield to the act of love of her own accord, but submitted to it rather with pursed disapproval, as though she were a martyr and I, her husband, an evildoer. Even today, when I remember it, the old resentment awakens. We Baglioni are not men to be taken on sufferance by any woman, were she a thousand times more exalted than the Conti thought themselves.

This was the uncertain way of it through the years preceding the night of the Great Wedding Massacre. At worst, there were weeks and months of avoidance and galling silence. At best, there was a cautious mutual courtesy which, at times, warmed into a fleeting frail amiability, as the noon sun in frozen Scythia briefly thaws the icefields for an hour before it sinks into the sea. In the meantime, the endless business of the outer world had kept me pleasantly occupied so that I forgot my sour house in the warmth of coursing contention with the enemies of the House of Baglioni.

If the life between Ippolita da Conti and myself was without savor, that between my father and his wife had been no better. As with the father, so with the son. Madonna Francesca had borne her own burdens in her marriage with my ever-absent father. She had finally escaped into a small gray world of her own, spending all her time with the nuns of San Francesco, telling her beads there and the legends of saints. I went to visit her in the convent on rare occasions. Though nobly born and well tutored by her father, she had relapsed into superstitious austerities and besotted mortifications in this convent, as a thing pleasing to God. She and I had nothing to communicate to one another. We no longer spoke a common tongue.

Like Ippolita da Conti, my mother never throve among the Baglioni. But Ippolita's resistance had always been spirited while my mother pined to a gray and feeble shadow, lamenting that the Baglioni were succubi who had absorbed and devoured her. She did bear Ridolfo Baglioni three lawful sons and my four sisters. Troilo, my elder brother, being a cleric, counts for nothing; but she bore my valiant brother Simonetto, a very Mars, and also myself. That was her distinction in life and it was sufficient. Beyond that, she was too ineffectual a soul to cope with the world. On the night that she passed from this to what she devoutly believed would be a better world, I was far away at the wars. So peace be with Madonna Francesca of Castel San Pietro, the mute slave of Nature who brought me into this world.

When I went into the convent, the portress directed me to Ippolita's chamber in that wing which was occupied by well-born guests of the convent. I entered and there I found Ippolita at her private orisons. A little window, high in the wall, permitted the narrow and grudging entry of some rays of sunlight. Beyond a prie-dieu, a crucifix, and a pallet, the chamber was bare. The nuns of San Giuliano took no care to cosset their guests even if they were queens or Conti. Ippolita looked up, smiled with no warmth and finally said, "I am glad to see you returned and well."

"A good welcome, Madam," I said.

"I have no better," she replied, rising from her knees. Then she walked about the chamber for a space and continued: "These recent events have brought us to a parting of the way. What I have seen has turned my blood to ice. If I remain, all of you will destroy me as they destroyed that forlorn soul, your mother, who was thrust among the damned Baglioni as a poor defenseless stranger."

"Madam," I said, "what has my mother to do with us?"

"This place puts me in mind of her lonely years in the Convent of San Francesco," replied Ippolita. "I was with her when she died, forgotten by her sons and by my lord Ridolfo. She cursed all men and you together with the rest. Such a son as you were to Madonna Francesca, such a husband have you been to me." I would have replied, but she raised her voice and went on: "Nor do I intend to be broken as she was. I am of a different mettle, so do not try to hold me."

I said I had a husband's right to do so but she retorted: "You will not have your way. I am leaving you. My father and brothers are strong and will support me. They have come to abhor all of you and admit now that they erred in marrying me not only beneath my rank, but to the kinsman of murderers and a murderer himself."

I replied that she was charging me unjustly but she continued, saying that she would take our sons and return to her own people and the light of Rome. To which I rejoined that, if she went, she would go alone.

Ippolita turned very pale at my words and said: "They are also my sons and I am their mother who yearns over them."

"Then yearn well," I said, "for they belong to the Baglioni and you will never see them again."

Ippolita forbore to reply. To hold male offspring, we would, if need be, have cut the Conti into a thousand pieces. She knew this well enough.

So the fragile thread was finally broken and only a gulf of cold enmity remained between us. "Go in peace," I said. "I have too many enemies before to be concerned with those behind me. My house is a draughty retreat but it should at least be a safe one, which it will never be as long as you are in it. Go, before others do you an injury when I am not here to protect you. Let us separate quietly."

Ippolita laughed and replied, "It is easy for you to turn away. You are not a man but a block of stone. You think that you see clearly, but by your lack of love you are as blind as those beggars who sit in the courtyard of this convent. Remember me, my clever husband, when your nature finally destroys you."

Ippolita returned no more to the city. She remained in the convent, awaiting her Conti retainers there. She took leave of Malatesta and Orazio — a bitter farewell it must have been for her. And on the same day that she parted with our sons, she and her Romans rode out of Umbria forever. She returned to her father's house and, as I was informed, she was received by the Conti as one who has ridden with honors out of a beleaguered castle.

That is how, in the contentions of their parents, my sons were raised motherless. They remembered Ippolita but they never spoke of her again, at least not to me. They buried their hearts and resumed their studies in the art of war which Simonetto and I had already imposed upon them two years before. Our household, as you have seen from what took place so recently, was an uncertain quicksand. Malatesta and Orazio learned early to walk among the bogs of dissimulation in men's hearts and still survive. They learned in childhood to be patient and impassive, to master their feelings. From me, they learned a skill in arms. By the time they were twelve and fourteen, they excelled in the sword and the poignard and were skilled horsemen. I took Atalanta's advice and sent them away to Venice to live with my sister, Panthasilea, and her husband, Bartolomeo d'Alviano.

A bleak beginning, truly, but useful for the life we must lead.

8.

THE RECONSTRUCTION

THE GOAL for which men hoard, strive and walk so circumspectly before God is the joy of wallowing periodically in drunken war, in brutishness and destruction. Yet all pleasurable regressions into beastliness eventually come to an end. Perugia's debauch, in which the citizens had tasted all of the pain and none of the pleasure, also came to an end. With aching heads and empty bellies, they girded themselves to reduce their filthiness to order, to bury the dead, to feed the living, to patch some truce with God and to return to work.

Since the greatest destruction (aside from the ruined Ward of Sant' Angelo) had occurred in and around the Cathedral of San Lorenzo, I ordered the house of God cleansed and repaired. The soldiers were paraded in the great piazza before the cathedral and the bishop entered preceded by priests, choristers and censer bearers. Then Morgante, Gentile and I, together with Vitellozzo Vitelli, followed and knelt in prayer before the coffins of our kinsmen.

Thereafter workmen, under the direction of the cathedral canons, washed the portals with wine, and the cathedral was rededicated to the service of God. The purification of the cathedral in the presence of witnesses marked a solemn break with the past. Such ceremonial pageants are desirable for calming the people, for reassuring them that their comfortable and customary world has not departed from them.

Now, since men live by symbols, I commanded that portraits of Carlo Baglioni, Girolamo della Penna and Filippo di Braccio be prepared and hung in dishonor, head downward, on the façade of the Palace of the Podestà. This is our traditional way of declaring that such and such a one has been excluded from the community of men. Moreover, we acted out another and more robust symbol. We split the houses of the traitors down to their foundations. Remembering Atalanta with good will after so much bitterness, I spared her dead Grifonetto these ultimate infamies. As for the houses of the other three traitors, the workmen clambered to the roofs, cast down the chimney pots and stripped away the copper sheathing to a width of three or four feet. Then they dismantled the inner timbers and joists to a like width. Thereafter, the masons set up their scaffoldings within. They brought down that gaping gash from the roof along opposite walls. They hacked at plaster within, cut away the supporting joists and removed the dressed stones and carvings on the outward face of each house. In the end, each house was riven from earth to rooftree as though by the lightning bolt of a vengeful archangel. These dismantlings consumed the whole of a week, and when they were complete my cousins and I went with the Priori delle Arti and the exorcists to lay a curse and bring matters to a good ending. We began with the house of Carlo Baglioni. The exorcists spat into the cold black hearth and intoned:

"We are in a place, unholy and unclean. Let this house stand forever empty, riven and accursed. Let it remain a dungeon for the restless ghost of Carlo Baglioni in the hour of his death. Let this house fall into dust only when his soul descends into eternal hellfire. Let the voice of children never more be heard in this house, nor the voice of women, nor the voice of any living thing.

Let nothing enter here save the driving rain, the howling wind, the plague-rat and the slimy serpent. Let this house be a perpetual desolation, the breeding-place of nettles and salt-pits."

Then one among them preached upon the text of Isaiah:

> From generation to generation it shall lie waste;
> None shall pass through it for ever and ever,
> But the cormorant and the bittern shall possess it;
> The owl also and the raven shall dwell in it.

And the others lifted their voices and chanted:

> And it shall be a habitation of dragons,
> And a court for owls.
> The wild beasts of the desert shall also meet with
>   the wild beasts of the island,
> And the satyr shall cry to his fellow,
> The screech owl also shall rest there
> And find for herself a place of rest.
> There shall the great owl make her nest
> And lay and hatch and gather under her shadow,
> And there shall the vultures also be gathered,
> Everyone to his mate.

The words rolled through the mutilated chamber like the sullen echo of distant cannon, and as I listened I felt a deep cold in my heart. And so we went in the space of one day from the house of Carlo Baglioni to those of Girolamo della Penna and Filippo di Braccio.

Among the idle witnesses present were many butchers, tanners and flayers, for the vulgar are ever drawn to that which is gross and gloomy. These people brought in and would have strangled a bound black dog on the hearth of Carlo Baglioni's house, saying that the spell was for naught without a suitable sacrifice. At this, the chief exorcist shouted that we were gathered to curse a house in conformity with lawful ceremonies and not by filthy pagan rites, and my servants drove these men from the house with blows.

The expenses of these ceremonies and strenuous dismantlings were considerable, yet they were not wasteful. One must weigh the labor involved against the impression obtained. The people were much edified by these lugubrious and thunderous purgings, for such spectacles are the common man's poetry whereby he carves himself meanings in an indifferent world.

In conclusion, I commanded that the furniture in the principal chambers of the Baglioni palace should be shrouded and the walls hung with black. All retainers of the House were ordered to don and wear black garments, even to their horse-housings, their bannerols and lance pennons. The bedchambers of my murdered kinsmen were blessed and exorcised for the appeasement of their vengeful ghosts. Thereafter they were bricked up and sealed forever. All music, dancing and public feasting was banned in Perugia indefinitely. The city walked on tiptoe and spoke in whispers.

Having honored God and the dead sufficiently, Morgante, Gentile and I turned our faces to the things of this world. Gentile's preoccupation at this time was his connubial and dynastic ploughings, seeing that he had lost so much time in the service of the Church. He therefore left without delay for Pacciano. Morgante and I remained to reorganize the government of Perugia. Our first act was to wrest all power away from the Ten Men of the Arbitrio. Each of Perugia's five wards had always sent two representatives to the Arbitrio and, in the past, the House of Baglioni had always controlled six or more of these votes. The fact is that the Arbitrio had been rendered inoperable. Because of so many deaths and flights, the della Penna and the Corgna were unable to send qualified men. Morgante and I therefore laid pretense aside and took the powers of the Arbitrio into our own hands. I do not wish to bore you with a detailed disquisition concerning political techniques and if you have found me tedious to this point, I must remind you that these matters were no cobweb of dreams but the daily practice of politics. I have more to tell and a limited time. Besides, you may learn more here than from reading the poets. Their tale is spun from fog; mine is anchored in fact and necessity.

As I say, Morgante and I were in no mood to humor the Priori delle Arti by observing the forms of self-government. We laid the amenities aside and gave them one choice, at sword point, so to speak. They accepted the new order reluctantly. So did the noble families, who had all lost blood. There were no della Penna left in the city; seven of them had fled with Girolamo. Four of the Corgna and five of the Ermanni were with the exiles. The Antignolle and the Ranieri had lost men, and so it went.

I found the work of reconstruction irksome and have always preferred active soldiering. I left the spadework to Morgante, who had a flair for such duties. The Italian states condoled with us by letter and envoy. We listened, without necessarily believing, and replied appropriately.

Morgante restored the good humor of the Priori with gradual small concessions. He gave the bargellos — the sheriffs — a free hand to do their own judging as well as hanging. He set up an inspection system and beheaded twenty grafting officials while the bargellos hanged looters on the spot. We issued a number of new regulations: no renting of houses for prostitution, no keeping of private whores, no drunkenness, gambling, sodomy or brawling in the streets. It was ambitious, as are all reform programs at the outset. We enforced a curfew and ordered all shops closed on holy days under penalty of fine. In my experience, nothing is more effective than fines. Men weep less for the loss of their heads, less for the honor of their wives, than for the loss of their purses. Finally, we dismissed lax magistrates and replaced them with ambitious climbers, men wholly dependent on us, who labored diligently to deal summary justice.

Three of Morgante's personal friends were arrested one night for brawling and resisting the bargello's men. He ordered that their heads be cut off, for which reason the citizens came to believe Morgante's declaration that he cared nothing for personal popularity. In truth, the humbler the plaintiff, the more Morgante exerted himself to obtain fair treatment. The citizens began to compare him with his great brother Braccio. When he died of a lung fever two years after this time, I was accused of having poisoned him out of jealousy. Indeed, it is one of the present charges against me, but I can only say that I admired Morgante and his blood is not on my hands.

I have mentioned that Guido Baglioni had a son named Marcantonio. This Marcantonio pursued the dual profession of valetudinarian and courtier to the Neapolitan Crown and had been absent from his native city for many years. We duly sent messengers to Marcantonio with news of the Great Betrayal and he finally returned to Perugia. Our kinsman's long sojourn in Naples may have imbued him with the theatricality of that nation. When he saw with his own eyes the effects of the massacre, he howled, sobbed and beat his forehead. He tore his hair and swore that he would raze the Ward of Sant' Angelo to the ground, yea, that he would plough it under and sow it with salt. And so by his daily lamentations he continually interrupted the conferences between Morgante, Vitellozzo and myself.

We sat closeted on one such occasion, struggling to reduce Perugia to some order, and Vitellozzo was saying: "You will need much money, gentlemen, much money to refortify the walls, mend the roads and repair the gates."

Now came Marcantonio breaking in on our counsels without

notice and roaring: "I will destroy Perugia and utterly waste it!"

Morgante was greatly angered by this interruption. "My brother," he said, "Vitellozzo, who has a talent for havoc, has already done what you now propose to do. Today is the first time I have ever heard such sweet sane water issuing from his muddy fountain. Let me enjoy it in peace. You will oblige us by mourning elsewhere in decent privacy."

Vitellozzo was wholly unabashed by the bad character which Morgante had given him. "Signor Marcantonio," he said, "where were you when we needed you most? Why were you not here taking blows when they were being distributed?"

Marcantonio replied haughtily: "You know well enough that my illness required that I take the baths at Naples. My physicians ordered it."

"Take another bath then," said Vitellozzo. "It will do you good." He turned to me. "As I was saying, Gian, you need taxpayers, citizens with confidence in their government's word. You must convince the refugees to return. Show them that your government is one of immutable laws, not one of wayward and capricious men."

"Out of the jaws of wolves shall issue righteousness," said Morgante.

"Even a wolf has sense when his belly must be filled and his cubs bedded down," said Vitellozzo. "Call a truce on vengeance, gentlemen. It is a luxury and you are now beggars. Swallow your pride, fill your gullets with sour wine, if need be, and call the sinners home."

Marcantonio interrupted in a hollow voice, crying: "Shall I permit the slayers of my beloved father and of my brothers to escape? Never!"

"The parlor has been scrubbed, brother," said Morgante, "and your belated wailings will only serve to sloven it again."

"Nor do you know what toil they have had restoring this pig-sty of sorrows," added Vitellozzo.

"Their ghosts will return from the tomb to haunt me," wept Marcantonio.

"An excellent line," said Morgante. "Save it for the whore-houses of Naples. As for ghosts, they have all been laid and you will serve them better by not tearing up the ground like a wild ass. This is Perugia, not the Neapolitan theater. Keep your fe-vered paws to yourself. As long as we hold power here, we in-tend to live with the people in peace."

"He is right, Signor," said Vitellozzo helpfully. "Your brother and cousin have been through a very difficult time."

Marcantonio rose, saying bitterly, "Seeing that you are men without sensibility and without honor, there can be no spiritual communication between us."

"I suggest you return to Naples, brother," said Morgante. "From what we hear of it, it is a place more agreeable to your sensitive temperament than the garrison climate of Perugia."

Marcantonio stalked out without replying and Vitellozzo cried briskly, "Let us return to work."

I looked through the windows of the Municipal Palace, where we sat, and at the spikes around Pisano's fountain.

"In the old days," I mused, "those spikes were always fes-tooned with the heads of the Opposition. Now they are bare, for the first time in many years."

"That is because we are becoming civilized," said Vitellozzo.

Morgante and I followed Vitellozzo's advice. It was wholly sound and one should always take good counsel no matter how polluted the source. We invited the noncombatant refugees to return home. We promised reimbursement with interest to all those whose goods had been pillaged in the late fighting. We appointed judges to adjust claims and to restore stolen property.

Vitellozzo was one of those judges and performed creditably. Will you believe it? Vitellozzo was two men! His wits were clear at this time and his heart tranquil. We published a blanket amnesty, guaranteeing everyone, even the Sant' Angelo Ward, in life and goods — everyone, of course, except the principal traitors and their partisans.

We kept our word, and people began drifting back to pick up their lives. The conspirators and their friends opened negotiations to join forces with the Oddi and continued living in Urbino as exiles. Guidobaldo da Montefeltre of Urbino had certain pretensions as a civilized and enlightened prince. We resented his protection of the murderers, and Morgante composed and dictated a letter like a stew, throwing into it all the vegetables he could find. He sidled to his point with a series of monkish propositions, illustrating them with rhetorical flourishes and learned precedents. Thus — rulers were appointed in Heaven. Subjects owed them love and submission. Governors and governed owed each other faith, loyalty and respect. Morgante cited a brimming potful of authorities which spiraled down from Holy Writ to the Fathers, the Schoolmen and the Poets with their Mirrors for Princes. Princes were also bound to deal fairly with neighbors. Morgante conceded past discords and unsettled disputes with the Montefeltre. He finally made his protest. "If your father, Duke Federigo (whose memory we revere in Perugia) were alive today, he would never have countenanced a nest of fratricides in his country. Honorable men do not treat with traitors. We ask you to expel them and save your own subjects from their infectious example."

I reproduce this from memory, which gives little idea of the letter's stately, cumbersome style. There was a musty flavor about it of the cloister, of pious mortification, for which I had no taste — but it served our purpose well enough. Guidobaldo replied reasonably, and expelled the conspirators soon after, though not for ethical reasons. I rather think it was because his fastidious esthetic sense took belated offense at playing host to the unsuccessful. Guidobaldo signified his gracious agreement with our views, but the subtle thread of patronizing benevolence woven into his response irked me. In this modern day, a Montefeltre of Urbino stands no higher and closer to God, or the Ultimate Perfection, or whatever one chooses to call it, than we Baglioni. There is no memory of the olden times in my bones and I do not accept the right of the Montefeltre to patronize me. Nor do I accept the view that every man has his niche and stratum in God's decorous Universe. As long as I live, I shall rattle the underpinnings of that Universe.

Perugia was in poor shape at this time, quite stripped of good fighting men, whatever their political beliefs. Italy has always been a pot of seething bitterness and Perugia never far from the glowing heart of it. Her chronicle is the more dark for being so senseless. The factions have contended in Perugia more persistently than anywhere else. With the plague of chronic warfare, she has remained lean and threadbare. She has lagged behind the general luxury of the peninsula. We Baglioni, I fear, have not performed as we promised, because of our self-devouring strife. This is the local problem only. For Italy as a whole, the prime cause of deviltry and discord, has always been the pope, or I should rather say the papacy as an institution rather than the pontiff of the moment. The papacy claims Perugia, Italy, Europe, the whole world. How is that? The priests have an answer. Answers are their trade. The Church trades Divine Wisdom for our faith and homage. The Church is the fountain of law, order and civilization. What a fountain! Look about you; the answer is plain if you have eyes to see.

But let us leave civilization and Divine Grace aside for a moment and return to something as mundane as politics. The pa-

pacy is the natural enemy of all states, including our small and
battered Perugia. I am in agreement with Machiavelli here, despite our differences on military matters. Some say popes have
their place as cupbearers to the state. I go beyond and question
their right to breathe. A state has one end — to survive. There
may be faiths to further that end but I would not include that
proclaimed by the popes among them. Of the three popes I
have served, the least unpalatable was Borgia, perhaps because
he set so little store by revealed mysteries. He and his son,
Cesare, were men like myself and of my way of thinking. They
saw men as they were, not as they ought to be. Cesare Borgia
was superior to our Italian princes, although at the time I strove
against him I could not see it, for my own neck and interest
were at hazard. Our own fears and ambitions blind us to the
greater good and the princes have always been more at fault
than the people, who are only an anvil for the princes to hammer on. Nor do I hesitate to include my family in this judgment.

Had Morgante lived, I think he would have succeeded in
transforming Perugia into a lean soldierly state to knife through
the dry rot and the soft belly of Italy's confusion and survive, for
arms are everything, and without them politics are a mere for-
malistic bable and a posturing. I wonder now if Malatesta will be
able to steer us off the rocks after I am dead. He may succeed,
despite the fact that there has always been a curse on the Baglioni. It has happened more than once in the past that the males
of our family have been massacred except for one unborn child
who survived — in each instance, a male child. From one feeble
spark, the fire caught again. On the whole, the men of our
House have not died in bed, which is well enough, but they have
usually died prematurely.

BOOK II

THE HOUSE OF BORGIA

1500-1503

9.

ALTOBELLO DA TODI

HAVING restored our power in Perugia, I gladly left the government entirely in Morgante's hands and went off to the wars. Like the sea, the wars are always there for a man to bathe in when he is so inclined. I elected to participate in a campaign which was being prepared against the House of Chiaravallesi in the neighboring contado of Todi. It promised to be a modest local affair and I entered it as a favor to my friends, the brothers Lodovico and Giovanni degli Atti da Todi. The Atti had been allied with us since the days of my grandfather, but my feelings for Lodovico went beyond the letter of treaty obligation.

These Chiaravallesi were headed by a certain Altobello who called himself Altobello da Todi, and by his cousin, Jeronimo da Canale. They were exiles who had been driven several years before from Todi by the House of Atti. In addition, Altobello and his cousin, though only in their middle twenties, were apparently quite mad. Their depredations and senseless atrocities in the Todinese had made them burdensome to our neighbors, the Atti.

I should also add that, while the Baglioni have always been Guelphs, the Chiaravallesi were an appendage, marital and otherwise, of the Ghibelline House of Colonna. I am uncertain why this should have been so, but Guelph and Ghibelline are as good labels as you will find anywhere to explain the smoke-blackened division of centuries among men. Men must stand on opposite sides of an impassable river. It is their nature to do so, just as wolves must howl. Perhaps the Guelph and Ghibelline parties were founded on the day that Cain killed his brother, which was the day, poets tell us, that war was born. Had these parties not arisen after our expulsion from Paradise, men would have doubtless invented others and given them a name.

We rode forth on this mission as bargellos after malefactors rather than as soldiers against an honorable enemy. I include it to acquaint you with the exceptional people with whom we contended in Umbria in those days. There was universal agreement on one point: that Altobello, the infant killer, was a prodigious pest. Men normally in disagreement on the time of day and the color of each other's hair were in accord on this matter — hence the cooperative spirit in which all joined to help the brothers Atti rid the world of Altobello. The Atti raised three thousand troops, a proof of their earnest intentions, for they were poor men. Vitellozzo brought another three thousand. Like the rest of us, he hoped to find rich pickings in Altobello's stronghold of Acquapendente, and, initially, he gave the rest of us little trouble. The condottiero Paolo Orsini contributed four thousand cavalry. I had been previously associated with Paolo, for we Baglioni were very close with the Orsini. I was to be associated with him again in the conspiracy of La Magione against Cesare Borgia, but that will come later. I brought more troops than any for I was the richest; most important, I brought the siege guns which proved the key to our success.

We assembled our army at Deruta and lay there ten days awaiting Paolo Orsini's arrival. He came finally in leisurely luxury, for he was an easy-going, almost an effeminate man, a lisper and a pouter. He fancied decorative rather than serviceable armor and the Atti brothers, in plain black plate, were decently rustic by comparison. For instance, he wore a little silver-gilt helmet such as they manufacture in Milan for the theater. It also pleased him to strut in a gilt cuirass which bore the goddess Venus in bas-relief, her pointed breasts jutting forth prettily.

Lodovico degli Atti, seeing this gaudy harness, raised his eyebrows and grunted disapprovingly: "One light sword cut will carry his Venus away. The bear of his House would have been more appropriate. An honest bear rather than a pagan slut, and not in gilt; at least in bronze."

Lodovico was one man who could grunt and sound prim at the same time. I esteemed him for his old-fashioned notions and found them wholesome. With his great height, his long forked beard and his severely controlled features, he seemed a patriarch from a simpler age. Yet he was not much older than myself. It was his manner. There was antique virtue even in the massive outmoded weapons which his people carried. But the Attis' best weapon was their quiet settled resolve to send Altobello to Hell by the most expeditious route. Lodovico's soldiers revered him and called him "Father."

"Since that day, three years ago, when Altobello slew my wife and children," Lodovico informed me, "I have had no other family. My soldiers are my children."

I knew the rest but he told it again, of his own accord, for it seemed to relieve his mind to do so. Lodovico was a man whom I voluntarily treated with the most careful courtesy.

"Altobello and da Canale swept into Todi one night in force while my brother Giovanni and I were away hunting. They carried off my wife, my youngest son and my daughter. She would have been thirteen now. My eldest son they stabbed in his bed and left a message impaled by the poignard driven through his heart. 'You can have your wife back when we're done with her,' it said, 'come to Acquapendente and welcome.' Giovanni and I went before Acquapendente and tried to bargain with Altobello when he appeared on the walls. I offered him all I could raise, ten thousand ducats of gold. He laughed and brought my wife out on the walls all naked. It was a freezing night. Altobello himself fixed the noose about her neck and kicked her off."

I supposed he would tell about his children and he almost read my thoughts.

"They beheaded the little ones on the battlements in our full view and flung their heads toward us. We have men with us who are widowers and childless through Altobello, men lacking fingers and some without noses or ears who fell foul of the Chiaravallesi, yet escaped. It is Altobello's custom to slay the little children out of hand by flinging them from the towers. He takes as much joy in slaughtering the young ones as he does in cutting down the young olive trees in our groves."

"I think we shall see some warm work in your company, Signor Lodovico," I said at last. "I am happy to be under your orders, for a captain with your motives will be a good one to follow."

"Yes, my reasons are good," agreed Lodovico thoughtfully, "yet let it be done temperately and carefully so that nothing goes amiss. You may be my junior in years but you know more then I about the management of your cannon. Only put us through a fair breach in those walls, Signor Gianpaolo, and we shall do the rest."

A few days after this conversation, our preparations were completed. We held a final review and marched toward the siege of Acquapendente.

The signs of havoc increased as we moved deeper into the contado. Isolated villas and farmhouses lay in ashes and cold charred timbers. We passed still smoldering manors from which escaped the sweetish smell of death. The road wound down into a small valley. Before a gaping empty hut, a peasant hung by his feet from his gatepost, his throat gaping and his face blackened by clustering flies. In the courtyard lay two children and a naked woman with her belly ripped open. Thus it went for mile after mile with no cattle, no chimney smoke and no sign of life. The scouts brought over a peasant they had started out of a hedge when they saw his movement. His face was emaci- ated, so knotted and sun-blackened he seemed a Moor. He might have been a young man but it was difficult to tell his age as he mouthed his toothless gums, the spittle drooling from his lips as he mumbled:

"They burned my village three days ago, or three weeks ago, I can't remember. They killed my father and wife. I hid so I am alive. They slaughtered the cows they could not take and they took all the wagons and broke the wine casks with axes." He sat staring with sullen indifference as we rode away.

The land was dead in a wide band around Acquapendente. Most had fled to Todi. The imprudent who remained had suf- fered that peasant's fate. We met other wanderers. "The Chia- ravallesi take no prisoners," they told us, "but slay out of hand all who come their way. The greatest devil is Altobello, who refuses ransom so that none may buy their lives, and it is his chief pleasure to torment those he seizes."

We closed the ring about the stronghold. On taking count, we had more than fifteen thousand people about the walls, which was a brave show for the taking of one robber. Madness is no bar to military ability. Altobello had one-fifth the number of our people, and until our guns arrived he made a shrewd de- fense and gave us a useful problem in siege warfare on which to exercise our wits.

Our cannon performed well. Altobello and da Canale, having no means for reply, sat and endured for five days. Without artil- lery, the task would have dragged for weeks since the walls of Acquapendente were of a hoary ancient strength. They rose from the cliffs as a continuation of Nature in her most convulsed mood. They showed a challenging malevolence which invited reprisal. I supervised the serving of the guns like a chief priest making sacrifice. Our cannon-gods found the straw heart in those walls while other companies mined below and blasted at the foundations with powder charges.

When the breach was made, the Atti brothers led the storming parties over the rubble-hills and up the swaying scaling ladders. As they went upward and through, we kept the defenders restrained with hails of bolts and heavy arquebus fire.

Da Canale made a stubborn defense. As we secured the breach and poured through, he and his men retreated toward the castle. Altobello was nowhere to be seen. Behind the walls, we found the town little more than a cluster at the foot of the fortress proper, a few streets with miserably grouped houses and huts on the far side of a broad moat encircling the fortress.

Da Canale and his people fled into the castle but had no time to raise the drawbridge and drop the portcullis. We had had time to bring the lighter French cannon through the breach and set them up, and thus we had the main entranceway under constant fire. We dragged the cannon forward across the drawbridge and quickly splintered and battered the heavy wooden inner gates. Vitellozzo and his horsemen galloped through into the inner courtyards, cutting down the Chiaravallesi. Da Canale barricaded himself in the main banquet hall on the upper story. We brought in small rams, broke down the double doors, and an indoor battle began. The Chiaravallesi behind a furniture barricade in the center of the hall defended savagely among tables, benches, napery and spilled wine.

To make room, the soldiers upended furniture and hove it through shattered windows into the courtyard below. Men lay sprawled, their heads pillowed in half-consumed platters of meats and fruit, with the floor all slippery with blood, wine and breads spilled from silver basins, the whole churned into mud. But the fight came to an end, and in the guttering light of some torches, combatants lay embraced among overturned tables. Lodovico finally knocked da Canale's sword from his hand and the Atti bore him down like a pack of hounds.

"Clear the floor," shouted Lodovico. "Pitch the corpses out of the windows and carry our wounded down the stairs." Then he turned to da Canale. "Where is your cousin?"

Da Canale laughed at this, and when a soldier sought to rebuke him with a kick, Lodovico admonished the man, saying, "Do not mistreat him more than is necessary but, rather, go to bring him a friar."

Jeronimo da Canale was a cold-eyed man of twenty-five or -six, of good height and strongly built. Everything about him was square — his face, his blunt-cut blond hair, and his axe-lipped mouth. The men of the Atti thrust him down on his knees, saying respectfully to Lodovico, for in no other way did men think of addressing this lord: "Signor, there are no priests in this wolf-den."

"Save your time and mine also," said da Canale from his bent knees. "I have no need of priests."

"You are a poor sinner and a most wretched man," said Lodovico earnestly, "and I would not see any man go under unshriven. Will you not, at least, pray awhile before the soldiers strike off your head?"

But da Canale knelt erect and stared before him with wide unblinking eyes.

At Lodovico's sign, a soldier swung da Canale's own sword in a flashing arc. The head went bounding toward the cold fireplace. The trunk doubled forward spouting blood.

Soldiers came up the stairs in a procession hurling bundles of faggots about the hall. Lodovico ordered them to scatter the floor well with gunpowder, saying that we would touch off the room when we left. When all was done to Lodovico's satisfaction, we trooped out of the darkened hall, leaving da Canale kneeling there as its headless guardian.

A mob of soldiers and townsfolk rioted among the flaring torches in the courtyard. They dragged a bound man in their midst and beat him as they went. Like Jeronimo da Canale, he was tall and blond. His face was battered and one eye had been gouged from its socket. Under his torn peasant's smock peeped a doublet of rich red silk.

"I found him hiding in my barn," shouted a farmer to all who would listen. "A poor devil of a soldier he said he was, fleeing from the battle. Then I saw the rings on his fingers. I brought him here and the rings are mine! The soldiers have stolen them from me."

"Altobello!" screamed the mob. "Death to Altobello!"

Someone jerked up the prisoner's arms to show his bloody hands to the crowd, with four fingers hacked away at the middle joint.

"To one side!" shouted Lodovico to the soldiers. "Get back! Let the people have him!" They swarmed over him with bill-hooks, with knives, clubs and their fists. Men wounded themselves and others in their eagerness. A heavy-set black-haired man brandishing a cleaver came running into the courtyard.

"That's Tomasso, the goldsmith," said one of the men. "Altobello raped his wife."

Tomasso shouldered his way to Altobello's already dismembered corpse and people ducked away from the wild-swinging cleaver. He clove the corpse's chest with an accurate blow, tore out the dripping heart and began to chew it. More people came running with cups and pannikins, shoving and shouting offers of a ducat of gold for his blood.

The soldiers began to laugh among themselves, saying, "Altobello sells higher than a suckling pig."

Lodovico degli Atti roused himself from silence. "Enough of this swinishness!" he roared. "Let's finish and be gone."

The soldiers remounted and began to herd the mob back from what was left of Altobello. Two by two, the heavily armored riders rode under the arch of the portcullis and over the drawbridge across the rubble-choked moat. Lodovico and the arbalasters waited in the courtyard. A full moon now sailed through the broken clouds and lit up the grim upper works and gaping windows of the fortress.

Lodovico turned to the arbalasters and ordered them to make their fire-bolts ready.

"Now send me a few, true and fair, through the windows of that hall which we prepared with gunpowder."

The arbalasters took careful aim and the flaring tow-heads of their fire-bolts flashed off like little comets. An instant later a tremendous rumbling explosion rocked the ground on which we stood. Orange flames shot through the gaping windows and a large section of the donjon wall collapsed down into the far end of the courtyard in a cloud of rubble, dust and black smoke.

A shout of exultation rose from the watching people.

"So perish the enemies of God and men! God save Lodovico degli Atti!"

"Amen," said Lodovico, crossing himself, "we have done our work and the dogs have gone down to Hell."

We watched a little longer to see that the upper reaches of the fortress were settling down to burn and crackle merrily. Then we turned and rode across the moat and down the hill, followed by a trailing procession of peasants and townsmen.

So I brought my first action since the Great Betrayal to a happy and pleasant ending under the leadership of Lodovico degli Atti. The Atti profited by it more than ourselves, but I was satisfied to have been of service to Lodovico. He was a grave, soft-spoken honorable man and a notable soldier.

The service which I rendered him in this affair returned to me manyfold three years later. Which demonstrates that God knew what He was about when He enjoined us to live in loving-kindness with our neighbors and to aid them whenever we can.

10.

THE BORGIAN CONDOTTA

I RETURNED to Perugia from the siege of Acquapendente in September, 1500. By that time, Morgante had fully restored the Baglioni power, by love, by guile and by force, so that all obeyed our decrees and regarded us not merely as defenders but as masters of Perugia. After Acquapendente I fought other campaigns in company with Vitellozzo and Paolo Orsini. I have forgotten many of them and will not weary you with a recital of those I do remember.

My fortunes rode high, and wherever I went I won victories. These, as well as the Chiaravallesi affair, enhanced my reputation. Ambassadors of the major Italian states began recommending me to their masters as a sound practitioner of the military art. I have since come to appreciate how mediocre was our Italian practice when measured against Spanish, French and Swiss standards. These nations have made Italy their workshop and test-ground during the past twenty years and they have achieved a gratifying proficiency in the art of destruction. The Italians at that time were so relatively poor in skilled captains that, compared to many, I was a virtuoso.

As for my own military ability, I have no illusions. Even today I have much to learn. But the soldier's trade will be superfluous in the City of God.

During the year 1500 I was in the world with both feet, and the princes of Italy were impressed. From the offers I received, it was evident that they had listened to their envoys with benevolent patience.

Pandolfo Petrucci of Siena, a timid crafty man with a scavenger's sensitive nose for the shifting breezes of Fortune, wrote to me promptly. He offered a contract to include all the cavalry I could raise, at double the customary rate. The Florentine Signoria, with which our family had satisfactory relations in the time of Lorenzo the Magnificent, also joined the bidding. They offered me a condotta of three hundred men-at-arms. Their contract was so hedged in with qualifying safeguards for themselves that even our lawyers, for all their delicate appreciation of human guile, had trouble understanding the stipulations. Whenever I have done business with Florence, I have come away with the feeling of being robbed like a peasant girl of her virginity. Petrucci's contracts were equally dubious. He paid gold in advance, however, and affected no virtuous airs. Petrucci's cowardice canceled his cunning and I was always able to bully out of him some future compensating advantage. Pandolfo Petrucci was a predictable and controllable quantity; that pleasing and classical prototype — an honest thief. Finally I had my eye on his infant, Francesca, for my son Orazio. The Florentine merchants, who concealed their craft behind a façade of lofty republican idealism, were more reluctant to part with their money. It was axiomatic that a contract made with them had value only to the degree that they could be forced to honor it.

As a result of heightened prestige, abler captains came to enroll in my companies. I recruited carefully and enjoyed a slight bargaining edge — ambitious soldiers were willing to join me for less than they asked of other captains, such as Vitellozzo. I was not more lenient but more consistent, and I paid punctually.

Further, I did not commit Vitellozzo's error of harrying non-combatants wantonly. Peasant hatred, needlessly aroused, recoils on the condottiero at the most inopportune moment.

I decided in favor of Petrucci. With the signing of the Sienese condotta, the competition for my services sharpened. Pope Alexander evinced a new interest and invited me to Rome. I obeyed readily, eager to view the possessor of those illogical spiritual advantages which so annoyed his secular princely competitors. If, thanks to popular superstition, he enjoyed an additional weapon in his pontifical thunders, it was a fact of life with which to reckon. I philosophized no further. As for the princes, how natural that two-eyed thieves should envy a thief with three!

In obedience to the Holy Father's summons, I traveled to Rome. Viewing the Vatican for the first time, I began to understand more fully why men claw so furiously for earthly power and glory. Nothing is sweeter to the human heart. I stood near a window and watched a throng of prelates and lay-petitioners. I did not have to wait long. While I was examining the halberds and uniforms of the rigid guardsmen, a smooth-faced elderly secretary in black came to me, bowed deferentially and requested that I follow him.

Pope Alexander sat writing behind a long inlaid table when I was brought in. In the mellow light of the wax tapers, he was venerably handsome. He finally looked up, adjusted his white skullcap and examined me with bold interest. Even seated, I could see that he was a tall man and his broad shoulders were imposing. He seemed closer to fifty than to seventy. Raising his right foot to a red velvet footstool, he motioned me forward, a good-humored smile lurking at the corners of his mouth. I knelt carefully and kissed his velvet slipper.

"Peace be with you, my son," said Pope Alexander in a vibrant musical voice, "with you and with your House."

"I am here in obedience to the Holy Father's summons," I replied.

Pope Alexander smiled broadly. "We reserve our circumlocutions for ambassadors and scholars," he said, "but you soldiers are a different story. We enjoy an occasional lapse into wholesome frankness. We need a captain of your merit in our service."

"The Holy Father is gracious," I replied. "He is doubtless aware that I have only now engaged myself in the service of the Sienese Republic."

"We are aware of that," nodded the pope. "We have already approached Signor Petrucci. For the love which he bears the Apostolic See, he has consented to release his valorous captain and lend him to the Church. As you see, my son, God smooths a way for those who labor in His service."

This prince was to Petrucci as the sun is to a candle. Plainly, I was dealing with a lord of great enterprise who would more than better Petrucci's figure.

"In that case, I am ready to serve," I replied promptly. "My life and skills are at the Holy Father's disposal."

"Spoken to the point, like a soldier," said the pope.

I asked for twice the sum Petrucci was paying me. Pope Alexander did not haggle with this estimate of my worth. He nodded and ordered his secretaries to draw up the contract immediately.

I recall this notable Borgian pontiff as vividly as on that day twenty years ago when I first met him. He possessed as quick an eye for good soldiers as for pretty boys and tender girls and, together with that, an irreproachable judgment in hounds and fine horses — certainly a flexible and generous taste. Moreover, he was compatible and eloquent even when doing violence to the truth. He was all that a prince should be, and our Italian assessment of him has been confused by ecclesiastical superfluities.

If a word may sum up Pope Alexander, it is "love." He loved beauty in all its forms so that even his carnality (that quality which the ancient Greeks revered in Father Zeus) was brightened by his sunny philosophy. Above all, Pope Alexander was *pater familias;* he loved his sons and his daughter with a passing great love. We should not enviously condemn those whose weakness is an excessive and exuberant capacity for affection, and I would write on the tombs of all those whom Pope Alexander brought low: "We slew thee for love."

Let us speak the truth on all occasions and admit that the nepotism with which this Spaniard has been charged is open to debate. His predecessors, Sixtus IV and Innocent VIII, lovingly raped the States of the Church to provide for their bastards. That was nepotism. Pope Alexander, instead, very lovingly raped the princes in the Romagna. Far from dismembering the Patrimony of Saint Peter to provide for his family, he strengthened and enlarged it. If I disapprove of the Borgia, it is for that reason and because, two years later, in the winter of 1502, Alexander and his son sought to slay me.

On that first afternoon, when our military business was done, the pope kept me in conversation, condoling in the murder of my kinsmen so that I found him agreeable and sympathetic, infinitely more so than his boorish and bitter successor. Roderigo Borgia was more gracious plotting harm than Giuliano della Rovere giving praise. But I speak of the man, not of the pontiff.

Seeing him so well disposed, I brought forth the letter which Amico Graziani had carried away from Perugia. "This missive was addressed to Your Holiness by my cousin, Carlo Baglioni," I said. "I took the liberty of intercepting it."

Pope Alexander glanced at the letter and grimaced fastidiously, saying: "It was Heaven's will that you should have done so, my son. It is just as well." Then he observed gravely, "With sorrow, we see on every hand men ground between the mill-stones of princely ambitions. We see lesser men, pawns, expiring painfully in the spiderwebs of dynastic contention. Though it pains our heart, there can be no avoidance of such evils. Political assassination is a melancholy and deplorable necessity in the furtherance of Heaven's mysterious works. It is to be entered into and employed soberly, prayerfully and intelligently. One ought not to disturb a status quo unless one is certain of improving a situation."

While I was savoring the pontiff's elegant presentation of the unanswerable, he fixed me with his large brown eyes, so warmly Spanish and yet so icy, saying, "This Carlo Baglioni, this cousin of yours, has wrought clumsily; therefore he is wrong and a grievous sinner. Who is he? We have never heard of him. Truthfully, Baglioni, your family has always been something of a trial to us, imposed by God, no doubt, but at least a legitimate trial, a calculable penance with which we have learned to live, as one lives with a boil on one's neck."

"Your Holiness has entirely lanced us with your graciousness," I replied.

Pope Alexander smiled. "Not quite, Baglioni, but we may still do so if you do not comport yourself. These conspirators seem to us no more than bravos with long swords, beggarly purses and vaunting hyphenated names. We prefer our customary sorrows to new and unpredictable evils. We prefer you, my son, to those who have sought your blood."

Pope Alexander was not a man to indulge in graceful observations for the pleasure of hearing his own melodious voice. In describing the Baglioni as a penance he was undoubtedly referring to a passage-at-arms he had had with Guido five years before. He had come to Perugia with a strong escort, was entertained, and coveted what he saw. He desired to see the goodly House of Baglioni assembled before him in one place. He was a lover of beauty he said, and had heard that the Baglioni were the handsomest people in the world.

"Holy and Blessed Father," said Guido on this occasion, "your slightest wish is our command."

He paraded the armed strength of the Baglioni, each company mounted, armed at all points and led by a resolute captain of the House. Seeing how the wind blew, the pope contented himself with graciously admiring instead of gobbling.

This jocund and majestic dragon blessed us fulsomely on his departure. We accepted his benedictions with suitable reverence. Pope Alexander had a long memory as well as a sense of humor.

Having completed all preliminaries with the pope, I rode to join his son, Cesare Borgia, at Deruta in Umbria. Cesare made a less agreeable impression on me than had his father. He was courteous but not friendly. His face and eyes remained coldly inscrutable. Nevertheless, in conversation with him, I was impressed by his freedom from religious superstition. He was one of the new men of whom I was inclined to be hopeful. Though young in years, he already enjoyed a reputation for audacious treachery. So much the better for his future prospects and for mine, I thought. But I was unable to feel any warmth toward him.

The headquarters camp at Deruta was crowded with Spanish mercenaries, short, swarthy, bearded men in the Borgian red and yellow. Their equipment was battered but well maintained and serviceable. They soon gave my Perugians cause for exercising patience. They sacked the neighboring villages and behaved like enemies instead of allies. My soldiers were quick to retaliate. Continual brawling began between the Perugian and Spanish soldiery, with nightly murders about the camp. The Perugian peasants groaned under the exactions of Cesare's

Spaniards, who pillaged their winter food supplies and took away all the wine. But that was not enough. What wine the Spaniards could not consume, they poured out. In addition, they deliberately fouled the casks with filth so as to render them permanently unusable. Though Cesare Borgia was fastidious in many ways, in this practice he was as much a vicious sloven as his people.

So he lay in Umbria recruiting, training and perfecting plans to besiege Faenza. He collected the usual crowd of pimps, scribblers, whores and artists about his camp. All came flocking in the hope of receiving some benefit from this lord who seemed so favored by Fortune. He held banquets each night and his friends molested the women and girls of the surrounding villages.

My troops were beginning to slip from my control out of sheer hatred of their Spanish allies. They leagued with the Perugian peasants to murder as many Spaniards as possible. When Spaniards straggled in the countryside, or wandered off on the wrong road, they never emerged. The peasants and my people slew them privately and buried them. I too was beginning to share in the general hatred for these Spaniards.

The winter of 1500-1501 was a bitter one. The Borgian army marked time in winter quarters, waiting for a thaw when they would commence the siege against Faenza. The strife between my troops and the Spaniards finally came to the attention of Cesare Borgia. He complained to me of the murders which my men were committing. I retorted that if the Spaniards were detested in Umbria, they had only themselves to blame. Cesare laughed and took this in very good part, saying that my attitude was understandable since I was native to this region. He ended by offering me the command of the coming assault on Faenza. I refused and added that since the army was now inactive and in winter quarters, I desired leave to attend to my personal affairs

in Perugia. If I remained, I feared we would come to open warfare with the Spaniards.

Cesare acceded to my request and added with a smile: "This
has been an inauspicious beginning and your people are plainly
in need of discipline. Look to it that they are more tractable by
spring or I shall ask the reason and demand an answer."

"My people are hot-tempered and stiff-necked. They are unused to your service," I replied.

"In my service there is only one master," said Cesare. "You
are looking at him. I have plans for your advancement and
profit when the spring campaign opens, but I expect unques-
tioning obedience to my orders. I do not hire condottieri for a
season or a year. If you and your troops are to serve me, it must
be with your entire hearts and minds. As you shall learn in
your dealings with me, I am not as other men, and my service
is based on rewards other than pillage and soldier's pay."

I forbore to reply, silently noting that these were high words
from one who had been a priest a short time before.

"Why must you return to Perugia at this time?" asked Cesare
casually.

"My cousin, Morgante, has summoned me urgently," I said,
and it was true. "Our enemies are harrying the contado again,
the old exiles of the Oddi party and the new exiles who are with
Carlo Baglioni. The House of Crispolti has joined their raids as
well. It is my intent, while your army remains in winter quarters, to seek out and crush these people."

Cesare Borgia smiled and stroked his small tawny beard. "By
all means," he said at last, "go and kill your Oddi and your Crispolti. It falls into place with my greater plans. Before I am
done in Central Italy, all of these petty tyrants will be sleeping
in their shrouds."

So I rode out of the Borgian camp, returned to Perugia by
December 18, 1500, and distributed my troops to winter quarters.

I had met Cesare Borgia. He was a young man of singular virtù who left as sour a taste in my mouth as his father had not. He was a man whom one might disbelieve at one's peril. I stored up in memory both the words and the man behind the words. This decision to regard him with the utmost seriousness saved my life when Cesare Borgia sprang the trap at Sinigaglia two years later.

11.

THE BATTLE OF CORTONA

AMONG the most determined enemies of the Baglioni were the Crispolti, who owned the town of Bettona. This ancient and well established feud had probably originated in nothing more serious than stolen cows and broken fences. I suspect that if you retrace the time-hallowed quarrels of princes, you will usually end with two louts bickering over a pig, and that is the history of man.

In these years, the House of Crispolti was headed by three able soldiers, Matteo Crispolti, his brother Fabrizio, and his son Metello. The family had been faithful allies of the Oddi for many years. When Carlo Baglioni fled from Perugia in July, 1500, he found his first sanctuary in Bettona. Thereafter, the Crispolti continued steadfastly to aid both the old exiles and the new exiles.

On January 7, 1501, Morgante and I received news that Carlo Baglioni was once again on the march. With Crispolti aid, Carlo hoped to join forces with the town of Foligno and start a new war. With the gallant Filippo Cencio, whom I had appointed my second-in-command, I rode out of Perugia leading several hundred men. We pushed hard toward Bettona in a sleet storm hoping to ambush Carlo. We also had garbled information that Metello Crispolti was somewhere in the contado waiting to guide

Carlo's troops to Bettona. It appeared that Carlo was also planning to ambush us as the opportunity might present itself.

We posted a doubled guard that night. I was pleased when Cencio wakened me from a light sleep before dawn, saying, "Our pickets have just taken a fine frozen fish. Metello Crispolti himself. Come and see our prize."

Metello was about twenty-six years of age. The sentries had bound his wrists and he stood defiantly among them, the sleet and rain dripping down on his blond head with his hair cut in the ancient Roman fashion. He may have fancied himself as a heroic antique tyrannicide and he held his tall slender frame proudly.

"Rack him, I say," said Cencio. "We may have less time than we think."

We threw Metello across a horse and brought him to the nearest town, Spello. There we stretched him on the municipal rack until he told us where he was planning to meet Carlo the following night. It continued to rain heavily all that day and into the night. We counter-ambushed Carlo's army and would have killed them all except that the rains put out the slow-matches of my arquebusiers. With his usual good fortune, Carlo escaped.

Since the Crispolti were not expecting us, it seemed a logical opportunity to assault Bettona. Metello's limbs were dislocated but he seemed otherwise uninjured. We tied him across a mule and pushed on. It was still raining before dawn, and we struck Bettona from three directions. These precautions turned out to be unnecessary. Only Fabrizio was on guard in the small Crispolti palace, with a few soldiers and servants. We overran the palace and killed him before he could offer any resistance. We carried the unconscious Metello indoors, laid him on the floor and began to search the place. It was actually a rambling fortified villa rather than a palace.

While I was trying to revive Metello, Cencio came down the stairs gripping a young woman by the arm. He threw a blood-stained poignard on the floor, saying that she had wounded a soldier who sought to seize her. He thrust her forward so roughly that she almost fell. "This must be Metello's sister, Laura," he said. "A handsome bitch but treacherous, like all the Crispolti."

The girl tossed back her unbound glossy hair and stared with defiance and anger. She seemed about eighteen or twenty and drew her nightdress closer to conceal her tall straight body from the calculating appraisal of the soldiers.

"Well met," I said. "I have been curious to see you."

"I do not reciprocate the wish," she retorted.

"Do you know who I am?" I asked.

"The great Baglioni," she replied. "A tale to frighten children."

At this point Metello, groaning and rubbing his wrists, struggled into a sitting position on the floor. Laura, showing alarm for the first time, ran over to her brother, knelt and put her arms about him.

Cencio strode over, placed his sword point against Metello's throat and said, "This is the dog who sheltered Carlo Baglioni. We should cut his throat and the girl's too, and burn the house over their heads."

Making allowance for Cencio's natural bias, his advice was reasonable and uncomplicated. It would have served Matteo Crispolti right to find the bones of his children on a pyre. Then I hesitated, perhaps because the girl was staring back with level eyes. I considered the ease with which this spirited creature could be reduced to charred and bleeding flesh. A disgust seized me which hung and hardened into reluctance. I asked Laura for her father's whereabouts. She continued in mute hostility and I said that Metello would be instantly killed if she did not reply. So persuaded, she admitted that her father was away campaigning with the Oddi exiles.

"Give him my compliments when he returns," I said.

Cencio turned to me in surprise. At that moment, I lacked his faith in the saving grace of bloodshed. Cencio was a physician with but one scalpel in his pouch.

"Madonna," I continued, "when your father returns, tell him that I have carried off his son. I will keep Metello alive to insure a welcome when I next come visiting."

I gave the necessary orders and Cencio, unhappily, had Metello hoisted to his feet and assisted from the room. So we departed for Perugia, leaving the girl with the corpse of her uncle and a roof over her head.

"That was badly done," said Cencio with some bitterness as we rode away with Metello still groaning beside us.

I reminded Cencio that Astorre had been my cousin as well as his master.

"We should at least finish our friend here," he persisted.

"Stop naming your blood-lust loyalty," I said. "I feel no inclination to kill anyone at the moment. Can you understand that?"

"If I did not know you better," rejoined Cencio, staring at me suspiciously, "I would say that you have been taken with the girl."

"That may be," I replied.

Cencio shrugged and we said no more.

It was possible that the seed was already in my mind. If not, the words of Filippo Cencio planted it there.

I was taken with the girl.

The winter of 1501 passed in a series of burdensome campaigns against the exiles through the length of Umbria. While I was trying to burn Carlo out of one fortress or another, my father finally died on Saint Constantine's Day, February 24.

My forces were so shrunken at this time that I decided to break off the pursuit and return to Perugia. Carlo took advantage of my absence from the field to harry me in other directions. He rejoined forces with the Oddi and captured the Fortress of Fossato near Lake Trasimene on Wednesday of Holy Week, April 7. It should not have been a difficult matter to hunt down Carlo. There were complications, however. The Florentine Republic, hoping to win some advantage for itself, began to send aid to the exile coalition. Nor was this all. The town of Foligno had previously joined the exiles and was menacing our flank. When Morgante and I turned on the Folignati, they screamed for Pope Alexander's assistance. He obliged them for a heavy monetary consideration and sent a legate to hold us in argument through the month of March. Needless to say, we settled nothing with the Folignati and they continued to plague us for six additional weeks, at which time we decisively smashed the entire exile coalition.

One week after Carlo's capture of Fossato, I began the assault against it. Unfortunately, it was difficult and impracticable to maneuver troops because of the heavy spring snows. I therefore marked time in nearby Gualdo while Gentile skirmished daily with the Fossato outposts. We finally carried Fossato, not by bravery or brilliance, but because of the low morale of the defenders. It so happened that we captured a column of infantry on their way to the relief of Fossato. Of these we killed all except one hundred men. The next day we brought these hundred prisoners before Fossato's walls in full view of the besieged and strappadoed* the prisoners until they died under the treatment. This tactic so unnerved the defenders that they

---

* Torture of the hoist, known as the strappado or corda. The practice was flexible and lent itself to many variations. Usually, the wrists of the accused were bound behind his back and secured to a rope passed through an overhead pulley. Hoisting and dropping him short of the floor resulted in shoulder-dislocation. In other forms, the hoisting rope was secured under the armpits and weights were attached to the ankles.

secretly abandoned the fortress, and, we were able to seize it with a minimum of loss. Actually, we would have had very little chance of storming the fortress without artillery. It was strongly fortified. Even if we had had cannon, we would have been unable to maneuver them in the snow and mire.

While I was continuously occupied in the field, Morgante was governing in Perugia and doing his work so well that all the citizens began to love him for his just administration of the laws. Morgante was still in the employ of the Florentine Republic at this time; that is to say, they retained his services on an annual basis as they had been doing for many years. Nevertheless, the Florentines were maturing subtle plans to break our necks as they had broken the necks of the Medici.

By the beginning of May, 1501, the Florentines had poured so much arms and gold into the exile coalition that Carlo Baglioni and the Oddi were ready to risk an open and decisive battle. That battle took place on May 5. In order to spur our people with a better incentive, Morgante and I promised them all the arms and spoils of the enemy, including our own share. This enlivened our Perugians and strengthened the natural ferocity of the Albanian stradiotti cavalry which we had hired. We agreed that Morgante should hold the infantry in reserve and bring it into the attack across Lake Trasimene at the proper moment. I led the cavalry up along the heights of Borghetto. When I saw the exile army down below, I ordered the black banners unfurled and gave the order to charge down the slopes. The fighting was hot and the enemy stubborn. When we were well committed, Morgante brought his infantry across and joined the fight.

I will not make more of the battle than is necessary. It went against the exiles and they finally broke. We pursued them as far as Cortona, killing several hundred of them and capturing, not only many prisoners, but herds of cattle and other valuable pillage as we harried the countryside.

This battle, which has since come to be known as the Battle of Cortona, broke the last pretensions of the Oddi to Perugia. We captured Pompeo degli Oddi, the chief of the Oddi clan, in the fighting and brought him into the citadel of Borghetto. He was a fine honorable man of the old-fashioned school of Lodovico degli Atti, and both Morgante and I admired him greatly. Although deeply moved by his lamentations over the fall of the House of Oddi and commiserating with him in his misfortunes, we nevertheless had him strangled on the following night. I do not speak here from both sides of my mouth. We abominated this civil war like a plague. It had destroyed some of Perugia's best men and desolated the contado. Yet we felt that if peace were ever to return, it was necessary to exterminate the exiles.

The victory at Cortona was a relatively substantial one. The few survivors of the exile army saved themselves by flight. As we moved over the now silent battlefield, we saw the armor and broken weapons strewn over the field among the slain horses and the mutilated and butchered corpses of friends and kinsmen. The land was stained with blood, the trees were cut down and the houses in flames. Here was only destruction and a sinister solitude.

Such were our modest parochial affairs, but at the time they loomed large and were the substance of our lives. Cesare Borgia did not interfere with them. He was busy with his grandiose plans for Central Italy, and in a sense we Baglioni were facilitating his greater designs.

Our triumph created local repercussions in Tuscany. The Florentines, who had hoped to fish in troubled waters by helping the late Pompeo degli Oddi on the sly, now sent us envoys and lame excuses. Morgante and I were in firm control and human enough to relish the about-face demonstrations of the Florentines. Since we had broken the Oddi and could deal with our Janus-faced neighbors from positions of strength, we relaxed in Perugia and accepted Florentine explanations at face value. We tendered a great victory banquet in Perugia to which we invited our friends and neighbors and all foreign envoys resident in Perugia. Vitellozzo Vitelli came from Città di Castello and the Atti brothers came from Todi. The anxious Florentine ambassador made an appearance at the reception which preceded the banquet, and Morgante amiably assured him that he harbored no ill-will and would continue serving the republic.

"Always give liars the opportunity to save their faces," Morgante told me later that evening, "if it is to your advantage to do so and if you have no better alternative."

"True enough," I replied, "but I am salting away my grudge for future use. I rather sympathize with Vitellozzo in his quarrel with the Florentines."

You should know that Vitellozzo Vitelli burned with a single-minded hatred of the Florentine Republic and planned revenge against it day and night. His reason was that the republic had murdered his elder brother, Paolo, in 1498. Paolo was a con-dottiero like the rest of us. Florence had engaged him to prosecute the war against Pisa. I had served under him during the early campaigns of that war, which was not concluded until 1509. The republic was dissatisfied with Paolo's conduct of the campaign and suspected him of double-dealing with the Pisans. They lured him back to Florence under pretense of consultation, arrested him and cut off his head the same night. Considering Florentine military flabbiness, I deemed their judicial murder of Paolo very rash. In fact, the primary reason Vitellozzo had entered Cesare Borgia's service was in the hope of being able to take revenge on the Florentine Republic. Cesare was perfectly aware of Vitellozzo's motivation. For the time being, it suited Cesare's plans to keep the Florentines apprehensive by threatening to unleash Vitellozzo against them.

Vitellozzo became drunk and abusive during this banquet. It may be that his mal francese had lowered his tolerance for wine, and when he was in this condition he was given to uttering indiscretions. Morgante and I therefore brought Vitellozzo into a private room where he might discharge his bitterness and drunken babbling in safety. "Now that the French have come to Italy," Vitellozzo shouted, "they have made an end of the farce and have taken Pisa. Now look at Florence, hanging to the French skirts, barking for Pisa, scratching fleas, demanding from the French what she was never able to take with her own arms. She balked to pay my brother what she called tribute and finally murdered him. Ah, those bankers! They can't use arms and they grumble to pay gold for the arms of others. They think gold will work every miracle for them. Their heads are sharp but their hearts are rotten and I shall tear their hearts out!"

"You are a fool," said Morgante dispassionately. "You are letting your anger and family pride make your politics. Your intemperate words and thoughts will end by hanging you."

"Nevertheless," I said, "Vitellozzo has some justice on his side. Morgante, you should join us under Borgia. Cesare wants you. He offers you commands at three times your Florentine pay."

"I would never work for Borgia," said Morgante. "He is an adventurer while the Florentines are stable consistent men. They are civilized."

Vitellozzo roused himself and opened his eyes. "Civilized?" he said thickly. "Her civilization is not worth the bark of a stray cur. Give me strength and let my enemies be civilized."

"Fine words," said Morgante contemptuously, "but you are not the man to implement them, Vitellozzo."

Vitellozzo did not hear. He was already snoring.

So it was that the Cortona victory had raised our reputations and increased still further the bargaining power of the House of Baglioni. The princes of Italy stroked their chins and nodded approvingly. They were beginning to take us seriously. Righteous men themselves, it was immediately obvious to them that we were likewise righteous since we had succeeded and beaten the Oddi. Have you not noticed how swiftly success is transmuted into goodness, beauty and every other virtue? The rulers began to smile cordially and to make room for us on the bench of justice.

"Not much room, it's true," observed Morgante, "a mere edge for half our talented arses, but, at least, on the same bench with themselves."

"When we prove our virtue and respectability by wiping out Carlo," I said, "they will give us space for the other buttock."

"How true!" said Morgante. "Our Italy has always been a land of golden opportunity for the virtuous."

I have said that Pope Alexander was a doting father and a lover of beauty. He was also passionately appreciative of successful men. When he heard of our victory at Cortona he sent me his blessing and a confirmation of my new contract with the Borgia at an even higher rate of pay. He also summoned me to Rome to discuss his maturing plans for the Romagna. Alexander was God! I departed Perugia immediately and pushed toward Rome at top speed.

Cesare was present when I was shown into the pope's private study. It was the first time I had seen father and son together. The stature of the former seemed to shrink before the driving ruthlessness of the latter. Pope Alexander was amiable although not entirely honey and mulled wine as during the previous audience. At one point, he stared through me with a steely smile as he said, "You are becoming a great man now and one of our most trusted captains. But, remember, Baglioni, when you deal with us, you are not dealing with Italians. We and our dear Cesare will expunge these Romagnol princelings from the face of the earth; those who defy us openly and those who run for cover. It is all one and we shall use any weapon that comes to hand." He raised his right arm majestically. "Our cause is a righteous one and entirely acceptable to God. We, God's Vicar on Earth, shall make all things right."

"When we're done," I assured him, "the Romagna will lie in the Holy Father's arms like a gentle sucking lamb."

Pope Alexander's good humor settled gently on his face like a benign mask. He raised his fingers in a gesture of benediction.

"We have confirmed our dear Cesare as Gonfaloniere of the Church," he said. "Be loyal to him, Baglioni, forward in God's work, and you will rise with him. Fail him, and the world will fall out from under you, yes, and Paradise also, for we are the beginning and the end."

Cesare Borgia was graciously patient and listened with attention as I described the battle which had established Baglioni dominance in Umbria. When I concluded, he said: "It is pleasing that you have been able to flog these Umbrian towns into line. There is no room in Italy for these snapping civic dogs, these brawling, squalling communities. They must be driven to obedience under one resolute prince. With the aid of talented men like yourself, I expect no difficulty in toppling the Romagnol princes during the coming year. They are frivolous, unintelligent and greedy. They have ambition without ability."

Pope Alexander sat listening and nodded approval.

Cesare Borgia warmed to his favorite subject. "All Italy is infected with the Florentine disease, with the idea that everything can be accomplished with money. Let me repeat that gold can never be a substitute for an army, well led and disciplined by an idea. Italy is a sewer infested with foreigners and adventurers. Italy's people are overtaxed, overworked, oppressed and misgoverned by petty tyrants. There are those here who hug themselves behind velvet hangings and count gold as they say in their hearts: 'I shall not be seen.' But I have seen them and I shall tear the hangings down."

Pope Alexander looked at his son with open adoration.

"My lord Cesare and the Holy Father honor me with their confidence," I said. "But before you dismantle the entire world, grant me another few weeks of liberty on my private business. There is one little town left and one family whose neck I should like to break myself. A small matter by your magnificent standards but important to me."

"Indeed?" said Cesare, smiling, "what place is it and who are the people?"

"The name of the town is Bettona," I said, "and the name of the family is Crispolti."

"Go, my son," said Pope Alexander. "Go with God."

Sitting here today and writing in my prison, I must smile once again when I think of Pope Alexander, that brave and stately Spanish dragon. He had a way with soldiers, and if the Church was loose in those times, so is she still today. At least, she had a capable master in that handsome old Spaniard. Even his subsequent enmity cannot minimize the opulent quality of this pontiff's temperament. He vibrated like an angel's harp, though the angel could have been Lucifer.

12.

LAURA CRISPOLTI

ONE OF THE important prisoners whom I captured at the Battle of Cortona was Matteo Crispolti. Why I neglected to execute him as Pompeo degli Oddi was executed, I cannot explain. Perhaps I may have been thinking of his daughter. Perhaps Fate was putting me in the way of a good deed because my credit was low in Heaven. In any event, such absent-minded neglect to kill Matteo may have saved my own life some time later, as you shall hear.

Since capturing Metello Crispolti during the first week of January, 1501, I had kept him a close prisoner in Perugia. He had recovered entirely from his taste of the rack and his captivity was a lenient one. In general I have always distrusted the impulsive killing of prisoners, and that which is dead is wholly useless for striking future bargains. Having taken Matteo, I sent him to Perugia under close guard to join Metello in captivity.

I now began to consider the disposition of the Crispolti in accordance with the new Borgian philosophy. I summoned Amico Graziani and asked his opinion. His advice was brief — when you take a place, you must utterly destroy the rulers of it. Strangle both men.

"There is a complication," I said. "Is Matteo's daughter also to be strangled?"

"That would be wisest," said Amico, "but if you are queasy, you could have her immured in a convent."

"It would be a pity to wall up such a handsome creature," I said. "She would wither away and die."

A shrewd smile broke out over Amico's moonlike face.

"Is that your complication?" he asked.

"I am interested in that young woman, despite myself," I said.

"You will find it expensive to mix such interests with politics," said Amico. "Are you certain?"

"What else can we do besides strangling her father and brother? Let us put such considerations aside for the moment."

"You can trade," said Amico. "Banish the men and take the girl hostage for their good conduct. It is not as tidy as death, though."

I summoned Cencio and told him to assemble 300 cavalry and 300 footmen. The following day we went off toward Bettona, carrying Metello and Matteo Crispolti in our midst.

We found Bettona undefended and ruled by a girl. There was no need for force. I dispatched an ultimatum and the Bettonese readily sent out ambassadors to parley. On the following day Amico and I gathered around a table in the citadel of Bettona with the Bettonese envoys and the three Crispolti.

Amico rose and read out the treaty which he and I had discussed during the march. It called for the perpetual banishment from Bettona of Metello and Matteo Crispolti. It demanded that the town put up a bond of three thousand gold ducats for each man, this bond to be forfeit if they ever returned. In addition, Bettona bound itself never to aid what remained of the two exile factions. It promised to receive a Baglioni governor and garrison. Finally, Madonna Laura Crispolti was to be surrendered to the House of Baglioni as hostage for the good faith of her brother and father in observing the terms of their banishment.

Amico had worded the treaty carefully. He defined the terms of the Crispolti banishment meticulously even as to the distances to which they might approach their ancestral place. He forced an acknowledgment that the Baglioni were blameless in the death of Fabrizio Crispolti. He listed by name the leaders of the two exile factions with whom Bettona was to have no future dealings and defined what the House of Baglioni would consider treasonable in Bettona's future communal behavior. He specified Bettona's tax liability to the Baglioni and projected it for the coming decade. All of these clauses were preceded and followed by the magnificent legalistic flourishes in which Amico Graziani took such delight.

When Amico read out the demand for Laura's person, all present looked up and stared at him.

Amico coughed delicately, asking: "Is there any question concerning this last stipulation, signori?"

He was laughing behind his gravity. There was so much space in his full fat countenance and so many hiding places that he was able to amuse himself as much as he wished while appearing outwardly portentous.

The Bettonese envoys intelligently retained their serious mien. As for Laura, she might have been listening to an announcement for her betrothal to a prince.

The demand for Laura's person was incongruous. It was as irrelevant as a protracted discussion of a peasant's pigs in a treaty between a king and a pope. It was additionally absurd because it could have no force. If the Crispolti ever decided to violate their banishment, the possible forfeiture of a mere female's life would in no way prevent it. There was no hostage-virtue in Laura; she was neither a lever to compel nor a fetter to restrain the acts of her men. The Bettonese understood this very well. They stared at Laura with cool objective shrugs in their eyes and accepted the phenomenon of illogical sentiment in any of its ten thousand disguises. Why not? Politics were explicable and love a lunacy, but the latter was a factor with which to reckon. The perceptive Bettonese accepted the possibility of the irrational, particularly since it would put them to no additional expense or trouble.

Love was an aberration to which intelligent men submitted gracefully. Even trees loved one another. They flourished when joined and withered when separated. Wild beasts doted passionately on one another and on humans also and pined to death when parted. Gods fell from Olympus and mere men went up to Paradise or down to Hell, all by the power of love. Magnificent princes were known to have fallen in love with wrinkled beldames and beautiful duchesses with hump-backed swineherds. If the supreme tyrant of the human heart was self-interest and the hunger for power, its co-tyrant was love in any of a million multifarious and grotesque shapes. Truly wise men resignedly accepted the monstrous comicality of the human heart in refining their political schemes. Hence, the envoys understood and held their faces impassive.

Matteo, the bear, lacking the quicker wit of his fellow townsmen, scowled at the demand for Laura and commenced to protest. I cut him short, saying: "You will agree because there is no alternative."

"What does my daughter say?" growled Matteo.

We all looked at Laura.

"If it will save lives, I accede," said Laura.

"You say that too calmly and much too readily," said Matteo, frowning. With a bad grace he scrawled his signature across the parchment in great ink-splotched letters.

I left Cencio in Bettona as temporary governor with most of the troops and rode back to Perugia with my new acquisition beside me. "Madonna," I said as we rode, "yours is not the worst of fates."

"Signor," she said, "I am inclined to agree with you. I have become tired of Bettona and would like to see something of the world."

"As long as you preserve the formalities of your status," I said, "you are welcome to as much of the world as you may see in Perugia."

"What if Metello and my father break their oath and return to Bettona?" she asked. "Will you have me strangled, Signor Gianpaolo?"

I looked at the white column of her neck above the well-curved bosom and replied:

"God forbid that such thoughts should enter your mind."

"God notwithstanding," she said, "I have heard that the Baglioni are very adept at snapping the necks of honest people."

"Mere gossip," I replied. "You are not a prisoner. You and your women will have your own quarters and no one will molest or hinder you in your movements."

"Do I have your knightly word for it?" she asked gravely.

"Madonna," I said with an equally serious face, "you have my knightly word for it."

When we returned to Perugia, I saw her settled in the palace and gave orders that she was to be shown all courtesy and obedience as an honorable guest. I had already discovered one fact about Laura Crispolti: she had salt in her brains.

I saw nothing of her in the next few weeks and, in discussing her with Amico Graziani, agreed with his observation that she was not sorry to be done with Bettona. The widower Matteo Crispolti was unfit company for females, his daughter or any others. There was the unwashed reek of war about him. He was a tough leathery warrior, more interested in hanging people than in giving them a civil greeting. And the fire-eating Metello was no more than a younger copy of his father. "I have done well to take her away from that pigsty garrison," I said indignantly. "It was no place for a delicate young woman."

"Your sentiments do you credit," said Amico dryly. "Is this place an improvement?"

"Perugia is a world by comparison," I said. "She will at least have the company of ladies here. What do you think of her, Amico?"

"I never try to plumb the mysteries of another man's taste," he said carefully. "If I did not know you better, I would venture that you are entering a premature dotage."

The year of 1502 opened with a blare of martial trumpets. I helped to plan the Borgian campaign against Giulio Cesare Varano, the tyrant of Camerino. Later that year I took part in the fighting. When I spoke earlier of those who had conceived the Great Wedding Massacre, I had reference to old Varano. He was Carlo Baglioni's maternal grandfather and the theorist of the massacre as Carlo was the executioner. So all things came to pass, and two years less a month after the massacre, I witnessed Varano's execution. He was quietly strangled in a prison cell some weeks after we captured Camerino for the Borgia arms.

During these early summer weeks of 1502, I had further arguments with Morgante on the score of his stubborn loyalty to his Florentine paymasters. So did Cesare Borgia, who continued to write letters to Morgante and to raise his inducements. Fortune, however, settled the matter that summer in quite another way. Morgante contracted the sweating sickness on the marshy shores of Lake Trasimene, where he was encamped with his troops. As he grew worse, he was moved to the higher ground and better air of the Castle of Pacciano. When I came to visit him at Pacciano, he was far gone and growing worse. He lay in bed, his long splendid hair dulled by disease, his eyes sunk deep in their sockets with fever and his cheeks so gaunt that he already resembled a death's-head. One week after my visit, Morgante was dead.

Cesare condoled but also twitted me concerning Morgante's death, saying, "All the choice gossip has it that you poisoned your cousin."

I replied that such gossip was customary, almost a convention.

"Now you know how it has been with me," said Cesare. "I have been accused of having poisoned everyone from bishops to kitchen scullions, families, whole villages. For such industry, I would have needed regiments of apothecaries instead of soldiers."

"You must be philosophical," I said. "This is the price exacted by fame."

"True," said Cesare, "one must suffer for being a patriot. Still, there is a basis for it in your case; your opposed military interests, for instance; you with the Borgia and Morgante with Florence. Then there was also the possibility of future discord as co-rulers of Perugia."

"Morgante died of something more mundane than poison," I said patiently. "The polluted waters of Lake Trasimene, in fact."

"That sounds as reasonable as the poisoning theory," said Cesare, "but it is not as amusing to the people."

I told him that I would have to leave the field immediately to attend Morgante's funeral in Perugia. Cesare told me to go with God, saying that one should never neglect to pay one's last respects to a kinsman.

Now Morgante died on the seventeenth of July in the year 1502, and I escorted the body to Perugia, where it was interred with full honors, pomps and solemnities in the Cathedral of San Francesco. Our Communal Professor of Public Eloquence, Signor Francesco Maturanzio, delivered the funeral oration, declaring that Perugia was poorer a citizen of infinite bravery, prudence and good judgment. The Florentines — and it was true — heard the news with deep sorrow, for they recognized that they had lost a captain of noble qualities and exceptional faith and loyalty toward their republic.

Morgante had been a man of comely and impressive stature which, together with his imposing presence and marvelously proportioned frame, moved all beholders to admiration. Now that the embalmers had prepared the wasted mortality of what had been my cousin and clothed it in black satin, my kinsmen and I placed his silver helmet of command and sword in the casket beside him. Over his hands, I drew gloves of soft black leather and set his seal ring on his right forefinger. The casket was massive, of curiously carved Moorish woods inlaid with silver and gold. Twenty soldiers in black armor set their shoulders under the poles and so they bore Morgante into the Cathedral of San Francesco and placed the casket on a catafalque before the altar.

While I was attending the high requiem mass, Laura came to me unobserved. This was easy of accomplishment since the cathedral was filled with a great concourse of mourners, the devout and the curious who had come to pay their last farewells to Morgante Baglioni. Laura touched my arm, drew down her veil and said very low:

"Ten men are waiting to kill you as soon as you emerge from this cathedral. I have reason to believe that one of them is my father."

Before I could question her, she disappeared in the throng. I whispered what was afoot to Filippo Cencio, who knelt beside me. He slipped out quietly and posted guards about the cathedral portals with so much cunning that his actions went unnoticed. When we came out of the cathedral, Cencio walked close behind me, and just as Laura Crispolti had warned, the would-be assassins ran forward swiftly to strike. But Cencio's soldiers bore down on them even more quickly and disarmed

them before they could act. One of the attackers was indeed
Matteo Crispolti. The others were Carlo's partisans who had
stolen into Perugia during the distractions of the processions
and the obsequies.

"Do what you want with Carlo's people," I told Cencio, "and
tell me nothing. I do not care to know."

Cencio, who above all men had loved and served the late
Astorre, smiled and said: "They will vanish from the earth as
though they never lived."

"Just bring Matteo Crispolti to my house," I said. "Because
his daughter gave us warning, his fate hangs on a different
hook."

"If you are prudent, you will kill him," said Cencio. "There
is no good in the Crispolti except when dead."

But I was curious to find the root of the matter, and when
Matteo Crispolti was brought in to me with his hands bound,
I said, "Welcome, Matteo, what brings you into forbidden ter-
ritory?"

Matteo shrugged and maintained silence. When I asked him
if Metello was with him, he continued to stare and spat at my
feet. "Since you have seduced my daughter," he said at last,
"I consider my decree of banishment void."

I told him that it was his daughter who had put him into my
hands. He changed color and although his lips were silent, his
eyes called me a liar. I told him that he had both the odor and
the wit of a mountain goat and that there was nothing about
him that a daughter could love, for which reason he need not be
surprised that his daughter had betrayed him. I pointed out,
moreover, that in doing so she was making amends for the oath
which he had broken. Then I brought in Laura, who confirmed my words. When she had done, Matteo cursed her with
very hard oaths, calling her a whore and a traitor. Laura replied quietly enough that, if she was a traitor, it was to save

his honor. She also reminded Matteo that I had kept my word and spared both Metello and himself when I could have killed them both out of hand without reproach. Finally, said Laura, since the Crispolti were as good or better than the Baglioni, they should not be remiss in matters of honor.

I laughed to hear such fine wisdom from the lips of a mere girl and said, "Well, Matteo, you have lived to see your daughter instructing you in the nice points of honor."

Matteo retorted that she was no longer his daughter and that if he ever won free, he would cut her to pieces on the path of filial duty. I chided Matteo for such harsh words, saying that even the bears in the mountains were kinder toward their young and finally suggesting that he beg his daughter for his life since it was in her hands.

Had I set out deliberately to goad Matteo Crispolti to run on his destruction, I could not have chosen my words better. I know these mountain barons well. They set little store by their lives and infinite store by their pride until they show all the feral rage of beasts without any of their accompanying virtues. I think that I would have had Matteo Crispolti killed as a practical measure, for these men can neither be tamed nor trusted nor reconciled. But Laura knew her father's utter inability to unbend — which is a great weakness — and, seeing how the matter was tending, she began to plead for his life. She moderately pointed out that if Matteo were executed his blood would be on her hands, that it was a daughter's duty to plead for her parent's life, that it was necessary at times to return good for evil, and so many other eloquent and lawyerlike arguments that I felt I had chosen well. Since Laura had such an apt mind to match her comely body, I decided to risk sparing Matteo for the sake of winning her entire good will. So, without accepting a word of her arguments, I said: "You have made a very telling defense and, if this is what you want, I will accede to it."

Matteo, being what he was, cared nothing one way or the other that his life was in the balance, but Laura was taken off guard by my apparent complaisance. Seeing the wary doubt in her eyes, I said, "I will give him a horse and a spare mount, a sufficiency of money and twenty-four hours safe-conduct to pass out of here and over the borders into Tuscany. Let him go where he wishes and never return to Umbria. Is this acceptable to you?"

Laura replied with slow grudging surprise that it was very fair, if I meant it.

I saw with pleasure the solvent of my crafty good deed beginning to work in her eyes and was already hugging the future in my thoughts. It therefore struck me as no more than laughable when Matteo, still bent on his destruction, burst out, "It will not save you if I ever catch you, nor this whore who is no more my daughter. I will flay you both like a pair of sheep. Yet I accept your safe-conduct, so tell your soldiers to untie my hands and let me go."

"I thank you for your courtesy and graciousness in accepting these terms, Matteo," I said, "and so does your daughter."

And, indeed, I could not help admiring his courage and his temperament, which was like that of brutes who know neither fear nor hesitation, appropriate in wolves but grotesque in men. He gave orders like a victorious captain instead of a prisoner, for such people know no other way. Laura was embarrassed by his stiff-necked demeanor but I assured her that having given my word, I would not retract it. Matteo was leaving me his daughter in hatred, like a sack of serpents, but I thought otherwise and was already turning his enmity to good account in the wooing which had begun.

After my people had unbound Matteo Crispolti, I ordered that he be provided with the things which I had promised him, together with the safe-conduct in writing, and he strode out arrogantly without a word of thanks or farewell to either of us.

His conduct gave me further pleasure, seeing that it would advance my credit with the girl. Laura, being a woman, began to weep for the first time since I had known her. She upbraided me — I was the author of all her sorrows, had driven her father and brother into bitter exile and had scattered the House of Crispolti. All of this was true enough. She bewailed her misfortunes, cursing me and herself, saying that she was the most miserable of creatures and that she loathed me who had brought these evils upon her.

I said to her very comfortably that I had no desire to perpetuate the bitter hatreds which had burned so long between our two families, that, like herself, I was seeking only to bring such senseless feuds to a conclusion and that I was unwilling to hold her against her own will. At this she grew calmer and pointed out that in the eyes of her kinsmen she was indeed a traitor, despite the fact that she had tried to do good, that her own people would reject her from this moment forward and that she had nowhere to go.

"Yet, if you prefer to leave," I said, "I will give you money and an escort. My cousin, Atalanta Baglioni, is an honest woman. Go and live with her at Castiglione del Lago. Or go to Venice and live with my sister, Panthasilea, and my brother-in-law, Bartolomeo d'Alviano. He is short, ugly, bald-headed and has never been known to look at another woman but his wife. You will be safe enough there."

Laura dismissed my suggestion, saying that she would not better her lot by running further. But by now, my fine outpouring of Christian charity and forbearance had softened her sufficiently so that she hesitated and did not know what to say further. I noted that together with her fearlessness, she had a noble nature which she could not have received from her bear of a father, and that she was one of those magnanimous souls who are more ready to believe good of people than ill.

She finally admitted that I was not the iniquitous monster in which she had been brought up to believe and that she did not think that I would injure a woman who was now all alone.

In reply, I praised Laura's courage and good sense, rather than her beauty, saying that if she would trust me a little longer, I would prove to her satisfaction that my intentions toward her were friendly and honorable. I added that she had saved my life and that I was her debtor.

"I have no choice but to believe you," she said, "since you have already given me your knightly word."

I found this second reference to my knightly word as comical as a legless beggar, and at that moment, she pleased me more than ever. It was a revelation of her naked youth and inexperience, which she had overborne by a manly spirit. With some effort, I restrained myself from praising her further, for this was not a woman to be won with mere words. I composed my face and said: "I will pledge my knightly word once again."

Laura mulled over my reply very earnestly and finally said, "I accept your promise and will remain here — with Madonna Atalanta."

So I sent Laura Crispolti with a strong escort to Atalanta, who had retired to Castiglione del Lago, our castle on Lake Trasimene. I sent strict orders to the people there that she was to be shown every courtesy and obedience. I was satisfied by now and determined that this woman should be my future wife. How I hoped to accomplish this, seeing that I was still lawfully married to Ippolita da Conti, I did not know. Of one thing I was certain — I intended to hold this girl, not by force but by good will.

In the ensuing weeks, I spent some brief and formal days with her and Atalanta at Castiglione. Having planted the first seeds of friendship, I took no more for granted and moved carefully, pleased to feel my heart beating once again. The hope of love is a rare pleasure and hard to come by. It makes the days pass lightly and dissolves for a time the world's ugly face. I had grown tired of the great and filthy world and called to mind the maxim of Domenico Boccamazzo, who in later years became Pope Leo's master huntsman. "The first step in snaring a rare creature," said Domenico once, "is to disregard it." I had come upon such a rare creature, cast out of her lair by the hateful fortunes of war and human contention. I hoped by patience and discretion to bring this creature into my hands of her own free will.

If Laura regretted her decision, she did not show it, or, at least, having a philosopher's head upon her young shoulders, she made the best of her predicament. I thanked Matteo Crispolti in silence and swore that I would make his daughter my wife when the times permitted.

Yet the world and the times had other plans for us. While I was still at my cautious wooing of Laura Crispolti in Castiglione del Lago, messengers arrived from Cesare Borgia recalling me to the army. Together with their verbal orders they brought dispatches from Cesare in which he wrote with urgent displeasure that I had delayed long enough. I showed Laura these orders and took my leave, and it may have been that she was sorry to see me go.

So, both contented and discontented all in one, I gathered my men and rode eastward toward the Borgian camp. I had been torn from my wooing like a cutter from the carving of his favorite gravestone. Yet I also knew that if and when I returned, the gravestone would still be waiting.

The citizens of Perugia had mourned Morgante with genuine sorrow. He had given them for two years that rare spectacle, a just and efficient government. And Florence also mourned because Morgante had rendered it full value and was a better man than it deserved. I was now alone in Perugia and already missed Morgante's sense and steady hand. Cesare Borgia's affairs were burgeoning and developing swiftly. It was at that time, as soon as I rejoined his army, that Cesare ordered me into the long-delayed assault against the Varani of Camerino. While I was still mired in the fighting there, Cesare, with other troops, feinted with subtle treachery and snatched the Duchy of Urbino from under Duke Guidobaldo's nose. All Italy applauded the brilliant maneuver, but the bolt had fallen too close to home and it worried me. At the time, however, I was already committed to the action against Camerino; therefore I swallowed my misgivings and drifted along. The successful coup against Urbino pushed up Cesare's reputation by several notches. I began to speculate on when it would be Vitellozzo's turn and when it would be mine.

My personal hopes in Cesare Borgia began changing direction at this point. It was now obvious that he aimed at nothing less than the mastery of the Romagna, the Marches and Umbria. A very fine goal, but where did the Baglioni fit into such plans? Would there be a place for me, or would my own head eventually roll? And if there were a place for me, for how long and at whose pleasure? States were mortared with blood and omelets were made with broken eggs. Yet I felt an insupportable prejudice against being broken into some royal Borgian omelet.

Abstract political theory collided with my personal interest, and I began to worry in earnest.

13.

THE DIET OF LA MAGIONE

In August, 1502, Cesare Borgia ordered my fellow captains and me to attack the Bentivogli of Bologna. I was satisfied that we were in trouble. A warning bell had been ringing all summer and we had not listened to it. We had signed a treaty of amity with the Bentivogli at Villafontana on Cesare's behalf, although I will not pretend that we were technically bound to honor our signatures. My own motives, at least, involved the modest practicality of self-preservation rather than honor. If Cesare was planning to topple his dear friends, the Bentivogli, with whom he was in loving accord on paper, why should we not be next? It was now obvious that Cesare was planning to digest all of us individually. I broached my fears to my fellow condottieri, Paolo and Francesco Orsini, the illegitimate scions of the Roman House of Orsini. They agreed with me. Their uncle, the cardinal Giovanni Battista Orsini, had already informed them that he had secret information that Pope Alexander was plotting the destruction of the House of Orsini. I wrote to the cardinal and we arranged a conference.

Cardinal Orsini owned a fortress at La Magione, nine miles from Perugia and overlooking Lake Trasimene, which had originally been a chapter house of the Knights of Malta. On September 20, 1502, all of us who had reason to feel ourselves threatened gathered at La Magione. The three Orsini and Oliverotto Euffreducci, the Tyrant and Butcher of Fermo, were already present by the time I arrived. Not waiting for the others, Cardinal Orsini opened the meeting formally, saying: "In summoning you here, I am sharply aware of the fate of the Romagnol rulers already overrun by Cesare Borgia. I wish to remind you of it once again and you will do well to keep it in mind. That criminal intends the total mastery of Italy and the fate that awaits us at his hands is already clear. Now that the Colonna have been crushed, our House momentarily expects to be attacked by Cesare and his father. I think you appreciate what we can expect from him before very long."

The cardinal was interrupted by a disturbance at the other end of the room. The doors were flung open and attendants carried Vitellozzo Vitelli on a litter toward the conference table. He lay with his eyes closed and his features were puffy and livid. Vitellozzo was an ailing man and the thought occurred to me that if Cesare did not finish him, the mal francese would. A few minutes later the condottiero Ermes Bentivoglio entered. He came as the representative of the immediately threatened House of Bentivoglio. With Ermes came the Sienese law professor Antonio da Venafro, representing my old friend and sometime employer, Pandolfo Petrucci. I knew da Venafro slightly. He was reputed to be the wisest man in Siena, always excepting his employer, who was certainly the better thief.

Oliverotto Euffreducci's burly frame sprawled in a chair facing me across the table. He chewed on his long mustaches as though they were personal enemies and spat over his shoulder several times without regard for the presence of gentlemen. Perhaps you have heard how he gained the rule of Fermo by murdering his uncle. It is instructive as a piece of low cunning. It called for courage of a gross sort, which Oliverotto pos-

sessed in good measure, but no particular intelligence. He had
been apprenticed in the soldier's trade under the Vitelli since
boyhood and had risen in their service by energetic guile. He
was sufficiently able within severely defined limits. It was not
the butcher in Oliverotto which offended me as much as the
boor.

"Soon it will be the turn of the Baglioni and the Vitelli," the
cardinal was saying. "If we do not unite and take some action
to protect ourselves, we are dead men. We shall inevitably suffer the fate of Catherine Sforza, of the Manfredi and the Varani."

Cardinal Orsini now put the meeting in my hands. As I
studied my listeners, they did not appear promising. Da Venafro, tugging at his forked beard, resembled an astrologer con-
cocting a horoscope to please his patron. Paolo Orsini lisped
and pouted. Oliverotto spat, pared his fingernails with a dagger and yawned audibly. Vitellozzo lay on his back with his
eyes shut and breathed stertorously. Cardinal Orsini stared at
Oliverotto with fastidious distaste.

I rose and advised my associates that we were gathered to
concert measures for the defense of the liberties of Italy. All of
them solemnly applauded my sonorous description of a non-
existent abstraction. I continued, saying that in order not to
be devoured separately by the Borgian dragon it was necessary that we act together like true brethren. There was no more
living with Cesare, I warned them; if we did not make some
decision and commit ourselves, we were done. "Vitellozzo," I
said, "you will be next, and you, Oliverotto."

Here Vitellozzo groaned and stirred on his litter, mumbling,
"Perhaps we should wait. In less than a year Cesare may be dead
or a prisoner."

Francesco Orsini laughed at this, saying that the mal francese
had endowed Vitellozzo with second sight, and that he was in-

dulging in costly and wishful thinking. Cesare had done the House of Orsini the greatest harm, said Francesco, and he wished to make some specific and constructive proposals.

Oliverotto interrupted at this point, sheathing his dagger and crashing his steel gauntlet down on the table. He roared that he spoke only for himself, cursing Cesare Borgia for a gutter-born papal bastard and vowing that he would personally let three feet of steel into him.

"You should give Cesare Borgia credit for intelligence," said Francesco Orsini to Oliverotto. "He is not like your uncle — to be taken like a partridge at a banquet."

I agreed with Francesco's observation, pointing out that Cesare Borgia was more intelligent and talented than any man in the room. "Bravos like Oliverotto are the least of Cesare's worries," I said. "He picks his teeth with them after breakfast. It is plain, Oliverotto, that you are not accustomed to polite company."

Oliverotto rose, kicked back his chair and whipped out his sword, which brought the others to their feet with their hands on their sword hilts. I banged the table for order and Francesco Orsini laughed and shouted that since we were statesmen and not drunken lanzknechts, we should put up and return to our discussion. Vitellozzo, clinging to the edge of the table for support, sat up in his stretcher cursing Oliverotto and vowing that he would have him hanged out of the castle window. At this, Oliverotto stared at his old master and began to laugh while Vitellozzo fell back spent on his litter.

"Holy Saints!" said Oliverotto, chuckling, "our friend Vitelli is in no condition to wipe his own nose, much less hang me."

I finally brought the meeting to order and Francesco Orsini took the floor, proposing that with a thousand horse and seven thousand foot at our disposal, we were in a position to attack Cesare Borgia immediately. He suggested that Ermes Benti-

voglio attack Imola, where Cesare lay, from the north. The
rest of us ought to combine, drive against Urbino from the
south and so restore Duke Guidobaldo.

Everyone present agreed to our plan of action. It was a
good one and could have succeeded, for Cesare had been caught
short with only some three thousand men. Had my associates
been men of character, it would not have failed. I except
Francesco Orsini here.

We separated and rejoined our forces. Even as we began to
move, the Urbinati revolted and recaptured the supposedly
impregnable fortress of San Leo. By the end of September, all
Urbino was in arms against Cesare. The revolt spread to
Camerino and the Borgian garrison there was massacred. If
Cesare was surprised, he did not show it. He did dispatch envoys, however, seeking a reconciliation with us. I warned my
fellow captains not to trust Cesare, saying that he was playing
for time until the four hundred lances promised him by King
Louis arrived from the French camp.

We won the first round and put Guidobaldo back in Urbino.
A Borgian garrison still held out in Gubbio but that was all.
Cesare marked time and began to court Paolo Orsini, the weakest character among us. Then Pandolfo Petrucci, who could
never resist the delectation of bad faith, sent secret envoys to
Cesare and made private terms. I do not condemn Pandolfo;
the crookedness was in his marrow. Paolo Orsini visited Cesare quietly in Imola and brought back the terms which he
offered to all of us. They seemed fair enough, but I said to the
captains, "You are gullible sots if you believe that Cesare will
do as he says." And to Francesco Orsini, I said privately, "Let
Paolo go to the Devil if he wishes, but I regret to see you deceiving yourself. You will regret this."

Francesco shrugged with a dark frown on his face and said
nothing.

Then it was Bentivoglio's turn to capitulate. Only Vitellozzo, Oliverotto and I held out. Our position daily became more precarious. Aside from the cowardly, short-sighted and self-seeking attitude of our confederates, the Romagna had not revolted against Cesare as we had hoped it would. The truth is that the people of the Romagna did not care who ruled them. They had been ruled too long and too badly by too many incompetents. Their only desire was to see all princes kill one another.

Vitellozzo's confidence finally weakened. He was a coward at heart, but I am more inclined to charge it against the mal francese, which has beclouded the judgment of better men. It was Cesare Borgia who once said of Vitellozzo: "I do not recall ever having seen him do a single thing worthy of a man of courage and honor. His constant excuse is his mal francese. He is good only to destroy places that have no defense, to plunder feeble civilians and to plot treacheries."

With Vitellozzo fallen away, I was left alone. Oliverotto was personally odious to me, and in any event he could be counted upon to follow Vitellozzo's lead. I stood by trying to decide my personal course of action while my former associates, one by one, made up their differences with Cesare Borgia. The quarreling lovers were finally reconciled. Oliverotto and the two Orsini captains met Cesare at Cesena to receive his new orders. He ordered them to assault the city of Sinigaglia, as a part of his earlier plans interrupted by our disaffection. Eager to show their good will, Oliverotto and the Orsini captured the town. Now Cesare, radiating friendship and brotherhood, invited all to meet him at Sinigaglia to celebrate and to lay plans for future glories.

I came to Vitellozzo's headquarters and watched him making ready to leave for the love-feast with Cesare Borgia.

"Why does he insist on meeting you all personally?" I asked. "That was not part of the agreement."

Vitellozzo replied almost sheepishly that since Cesare was

the supreme commander, it was necessary that he confer with all his captains concerning the coming campaign.

"You sound like a country girl telling herself she is committing no sin in lying with the village priest," I said. "You have still to convince me. Do you remember when you came from Pantalla to help me regain Perugia two and a half years before? You did me a good turn then. Now I will repay it with some sound advice. Come with me instead of to Sinigaglia."

Vitellozzo shrugged and threw a green-lined cape across his shoulders. "Why should I?" he asked. "Where are you going?"

"First Gubbio," I said. "My people have Girolamo della Penna besieged and cornered there and I have some personal business to settle with him. And after that I am riding for Perugia. If the magnificent Cesare asks for me, you may tell him that I am too ill to attend his little reunion."

"I have given my word," said Vitellozzo with mournful heaviness. "Cesare promised that he would help me to revenge my brother's death on the Florentines."

"He knows your weak place," I said. "Who does not? Cesare is playing on it hard. Morgante and I warned you many times that you would break your neck if you continued to mix family feelings with business."

Vitellozzo did not seem to be listening.

"Do you really believe him?" I asked.

"I must go," said Vitellozzo.

"That is the mal francese speaking," I said.

"I must go," repeated Vitellozzo.

"Very well, go," I said. "But you will need more than ordinary good health to return from Cesare's banquet alive. Farewell . . . I do not expect to see you alive again."

I rode out of Vitellozzo's headquarters immediately in the direction of Gubbio. My fellow captains were clever men and had been warned repeatedly. Vitellozzo had smelled something, but his personal devil drove him on in spite of it. Paolo

Orsini was a fop and Oliverotto was a brute. If I sympathized with any one of them it was Francesco Orsini.

I kicked spurs to my horse and began putting as much distance as possible between Cesare Borgia and myself.

But my troubles had barely commenced.

Girolamo della Penna was serving with Cesare's Spaniards in the Gubbio garrison. As soon as I rejoined my people before the Gubbio fortifications, I began the siege in earnest to complete my business while Cesare Borgia was still reorganizing his forces. I was like a hunter who imminently expects to become a quarry himself.

The tough Urbinati mountaineers had scores of their own to settle with the Spaniards and were glad to assist. My men set the peasants to mining the walls and we labored together day and night digging ditches and dragging huge blocks of stone out of the walls with teams of oxen. In those days, the fading need for revenge still supplied me with sufficient driving power. What prodigious labors men can accomplish if the interest is adequate! No matter how huge those stones, I felt myself able to tear them all out of their sockets. I coaxed, encouraged and drove both my men and the peasants. In the end, we breached the citadel and the wall began to split. The Spaniards surrendered on good terms. I allowed them to march out of the citadel with their standards and personal arms, for I was uninterested in them. For Girolamo della Penna I would make no terms. The Spaniards cared nothing about his personal predicament. Unwilling to commit suicide, he gave himself up unconditionally. He surrendered, still in armor, with a sullen uneasy look on his swarthy face.

I advised him to strip off his armor, saying he would no longer need it, for I was returning him to Perugia in irons for a fair trial before the Priori delle Arti.

"You shall have the opportunity which you never gave to

Gismondo Baglioni," I said, "an opportunity to defend yourself."

I did not know how much time I would have in Perugia before
the Borgian army came in pursuit. But, as it happened, I was
given a sufficient interval to stage my final official act — the trial
of Girolamo della Penna. It was a good trial, with so many ob-
servances and safeguards that I was admired and compared to
the late Morgante. We are known for a fine legal tradition in
Perugia and have given the world many famous jurists, despite
the wry truth that we have not heeded our legal men too
closely. I decided on a public trial to show the people that
we did not deal in private vengeance, that we respected the
Priori and the forms of communal justice in Perugia. Perhaps
my heightened civic sense may have been due to the fact that I
was simultaneously looking over my shoulder waiting for the
pennons of the Borgian advance guard to appear. So do men
grow virtuous when their minds are uneasy!

Girolamo della Penna was twenty-eight years old at this time.
Despite his warlike reputation, he took his death sentence
badly. I was aware that he was not a coward and could only
conclude that he was disturbed at the prospect of being hanged
and quartered like a common peasant. I went to visit him in
prison on one occasion and spoke my mind to him.

"Such snobbery has always been among your weaknesses,"
I said. "If you were not always straining to prove yourself a
great gentleman, you would not be here today. It was such
vanities which involved you in the massacre in the first place."

But Girolamo ignored me, for he had taken to piety in an
impressive fashion. The Brethren of Mercy had given him an
image of Sant' Ercolano for the wall of his cell and he spent
whole hours together before it on his knees praying heartily.
Much of the time he did not bother to look up when I came to
visit him. If Sant' Ercolano did not hear him, it was not for
want of Girolamo's effort.

Such a display of exemplary piety and repentance must have softened me sufficiently at the time — that and my private worries about Cesare Borgia's intentions. I finally sent an officer to reassure Girolamo that he would die like a gentleman — by the sword. Girolamo continued disconsolate and I finally went myself to confirm the promise. It was better than Girolamo della Penna deserved. I will make no capital out of it, however, for it will store me up no credits in Heaven.

My personal promise cheered Girolamo greatly. He became like a man going to a bride instead of a sword. Such is the pride and the vanity of men! He smiled and asked for friars to prepare his soul and a barber to shave off his beard before he died. The spirit of good will became progressively contagious. I fell in with it and presented Girolamo with a handsome suit of black velvet and silver lace in which to die. So when he finally emerged in the prison courtyard, he made a brave show, walking with steady dignity behind the chanting friars, fingering a rosary and murmuring prayers as he went. Certainly a man should be given the opportunity to die well, for it is humiliating that he should have to be dragged amain to the block.

The witnesses who were present praised Girolamo's mien and my magnanimity. His head, having been parted from his body, was impaled on the spikes of Pisano's fountain, in accordance with the sentence of the Priori. Girolamo was forever beyond caring and I had done nothing with which to reproach myself.

Even as I was witnessing the death of Girolamo della Penna, a courier rode in to announce that the scouts of the advancing Borgian army were nearing the village of Marsciano. So in the instant of Girolamo's death, I had, in a manner of speaking, exchanged places with him. Now it was my turn to be a fugitive and a quarry.

I fled from Perugia that same night.

14.

THE EXILES

It was many months later that I learned — but only in a general way — of the beautiful stratagem which Cesare Borgia had executed at the city of Sinigaglia. I learned also how all Italians, especially those who should have known better, admired him for it. I repeat — they admired the wrong things for the wrong reasons. Cesare had managed his coup brilliantly although he was aided by the poltroonery and also by the dishonesty (and I must apologize for intruding such a righteous factor) of my associates, who deserved to die as petty failures. As for the people who applauded Cesare's guile in snaring and murdering his captains, the vulgar majority may be excused on grounds of ignorance. But those who fancied themselves sophisticated adepts at statecraft were juggling hot coals and flirting with perilous precedents. It is one thing to praise evil and call it good. It is another to accept the implications of such a stand. Which is why many who commit the sin of self-delusion often come to die like cattle with expressions of hurt surprise on their faces.

I fled from Cesare Borgia's vengeance like a lame sparrow in a thunderstorm, skittering across a vast black plain without shelter and without hope. Wherever I paused the lightning bolts crashed around me, singeing my bedraggled feathers.

Wherever I turned, I could see no way of escaping from the Borgia and from Carlo Baglioni, who had already joined them. But Alexander, that glorious golden pope, had warned me fairly: "If you fail us, Baglioni, we will cut the world out from under you, for we are the beginning and the end."

The world, in truth, was shaking under my feet.

Cesare Borgia wasted no time in seizing the Vitelli stronghold of Città di Castello. The Perugian Priori delle Arti bent in terror before the high wind of his ultimatum and begged me to leave Perugia immediately if I would save my life and the city from sack and utter ruin. They showed me the letter which Cesare had sent them from Corinaldo.

Cesare recounted to them the rebellion of his captains and damned me as the chief rebel — all of which was true. This, he wrote bitterly, despite the fact that he had treated us as sons and brothers. As for Vitellozzo Vitelli, Oliverotto da Fermo and the two Orsini, he had rid Italy of burdensome pests in executing them. He informed the Priori that he proposed to liberate Perugia from the rapacious and bloody tyranny of the Baglioni and place the city under his beneficent rule. Wherefore he exhorted the Priori to send him envoys and a like embassy to the Holy Father in order to render full and proper allegiance to the Apostolic See. Failing such steps, Cesare warned that it would be his painful responsibility to bring the Priori to a realization of their duty by force, which course would pain him deeply, because of the singular benevolence which he bore in his heart toward the people of Perugia. It was a fine letter.

By the stroke at Sinigaglia, Cesare had crushed all of us. Vitellozzo's kinsmen fled into exile. That connoisseur of the gracious life, Guidobaldo of Urbino, was once again a hunted man. I was suddenly powerless, without arms, money or troops. It was vain now to try to repel the victorious arms of Borgia, and yet it need not have been. Had we held together, we could have defeated Cesare. But it was too late for regrets and our only hope now lay in flight.

On January 5, 1503, therefore, Gentile and I, leading a procession of kinsmen, retainers and trusted soldiers, fled toward Siena. Within a few days, I learned that Carlo Baglioni had entered Perugia in triumph to coordinate the city for the new Borgian master. I do not mind deceiving others but object to deceiving myself and will therefore admit a truth — the Perugians were not displeased with Cesare's government. He was and always had been a better administrator than soldier. The majority of the citizens celebrated our flight by bolting the gates as soon as we had passed through and were on our way to exile. We departed with the bells of Perugia ringing in joyous mockery. Even while we were riding through the streets toward the Porta Eburnea, the citizens were waving banners and shouting, "Long live the Church! Long live Cesare Borgia!"

I hold nothing against Cesare Borgia except his readiness to sacrifice me. Others — yes; but at the time I considered myself an exception to the rule. I think I could have worked with and for him. I might have been willing to subordinate myself to a good leader and to a rational policy of unification and, certainly, to a policy of declawing Holy Mother Church. I say "I might." But I reflect on these matters through the shifting prism of memory. To be rigorously honest — I do not know. How can I recall my feelings after seventeen years? Would I have let slip the rosy apple of personal power so easily? It is not so simply answered. In my experience, human beings do not bow to a common cause to preserve life or goods or for any other reason. There are many prizes which men love better than life itself — their passions and appetites, their prides and what they conceive to be their self-interest — and the greatest of all human lusts is the lust for power. There are those who will let the world sink ruined into the deepest pit of Hell if they cannot hold power, and they will never hesitate. Let all the world go under but I must be first. My world or no world, for such is the nature of man. No creature, not the wolf nor the wild swine, is charged with such boundless feral pride. Will you still maintain, then, that God created Adam, and in His own image?

As the Borgian army marched into the Perugian contado, very few castles or houses escaped from the claws of the Spaniards. Those landowners who fell into Spanish hands were cut to pieces. The peasants were spared for forced labor to satisfy the exactions of Cesare's Spanish captains.

I sent messengers ahead telling Laura Crispolti to make ready. When I reached Castiglione del Lago with a small troop, she was cloaked and ready to ride. I came in weatherworn, for I had ridden hard through a freezing night, and for my exertions received no more than a civil greeting.

"Since my hostage-state has been canceled by Cesare Borgia's triumph," said Laura, "why have you come here?"

I said: "Would you prefer to remain under the rule of the Borgia?"

"Why not?" asked Laura with a smile. "He knows that the Crispolti have always been enemy to the Baglioni, for which reason he will protect and favor me. I have heard that he is appointing new men in Perugia to administer the laws — fairly — and new magistrates who are not submissive to tyrants and bravos. You are a fallen landless man, Signor Gianpaolo. Now it is your turn to go into exile and taste what my kinsmen have tasted at your hands."

Her words caught me shrewdly, like a dagger at the throat, but I took heart, seeing that she belied her own statement since she was clothed and prepared to leave.

I went over to her and took her hand, saying: "Everything you say is true. All I can promise is that, when the tide changes,

I'll give you back Bettona and make you my wife. Therefore come with me into exile."

"I have not been asked whether I would have you for a husband," said Laura. "You are in no position to build promises on an empty future, and, finally, I believe you are lawfully married to Madonna da Conti."

"She is my wife," I admitted, smarting under the first two blows, "but I shall seek dispensation from Pope Alexander to annul my marriage."

Laura laughed. "From the Borgia pope whose son is hunting your head at this moment?"

"He won't live forever," I said. "There will be future popes."

"Your fortunes may turn," said Laura, "but no one knows the future. For the present you have been declared rebel, a pauper, and all your goods have been confiscated into the Perugian treasury for the advantage of the Borgian governors. Why should I go with a beggar — and where?"

The sweat broke on my back for exasperation, and I resolved that she would leave with me if I had to carry her away by force. The harder she struck at me, the more my skin smarted to win over this fine rare beast of a female who clawed perversely as she felt her chains loosening.

I contained myself and said, "We are going to Siena and Pandolfo Petrucci's protection. And because this beggar needs you."

"No more?" she said. "You put it very grudgingly and you are still too proud."

"I've had no practice yet in humility," I said, "and, as for love, I will talk of that later."

"How fortunate I am," she sneered, "having that to look forward to. But now that we're equally gypsies and beggars, I find you more tolerable, and so I will go with you, but for my own reasons."

"And what is that?" I asked.

"Something more important than your promises," she said. "My father and brother have returned with Borgia's army, breathing fire and looking for both of us."

"I am not afraid of them," I said irrelevantly.

"Afraid or unafraid," she said, "if my father takes you, you will die slowly and very painfully. And he will kill me also."

"He spoke in the heat of the moment," I said.

"You should know my father better," smiled Laura. "If he promised to flay you like a sheep, a sheep you shall be. I will take you as the lesser of the evils," she concluded mockingly. "If I feel no love for Matteo Crispolti, it does not mean that I feel any for you."

Laura's words and demeanor gave no promise of warmth for the winter nights which lay ahead. Nevertheless I rode out of Umbria, perhaps forever, with a better heart because she rode with me. Spring would return to the land and also to this woman's heart. We rode hard in silence and rejoined the main body of our exile company at Chiugi; from there, we traveled more slowly toward Siena.

Pandolfo Petrucci's situation was as bad as mine. His comfortable secret agreement with Cesare Borgia served him not at all. I could have told him that. But what would you? Pandolfo could no more help his double-dealing than a fox can resist stealing hens. But Cesare was no man to keep faith with chicken thieves.

Now Pandolfo, being a tyrant, was properly furnished with all the pains and pleasures which pertain to that estate. He had a mortal enemy whose name was Baldassare Scipione. Baldassare was a condottiero, a Sienese exile and Pandolfo's chief rival. Pandolfo offered a fat standing reward for his private political thorn which we Baglioni had often and unsuccessfully

tried to collect. At this time Baldassare turned up from nowhere as Cesare Borgia's partisan. He reached Siena before
me and was stirring riots in Borgia's behalf against the Petrucci.
I was apprised of this development as soon as I reached Siena,
and leaving Laura at the home of trusted friends, I rode to
confer with the Sienese Priori.

"Our First Citizen is hiding under the bed," they informed
me. "We cannot guarantee your protection, Signor Gianpaolo.
Cesare is too strong and you are only an embarrassment to us.
Go with God by the way you came."

I went to the palace, coaxed Petrucci out of hiding and led
him to a window overlooking the piazza, where Scipione was
haranguing the people.

"Stop shivering," I said to the old man. "Cesare is still twenty
miles away and Scipione is present here only as his advance
agent. He's not ready to bite your head off — yet. He has first
to convince the people."

Petrucci shook with fear and also with indignation. "Do you
hear what he is saying?" he quavered, "and how the citizens
are replying? Ah, the ungrateful curs! Behold how they disown
a loving father who has spent his heart's blood in their service!"

"Cesare Borgia's only desire," roared Scipione down in the
piazza, "is to lead you from Petrucci's servitude toward liberty!"

"Death to Petrucci!" howled the crowd. "Death to Baglioni!"

"Mobs are mobs," I said to Petrucci, "and I think it is time
that we put in a good word in our own behalf. If we do not,
Scipione's rhetoric will heat them up to our destruction."

"No!" said Petrucci. "They'll tear you apart."

"It is worth a try," I said. "I am at least as persuasive an
orator as Scipione."

I descended the stairs into the courtyard and mounted my
horse. The gates were unbarred and I rode into the piazza, just
as I had come, in full armor.

As the mob milled and fell into a momentary confused silence, I shouted to them:

"I come here because your First Citizen invited me and because I am your condottiero and still receiving your pay. Siena hired me in good faith and I have returned to fulfill my contract."

This was true enough; Siena had lent me to the Borgia temporarily but I was still in Sienese hire. The mob grew quiet and I pointed to Scipione. "Who is this man? He says he is Sienese. He speaks your dialect and he dresses like you. But remember that his heart is not Sienese! I say he is a traitor in the service of that malignant Spaniard who now marches here. If you listen to Cesare's man, you will have a true taste of the whip and wish to all the Saints you had Petrucci back. Who is this Cesare, this Gonfaloniere of the Church? And what have you to do with the Church? Was ever the sovereign Republic of Siena a dominion of the Church?"

This finally won a scattering of belated applause and more silence.

"I will inform you about Cesare Borgia," I said more quietly. "I served under him and can tell you how he rules. Now, think well — do you want your women carrying in their bellies the bastards of his pox-ridden Spaniards, that scum that he has dragged here from every jail in Spain?"

"No!" shouted the mob, and the applause rose stronger.

"You know what has happened in my own Umbria," I continued, "the rapes, the abductions, the tortures. You will have a taste of that also. If you listen to Scipione, I will not be responsible for what follows and am ready to leave if that is indeed what you want. But when you do repent, it will be too late."

The reaction was better than I had originally hoped. I did not expect them to turn about completely and resist Borgia. Nevertheless, I was more confident that the prominent citizens, those who would make the decisions, were beginning to reflect seriously. A committee of the most influential men went immediately into secret session. Two hours later they announced their decision. "We have no choice but to negotiate with Cesare," their spokesman informed Petrucci and myself. "In the meantime, you and our First Citizen may take your goods and people and leave unharmed. Scipione has already left with the same message for Cesare."

"You are fools," I told the spokesman. "You are tossing the city into Cesare's lap. He will gladly accept, for he did not expect such an easy bargain."

Once again, Petrucci was all smiles and cheerfully set about ordering the packing of his money chests. I have never met a man with so little pride. Doubtless that is what carried him to the top of the civic hill in the first place. We all rode out of Siena together, leading a winding procession of wagons, riders and marchers. Laura rode beside me. Once she said, smiling, "I shall not mind this gypsy life when the weather turns warmer," and then she said no more for the rest of the day.

If we hoped for hospitality from the people of Lucca, we were disappointed. They were willing, but Cesare Borgia put immediate pressure on them to expel us. To save them embarrassment, our Perugians parted company with Petrucci and we moved on to Florence. Here, Pietro Martelli, the Florentine military commissary, found Gentile and myself and offered us service. Lacking another choice and from sheer weariness, we accepted. Martelli put his villa at my disposal, and it was just as well he refused payment for I would have been unable to meet the cost on such a palatial dwelling. Laura established herself in the wing farthest from that which Gentile and I occupied. It was plain that she did not wish to be disturbed, and I did not intrude on her privacy.

So we continued for a period of eight months through the spring and summer of the year 1503. I immersed myself in my duties and was away from Florence much of the time with Filippo Cencio, drilling troops in the garrison towns of the Florentine contado. Whenever I had freedom, I sought out Laura's company. As the weeks went by, her coldness gradually thawed into something resembling friendship — but no more than friendship.

Gentile tried my patience when he once said, "You have been at great trouble to bring away a very haughty woman. Who and what are the Crispolti that you are willing to spend so much pain over her? I remember the times when all the Crispolti were good for was to be killed."

"Such words come badly from the mouth of an ex-cleric," I retorted. "Where is the celebrated Christian charity with which you priests puff yourselves? Since we have already destroyed the Crispolti, I am only trying the greater feat of winning a Crispolti heart."

"Misfortune is making you soft and old," said Gentile, shrugging. "If your intention is to lie with her, you are giving yourself marvelous difficulty, since many ladies would be glad to pleasure you without thought of marriage."

"Well, should I ever need the services of a pimp, cousin ex-priest, I will apply to you," I said in ill humor. "In the meantime, it is this girl I want."

Gentile, who was famous for his thick skin as well as for his long silences, persisted unabashed, "Do you truly intend to marry her?"

"As soon as I can obtain dispensation from our holy shepherds in Rome," I admitted.

"You will have as much chance of obtaining a dispensation from this Holy Father as a Turk has of being cardinal."

"I disagree," I said. "Pope Alexander would sell cardinals' hats even to Turks if they offered enough money. Where gold is concerned, he can be majestically Olympian. But I have no money at this time and the girl chooses to be strict and pious."

"Then suffer and be patient," said Gentile.

I made no reply and congratulated myself, not on a talent of patience, but on the fact that I was not wholly obsessed by a need to have Laura. At no time, neither then nor now, has the flesh hung over my eyes and my understanding. If I bent myself to establish further communication with Laura, it was with the feeling that all experience was good, even the experience of being rejected and held off, of having one's lamentable weaknesses turned up mocking like a witch's pack of cards. I did not find it so great a mortification to be held at arms' length but neither did I convey this to Laura. She. enjoyed sufficient advantages with which to bedevil me since she had something which I wanted.

And so our life continued well enough through that summer.

During the third week of August, a cavalry trooper, dusty and staggering with weariness, brought me a letter from my brother-in-law, Bartolomeo d'Alviano, in Venice.

"I have just had news from Rome by the Venetian ambassador Giustiniani," he wrote. "I am relaying it to you as quickly as possible by Stracciabandiere. Take good care of him. He is my swiftest courier.

"Alexander, the marraño* pope, is dead. He died in Rome little more than a week ago and has gone to his reckoning. The accounts given of his passing are many. The vulgar say that he signed pacts with the Devil in return for the tiara. As usual, they are wrong, for the Devil would have come off poorly in a pact with Alexander. Also, the death-watchers swore that they saw a big black dog, red-eyed and slavering, standing by the bier with them. From which babble you may judge how edifying

---

* In Spain, a non-Christian who had professed Christianity in order to escape persecution; a term of reproach.

his death must have been and I consider it a slander on the honest canine breed.

"Panthasilea, whom Cesare Borgia seized in January in Castel delle Pieve, is still a prisoner in Corbara and we have much to do. I think it is time that you quit Florence and struck back. Malatesta and Orazio are well and send you a loving greeting and you will yet live to see them triumphant in Perugia. Rise up, gather your people together, get what help you can from the Florentines, ride from Perugia, massacre those scum who hold the city and utterly destroy them. I will follow and join you with all aid as soon as I am able."

I went immediately to show Pietro Martelli the letter. He read it with a small smile of relief and said, "We should take advantage of this. In serving yourself, you will be serving us, and I'll prepare the documents."

"Should there be a fight, we have no strength," I said. "We have a hundred cavalry and three hundred foot."

"Not enough," Martelli conceded. "I'll send on reinforcements immediately behind you. How soon can you depart?"

"Tomorrow morning," I said. "I can be in Castiglione Chiusino the following night, on the twenty-third, and at La Magione the day after, without difficulty. We will need at least five hundred infantry and crossbowmen."

"You shall have them," said Martelli, writing busily. "When you reach Magione, call a thirty-six-hour halt. We will have the troops meet you there."

He went to a ceiling-tall wardrobe on the far wall and came back with a white silk banner furled around an oaken staff. He unrolled enough of it to display the vermilion lion rampant on a white field.

"Take our Marzocco with you in token of our aid and good wishes," he said. "Plant it on the walls to commemorate the destruction of the Borgia."

I drank a toast with him and went on my way.

As Gentile and I rode toward Perugia the following day, we felt and saw the rising sea of change through every village we passed. Umbria's deep mellow summer calm was broken by the flow of armed men returning home from all directions. They were returning not only to Umbria, but to Romagna and the Marches. Guidobaldo was enjoying his second warm welcome from the Urbinati. The Vitelli nephews were riding home to Città di Castello. As the pope sank into his new grave, the Romagnol lords rose from theirs. Whether this was good or evil depended on one's viewpoint. I did not feel the Romagnols deserved such favorable fortune, for I reflected that none of them would have as much difficulty as I anticipated. Gentile almost read my thoughts. "I hear that Guidobaldo encountered no resistance at all in re-entering Urbino," he said with a touch of envy in his voice.

"The Romagnol princes are returning," I said. "They have forgotten nothing and they have learned nothing. But they are due for a surprise. Cesare has changed their cozy world."

In the past eight months Cesare Borgia had become the strongest man in Central Italy, not by his own generalship, but by the use of money and the skill of others. Yet this does not detract from his real ability. But now the circle had been completed and I was on the road back.

Martelli's promised aid did not appear at La Magione.

"Those Florentines are liars as well as bumblers," grumbled Gentile.

"It doesn't matter," I said. "In the end, we will have to depend on ourselves."

We pushed on toward Todi, and Lodovico degli Atti came out to join me with a strong cavalry force. He was a little grayer and as grim as ever. He embraced and kissed me on both cheeks in his grave old-fashioned way and said, "It is good to see you once again, Signor Gianpaolo."

"I will not ask why you are here," I said.

"There is no need," he replied. "Friends can speak with silence."

Lodovico's troopers seemed more beautiful to me than a bevy of nymphs, and Lodovico, following my stare, nodded grimly, saying, "They will acquit themselves, if only to please me."

Soon thereafter Bartolomeo d'Alviano arrived in Todi with a mixed force of footmen and arbalasters and I no longer had doubt regarding the outcome.

"So!" said Bartolomeo. "For a man who should have been strangled eight months ago, you look healthy enough, Gian. Have you work for me?"

"Yes," I said. "Put me back in Perugia."

He smiled. "Put yourself under my orders and I will do it."

"At your service," I said. "But bear in mind that there is a Borgian garrison of four thousand men in Perugia and Carlo Baglioni has been in command of it ever since Cesare captured the city. Carlo has every reason in the world to fight hard, and he has four times our strength."

"No matter," said Bartolomeo. "I learned my trade under old Virginio Orsini; so well, in fact, that he gave me his daughter for my first wife. It is not the number of men, it is how they are employed."

When Carlo Baglioni issued from the city to offer battle, we fell back before him in a series of patient feints and false retreats. Because of our numerical weakness, we sought at all costs to avoid a contest in the open field. We therefore continued to march and countermarch until we gradually maneuvered Carlo into an unfavorable position and forced him back into Perugia for a static defense. This is comprehensible when you consider that Carlo Baglioni, though personally brave, was no match for two wily professionals, two virtuosi, like Lodovico degli Atti and Bartolomeo d'Alviano. Theirs was the sound planning, and the final assault against the walls succeeded within two days because it was correctly conceived before it was launched. As in a chess game, the source of Carlo Baglioni's defeat was a small crack, an obscure fault which widened and deteriorated imperceptibly until his position ultimately collapsed. This is how most battles are won and lost — so I cannot rationalize the victory and say that the credit was mine and the fault Carlo's. I was swept along to triumph with the deep feeling that all of us were mere chips of wood swirling along in a swift and muddy stream.

From which we must conclude that the most meaningful force in men's lives is meaningless coincidence.

BOOK III

THE HOUSE OF DELLA ROVERE

1503-1513

15.

THE INFAMOUS CONCLAVE

THERE IS an ebb tide in the fortunes of all men when everything to which they put their hand withers and spoils. Such a tide caught me in the third year of the pontificate of Giuliano della Rovere because of my own defects and also because of political circumstances which I could not have foreseen.

While we are not entirely puppets in the hands of Fortune and can do much to protect ourselves from the vagaries of circumstance, there are moments when all the gods conspire in gleeful concert to accomplish our ruin. That such developments are coincidences without inner meaning neither solves our dilemmas nor salves our hurts. We tell ourselves that such grotesque mischances will never strike us, only others. But a moment arrives when we are the target. These malignant and improbable arrows are fashioned for a purpose, and when they pierce us we are wholly helpless in spite of all the pains and precautions we have taken to safeguard against the unforeseen. You need only consider the career of Cesare Borgia in this connection. He did all that he should have done in order to secure himself, yet he could not have anticipated that he himself would be helplessly ill at the critical moment of his father's death; and that moment was the beginning of his downfall.

Without spinning my theories too finely, let me only say that

Alexander VI, that pontiff so abhorred by the pious, departed this world leaving Holy Mother Church powerful and wealthy. He broke the Orsini and the Colonna, who until his time had immemorially menaced the Apostolic See. If he aggrandized his bastards, it was at the expense of the Romagnol princelings and at no cost to the Church. Certain troublesome persons who can never be satisfied will maintain that a good deed done without conscious intent cancels itself and is, hence, without merit. But they are subtle quibblers, for nothing is ever done without Divine warrant, or so the theologians tell us. If robbers overlook a coin in the church poorbox, their carelessness is ordained by Providence, which mysteriously suffers selfish clerics and all the world's evils. To those malcontents who still insist that Alexander wrought for his children rather than for God, I, who am no friend of the Borgia, reply — no matter; the effect is the same. Roderigo Borgia, who died Alexander VI, was a good pope.

Now came Julius II — born Giuliano della Rovere, that ex-vegetable peddler with his mal francese and his martial fulminations — to benefit by Alexander's sagacity while cursing Alexander for a marraño of evil memory. I could not withstand this new pope, thanks to the power which he had inherited from Alexander VI. So it was that he made swords from the honey which Borgia had stored, and by his rashness he succeeded in enterprises which would have daunted more prudent men. The wisdom of the first and the impetuosity of the second raised up a wind before which I was helpless. In the final reckoning it does not matter, for I was at all times a mere hireling, a fox among lions. Yet I cannot altogether go free; neglect as well as coincidence lost me my state and made me della Rovere's abject vassal for seven years. If I complain, it is against myself for carelessness and irresolution, that secret cowardice which prevented me from accomplishing della Rovere's death when I had him in my hand. This is greater than error, being a defect of character, but men whose time on Earth is short may examine their sores without reproach. I escaped from the consequences of that past irresolution as I have not escaped from the consequences of my present and lesser miscalculation.

When a man commits an irremediable political mistake, the world raises its eyebrows, shrugs its shoulders and moves on to better things. Such a man, being a dead pawn and off the board, need no longer be taken into anyone's calculations. There is nothing more ugly than error. When Cesare Borgia, in a moment of madness or weakness, trusted in della Rovere's promises, it was all finished for Cesare. When I, in a mood of self-destruction, trusted in Pope Leo's safe-conduct and entered Rome, of which I shall tell you in due course, it was all finished for me. I have already been dismissed, forgotten and interred by all sensible men.

There are always those who say that we condottieri are more apt at finding ways of avoiding than of fighting one another. The charge has merit. In my own case, it was not so much cowardice as a professional reluctance to solve problems violently which called for a nonviolent solution. The truth may be that I despised the motives of my employers as prostitutes despise their patrons, not on moral grounds but because of their illogical abuse of rendered services. As for other condottieri, I cannot say — there is rotten fruit in every profession and my own lends itself easily to a higher ratio of rot than many others, always excepting the priesthood.

The perils which I personally encountered arose not so much from the peculiar Italian practice of warfare as from other causes — my kinsmen, the singular volatility of Perugian politics, and the uncertain temper of my pontifical employers. Niccolò Machiavelli, who is so bitter against mercenaries, sees only one side of the coin. Mercenaries are but one symptom of a malignant disease — and that disease is the papacy and the princes of Italy. In the meantime, the mercenary is accused by all and most vociferously by those who hire and cheat him. How may a mercenary be trusted, asks Machiavelli, since his bond is worthless and he lacks feelings concerning the enemy he purports to be fighting? Who is fool enough to expect patriotism from a condottiero? True enough. I feel no loyalty toward any employer and am an evil effect spawned forth by an evil cause. In the great battle which was fought at Ravenna in 1512 there was no patriotism. It was a struggle of prince against prince, for wealth, cities and dynastic advantage.

I have often reviewed this list of tired charges and balance against it the querulous suspicion of potentates, their reluctance to pay, their haggling and their cheating. Some, like the Venetians, were better than others. The clever Florentines tried my patience most. Their luxurious timidity has always been self-defeating and the measure of their weakness has been their absolute distrust of others. Leaving aside military matters, these Florentines have never been able to organize their civil affairs properly and must be forever picking at their republican constitution as a dying man picks at his coverlet. Serving the House of Borgia, even when there was no fighting, was a hazard peculiar unto itself, yet I found the Borgia more consistent and more reliable than the Signoria of Florence. Peace be to Pope Alexander! May he find himself a cool place in Hell, if that is where he is. I was never certain whether he planned to decorate me with a golden chain or a noose, yet he never quibbled about the terms of a condotta and he paid handsomely. Above all, as I have often said, he possessed a papal temperament infinitely more sympathetic and agreeable than that Giuliano della Rovere who called himself Julius II.

But let us return to the past.

*   *   *

Once re-entrenched in Perugia, I went through the motions of cleansing the cupboards. I was gripped by a feeling of unreality and indifference. Unable to dispel it, I tried to evade it by furious activity. I refrained from sacking the Ward of Sant' Angelo, which as usual had been foremost in supporting all anti-Baglioni coalitions. Some people said that I was generous. The truth is that there was insufficient savor in revenge. There is only this about winning — it is better than losing, and since one must live, it is better to live as a victor. Beyond that, the best medicine is the blessed mindlessness of action, for thought is decay, and I was satisfied to plunge into the untangling of Perugia's affairs.

As soon as I had settled Laura Crispolti in the city, I summoned Amico Graziani. In Rome, the cardinals were still in conclave at this time. "I am sending you to the Sacred College with new credentials," I told him. "I want to be forgotten by Rome until I have had a chance to consolidate my position. We must discourage the cardinals from following up the late pope's encroachments on Perugia. We want obscurity and a reversion to the status ante quo. Do you understand?"

Amico replied that he understood perfectly.

"Then go and soothe Their Reverences," I said. "Tell them that all is well. Tell them we in Perugia are still the obedient sons of the Church and that it will be unnecessary for them to send us a legate. Offer them our heartfelt faith and devotion. Tell them whatever you wish but keep their meddlers away at all costs. You know the customary formula."

"I doubt if Their Reverences will annoy us at this time," said Amico, regarding me with his fat, sleepy cat-face. "They are still too distracted buying and selling each other's votes."

"Lie as well as they do," I said, "and with your usual eloquence."

"I doubt that they will desist from their electoral snapping and snarling long enough to listen to me," said my ambassador.

"But, in case they do, speak with feeling and reassure them," I said. "I do not want any legates prying in Perugia until I have had a chance to prune away this pestiferous underbrush of rebels. The contado is still crawling with Borgia's men."

"I do not think that the Sacred College will annoy you," said Amico Graziani. "They are too deep in their favorite sport — filling their pockets while they paw and snuffle around for a new pope. I have heard that Cardinal della Rovere has cleared the soldiers out of Rome. How he managed it, I do not know. The cardinals have torn the Vatican from Cesare Borgia's grip, but I think they may be too late. I don't doubt that he has already looted the papal treasury. Borgia's jaws are still strong even though his teeth are beginning to rot and fall out."

"Go with God," I told Amico.

"Willingly," he replied, "but since I am bound for Rome, I doubt if God will go with me."

I will not enlarge on the election intrigues of the cardinals in this particular conclave. The facts are sufficiently well known. On Alexander's death, thirty-seven cardinals gathered and the trading began. The three candidates were Giuliano della Rovere, Ascanio Sforza and Georges d'Amboise, the Cardinal of Rouen. Cesare Borgia favored d'Amboise and pledged him the votes of the Spanish cardinals, which he controlled. Sforza, who still shivered at the memory of the French prison in which his brother, Il Moro, rotted, hated the gallophile della Rovere and refused to come to terms with him. The popular feeling against the Borgia weakened d'Amboise's candidacy and the moribund Cardinal Piccolomini was elected as a compromise pope. He survived twenty-six days and the struggle recommenced.

Poor old Piccolomini had provided the red-robed hagglers with a breathing space which was now no longer possible. Della

Rovere began to chaffer in deadly earnest. At this point, Cesare made the fatal mistake of accepting the word of that man, the implacable enemy of the House of Borgia. Della Rovere promised that in consideration of the Spanish votes, he would guarantee Cesare's title to the Romagna. So della Rovere, the righteous reformer, traded briskly and merrily and bought his way to the tiara by the power of gold. "See to it that the election succeeds and do not worry," he is said to have told his friends. "Necessity forces men to do what they dislike while they depend on others, but once they are free, they act otherwise."

By such masked words, and I believe them true, della Rovere reassured the enemies of the Borgia that, once pope, he would keep Punic faith with Cesare, and so he did. And Cesare Borgia, who of all men knew the perfidy of human nature, permitted himself to be duped by his deadly foe. So this is how Giuliano della Rovere came to power on November 1, 1503, and took the name of Julius II.

But these events, so recently in the past, are as dead and dusty as the history of Troy.

As for my own affairs, after Amico's departure for Rome I busied myself with further housecleaning and destroyed the survivors of the Borgian garrisons in our contado. Not one of Cesare's men escaped alive. The Venetians moved in briskly to pick up the shards of Cesare's ruin in the Romagna. Between us, we organized a new defensive league of the returned Romagnol princes. A miserable, treacherous, apathetic lot were my associates, but from my viewpoint they were a lesser evil than rule by the Church. As one moves through life, the choice one must make is always that of the lesser evil. There are no good choices. Nevertheless, working with whatever tools came into my hand, I finally stabilized my rule in Perugia.

If I do not discuss my private life in greater detail at this time, it is because I do not judge it to be of sufficient weight. Laura Crispolti now showed herself more amenable to my overtures. The cynical will say that it was because I had regained power. But such a conclusion is too obvious. I say it was because Laura was convinced that I wanted her. This is the supreme consideration with women. We call it the essence of their charm in order to give our necessity for women a better name. Laura Crispolti was more honest than most and it has been my experience that women, being simpler than men, are less inclined to guile and wickedness.

This much I will tell. I went to speak with Laura and said, "Considering all the disorders and the uncertainties that beset us, I have little hope of obtaining an annulment from Rome of my marriage. Pope Julius has greater concerns than our problems and no friendship for the House of Baglioni."

"What then?" she asked.

"I have decided to wait no longer," I replied. "We must make our own marriage and live together as husband and wife, or we must part."

"I do not like ultimatums," said Laura, frowning.

"This is no ultimatum," I said. "You are free, wealthy and intact. I have kept faith thus far."

"You have no regard for our immortal souls," said Laura.

"For your soul, every qualm," I said. "As for my own, I have made private arrangements."

Laura continued discontented, saying that I spoke from defiance rather than love, that I was using her to strike a blow at the Church. I replied that I had no objection to the sacrament of marriage and promised again that I would continue to strive for the annulment.

"Does it mean nothing to you?" asked Laura.

"Only to the extent that you prize it," I replied.

Laura finally capitulated, although with many sighs, for

women are more docile to the chains of custom and belief than are men. Nevertheless, her heart and courage overcame her dread of hell-fire and we made peace.

You may therefore see that amid the general shadows I also found a rift of private light, for Laura accepted me of her own will. Holy Writ tells us of a patriarch who waited seven years for his bride — a notable feat! I waited only three years for Laura and found it long enough. When in good time she was delivered of a sturdy male child, I was infinitely pleased and ordained baptismal ceremonies such as had never been known in Perugia. The infant was born on the feast day of Saint Lorenzo. I commanded that the bells of Lorenzo's cathedral should sound a day and a night in honor of the occasion. Do not think there was a lack of muttering on many sides at the unprecedented magnificence of the baptismal ceremonies. Many citizens took the view that my display was ostentatious and unwarranted. I brushed them aside and decreed that the child be christened Lorenzo Ridolfo Troilo Baglioni.

I further arranged the infant's sponsorship at the baptismal font by the bishops of Perugia and Jesi, by Alfano, the communal treasurer, and by Francesco Maturanzio. These men, together with several other illustrious scholars, conferred sufficient distinction on Laura's son to satisfy me.

You may question why I went to such lengths in view of my opinion concerning the worth of the sacraments. To this I reply that my opinions were for myself alone and I would not foist them on another. The child was Laura's as well as mine. Had he survived, he would have had his own life to lead. But Fate did not see eye to eye with Laura and myself. Lorenzo died four months later during the Feast of the Purification of Our Lady.

Laura took the loss hard, saying that it was because she had borne the child in sin. I tried to comfort her, promising that I would give her more sons, but she was inconsolable and for many months thereafter she refused to let me approach her. She was the counterpart of her father, Matteo Crispolti, a strong character with an iron will, but I would not have had her otherwise.

Having told so much, I should add that I committed myself to this testament, prepared to relate my life without gloss, and so I have and so I shall. But Laura Crispolti is something else again and I find myself at times writing of her with an almost superstitious reluctance. This woman was above and beyond my life, a rare balm worthy of a better case than this sorry chronicle. Her fragrance, fixed in words, would be dissipated all too soon and I have little enough to spare of that which will beggar me without benefiting you. So, beyond what has already been said, let the matter rest.

16.

BARTOLOMEO D'ALVIANO

BARTOLOMEO D'ALVIANO remained with me in Perugia until, in
the autumn of 1503, the French-Spanish war boiled up in Naples. We parted company at that point. I chose the French
while he resigned his Venetian commission to serve the Spaniards under Gonsalvo de Córdova.

I had remained a long time in doubt as to where to cast my
lot and finally accepted the generous terms of a condotta offered
me by Cardinal d'Amboise, the French war minister and unsuccessful papal candidate. This condotta was actually under-
written by the Florentine Republic, which owed King Louis
XII sixty thousand scudi. However, as long as the money was
promptly forthcoming, I cared nothing for the bookkeeping
methods of my new employers.

As for Bartolomeo, it was natural that he should have elected
to serve Spain. Although he and I were so intimately bound by
kinship, he was deep in the councils of Piero de' Medici, who
was seeking to regain power in Florence and who was fighting
in the Spanish ranks. Thus Bartolomeo, supporting the Medicean cause, could not be other than hostile to the French, who
were supporting the Florentine Republic. But our professional
decisions in the choice of employers made no difference in the
warmth of the feeling between us.

I quit Perugia and Laura and joined the French camp in the Kingdom of Naples.* I smelled out the French collapse while it was still brewing and abandoned the campaign well before the end of the year. D'Amboise began writing me letters, impatient, annoyed, suspicious, and finally in outright anger. I wish I had them here to re-read; some of them were quite superior. When d'Amboise ordered me back to service, I replied that my Florentine paymasters were neglecting to remit my pay. When d'Amboise corrected that oversight, I found new excuses. He and King Louis had a heavy investment in me. They were fighting thriftily to extract some benefit for their money, but I would not fight because I was convinced that the French were doomed in Naples. D'Amboise finally lost his temper in writing, which pleased me and confirmed my feeling that I was playing my hand correctly. My heart was neither with Frenchmen nor Spaniards nor churchmen nor Florentines — only with the House of Baglioni. As long as the Baglioni remained intact, it made no difference to me who won or lost in Naples. I detested all the princes with impartial sincerity and felt that no treachery was properly treachery in dealing with them. The angrier d'Amboise's letters, therefore, the more cheerful I felt.

My premonitions of French defeat in Naples came to pass soon enough. To comprehend the full tale of it, you will have to bear with me and listen to a little recent history. It is important and has a bearing on how my fortunes fell out after Cardinal della Rovere got himself well settled on the papal throne.

In that autumn of 1503, King Louis had a fine army camped on the Garigliano River facing the Spaniards under Gonsalvo de Córdova and d'Alviano. The weather was foul with heavy

* A distinct political subdivision as shown on the map. It was also known as the Regno or the Kingdom of the Two Sicilies.

rain, flooded river banks and sodden fields. The troops began to sicken in the polluted mud and die. King Louis provisioned his people so wretchedly that, aside from sickness, the army dwindled daily from desertions. I remember when I was there how the tents stretched in disconsolate rows under a sullen leaden sky and the rain fell with persistent malice. The camp streets were an impassable mire. Only the captains kept somewhat dry, for their tents were pitched on a well-drained eminence and had wood floorings. But the soldiers sat and cursed in stench and misery. The latrine trenches, dug and maintained by prisoners of war, overflowed into the tents. After that, the camp fevers struck. Have I said enough?

At that point I left and so did many of the Gascon, Swiss and Italian units. A hard French core held their stockades stubbornly against d'Alviano's attacks. D'Alviano finally broke the stalemate and his plan was simple enough, as he related it to me later. He brought in companies of peasants and built floating boat bridges near Susa, four miles below the French outposts — all of this in heavy rainstorms with many peasants drowned. While Gonsalvo mounted a diversionary attack, d'Alviano led an offensive across and took the French from the rear. Of course he was helped by disease, rain and bad food on the French side, but he raged through their camp and broke their spirit. The Spaniards had their own miseries. Their impatience made them evil-tempered, and the surprise degenerated into a disaster for the French. Of the survivors — beggars and starving refugees — few returned home. You may judge then whether or not I was right in quitting King Louis before all of this came to pass.

Having received what he wanted, King Ferdinand discharged all his captains. When he offered d'Alviano continued employment at one half the former rate, my brother-in-law quit in anger.

"Can you conceive such rank ingratitude?" he wrote. "I won him Naples, the white city, the broad bay, and the blue sea before it. I got him Naples to wallow in, to tax, grind and enjoy. Gonsalvo was ashamed, for he is a man of honor himself and it is his fate to serve this Ferdinand who is a cozening cheat, so consummate a liar and scoundrel that even Pope Borgia lost a few fingernails in bargaining with him. Did I ask so much? A duchy for myself and handfuls of gold for my men, who bled, shivered and dug trenches, knee-deep in water, for the greater glory of Spain? All I asked was a renewal of my condotta at the same rate of pay. When in all the history of Italy has a victorious condottiero made such a modest request? Gonsalvo agreed that I was reasonable but excused himself, saying he was only the servant of his king's pleasure, his king, who lacking even the grace of a merchant in his damned haggling, dismissed us like dogs. I told Gonsalvo, for all that he was the Great Captain, I would no longer soil my honor by serving Ferdinand. Let the king choke on Naples! Let it lodge in his royal and pious throat like an heretical fishbone so that when he calls on God to confirm his sovereignty, it will silence him. Such a prince is he that he will not keep Naples long, for he is too mean-spirited, and when he has run out of captains to cheat he will end by cheating himself. All of this I told Gonsalvo and also that, even as the king had served me, so would he, in the end, serve Gonsalvo and throw him aside like a dirty clout."

D'Alviano and his troops rode homeward from the wars. I traveled south and met them thirty miles beyond Rieti. D'Alviano was in a foul humor. "I have lost men and beasts steadily ever since leaving Naples," he told me. "Fifty men against the Colonna three days ago and as many horses. My troopers are my eyes, my capital, my stock-in-trade. Fortune spits in my face and pulls my beard. Look at them!"

And, indeed, the arquebusiers marching by seemed war-weary. Their parti-colored uniforms, in the Orsini red and white with puffed slashed sleeves, were torn and shabby. Their weapons were rusty, broken and corroded. The pikemen and the baggage train went by. The carters goaded the great oxen and the massive ironshod wheels of the wagons turned ponderously in the dust. Then an officer rode up to report that the troops had bread and cheese and dried peas crawling with worms, these rations for seven days only, and no ammunition for the arquebusiers.

My brother-in-law d'Alviano, peace be to his departed soul, was a bristling peppery little man, with a bald head, overlarge for his body, and a broad crooked scar running transversely across the skull. But he had a heart as great as his body was small. He expounded his ideas as we rode along. "This is the life of a soldier of fortune. All want our swords and when they can they gladly cheat us. See how the king of Spain has served us after we won that rich kingdom for him! How many of our men are there behind us bloating at the bottom of the Garigliano? By God, in this Italy where every pig, every prince and priest, has his snug stall of knavery, we shall also have ours. We have just had our skulls cracked together, but there will be other times and other occasions. I measure plans sorting with the dignity of our House and our true merit and hope to make us all rich."

One of the officers riding with us agreed, saying, "God knows, we need some turn of the wheel. We have been battered and starved so long, we forget what it means to sleep in a bed, even a dirty bed. Look at the gear of the people. Look at the coats of the horses. Boneyard cavalry!" That was true enough. I had seldom seen such a collection of hangman's nags.

"Your troubles are over," I told them all. "I am rich again with the gold of my Florentine condotta. I shall re-equip you.

And when we are ready, we shall turn on Florence and tear Pisa away from her. This is the guts of my new venture." I savored their sudden smiles. "What do you say to it?"

"You come like an angel!" cried d'Alviano. "When do we start and where are we bound?"

I informed him that we were going to meet Cardinal de' Medici in Perugia. Piero, his elder brother, having drowned in the Garigliano, the cardinal was now the Medicean spearhead against the Florentine Republic. I said that Pandolfo Petrucci was also interested, seeing that there was a bit of free meat to be torn away from his neighbor without hurt to himself. I added that I could not think of any people I would separate more cheerfully from Pisa than the Florentines, that it would be a pious work with the connivance of the Pisans themselves, who would sooner bow to the Devil than to Florence, and finally that it would serve the Florentines right for their bad faith and broken promises.

"How right you are," said d'Alviano, "Double-dealing is the blazon of our Italian politics. The finest virtuosi in that art are the merchants of Florence, or merchants anywhere. That is the very mattress on which commerce is carried, and one merchant is a match for fifty soldiers in any lists. But it is also true that not everything can be done with talk and money. Those people, with all their cunning, have made a botch of the Pisan campaign and cannot finish the task. I agree with you, brother, let us do it for them. It is manifestly God's will and we ought not be overmodest about engaging God's interest in our business. Everyone else does so. But what of your plighted faith as Florence's condottiero?"

"No faith," I answered. "We already have an antidote for the poison of broken faith in the person of Cardinal de' Medici."

"The priests ought to know, being experts in larceny," said

d'Alviano. "To my mind, Medici has a better title to Florence than those wretched republicans. I would only wish he had more gold. A good case is not enough — not in Italy. What we need is gold, gold and more gold, if we are to mend our shoes and plug every leak in the roof."

That was the genesis of our plot against Florence. It was a good one and we refined it in subsequent meetings at Chiugi with Petrucci, Cardinal de' Medici and the Vitelli nephews. The Florentine Signoria, still unaware of the stew that we were cooking up for her, now began where d'Amboise had disgustedly ended. The Signoria's secretary, Niccolò Machiavelli, demanded that I report for service before Pisa. When I showed d'Alviano the letter from Machiavelli, he snorted and laughed:

"Let the world split, the mountains crumble, and the moon halt in its course! Let God declare He is tired of the world and plans to repopulate it with intelligent apes! Those money-changing Florentine slugs will crawl forward, mindless as ants, toward the occupation of Pisa. Let them simmer, Gian! Put them off! Tell them that the Priori insist you remain here. It is true, is it not? Look! the snivelers want to know what I am doing in Perugia; they are grieved about the company you are keeping. So they feel that their condottiero should not be having relations with one of their open enemies, do they? Ah, but they have no choice in the matter."

D'Alviano was right; the Florentines had no choice. I held a good hand and intended to extract the last ounce of advantage from it. I held Perugia in my fist, and with it the best reservoir of fighting men in central Italy. And Perugia, by virtue of geography, was Florence's bastion against Spanish power to the south.

States have, or should have, no personal pride to be wounded. The gentlemen of the Signoria would smile patiently and bite their fingernails because they had no alternative. Florence was undeserving of better treatment. She had long ago chosen to base her foreign policy on gold rather than on the arms and courage of her own citizens. No condottiero could esteem a state which was so bereft of self-respect and so wholly dependent on the good will and loyalty of a hired stranger.

If I needed justification, there was my old commander, Paolo Vitelli, whom Florence had so lightly shortened by a head less than seven years before. I looked forward to paying out the Florentines for that moldering reproachful head. Above all, I remembered their perfidious support of the House of Oddi against us during the spring of 1501.

17

NICCOLÒ MACHIAVELLI

NICCOLÒ MACHIAVELLI was a practitioner who aspired to cure the ills of the Florentine Republic. He was a student of men and affairs who strove very earnestly to exorcise the Devil. But the Devil, a perceptive jester of considerable experience, put his confident trust in Machiavelli's superiors. I had already met some of these scions of the great moneyed families. There were able diplomats among them, conjurers whose talent for petty dispassionate reflection had been refined into impotence. They were astute pismires, infinitely intelligent dung-beetles who confused gamester luck with a mastery of the stars, who knew all and understood nothing. Their enemies will tear off their legs some day and leave them on their backs to expire — still smiling subtly into the sun. No sage can smile as subtly as the fool who has achieved perfection.

But Niccolò Machiavelli was not one of these. His merit lay in the truth that he was a dreamer, a vulnerable and rebellious poet who thought himself a politician. If ever a man sold himself too cheaply to the sluttish world it was Niccolò Machiavelli. He knew his fellow men, but his heart seduced him into the comical error of casting pearls before swine.

The result of all our juggling and plotting in Perugia was that Niccolò Machiavelli came calling on me and presented his credentials. He was a man slight in stature, with a lean, clean-shaven face, hollow cheeks, the skin pale and stretched tightly across high cheekbones. His eyes, as he spoke, were sparkling black buttons of animation and I thought — his must be a thankless task as roving clerk for a government of merchants. Yet I did not underestimate his skill, nor he mine, and we felt our way cautiously like swordsmen testing one another.

"Since we are old birds at this business," I finally said, "let us dispense with further compliments. Is it to your liking, your new trade as courier?"

He refused to let himself be chivvied and retorted, "That is my trade, as you call it, and the Signoria thinks enough of my talents to give me full scope in forming the messages I shall carry back."

"They are fortunate to have you," I said truthfully. "I hope they pay you as you deserve, though I doubt it. Now what is it that you want?"

"You are blunt," said Machiavelli, "and I will be, too. Do you or do you not intend to honor your agreement with the Signoria?"

"Not so fast," I said. "You come to business like a drunken lanzknecht at a pot of beer. I have a pair of questions which have long intrigued me. How did Vitellozzo and Oliverotto actually die in Sinigaglia? I've heard some versions but never from a true eyewitness."

Machiavelli shrugged and said, "Why, it happened almost two and a half years ago, although it seems more like a quarter century. The history of failures fades quickly from one's mind. I was an unwilling witness."

"No doubt," I said. "You love violence only in ink."

"My own temperament and the weakness of my own humors in no way beclouds my true estimate of the world's ugly face," said Machiavelli. "I abhor blood and always shall. In any event, the end was drab and mean. Vitellozzo died badly. Both he and Oliverotto were seized and bound as soon as they entered the banquet hall of the Bernardino Palace in Sinigaglia." He smiled with wry satisfaction. "How right I was when I wrote to the Signoria that those men would be dead by morning! With a man like Cesare in command, there could be no other ending." He stared at me mockingly. "But why have you so great an interest? You behave like an innocent citizen hugging himself at the execution of a guilty one."

"You are a good teller of tales," I said. "Continue."

"Just before dawn on the first day of the new year, they were strangled by Michelotto," said Machiavelli. "You know him — the duke's man with the butcher's face and hands like knotted hams. He sat them together, back to back, and killed them with a cord and a stick of wood. A simple economical device fit for killing such brutes. Vitellozzo begged Cesare's intercession with the Holy Father for a plenary indulgence for his sins."

"What an optimist to depend on Pope Alexander for that," I said. "A legion of saints could not have laundered Vitellozzo's soul."

"He had faith," said Machiavelli dryly.

"Which you and I lack, Messer Envoy," I said. "And what of Oliverotto?"

"Even worse," said Machiavelli. "He bawled for mercy, shook with fear and died like a three-carlini whore. He swore that he had never intended Cesare any harm and that he had been misled by you."

"Now that is very droll," I said. "Since you know something of Oliverotto's reputation, you will appreciate it."

Machiavelli permitted himself the smile of a discreet elderly cat, saying, "You refer, no doubt, to Oliverotto's murder of his uncle, Fogliano?"

"To that and other things," I said. "And what did your duke have to say about such fine doings?"

"That Italy was richer for being lighter of such rascals," said

Machiavelli, "that posterity would never believe that such an absurd system ever existed in any country, I mean, of course, the condottiere system, and finally that he had done no murder but a fine surgical operation in ridding Italy of such scum. I agreed with Cesare then and still agree."

"I am fairly familiar with your views of the condottiere system," I said.

"I do not mind repeating them," countered Machiavelli. "You mercenaries have an unwritten law to avoid killing one another. We never know when and if you will honor your contracts. We have proof that the captains wink at the disloyalty of their troops, that you drag out campaigns for as long as the employer can be cozened to pay. And when higher pay is offered, you change sides as lightly as whores change lovers."

"I like a man who speaks his mind boldly," I said. "As I respect the laws of hospitality, I shall restrict myself to verbal arguments. Come, Machiavelli! Would you have us shed our blood in earnest to implement the intrigues of those fumbling amateurs you call statesmen? No one knows better than you that your masters are worse than dishonest — indeed, they are thoroughly incompetent. Would you have us exert ourselves to further policies which they can neither understand themselves nor explain to others? For mere pay? I dignify these petty day-to-day improvisations by describing them as policies. I will only say that those who would command loyalty need not be men of honor themselves but at the very least, they should be able to act in a consistent fashion."

"You will not shunt off this evil by bringing up another," said Machiavelli stubbornly. "Because of you we have become the butt of the world. You are faithless at all times and worthless against the soldiers of the barbarian. I have seen mercenaries too often throw a country into chaos by their treachery. They serve for gold alone and care nothing for the hearths they have been paid to defend. Since their own homes are safe and far away, they cannot be other than unreliable."

"Granted," I said. "I would certainly fight harder for my Perugia than for your Florence. But your gentlemen of the Signoria are still a sorry lot. There is so little charity and Christian love in their mealy sniveling souls that they would sooner go down in ruin than allow the least advantage to a neighbor. The sum and total of Italy's disease is magnified tenfold in your clever merchants. A fig for your rotten republic, Machiavelli! Remember me when she collapses and remember, too, that we are only the aftereffect of your own sloth, cowardice and self-deception."

Machiavelli shrugged his shoulders and smiled. "You have a point," he said calmly, "but it does not cancel out mine."

"Well, well," I said. "We could go on with this argument all night, but why should we? I admire your skill and intelligence. What a pity that you are serving the Florentine Republic! Do you know, I hoped to see an end to it, at one time, through Cesare Borgia?"

"I hoped for even more from that duke," said Machiavelli, again with his wry self-mocking smile. "As princes go, he was able with the best. He did all he should have done until Fortune went against him."

"If that be the case," I said, "he need not reproach himself for his omissions and may die in peace — that is, if he is not already dead."

Machiavelli said musingly, almost to himself, "I have studied his career. He accepted dangerous odds, for he was racing with the Devil, if we must give malicious Chance a name. He walked a tightrope, one end of which was held by his father, the pope, and the other by King Louis. Cesare's need was to cross the rope before Alexander died or Louis grew bored. What a foundation for a new state! He killed the Romagnol princes against a jealous schedule and the Devil was prodding his ribs to move even faster. He built well, as you may see from the truth that the people of Imola, Cesena, Forli and Faenza were contented with his equitable rule. Had it not been for his sickness he might have escaped the critical tyranny of time and of dependence on others. But what made him agree to della Rovere's election surpasses my understanding. Once he did so and turned over his fortresses to the pope, he was doomed."

"If Cesare still lives," I said, "no doubt he has time enough to consider what he should have done. But let us return to our own business. The truth is that I cannot leave Perugia to help your Signoria. My enemies here are kicking up their heels again. I ask you in good faith to cancel my contract. Would this not be better than taking your pay and then quitting suddenly to quench the fires in my own house? My counselors say that I am not bound. I ask to abrogate the contract without penalty."

Machiavelli mistook my amiability for weakness and he bore in. "Your reputation will have the worst of it if you default," he said sharply. "There are plenty of good captains who would be pleased to serve us."

"Indeed yes," I said. "Now that the wars are over in Naples, you can have your pick of every unemployed bandit."

"Some day," said Machiavelli, "we will no longer depend on condottiere bandits but on ourselves alone."

I laughed. "By all means! On that glorious day, your Signoria will make soldiers out of dyers, carders, bookkeepers and exchange speculators."

He turned pale with anger. "No! Out of Florentines and patriots whose only ill is their lack of military experience. But we will remedy that. We shall inspire patriotism in their hearts. When they have learned to defend themselves, they will learn a new self-respect."

"I wish you luck," I said. "From what I have seen of merchants, they are born dead to self-respect. They have one passion and one disease, and that is the love of profit."

"We will cure that disease before you cure your own," said Machiavelli. "There is no cure for you. If you break this contract, your reputation will be worthless and no one will engage you. As for your counselors, the affairs of state are none of their concern. Any soldier who respects his armor and wishes to wear it with honor would never risk the loss of men's faith in him. And that is what you risk."

"My affairs are in a sorry state when I need lectures on honor from a pack of wool peddlers turned statesmen," I replied. "However, I do not reproach you with it personally. You are only their spokesman, and speaking in frankness you are too good an instrument to be misused in their greedy hands. I have given you my answer and it is my final one."

As soon as Machiavelli left, I turned all my attention to the plot against Florence. I had had his reports to his government temporarily intercepted. He had surmised our plan correctly enough — truly, a sagacious man whose services Florence did not deserve! As I sit here in Sant' Angelo I often think of him and wonder if he is still alive.

Under d'Alviano's military leadership, our chances for success were good. Giovanni de' Medici, the mild and splendid cardinal, lent an aura of respectability to our enterprise. Pandolfo Petrucci, that chronic and timid subverter of ewe lambs, was less respectable, but his gold was backing us as heavily as my own. On balance, I expected no complications.

Cardinal de' Medici summed up our plans at a final meeting in Perugia. "Our objective is to wrest Pisa from Florence. Once we have entered Pisa, the people will assist us by revolting against the garrison. D'Alviano will commence open operations by harrying the Florentine frontier. We bind ourselves to aid

him secretly in all ways. If the first thrust succeeds, we shall
expand the offensive."

A good beginning — but d'Alviano's proverbial bad luck pursued him. In August of that year of 1505, the Florentines defeated him near San Vincenzo. He received a painful face
wound and escaped capture by fleeing to Siena. The Florentines exulted. I congratulated myself at first for not having
shown my hand openly. My second reaction was one of dismay.
I was like the hunter who has fired his last bolt at a wild boar
and has missed.

Our bouquet of sanguine enterprising thieves, touched by the
frostbite of defeat, shriveled, blackened and fell apart in silence.
Each of us ran for cover. Cardinal de' Medici waddled off in
sedate dignity to hide behind Pope Julius' protective skirts.
Pandolfo Petrucci fled to cower in Siena. I slammed shut the
gates of Perugia and prepared for the worst. It was Florence's
turn and she squeezed unmercifully. She was aroused, ready to
braid her gold into a golden noose with which to strangle me.
King Louis XII, whose royal fat nose I had tweaked during the
Neapolitan campaign, had finally become aware of me as a live
and very distinct individual. There are some who might consider it an honor to be personally cursed by the Most Christian
King of France. As for myself, I am not that avid of royal attention. Indeed, from what I have seen of King Louis' blundering in Italy, I can only say that it is a pity that his mother did
not miscarry when she bore him.

In the meantime, Louis was complimenting me with his
august recognition of my existence. A villain he named me, a
liar, a bastard and a blasphemous, insolent petty brigand. I
have already expressed my views on the state of bastardy and
have demonstrated that it need not be a dishonorable one. As
for the other royal epithets, what shall I say? They were, at
best, tedious and unoriginal but then one cannot expect the

fertility and the passion of poets in dull fat kings. King Louis swore by the tombs of his royal ancestors that he would hang Pandolfo Petrucci and myself by our feet from a common gibbet with our entrails draped around our necks. And, finally, he cast aspersions on the genealogy of the House of Baglioni. The last was mere pointless trivia, for it is only by accident that one man rules France and another the hill town of Perugia.

The king's anger endowed me with a certain notoriety but I was given little time to enjoy it. King Louis and the Florentines now joined forces in a mutual harmony of wrath. They opened their hearts and their purses to one another all for the high purpose of stamping me out flat on the cobblestones. You may see how serious they were. When men show the color of their money, they are no longer joking.

But that was only the beginning. A pregnant sizzling cloud of ecclesiastical choler rose in the background — the relatively new pope, the hitherto quiescent successor of Pope Alexander. Julius II, that hot-headed ex-onion peddler, burned on his own account to reclaim Perugia for the Holy See. As though I did not have enough, he too joined his papal thunders to the clanging racket of the French king and the Florentine Republic. King, pope and republic set up such an infernal din that all Italy became admiringly aware of me. Men everywhere regarded me with that sympathetic interest which they bestow on one who obligingly permits himself to be hanged for their entertainment. Pope Julius was welcomed to the feast of vengeance. He was showered with gold and soldiers as the means of chastising me. He graciously accepted the gift of five hundred lances from King Louis and sounded the keynote:

"Leave this Baglioni to us! He is only the first on our agenda. We shall destroy all of our domestic tyrants, all of those bandit signorotti in the Romagna and in Umbria who impede the

Holy See. We shall recover Perugia and Bologna also. And that shall be only a beginning."

I sharpened my sword, tightened the bolts, prowled behind the walls of Perugia and waited for the blow to fall.

Impending trouble made it imperative that I be in close touch with the Priori delle Arti. I therefore came from the villa in San Pietro to lodge in the Baglioni palace. Laura accompanied me reluctantly.

The memory of the Great Betrayal had made the palace an inhospitable, if not an uninhabitable, place during the past five and a half years. No one spent a night there without good reason. When we entered, I said in jest to Laura that a Crispolti under such a roof should feel like the Devil in church. To which she retorted sharply that a Crispolti under this roof was like an honest man in a den of thieves. So I refrained from further jests.

I think the massacre had stirred the quiescent ghosts, for nothing brings sleeping spirits trooping from the shadows like fresh violence. There was ample place for them to wander by night in the broad and silent halls. I sensed ghosts arrogant, vengeful, resentful or merely curious and lonely, come from the wicked past to join the newcomers.

Laura and I walked in the cloistered dust seeking a suitable bedchamber and there were few enough, for each place was burdened by some memory or defect. The death chambers of 1500 were now sealed vaults and others had been stored to the rafters with useless furniture. Moreover, Laura refused to consider the room which Ippolita da Conti and I had occupied.

For want of a better, we finally selected the chamber in which my great-grandfather, Pandolfo, had been stabbed to death in 1393 by the burghers of the Raspanti faction. Though Pandolfo had quit this world so unceremoniously, I think his ghost was in no way malignant and even pleased that we should rest in his bed. It was massive, a veritable chamber within a chamber, fashioned of precious woods, carved and gilded, and so high that one mounted four steps to enter it.

Having cleansed and aired the chamber, the servants renewed Pandolfo's couch with as many furnishings as would have sufficed for three ordinary beds. To dispel the gloom and chill, they brought in candelabra. Then they carried in logs and kindled a great fire in the hearth at the far end of the chamber. After one hundred and twelve years of dank silence, I cannot but believe that Pandolfo's shade was flattered to see a comely young woman lost in the depths of the bed in which he had expired under thirty well-driven dagger blows.

Laura remained small and half-hidden among the pillows while the flickering flames cast her distorted shadow on the hangings behind her. I paced before the fire considering her predicament if things should go badly. The world was a poor place for orphans and even for lawful widows like Atalanta. It was an intolerable place for those like Laura who lacked the fragile shield of the laws and the sanctions of Holy Mother Church. It occurred to me that if I were taken she would fare like a sparrow on a winter night.

Since such matters cannot be concealed from women, Laura finally took note of my silence and said, "What wall have you pulled down on yourself this time? Into what pit of your own digging have you stumbled?"

I told her how matters stood, assuring her that she could rest soundly and so would I. If a man could not sleep in the midst of danger, it was better that he should not wake in the morning.

"I think you are singing in a graveyard," she said softly. "In the meantime, this bed is big enough for the twelve apostles. Come to bed, my boastful Gian, and let me see your face."

We continued to discuss the problem far into the night.

"I am Fortune's own child," I said. "I have escaped from the Great Wedding Massacre, from five great battles, fifty ambuscades, and the long arm of the House of Borgia."

"Then I fear that God is preparing to break your neck," said Laura.

"Not so," I replied. "This danger will likewise pass. But if I am taken, go and live with Atalanta."

"Atalanta is herself a Baglioni and belongs in this place," said Laura, staring up into the blackness of the great chamber. "But I am like a spirit in limbo. I seem to have fallen between two ladders."

"Let it be on my head," I said. "I thrust you off."

"I went more willingly than you know," said Laura. Then she seized me by the hair, adding fiercely, "See that you keep this head on your shoulders. I have come to have some regard for my bad bargain."

In that instant, the candelabra beside the bed flickered and was snuffed out by a gust of cold wind. Laura was startled and threw her arms around me in the utter blackness.

"It is my old ancestor, Pandolfo," I said. "He savored your joke and has extinguished the candles with his laughter."

"I meant no joke," said Laura. "There is no comfort in a woman's life, only a succession of prolonged uncertainties."

I told her to have courage, that she was now a wealthy woman and that the world was wide.

But she only replied: "See that you survive, if I am to survive. For the rest, I regret nothing."

Later we fell into a deep sleep, but when I woke at dawn I was still in trouble, as you shall presently hear, for consider that a cat, even a Perugian cat, is no match for a pack of hounds.

18.

GIULIANO DELLA ROVERE

Amico Graziani, that prince of diplomats, was a pillar of bronze bound in layers of gracious jocund fat. He ambled in with a complacent smile when I summoned him on the following day and said, "I've been wondering when you would call on me. You have been chewing your nails and talking to yourself for over a week."

"Pope della Rovere is tightening the ring around me," I told him. "I need a man in Rome who thinks like a fox and argues like a nightingale."

"I don't think our pope listens very much to nightingales," said Amico. "He's too busy eating them."

"He may listen to you," I said. "Go to Rome and see what you can find out."

"I have a delicate stomach," he said, patting his belly and grimacing with distaste. "Must I?"

"Yes, you must," I replied. "Such sensitivity ill becomes your fortress of fat. Hold your nose, if you have to, but keep your eyes and ears open. And clack that tongue of yours where you think it will do some good."

"I shall need plenty of gold if I am to root out any information," said Amico. "You know the tastes of our prelates."

"Draw what you may need from the communal treasurer,"

I said. "This is state business and the Priori will approve it."

Amico heaved himself up and stared at me with his sagacious little eyes. "Don't raise your hopes too high," he said. "This pope's fingers are old and dry, but he has the humor of an angry bear. Guard your throat, Gianpaolo, for he means to tear it out."

I did not reply.

"I'm becoming too old and fat for these ventures," continued Amico, "and I no longer enjoy fishing in God's Roman cesspool as I once did. I am too tired."

"Go for my sake," I said. "You're my only reliable workhorse."

"You have wheedled me into it," sighed Amico.

I received Amico's first dispatch by courier three weeks later. "Rome is still Rome," he wrote. "These prelates are haughty before all the world. They stare down at us and treat us like men of small account. They are still rollicking in the loose and merry tradition of Alexander VI and Innocent VIII. Pope Julius is God's Chief of Staff and the Vatican has become a general's headquarters. I am reliably informed he intends to drag his cardinals along and teach them the rudiments of soldiering, if only to reduce their jowls. All the world is here in this squirming nest of serpents struggling for the Pope's favor; clerics, laymen and, above all, new ambitious captains, whom the pope favors above priests. It is a most unlikely shrine and the heart of this clawing tangle is the Pope's antechamber."

After another week, a further dispatch arrived: "It is well for you, Gianpaolo, that Cardinal de' Medici has the Pope's ear. Everyone is surprised, for the Pope is rarely predisposed to rich men's sons and nobles. Not that Medici is a nobleman, but he has the agreeable manners and style of one. There are many here who call him a shallow, frivolous sycophant. That is largely envy and it is immaterial. Medici is a polished, tactful man with a trick of calming the Holy Father's vile temper. He defends you at every opportunity and has smoothed our way."

I did not hear from Amico for the following two weeks and busied myself all the more drilling my troops. Amico's third report finally arrived. "We were at last brought in and presented to the Pope," he wrote. "He examined us as though he were a commander and we, soldiers on parade. Yet he made a small effort to be gracious, saying he had a friendly remembrance of Perugia. He mentioned that, during the time of his youthful poverty, he lived in our Monastery of San Francesco and gave lessons to our young scholars for his daily bread. However, when I presented the usual petition for the reconfirmation of our ancient privileges, he tore it from my hand and flung it to the floor, knocking over a flagon of wine from the table. He was sixty-two! he shouted, pounding the table; he had much to do and little enough time. The reduction of Perugia, he said, was but the first and the least of the tasks which God had imposed on him!

"It is marvelous, Gianpaolo, how these priests are always involving God in their politics without Divine sanction. He demands that Perugia resubmit herself unconditionally and that the Priori surrender your person. When I tried to defend the House of Baglioni, observing that his information had been exaggerated by those who seek to injure the Baglioni for their own wicked motives, he interrupted and cursed me roundly. He calls you an infidel and an atheist and swears he intends to exterminate all the ruling families in the lands of the Church whom he calls banditti. Cardinal de' Medici, who was present, spoke up at this point. You could always be eliminated, said the Cardinal, but, alive, you could be of greater service to God in the more important Bolognese campaign which the Pope intends. The Holy Father finally subsided, grumbling that for

a criminal you are far too well supplied with friends and influence. But I think he will come around; he needs your troops
and experience. 'Think of Baglioni only as a captain,' said
Medici, 'since his employment will further the plans of Your
Holiness and of the Divine Will.' The Pope found nothing
unusual in this order of precedence and is plainly in agreement
with it.

"In the end, he agreed to spare your life — provisionally —
saying he would arrive to take possession of Perugia in the first
or second week of September. But we shall have to surrender
Castiglione del Lago, Passignano and Castel delle Pieve to his
castellans. When we demurred, he damned us for wicked infidels and threatened to hang us after he took Perugia. We
submitted. The Pope is halting first at Orvieto. You are to
present yourself there and make submission. Guard your neck
and play your part well. He is violent and quite capable of doing all he threatens."

I received a final report from Amico. "We have gained another ally — Francesco Alidosi, the Cardinal of Pavia and the
Pope's favorite. Gossip has it that he once saved the Pope from
Borgia poison. These stories of venom in high places fascinate
the vulgar but none know the truth. Alidosi shared the Pope's
French exile and is now the strongest man in the Vatican. Nor
is he an upstart but comes of a good Imolese family. His black
eagle with the white lily on its breast is certainly older than
della Rovere's oaktree. He gives luster to the Pope's house, for
being a gentleman he has a way with artists and a good taste
where the Pope has none of his own. I have conferred with
him and we understand each other very well — for a price.
Therefore, send us even more gold and it will return to you
tenfold.

"Only yesterday, Alidosi told the Pope: 'If Your Holiness is
to reform the clergy, drive the barbarians from Italy and crush

the signorotti, you will need strong pliable tools. Though the Baglioni are unworthy vessels, the Holy Father would do well to employ them for the greater glory of the Apostolic See and the furtherance of God's Will!' Alidosi always sounds the note of glory in the Pope's ear and the old man invariably rises to it like a snorting charger. In short, the Pope is fully persuaded. Now he says that you shall live and serve him as a probationer under the surveillance of Guidobaldo of Urbino."

Amico Graziani had done his best. My freedom of action, however restricted, was no longer in the balance. My sentence had been suspended.

With Guidobaldo at my side and a hundred horsemen behind me, I rode into Orvieto at vespers on the first Tuesday in September. We swept into the square but our housings and bannerols were subdued. The rattle of horse hooves and the fluttering of standards did nothing to liven the spectacle. The trumpets were muted and the drums silent. My people remained grave and sober, as I had ordered. Guidobaldo's long solemn face, sallow and drawn from his illness, suited well to the occasion. I have the right sponsor in this duke, I reflected, for his visage could admit us both into a nunnery without question.

Carpets were spread over the piazza and, in the midst of these, a throne for the pope. Here he awaited me, surrounded by his prelates and captains. I dismounted at the far end of the piazza with my people. Then we knelt together just as Guidobaldo had rehearsed us, though the original suggestion for this mummery of repentance and reverence was Alidosi's. It was act or die. Given such a choice, most men will find in themselves some untapped fund of thespian skill.

I approached alone, knelt, kissed the pope's slipper and said: "I have come as the Holy Father's vassal, to implore forgiveness and to vow fealty to the Church without reservation."

He gave me no benediction, saying, "You are more fortunate than you realize, better furnished with friends than you deserve. If you had as many Heavenly intercessors as you have here on earth, your place in Paradise would be as firmly assured as any saint's."

"If I have given Your Holiness cause for offense in the past," I said, "I hope, by my future good conduct, to dispel your displeasure and to make atonement by my service to the Church."

"We do not believe you," he retorted bluntly. "Your family is a nest of serpents and dragons. In all the dark history of Umbria and Romagna, no House has wrought such mischief as your own. If you think you listen to a senile dotard, disillusion yourself. You Baglioni are thieving strutting princelings. You are outlaws and always have been. If we die before we have done with you, another pope will tear you out, root and branch."

He shimmered red before my eyes and I said in spite of myself, "Then why am I here before you?"

"Hold your tongue," he snapped. "We will phrase the questions. Have our orders to the Priori concerning your fortresses been executed?"

I regained control and said carefully: "All has been done as Your Holiness has commanded. The strongholds have been transferred to your castellans. I await the Holy Father's commands and shall obey his further orders."

"That you shall," said the pope, "to the utmost measure. Your sons, Malatesta and Orazio, shall go hostage for your future good behavior. We charge our Gonfaloniere, the Duke of Urbino, with their safekeeping. Let this also be recorded in writing."

I would have spoken but he waved me silent.

"We further demand seven hundred and fifty seasoned cavalry from Perugia and all of the artillery which Cesare Borgia abandoned when he left your country. Finally, Baglioni, if you fail us in the smallest measure, yea, if you so much as sin venially, we vow here in the presence of these illustrious witnesses to hang you high as Haman."

This artillery to which the pope referred was the finest in Italy, not excluding that of Alfonso d'Este. He is tearing my eyes from my head, I reflected. One way or another, I shall retrieve those guns and live to fire them over his grave.

Not all of the Oddi and the della Penna had been exterminated in their successive encounters with our House. Some had managed to survive the attrition. They stirred anew in their exile and emerged to warm their bones in the sun of the pope's favor. To them and to the whole world, Pope Julius announced from Rome: "We seek power, not for personal profit, but for greater glory of the Church. We are no nepotist. The corruption of our predecessor is hateful to us." He reminded his listeners how he had overawed the Colonna and the Orsini, how he had chilled the Roman netherworld by his summary methods.

"His Holiness has done good work here in the city," Amico had written in one of his dispatches, "for he has scourged the whores out of Rome and has been lopping off the heads and hands of evildoers with a very good will. He thunders daily in public audience that he was raised to the tiara to cleanse the filthy stables of the Church and to crush the contumacious princes so that they shall crawl on their bellies before him and grovel in the dust. These are brave words, Gianpaolo, and your enemies believe them because it is in their interest to do so."

So it came about that, on his journey toward Perugia, Pope Julius halted at Passignano, where the exiles flocked around him.

"Be of good heart," he exhorted them. "You shall again enjoy that which was yours! We intend to destroy the Baglioni and to rule Perugia through our legates."

My enemies, beggars fresh-risen from the tomb, bleated their thanks to the pope. It was the bleating of wolves whose teeth had been drawn. These Oddi and their friends were human preda- tors, breakers of promises, men of blood certainly no whit better than the House of Baglioni which had expelled them. I will make no dogmatic assertions regarding the incorrigibility of the human species. However, had the Oddi won the struggle with our family, their vengeance would have been less restrained than that of the Baglioni. In the meantime, Pope Julius played God to his heart's desire. Had I not been the target, I might have found it as good or better than any comedy contrived by the poets. Pope Julius combined self-confidence and a deficiency of humor in equal degrees. Lacking a sense of the absurd in human affairs, he was able to carry off the role of a wrathful new-risen Habbakuk. He was already taking credit for a groundwork laid by the Borgia. Pope Alexander, for all his love of pleasure, had been an expert administrator — and, weighed against this ob- streperous Jupiter from Savona, the Borgia pope had been a courteous reasonable man.

While I sat in Perugia waiting, Pope Julius exhumed the exiles. He cut away their shrouds and reclothed them in robes of honor. My emboldened enemies began to laugh and to wag their fingers.

"Keep a list," I told Gentile. "When the time comes, we'll cut off their lips and let them laugh forever."

In the meantime, the gossips of Perugia were measuring the distance my jaw had dropped. Still others measured the depth of my grave. "He groveled in the dust at Orvieto," they told one another. "He ate dung, wept bitter tears and bawled for mercy."

I had lost my power, it is true. A new faction waited eagerly to tear out my heart and nail it smoking to the portals of Sant' Ercolano. Pope Julius had the whip for the moment. For all that, the soldiers and the faction leaders of Perugia were still with me. With courage, I hoped to ride out the storm. But the tempest was blowing hard and I saw no way of escaping the pope's service in the Bolognese campaign.

Thus I sat in the autumn of 1506 and waited for ecclesiastical vultures to squeeze me from my own house, by grace of French arms and Florentine gold. Now that I was about to lose the palace, I viewed it with a new appreciation. I strolled restlessly through the arcaded courtyards and the echoing corridors. I loved it all anew, the mosaics, the statuary, even the cunningly molded door frames. I paused in the shuttered library with its hundreds of rare books, the happy loot of so many campaigns. A portrait of the goddess Perusia hung there; I had moved it from Grifonetto's palace following his murder. This matron supposedly symbolizes our ancient and august city. I failed to appreciate her, for to my mind it was a diminution that anything female should interpret Perugia. A wrathful old man in armor — Julius himself, perhaps — but hardly a woman. The painting had been made by some fool of a foreigner; certainly not a Perugian.

Though the chambers of Astorre, Simonetto, Gismondo and Guido were sealed off, their brooding ghosts still haunted the palace with a palpable malevolence. Take my word for it; I saw them there and spoke with them. But I did not fear them, for their ghost is my ghost. How can a man fear himself? The House of Baglioni is accursed, they told me, and I answered them: accursed or not, our House is none of the pope's affair. To this they gave a shadowy approval and seemed mollified. When I meet them again, I shall explain my predicament. Where, I cannot say, but I shall meet them.

The somber desolation of the palace lent itself to such visitations. Since the death of Morgante and my father, I kept only a few caretaker servants there. As I have related, Laura and I preferred the villa in the San Pietro Ward. In the dimness and the corpselike silence of the great banquet hall, I heard again the voices of buffoons, dwarfs, librarians, soldiers, gentlemen-in-waiting, and women singing in chorus. I turned reluctantly to review, with Laura's help, the plans for Pope Julius' living arrangements when he should arrive. He was pre-empting the Palace of the Priori for his own use.

"Where does he expect the Priori to go?" asked Laura.

"To the Devil," I said. "You know della Rovere. And his prelates are commandeering every large house in Perugia, those of the Perinelli, the Corgna, the Ubaldi, the Tancreducci and the Oddi. Even Braccio's old palace is being taken over and every monastery within and without the walls."

"My poor tyrant," said Laura.

"Your poor beggar," I replied. "If I have to feed this horde of clerical locusts for more than a week, I will be bankrupt and as poor as when we were in Florence three years ago."

"Think of it as an enemy occupation," said Laura, "and you may find it easier to swallow."

"It is good that you are here with me," I said. "This palace seems filled with creeping black hands which reach out after me."

"Then let us leave here and return to the villa," said Laura.

"There is one final piece of business," I said. "Guidobaldo is visiting me here tonight in his official capacity to discuss preparations for the pope's entry tomorrow. I wish you to meet him and to remain for our conversation. You have the intelligence to profit by such experience."

"If I knew you less well, I would call your manner patronizing," said Laura with a smile.

The Duke of Urbino arrived punctually at the agreed hour. We concealed our mutual dislike with urbane preliminaries as I presented Laura to him. Guidobaldo's face was lined and yellower than ever.

"You appear weary," I said. "The pope has burdened you with a heavy responsibility."

"I did not request to be Gonfaloniere of the Church," sighed Guidobaldo, "but he insisted on appointing me to the post. I am only an unambitious scholar at heart and would have preferred to live with my books."

"Fortune favors those who do not court her," I replied.

"How do you mean that?" asked Guidobaldo, and I said:

"I mean that you, who took the lesser risks when Borgia raged in power, have reaped the greater rewards. Yet you've accomplished it without effort."

"Bitterness little becomes you and little harms me," said Guidobaldo stiffly. "You brought this down on your own head and have none to blame but yourself. As for me, I have always been content with my lot and have tried to live by my father's precepts."

"Your late father would hardly have approved the gap between his precepts and your actual practice in persistently supporting my enemies," I retorted.

"I am here to discuss the pope's business, not my own," said Guidobaldo with chill in his voice. "I now inform you that I shall have three hundred arbalasters in position at dawn before the Holy Father enters the city."

"That should be sufficient," I said.

"I hope so," said Guidobaldo. "So let me give you some friendly advice: Attempt nothing rash."

"I've given my word," I said.

"True," said the duke, "but you also have a certain reputation."

"As does every ruler in Italy," I said. "This is the land of lies and every prince is a father of lies. Spare me your dainty aversion to the truth."

The rising flush in Guidobaldo's face clashed uneasily with

his yellow skin. "Your garrison is still strong," he said, "and I want only to avoid trouble."

"When have you ever sought it?" I asked. "But abate your fears — enough Perugians have a misguided devotion to the papacy and, thanks to you, my cousin Carlo and his followers are still a menace. In truth, I know of two ways to save my state. One is by force and the other is by submission. I have chosen to submit and trust in you. You're that *rara avis,* an honest man." Guidobaldo flushed and turned pale. "Do your duty," I said. "Your time is short and you'll smother soon enough in the coils of your own passivity."

I knew Duke Guidobaldo in those days better than he knew himself. I knew how far I could bait him. He died of his chronic malignant disease two years after our meeting. His death, however, did not improve my own dark fortunes. When he left on that evening after our conversation, Laura, who had been listening silently, said to me, "I suppose you are proud of the manner you cudgeled him about with words."

"For want of something better," I said. "He and his kind sicken me. I've no illusions about them nor about this frantic Italian barnyard in which they strut."

"There is little you can do about it," said Laura soberly. "You are merely an obscure condottiero."

As usual, she was right. I was no better than that pathetic dreamer, Niccolò Machiavelli, and already I had caught a glimpse of my ultimate fate. I would be ground to powder between ponderous impersonal millwheels.

And, now as I sit here and write, the grinding has long since begun. . . .

19.

THE TRIUMPHAL ENTRY

As I HAVE already mentioned, the city of Perugia has a genius of her own, and if I refer to her as a woman, it is only to observe the conventions and not because there is anything feminine about her spirit. As a city, she has always cared little for the civilized morning which has supposedly dawned radiant over Italy. Her house doors are built low for better defense. Her palaces are oftener spaced with slits than windows, the better to welcome visitors with showers of whistling bolts. She is suspicious, particularly of warlike prelates, for many such priests with mischief in their hearts has she seen pass under her arches.

Perugia wore her customary scowl on the day of Pope Julius' entry. A cold rain fell and a chill wind scudded through the streets. I sat my horse in the newly swept piazza before Lorenzo's cathedral, staring with bile in my mouth at the triumphal arches which had been hastily erected as welcome. The papal litter finally came into view at the far end of the piazza. Some twenty prelates on mules were crushed in around the litter by the press of the people, and soon I could make out the pope as he shouted greetings in his noisy manner and blessed the throng. Filippo Cencio, who sat beside me, said in surprise, "The pope's guards must be further behind. Perhaps the mob has cut them off."

In the meantime, the multitude shouted amid waving banners and strewn flowers. They struggled to approach the litter while many knelt on the pavement and prayed.

From the far right on the edge of the crowd, Gentile came struggling toward us with ten horsemen. The people gave way reluctantly before the hooves and the expert whips of the riders. When Gentile finally reached me, I said to him:

"It appears that we have our pope bottled up. Circle back with your people behind the litter. There are five of us here. You have another ninety men behind the entourage, which should be sufficient. Fire one signal shot when you're in position, then charge the mob behind the prelates and cut your way to the litter. Tumble the pope out of it, and, in the confusion, we will do the rest. I do not know what has happened to Guidobaldo's careful protective arrangements, but here is our chance to remove della Rovere from the board."

"Give Guidobaldo credit for intelligence," said Gentile. "Look behind you at the cathedral. Some three hundred of his arbalasters are aiming directly at you this moment. You might hack your way to the pope, but you would leave this world with him."

"Only do your part and let me worry about Guidobaldo's men," I said. "He will not risk killing the pope to shoot at us. Where is the rest of the papal guard?"

"Two miles back," said Gentile. "The crowd cut them off."

"Then do as I order!" I said. "We can at least take Julius as prisoner and put him in the fortress for bargaining purposes."

Gentile looked sullen and reluctant.

"You are wasting time," I said. "Go!"

An uneasy interval dragged by while we waited in vain for the arquebus report.

"Look behind you," said Cencio. "We have company. The pope's guardian angels have come out to join us."

Guidobaldo's arbalasters emerged from the cathedral and ranked themselves behind us with their weapons cocked and ready.

The litter progressing down the piazza finally approached us. "Long live the pope!" screamed the people about him as they pushed against the laboring litter-bearers. Pope Julius raised his right arm and blessed them. As he passed, he stared at me with a malicious twinkle in his small red-rimmed eyes.

Gentile and I had words that night.

"Why did you not obey orders?" I asked him.

"I am not yet reduced to killing popes," he said.

"It would not have been your task, priest-lover," I said. "We would have accomplished that at our end."

Gentile did not reply and I continued, "You mean you are incapable of such sacrilege. Is that it?"

"If you wish to so state it," said he.

"We have worked together for a long time, cousin," I said. "But today's disservice expunges our long friendship."

"Guidobaldo's people would have killed you all in any case," Gentile muttered.

"I should have known better than to depend on an ex-cleric," I said. "The Church got to you before the House of Baglioni and now the canker is showing."

"I am a soldier, not an assassin," replied Gentile reluctantly.

"You're also a trimmer!" I said. "And, now that I think of it, you have always been one."

I might have said more. I might have said many things, but I was too angry to trust myself. In that moment the mutual antipathy between us rose and came forth like Lazarus. We worked together for some years more but I think now he was always my secret enemy at heart. I hold us both responsible for our failure to kill Pope Julius when we had him in our palm.

I tried to assuage my feelings at the time by telling myself that I would have gained nothing by killing the pope, that the citizens and the exiles would have killed us in turn. But I was not convinced by my own hollow rationalizations. By way of comfort, I told myself that it mattered little, that the pope would not live long. Deep in my heart, I knew he should have been killed then and there.

In the final analysis, it must have been my own cowardice, which took the form of careless neglect to plan the deed properly.

Niccolò Machiavelli came visiting me at the villa in the San Pietro Ward on the following night. He was more sleek and self-assured than he had been a year before. His dress was richer. He carried his head high and he spoke with force. His greater assurance, and my awareness that the distance between us had lessened, gave me cause for irritation. As I had gone down in the world, he had evidently come up. I was so accustomed to thinking of myself as stronger — that is to say, better — than Machiavelli that his new prosperity was an affront. When a given circumstance has accommodated itself to our preferences, we are disturbed to see it rebel against comfortable precedence, insolently demanding a second solution. That is why rulers grow sincerely indignant when subjects complain. That is why shepherds fume at their skeptical sheep and masters at their recalcitrant workmen. And that, no doubt, was why Jehovah was forever barking at the stiff-necked Children of Israel. The status quo is right because it fits our convenience so pleasantly. The Truth is our pleasure, a whore's white-mounded belly, a mere saddle on a docile palfrey. So I fell to cursing inwardly and laughing at myself all in one. Machiavelli was quick to recognize the slippage and the realignment of the forces between us. He enjoyed it.

"The world seems to have treated you well since our last discussion," I greeted him. "You have become a great man in Florence, or so I have heard."

"They load my shoulders with all the disagreeable drudgery which no one else will undertake," said Machiavelli complacently. "As though I had not work enough organizing a militia, the Signoria has ordered me here. I have fared miserably ever since I joined the Holy Father's entourage at Nepi."

"I hear you have become quite the minister of war," I said.

"I have been modestly successful," said Machiavelli. "Our Florentines are not as backward about learning the soldier's trade as you had hoped."

"Are you here to crow over me?" I said.

"Not at all, merely to pay my respects. My presence here is as an official observer. I go where I am sent. I had thought myself beyond surprise, but I still learn something new each day."

"Indeed," I said, "and what have you learned this time?"

"That there's a gap between your practice and that of your late preceptor, Cesare Borgia. I think he would have played the hand somewhat differently."

"What do you know of the way I played my hand?" I asked.

"Would you have me believe that good faith or good will stayed you from killing the pope?" asked Machiavelli.

I did not intend to tell Machiavelli the real reason for our failure to kill the pope. It could only advertise our weakness and give the Signoria an additional advantage over us. If there were discord between Gentile and myself, the Signoria would immediately exploit it. I simply said: "A careful analysis of the forces arrayed against me contraindicated any action against the pope. I have considered it to the point of tedium and its repetition wearies me, and why I should tell you anything, I don't know. You are nothing to me. Yet I'll remind you that the uncertain temper of the people, the menace of these ravening repatriated beggars whom the pope dragged here, the presence of Guidobaldo's soldiers, yes, and the hostility of the Signoria — all of these things decided me against the attempt."

"Quite an array," said Machiavelli. "That is why Fortune favors the bold. If every man had the courage to seize her by the forelock when things looked blackest, why, we'd have more kings than cobblers among us." He shook his head almost sorrowfully. "Ah, Signor, what a slip we have here! Think of the eternal fame you might have won by killing the pope, fame for all time, and rich booty also! Men would have sung your praises and the majesty of your deed would have overshadowed its infamy."

I think his words irritated me all the more because I agreed so thoroughly with them. I could only reply: "You speak like a poetaster. Fortune favors the bold, not the harebrained. As for booty, your words are fit for one of those condottieri whom you affect to despise. Fame is evidently something of which you've never had enough, since you reach for it like a hungry peasant after a sausage. What is this fame of yours but an appetite for praise and a striving after vanity? For the rest, you speak like a clerk, not like a soldier. What is so easily scribbled on paper is otherwise when put to the clock and the test of bloody practice. True, I could have surrounded that brash old man who was trusting to luck and the awe aroused by his pontifical brayings. But a soldier would never have put his neck in such a noose."

I watched for the effect of my words and had a strong impression that Machiavelli was pretending to believe what he was too intelligent to swallow. He let me down lightly and permitted me to save face. "What a pity, Signor Baglioni! Popes are not killed every week or, I should say, the opportunity does not present itself that often. Though they are mere temporal princes, every whit as fallible as the others, they are held in superstitious reverence. Your act might have lifted the scales from the eyes of the people. Posterity would have raised statues to you."

"I'd rather scale fish than the eyes of the people," I said, savoring my sour appreciation of Machiavelli's tact. "Let them lie blind like newborn kittens. My interest is in the present. I have not the itch for posthumous fame. The deed would have been spectacular but its immediate efficacy doubtful. I deal in probability, not prophesy. This pope is sixty-two and wishes to play at war. Who knows? A chill, a seizure, a fever, any of these things, may carry him off. Perhaps the Devil will take him this winter at Bologna. No, I prefer the present gamble to any new furies that might have been unboxed by his murder."

I spoke with so much conviction that my words had an almost hypnotic effect on myself. Almost, but not quite. Pope Julius, decently dead, would have been the best of all possible solutions, said my heart. Machiavelli smiled acceptingly, which annoyed me all the more. There is a point where tact becomes excessive. He feels sorry for me, I thought, and I added: "Stop playing the omniscient theoretician, Machiavelli. Killing popes is not the same as organizing an army on paper. I've done what I've done. If I have miscalculated, my head will pay the penalty."

"You may be a better prophet than you know," said Machiavelli, rising to leave. "Perhaps we shall have an opportunity to re-examine our views in the future."

We did so six years later, and, as usual, that clever little man was correct.

The day before Gentile and I were thrust out of Perugia as veritable conscripts in the papal service, Pope Julius celebrated a pontifical mass of thanksgiving in the Church of San Francesco, in the presence of Duke Guidobaldo and all the cardinals. Also present at this service was Francesco Gonzaga, the Marquis of Mantua.

It was Julius' intent that Guidobaldo should lead the army

against Bologna. Guidobaldo, however, pleaded illness and rec-
ommended his brother-in-law, Gonzaga, as a competent general.
There is no doubt that Pope Julius privately disagreed with this
estimate of Gonzaga's ability. Nevertheless he conferred the appointment on Gonzaga. He did not and could not trust me and
he was too impatient to seek for another commander. Gonzaga
had quite lost his reputation at the Battle of Fornuovo in 1495,
when, despite his superior forces, he permitted the French to
make good their retreat from Italy. Since that time the noble
marquis had found no military employment. He sat by the fire,
shrinking in the shadow of his insufferable wife, nursing his mal
francese and his tarnished glory. As is the case with these nobly
born asses, he got on better with hunting hounds and his
blooded Barbary horses than he did with men of wit and learning. His appearance was as dubious as his intelligence. He was
a stunted little Moor of a man on whom had settled all the ancient sins of the Gonzaga.

Francesco Gonzaga obeyed the pope's summons with delight
and reached Perugia on September 17, 1506, with two hundred
cavalry, a few days after the pope had entered Perugia in triumph. This was the man, then, a composite of all that a prince
should not be, who was appointed my superior for the forthcoming campaign against Bologna.

Following the great thanksgiving mass, Pope Julius ordered a
forcible reconciliation of the feuding families of Perugia. Gentile and I, together with our partisans, were reconciled at the
altar with the Oddi and their followers. The oath which we re-
cited was composed by Pope Julius himself and it was lurid in
the best ecclesiastical tradition. The simpler and the more devout of the congregation blanched as they listened to the litany
of frightful curses and dooms which would fall upon any who
violated the terms of the covenant. Doubting the efficacy of this
thundering oath of his own composition, the practical pope

added the requirement that a bond of five thousand ducats be posted by each of the feudists to keep the future peace. I watched our treasurer count out ten thousand ducats for Gentile and myself and agreed for once with the pope. Gold is more binding and more persuasive than anathemas and almost as good as steel. I tell you that this reconciliation ceremony was a play within a play. Whatever the strangers hoped, we Perugians in the church knew in our bones that nothing would come out of all this peace-making and oath-taking. Whom do I call strangers? The pope, of course, and those such as Guidobaldo and Gonzaga who were his followers.

Perugia is a small place but it is a jealous secret world, and what we see, hear and feel in our blood, the foreigner in our midst can never experience. If ever there was a prototype of the blind, deaf, clumsy foreigner, Pope Julius della Rovere of Savona was that man. As always in the past, we of Perugia swore with our tongues but not with our hearts. For Perugians, above all men, will never yield up their cherished hatreds and their insatiable need for revenge, not for any king, not for any pope, not if they are eternally damned for it. Perhaps the pope sensed this native feeling, but I doubt it.

There was a deep bitterness in the pope's face as he listened, with his head lowered, to the recital of the oath. I think I also caught a momentary sadness which refined the grim coarseness of his features. Perhaps I felt a twinge of remorse in that instant, but I thought of the ghosts in the Baglioni palace and hardened my heart. At that moment, the pope may have felt he was doing God's work, according to his lights, and that he was being mocked behind his back by wicked and perverse children. Yet I thought then, and still say, that we Baglioni need no spiritual fathers to tell us how to live and think. We can take responsibility for our own acts without the intercession of the popes.

20.

THE WINNING OF BOLOGNA

DURING that year of 1506, winter came earlier than usual to the passes of the Apennines. On a day in early October, Gentile and I rode in the pontifical army, bound for Bologna and the expulsion of the Bentivogli. We rode in silence for the bitterness between us. Muffled to the eyes in rough woollen cloaks over our armor, we held our reins loose and the horses picked their own way over the treacherous ice-coated windings of the mountain road. Occasionally a beast slipped on the loose frozen gravel and started a shower of stones and muddy ice over the sheer cliff.

The weather, always bad at that time of year in the mountains of Romagna, worsened in the late afternoon and a freezing rain began to fall. A snow-promising wind howled down from the distant blue peaks and I ordered my men to dismount and lead their horses. The sky lowered and the men tramped by in a straggling double file. We wound through the passes in the gathering dusk till the dim glimmering lights of the village of San Luca showed below at a mile's distance. A milling nondescript rout brought up the rear of the fighting troops. It was a hodgepodge of artisans, carters, porters, cooks, smiths and personal servants. Then followed a train of supply wagons and extra mounts. One adjunct of an army on the march was lacking in this one — a rabble of soldiers' whores and the courtesans in carriages with their private maids. We were chaste warriors of the Church. "There shall be no harlots in our host," had decreed Pope Julius. "If we find one here, she shall be flogged through the camp, and the man who brought her shall be hanged from the nearest tree."

Pope Julius had brought his prelates with him, and the sense of Amico Graziani's first dispatch came to mind. Julius sternly denied them the comforts to which they were accustomed while traveling in the service of God. These clerics, astride their mules, had finally commenced their reluctant careers as valiant soldiers of the Church. They lamented as they rocked along, frozen, famished and half dead with unaccustomed fatigue. Their beasts slipped and slithered near the edge of the ice-rutted road and they muttered prayers of singular sincerity while struggling to guide their mounts from the yawning edge of eternity. In a burning haste to reach Bologna, the pope begrudged the few days we had spent in Urbino. He was no man to sit on silken cushions and listen to the polished idiocies of Guidobaldo's courtiers. Winding away from the duke's pleasant palace, the cardinals looked back sad-eyed at the civilized fleshpots they were abandoning. Most of them had remained in bed during that respite, resting and warming themselves. Back on the road, they audibly cursed Julius and his vulgar passion for conquest. They cursed this savage Romagna, the filthy roads, the perverse climate, the blisters on their consecrated backsides, and the Bentivogli of approaching Bologna.

The pope was in twenty places at once, swearing more like the sailor he once had been than the head of Christendom. He barked at the carters and the muleteers. He damned the soldiers and their officers. His language to his unhappy brethren in God became increasingly uncanonical. "Keep your rumps moving," he roared. "We halt for no one! Maintain the pace or freeze in the mountains and be damned!"

I have said I would tell the truth. The common people did

not object to Julius. On the contrary, he sat lightly on their backs. They laughed at his jokes, they rolled their eyes and poked each other in the ribs. All of them, even the leathery Romagnol porters who went about like shaggy half-naked apes, knew Julius was bound for Bologna. To his business there, they were indifferent. Yet they seemed to enjoy the spectacle of the effete curial robbers being kicked, harried and spurred forward over the mountains like a drove of ecclesiastical swine. The Romagnols gave Julius a new title, a comradely nomignolo, which, roughly translated from their barbarous guttural dialect, signified, His Holiness, the Swineherd. This name drifted upward to the pope's ears. He spat into a freezing puddle and growled: "It's as good a name as any we have had and doubtless more flattering than those we do not hear."

We halted that night at San Luca, some eighteen leagues from Bologna. The common ruck found shelter in wagons, in barns, sheds and stables. Many erected tents and built fires in the frozen fields. Together with the pope and his cardinals, we crowded into the only inn in the village. It was a low rambling structure, at one time a large stable, rat and vermin-infested with a sour fetid stench. A fire blazed on the hearth in the spacious stone-flagged kitchen and several local louts sat on benches drinking wine. Booted, cloaked and hooded, Pope Julius stamped in and roared:

"Out! Out! Everyone out! This inn has been requisitioned by the pope and by God! Ho, there! Innkeeper! Come here and be damned!"

You will note that, in all his dealings with the Host of Heaven, Julius invariably shouldered his way to the head of the procession and gave himself precedence over God. I do not judge that this was due to his pride, his terribilità, as some would have it, but rather to his innate vulgarity. Julius was many things, but he was never a gentleman.

The rustics at the fire goggled and gawked at Julius in wonder, though not in fright, for these mountain men are a sturdy
independent lot. Doubtless they had never seen a bishop, let
alone a pope. Some of them, wholly unimpressed, laughed and
asked, "Where shall we go?"

"Go?" he roared, "go? Go to the Devil, go home and sleep
with your wives. Out, you imbeciles! Out of here, by God!
We've work to do."

The host, quivering with pride and excitement, crowded his
local patrons out the door and bustled to obey Julius' commands. He did not know the identity of our noisy Vicar but he
must have decided that this was some great lord from the way he
shouted and flung his orders about. The innkeeper's instinct in
such matters is always sound.

Into the inn came four sad-faced strangers, their noses pinched
and blue with cold. They identified themselves as messengers
from Bologna and begged for audience with the pope. We were
all about a rough wooden table at the head of which sat Julius
with a horse blanket about his shoulders and his bare feet immersed in a pan of hot water. His cloak was steaming and dry-
ing before the kitchen fire. He sighed with satisfaction and ex-
haled wheezily. Before him had been set a loaf of native bread,
as forbidding as the Romagnol mountains, a stone jug of wine
and a broken joint of cold pork.

"It is our contention, gentlemen," Julius was saying, "that the
Italians, while not cowards, have forgotten how to fight on foot.
Their skills of war have withered and what they call field tactics
are nothing more than equestrian ballets, as stately and as useless. We know our people; they are much too clever to learn
anything new. When the times are ripe, we shall bring Swiss
footmen into Italy, men who are such masters of the pike that no
Italian or even the French will withstand them!"

We nodded and yawned, but the pope, caring nothing for our

disinterest in his military theories, kept on stubbornly. An officer brought the Bolognese strangers into the kitchen, approached the pope and said: "Holy Father, these men say they are from Bentivoglio and beg to speak with you."

Julius put down the joint and wiped his mouth on his sleeve. "From Bentivoglio, are you? Have you come to capitulate?"

"Holy Father," said one of the messengers, kneeling, "we have traveled here from our lord Bentivoglio, to parley with Your Holiness."

Pope Julius' face darkened.

"Parley!" he barked. "Have we struggled over these mountains to parley with that impudent upstart? We'll hang Bentivoglio in chains first."

He called loudly to his guards. "Arrest these people! Put them in irons and carry them along. When we reach Bologna, we'll cut off their heads and hurl them over the walls into Bentivoglio's face." The guards escorted the unhappy messengers from the kitchen and the pope went back to his lecture on tactics. A fit of yawning rendered his discourse unintelligible. He rose reluctantly and went off to bed.

"That's what I call a very devil of a pope," said one of the captains. "He has slow-matches in his miter and gunpowder in his breviary. What are your thoughts, Baglioni?"

"I find his heroics tiresome and raucous," I replied. "If he has lasted as long as he has, it is because he has good captains and the times favor his brashness."

"They certainly favored him when he came to visit you in September," gibed the captain. "From what we hear, he reaped you as Captain Joshua reaped Jericho."

"The Holy Father roared 'Anathema,'" said another, "and all the Baglioni fell down flat."

The company about the table dissolved into laughter.

As you can perceive, this was an uncomfortable time for me.

Yet my spirits were higher than in Perugia, perhaps because of my activity and responsibilities. I was supposed to be a probationer, almost a prisoner under constant scrutiny. What with foul weather and the logistical problem of bringing the army through the mountains, Julius shelved his hostility and assigned me the task of keeping the army orderly. Whatever else this soldierly pope knew, he was ignorant of the art of logistics. The worse the weather, the more hopeful I felt. This will be a good winter for cooling overheated old men, I thought. May the Romagnol frosts crunch his lungs and silence him. In a more impersonal fashion, the other captains would not have been averse to such development. They, too, were beginning to find the pope a nuisance.

In the meantime, I had received reports that my affairs at home were not entirely desperate. For all that Julius' people controlled the contado, my supporters continued to dominate the city and the returned exiles remained fearful despite the assurances which the pope had given them. Should the pope die, their future was grim — and so it eventually turned out. Perhaps it is just as well we did not kill the pope, I thought; the Romagnol climate will do it for us.

I reflected on these matters as I lay on a pallet in the inn at San Luca and felt myself growing drowsy. I cursed the corrosive sterility of my life. I cursed Italy, her princes and her people, but it was not on account of Giuliano della Rovere and the things he was seeking to accomplish. I did not feel that he would succeed. Like many before him, he eventually disappointed — and was disappointed by — the volatile, many colored beast of the Italian people. If a brief thought may sum us up it is that we lack self-respect, which I think we lost in the dim times of the barbarian invasions. The only way to keep us loyal is by continued success. The only thing we respect is a strong rein, a point which Cesare Borgia well understood. In the moment that Pope Julius began to slip and weaken, he would lose his hold over the petty imaginations of our complacent Italian realists.

My only satisfaction was in recalling my separation from Laura. She neither wept nor wasted words but she could not mask her eyes. I told her that she could not remain alone in Perugia for very long. Sooner or later the new people whom the pope favored would try to kill her for my sake. If her father and brother still lived they would turn up in Perugia, and the papal legate would be unable or unwilling to protect her.

"I'm no more afraid of that than I should be," had said Laura. "I wish to be with you."

"If we take Bologna and I think we will, I'll send for you immediately," I had replied. "We will make our home there until the wheel turns again."

And so I had gone into exile once more with a better heart.

We finally emerged from the mountains in a driving rainstorm and entered Cesena, where the pope set up his headquarters. Cardinal d'Amboise arrived soon after to arrange French assistance for the attack on Bologna, if it should come to that. He rode in with a bustling train of lords, soldiers and attendants. He made a point of coming over to me and saying: "I think the Holy Father was overgenerous in sparing your life and my master, the king, concurs. I hope you fight better for your new lord than you fought for mine."

"It will not be difficult to better the French performance on the Garigliano River," I answered.

"You are an insolent failure," said d'Amboise.

"After you, reverend cardinal," I said, "for you will never be pope no matter how hard you scramble."

During the last week of October the weather turned cold and my soldiers became restive. The Signoria of Florence had loaned Pope Julius several companies of Albanian stradiotti, and sporadic brawling broke out between them and my Perugians. My people killed a dozen of the stradiotti — in self-defense, they claimed.

Francesco Gonzaga summoned me to his tent. While I waited, he clanked back and forth in armored bandy-legged majesty, lashing himself into a rage. Then he drew himself to his full height, opened and closed his thick lips several times and glared up at me. I would not call Francesco Gonzaga a conventionally ugly man, but he gave an impression of deformity. He was a full head shorter than I and resembled nothing so much as a Moorish stableman. Had he been born a groom instead of a marquis, he might perhaps have been happier, for the weight of the world confused his poor wits.

He shouted that he was still in command of the army, to which I replied that I was not disputing this truth with His Magnificence. Thereupon he accused my men, whom he called ruffians, of having slain fifteen of the pope's soldiers. "What have you to say to that?" he cried. I replied that only twelve had been slain, that my people, having been attacked without provocation, had no choice in the matter. If the stradiotti said otherwise, they were liars and I preferred the word of a Perugian to that of an Albanian muslim.

Francesco Gonzaga's face darkened. He bared his yellow dog-teeth and pounded the table. He shouted that I was under his orders by the pope's command, that if I continued insolent he would have me arrested. I asked Gonzaga who would fight the pope's war in that case and he replied ingenuously: "I will. I have a reputation."

I observed that he must have obtained a new one, seeing that he had lost the first at the Battle of Fornuovo eleven years before. Gonzaga's African eyes bulged wider. The veins in his forehead thickened and blackened and he seemed about to collapse with a seizure of the sickness of Hercules. Then his anger suddenly dissolved like a summer shower, and he entreated me to make his task no harder than it was already. Here I began to laugh and Gonzaga joined me, throwing his head back, his mouth wide open and the thick red lips moist with spittle.

I assured Gonzaga that I was not seeking trouble out of mere perversity. I was weary of being ordered about by every ribboned courtier who had the pope's ear. And I reiterated that the Albanians were responsible for the bloodshed and not my Perugians.

Gonzaga sighed with relief and said, "Very well, Baglioni, I will accept your version of the incident. But get your people into another camp if necessary and keep them away from Albanians. As long as I hear no more about it, I shall be satisfied."

I left in a better mood. It was difficult to remain angry very long with this diseased little pug dog of a marquis. He was essentially good-natured. He loved his falcons, his packs of hounds and his race-horses, which were of a breed at least as illustrious and ancient as that of the Gonzaga. And, as an afterthought, he had a careless predilection for camp whores, by whom he had been furnished with the mal francese, to the distress of his strong-minded wife. He was not malicious, merely stupid, and toward an honestly stupid man I tend to feel a certain tolerance. Because of this, I did not object to the drudgery of keeping the army viable while he enjoyed the credit.

With Marcantonio Colonna, who led a third important contingent of the army, I had as little to do as possible. He was a far different proposition than my friend the marquis. Both men outranked me, not only militarily but in the pope's favor. This last is an understatement since I was in the army as a probationer, on sufferance. The papal reprieve could have been revoked at any moment. Aside from the fact that the Colonna were among the traditional and most competent enemies of my

House, it was a matter of discretion to walk narrowly, to guard my tongue with Marcantonio Colonna and to perform my duties with impassive alacrity. I called a staff meeting and reviewed the Perugians.

"Discipline yourselves," I told them, "or I will be forced to do it for you with nooses and the nearest tree. Hold to yourselves and keep far away from the stradiotti." My people took the lecture kindly. When the Albanians tried to provoke them thereafter, they walked away. It is plain that their love for me overrode every other consideration.

Following d'Amboise's departure, Pope Julius summoned us for a conference.

"Gentlemen," he said with his customary bluntness, "though Bentivoglio thinks otherwise, his friends, the French, are aiding us. We shall strike Bologna from the south while d'Amboise's forces simultaneously assault the city from the north. As for Bentivoglio, we neither plan nor hope to capture him. Let him go to the Devil! His person will advantage us in no way. D'Amboise will arrange for his escape through the French lines. Bentivoglio is already so frightened that he will flee there like a blind rabbit."

Cardinal de' Medici could not resist a smile of satisfaction. "Is Bentivoglio then truly unaware that the French are betraying him? How mysterious are the ways of Heaven! I cannot but help remember, Holy Father, Bentivoglio's unchristian mockery of myself and of my dear late brother, Piero, at the time when we fled from Florence eleven years ago."

Pope Julius chuckled with light malice, saying: "Bentivoglio's wits are so fuddled with fear that he will plunge toward any avenue of safety which presents itself. Now it is his turn to weep, and weep he shall. We intend to excommunicate him in such terms as will singe the brush from his head. He is a rebel to us, and to God, with all that the term implies." Then the pope's roving petulant eye sighted me at the far end of the conference table. "Ah, Baglioni, is that you?" he growled. "You're also a rebel but, at least, you're not a coward. A damned ruffian like all your House, but not a coward."

"I thank the Holy Father for this expression of his approbation," I replied.

"We've had good reports of your zeal from Cardinal de' Medici," said the pope with vinegary benevolence. "Continue as you have thus far and we will have less cause to quarrel with you."

He turned to the captains at large. "A fair beginning, gentlemen, but too good to last. None of our future enemies will repent, as has our friend, Baglioni, or prove a poltroon like Bentivoglio. Stern trials lie before us."

"Holy Father," spoke up Francesco Gonzaga, "for the love which my House bears toward Madonna Ginevra Bentivoglio, grant her permission to remove her goods from the city so that she may not go forth naked into the world."

"Very well," said the pope. "Take it upon yourself and notify her. She may take her husband and her loot out of the city." He shook a jeweled forefinger at Gonzaga. "But should she still be in Bologna when we enter, we will treat that bitch, not as a legitimate ruler — which she is not in any case — but as a criminal, despite the fact that she is a woman."

Gonzaga's slack lips parted and his yellow Moor's eyes bulged wider. Pope Julius frowned and his face darkened. "It is clear that we do not speak the same language," he said in a grating voice. "You noble robbers always hang together. Your only religion is your self-interest. How have you, the well-born, come by your quarterings and your coronets? We can tell you. You stole them or bought them with blood, a fact you have conveniently forgotten, as though Time put a gloss of righteousness on your villainies." He studied Gonzaga's face thoughtfully and suddenly began to laugh. "We don't think you have forgotten anything. It is simply that you never knew." He stared around the table and continued: "And none of you will be any better than the Bentivogli. As long as you can steal away with your paintings, your jewels and your money chests, you will all be content enough and to the Devil with the people."

I recalled Petrucci's flight from Siena three years before, and my own also.

Pope Julius had made a very nice point.

One month after these events, on the eleventh of November (for it was Martinmas Day) my cavalry and I rode into Bologna as part of the triumphant papal army. Gentile was not with me. If I recall, the pope had given him leave to return home. The rift between us had not healed and was to break forth again even more virulently.

The papal standard bearers led off the procession. They were followed by Francesco Gonzaga, Francesco Maria della Rovere, the pope's nephew, and Guidobaldo da Montefeltre, who was still fighting his losing battle against illness. Behind these gentlemen rode their attendants and household troops, and after them followed the Sistine choir and the Host, over which a rich canopy had been spread. Then came Pope Julius himself, wearing his silken robes and jeweled tiara. We, the minor captains, followed the papal train, leading selected units. Along the broad flower-strewn avenue leading toward the Church of San Petronio, the Bolognese stood four deep and roared applause as the pope was borne aloft toward the church on his *sedia gestatoria,* to seal his possession of the city. Bentivoglio was out and the pope was in. "Long live the pope!" cried the people. As we moved along, the curial attendants marching beside the *sedia,* scattered a golden largesse of coins bearing the inscription:

"Bologna has been liberated from its tyrants by Julius." The people could not read Latin, but their fingers lovingly read the weight of gold. Julius' profile on the coins was gracious and perfect in their accepting eyes. No face more beautiful than the face on a coin. They proceeded to demonstrate their approval of the new regime by pillaging not only the hastily vacated Bentivogli palace, but also the art treasures which sorrowful Ginevra had left behind.

I have often noted that the mob's customary mode of self-expression is a cheerful destructivity. It destroys to show joy, and once again to express displeasure. Perhaps it is capable of creation, if one can call fornication and casual reproduction creation. It is noteworthy that seven months after this triumphal entry, Gian Giacomo Trivulzio and Alfonso d'Este recaptured Bologna, expelled Pope Julius and restored the Bentivogli to power. The people bawled: "Long live Bentivoglio!" just as heartily as they had bawled: "Long live Pope Julius!" And they pulled down Pope Julius' bronze statue just as zestfully in May as they had smashed the monuments of the Bentivogli during the previous November. Citizens, like little children, possess a great deal of mischievous energy. The prince who neglects to tap it does so at his peril; they will pull down his palaces and, finally, his head.

Ergo — the best citizens are weary citizens.

In this way began my third expulsion and exile from the city of Perugia within a period of six years. It was to last more than seven years, for I did not regain Perugia until after the death of Pope Julius in the winter of 1513.

But Bologna was a fair fat city, and when not campaigning in the pope's service, I made a good nest there. It was a better one than I had ever known. I purchased a house in Bologna and received Laura there on Christmas Day of the year 1506. My life settled down into a pleasant routine of garrison duty and unimportant campaigns. I took no part in the Battle of Agnadello in 1509, during which Bartolomeo d'Alviano was captured and went into French imprisonment for four years. These were my years of relative peace, and since they were so warmly eventless, my remembrance of them is a cracked mirror. We are quick to recall the evil and apt to forget the good which has befallen us in our lifetime.

On several occasions, when it seemed that Pope Julius was in a complaisant mood, I approached and requested that he annul my marriage to Ippolita da Conti in order that I might lawfully marry Laura Crispolti. I had learned that those without power must bend, and bend I did. The pope refused me with grim steadfastness. He was a hard man and unrelenting toward his enemies. In this, he was correct; I was his enemy.

I took Laura Crispolti for my wife in the eyes of God, if not in the eyes of Holy Mother Church, with which state she had to be content. It is possible that the dream of Niccolò Machiavelli will some day come to pass; the Church will be smitten under the fifth rib and the arrogant tyranny of Rome will be brought low in the dust.

And so my life continued until I was summoned from the warm bed of domesticity in the winter of 1510 to the siege of the Fortress of Mirandola.

Departure for the wars comes in every form. There are departures in sun-dappled courtyards with trumpets blaring, drums rolling and horses neighing, impatient to be gone. There are grooms and kinsmen, women making a great yammer from the windows and friars blessing the village boys bound on their first campaign. Perhaps these are best, for they are of such a noisy confusion that one cannot hear one's thoughts. Then there are small and secret departures launched in the dead of night with blackened faces, muffled hooves and wordless signals. Such departures are also good, for the business in hand takes overriding precedence and there is no time for reflection.

The departure for Mirandola was still another experience. Laura rose with me before dawn on a bleak chilly day in late November and saw to the packing of my gear. When I admired the dispatch with which she supervised the grooms, she reminded me that she had often performed a like service for her father and brother. When all was done, we broke our fast together before a fire in the bedchamber. Laura masked her feelings with a cheerful manner and could not come close enough. She was swathed in a red velvet robe trimmed with marten fur. I gathered her in my arms, and her hair coiled about her head and bound with a fillet was like the perfumes of the East. I told her I had done nothing to deserve such good fortune.

"That may be," said Laura, "but a woman must have someone to love. You must accept with a good grace what I offer, for that is the first duty of a man."

Her words challenged the gloomy gray morning, thrusting back morbid thoughts and a sense of doom.

"I will set my heart to it," I said. "Winter and war and all things come to an end. I do not like sad partings."

"You will never have them from me," replied Laura. "Go with my love. I fear nothing and will wait for you."

My men and I mounted in the courtyard. The horses stamped and their hooves rang clear on the frozen cobbles. We rode out on the highroad and my last thought was of Laura framed by the window in her bright red robe.

21.

THE FORTRESS OF MIRANDOLA

WHILE I served Pope Julius in the Bolognese and in the Romagna in those years, I was his military hostage, supervised and spied upon by his ecclesiastical commissaries. If the papal legates controlled the government of Perugia, I nevertheless continued in correspondence with those of the displaced Priori who were opposed to the rule of the Church. Most of them were my secret friends. While apparently bowing to the will of the legates, they sought my ideas from afar so that even in exile I maintained a skeleton political structure in Perugia against that day when I should be able to return openly. Pope Julius, for all his tenacity, was growing no younger.

In the autumn of 1510 Pope Julius was warring against the French and Alfonso d'Este, the Duke of Ferrara. In order to make good his drive against Ferrara, it was necessary that he reduce the Fortress of Mirandola, which lay some ten leagues to the west of Ferrara and an equal distance in a northwesterly direction from Bologna. Thus, Mirandola comprised one corner of the Mirandola-Ferrara-Bologna triangle. The fortress presented a troublesome problem during the final days of the year 1510. It was being defended by the Countess Francesca Trivulzio, the doughty daughter of Gian Giacomo Trivulzio, the Milanese condottiero in French service. Countess Trivulzio appreciated the natural strength of Mirandola as well as we did and held on with grim confidence. Our besieging papal army, had dug a system of trenches and erected breastworks palisaded by sharpened stakes which zig-zagged in a drunken circumference, almost encircling the fortress. The vast bulk of Mirandola loomed eerily out of the frozen gray mists of winter.

Throughout December, the weather turned so foul that Mirandola was entirely fog-shrouded for days on end. Shortly after Christmas, a heavy snowfall began and continued intermittently for four days. Five feet of snow filled the trenches and a bitter cold followed the storm. My Perugians cursed, floundered and slowly dug out the guns and wagons. The animals which we were unable to reach perished of cold and hunger. The palisades were buried under drifts which sifted up before the trenches, driven along by the biting winds. Mirandola, when we could see it, scowled down on the slate-colored winter landscape. Countess Trivulzio had no need to parade her small garrison on the snowy battlements or to scan the murky horizon for aid. Winter was her ally and she sat snug in the fortress donjon.

The papal captains lived with their people in the trenches. I had a dugout to myself and rolled from my pallet each dawn, at which time my orderly brought in a snow-packed bucket to be melted for water over a charcoal brazier. He cared for my equipment and cooked for both of us. This last he did well, considering his lack of utensils, and I was careful never to ask what I was eating.

Five weeks of a hard winter passed and we still made no dent in Mirandola's bulk. Through the first month of the new year we steadily lost men and animals to frostbite and lung fevers. Mirandola squatted athwart the road to the Estensi lands like a stubborn dragon. It stuck in the pope's throat (though not in mine) like a perverse granite fishbone. I say "not in mine" for I cared no more for the pope I served than for Alfonso against whom I strove. As for Countess Trivulzio, she was merely an abstraction of the immediate tactical problem. It was enough for me that while waiting for Death to carry off Pope Julius, I was able to practice my profession.

Beyond the hope of regaining power, I extracted a certain comfort from soldiering. I found relaxation each dawn in the discomfort of the trenches, warmth in the frozen air and promise in the retreating darkness of the night. My post looked out on a desolate winter landscape. The trenches with their frozen earth parapets stood out clearly against the snow and the line of stakes rose over hillocks, dipped into hollows and disappeared into the silent morning mists. Such prospects have a meager beauty of their own. I enjoyed them as best I could while studying the mist-dimmed bastions of Mirandola, which reared into the leaden heavens like a disapproving granite horse.

One month after the new year, the pope, newly risen from a sickbed, arrived to inspect us. He stamped about in the muddy trenches with his physician, Shemuel Sarfatti, running after him and wringing his hands. "I cannot answer for the life of Your Holiness," the old healer was crying, "if you disobey my orders. The cold and damp of this place will kill you."

"Take yourself home, Shemuel, and stop bothering us," said the pope mildly enough. "If God wished to remove us, He would have done so long ago in spite of your nostrums." He scratched his scraggly half-grown beard and a new color came into his sunken cheeks as he snuffed the sharp icy air in the trenches. Then he turned to me and said: "Take us on a tour of the guns."

When we reached the snow-buried gun emplacements, the pope's exasperation broke out in new maledictions. Between hacking coughs and constant spitting, he croaked: "Why have not these cannon been dug out? Where is the ammunition and what are your cannoneers doing?"

"My experienced men are down with fevers and frostbite," I said. "The few who are fit for active duty are spread thin in other posts."

"Then spread them thinner," he retorted. "You can always get a little more work out of a man if you are willing to drive him, and it is evident that you are not, or by now you would have had this artillery uncovered and in operation." He glared at me, hammering his staff for emphasis. "If you can do no better, Baglioni, you are unfit to command troops and we shall send you to the rear in disgrace."

Despite my personal indifference to his plans, I could not help but admire the pope's driving preoccupation with the need for action. He seemed to take it for granted that I shared his passionate interest in the reduction of Mirandola. My quarrel with him was sufficiently deep so that I no longer took his sharp tongue and villainous temper seriously. I was willing to concede privately that had he been thirty years younger, he might have made a competent captain.

The pope's hot-tempered thin-skinned nephew, Francesco Maria della Rovere, did not accept the old man's goadings and baitings with an equanimity equal to mine. He often turned white with rage under the pope's abrasive promptings. I shall have more to tell about Francesco Maria. In the meantime the pope was popular, as usual, with the common folk of the army. He set up his personal headquarters in the kitchen of a ruined convent at an angle of the trenchworks within range of Countess Trivulzio's cannon. A day later her gunners plumped a lucky shot through the gaping roof of the desolate nunnery. As was his custom, Pope Julius had dragged some of his reluctant prelates to the theater of our operations. They begged him to retreat beyond artillery range "lest Heaven, angered by his rashness in thus exposing his august person, turn away from him, to his ultimate destruction." The pope responded by striking his martial pose and saying: "That unholy woman up there in the fortress manages her cannon as she does her sewing needle."

"Then she manages them well indeed," said those about him.

"We do not mean that at all," snapped Julius, "but the very opposite. We fear no bodily harm and are secure in God's protection until our mission is accomplished."

During those days I often speculated when God would weary of the brash importunity with which the pope took Him for granted. I can only surmise that God was deaf, excessively patient or away elsewhere. But it is plain that up to this point the Divine Plan did not encompass the reduction of Mirandola. The pope gave his prelates grudging permission to withdraw well behind the breastworks and to quarter themselves in a cluster of deserted stables. They did not wait for their master to urge them and hurriedly retreated with their mules, their chests and their servants to suffer in the draughty stables until the pope's madness would have been satiated.

As the temperature fell once again and my people struggled to hack the ice from their gun positions, the old man's spirits rose. Instead of relapsing, as old Shemuel had feared, the pope throve on hardship. His coughing lessened and his oaths strengthened. He became a common sight, waddling through the trenches in a gray woolen cloak that reached to his ankles, while his face, except for the bristling beard, was hidden by a pointed hood attached to the cloak. I have mentioned his relationship with the people. He shared their messes, listened to their stories with more patience than he accorded the captains and gave them money from his purse. There were moments when I felt myself almost tolerant of him.

It was due to Pope Julius' urgings that the gunners gradually put their shoulders to the attack and began to hammer Mirandola with patient toiling accuracy. He would stand behind them for hours on end, sword in hand, urging them to even greater efforts, saying: "Once in the castle, children, we promise you drink, warmth and riches. None shall be spared! We shall give no quarter! We shall put them all to the sword, not excepting that harlot of Mirandola."

The fact is that when we finally took the fortress, Julius was civil enough to the Countess Trivulzio and permitted her to leave unharmed. Nor did he ever behead Bentivoglio's people who had come to parley in San Luca. I have no quarrel with that. Such clemency is an admirable enough trait in a priest, though its erratic practice in a soldier is ill-advised.

By the last week of January, the incessant pounding of the guns had breached the southern bastion of Mirandola. Milder weather set in and now we labored in thawing mud, and the thunder and crash of the cannon continued by day and night. As the pope stood with our people one morning, a broad section of the bastion collapsed in showers of fire and clouds of dust.

"Forward!" shouted Julius, raising his sword. "The way to carry a fortress is with the sword. We shall be first through the breach!"

He tucked up his cloak. My cannoneers heaved his pontifical haunches over the parapet so heartily that he fell on his face into the mud. He struggled to his feet, waving the sword and shouting: "Follow us!"

A straggling, ever multiplying host of pikemen, arquebusiers, arbalasters and gunners came climbing out of the trenches and headed for the breach. The garrison offered only a token resistance and Pope Julius was hoisted through the breach in a basket.

The road to Ferrara now lay open. As it turned out, the capture of Mirandola was only the beginning and not the end of our labors.

This fortress which we took with so much toil was torn from our hands a month later by that skillful captain, Gian Giacomo, the Countess Trivulzio's father. By the middle of May, 1511, Gian Giacomo Trivulzio compounded the insult by driving us out of Bologna. The pope retreated to Ravenna to lick there the realization of his defeat, and he carried me along. The government of Bologna had been entrusted to Cardinal Alidosi. Alidosi had already explained the loss of Bologna, and Pope Julius apparently accepted his favorite's version of the affair. I was present with Cardinal de' Medici and Alidosi when Julius summoned his nephew, Francesco Maria della Rovere, to present his version of the defeat.

"The brightest jewel in our crown has been lost," said Pope Julius, "and you were both chargeable for it. We intend to learn the truth and to hear what our nephew has to say."

Alidosi replied with assurance: "I reiterate what I have already written in my dispatches and charge the nephew of Your Holiness with this loss and with other things besides."

"What other things?" said Julius, looking very black.

"With having engaged in traitorous commerce with Trivulzio and the French to his own profit and to the grievous hurt of the Apostolic See," said Alidosi calmly.

If I had any previous doubts that Alidosi was a master liar, the profound sincerity of his words dispelled them.

The pope scowled expectantly at the now livid Francesco Maria, who launched forth angrily: "Cardinal Alidosi wasted no time in reaching your ear first so as to put me at a disadvantage. Nevertheless, he lies and I can explain it."

Pope Julius waited in ominous silence.

"The common gossip of all Italy is that Alidosi himself had this traffic with the French which he imputes to me," said Francesco Maria. "Listen well, uncle, for I speak the truth. I was moving in the direction of Ferrara to give battle to Trivulzio. He avoided me and turned south toward Bologna. We raced toward Bologna by forced marches and I arrived at Casalecchio three miles south of the city before him. By that time, Trivulzio was at Ponte Laino, five miles north of Bologna. I immediately notified Cardinal Alidosi in the city of the situation and offered to reinforce his garrison against Trivulzio's imminent attack."

"What help did you offer him?" asked Pope Julius.

"Cannon and some two or three thousand men," replied Francesco Maria. "Cardinal Alidosi had no more than twelve hundred men behind the walls of Bologna. Yet he declined my assistance. Does it not seem strange to you?"

"Get on with it," said Julius.

"Cardinal Alidosi informed me that he required no aid, that all was well within the city. When I insisted once again on reinforcing the papal garrison, my officers, deceived by Alidosi's assurances, finally dissuaded me from my plan."

"That does not relieve your responsibility," said Julius.

"From our camp we heard shouts and fighting during the night," continued Francesco Maria, "and by dawn it was too late, for the French with their Bentivogli partisans were already through the gates — which must have been opened to them by treachery. I retreated immediately, beating off French attacks, and made camp between Forli and Cesena, losing only my baggage train."

"Is that all?" asked Julius.

"I beg Your Holiness to believe me," said Francesco Maria. "It is plain that the cardinal deliberately hindered every effort by myself to relieve Bologna and he lost no time in speeding his report to you."

I listened to this exchange with great interest. There were open rumors at this time — better still, verified rumors — that among other tricks Cardinal Alidosi had deliberately posted Bentivogli partisans at the critical gates on the night of the French break-in. Following this, he sent off his story to the pope, pretended panic and escaped to his estate in disguise. That is how the story went.

The pope turned expectantly to Alidosi, who said: "Most humbly and sorrowfully, I charge the nephew of Your Holiness with treason in that he sold Bologna to the enemy."

Pope Julius turned grimly to his nephew. "The Cardinal of Pavia's word is good enough for us. Proof! Give us proof of your charges, Francesco."

"My own word," shouted Francesco Maria, "which is better than that of this traitor. I have also heard that he deliberately oppressed the Bolognese to encourage an internal uprising against papal rule and facilitate the French entry."

Francesco Maria's defense and his show of temper heated the pope's own anger beyond recall. Yet he tried to control it, saying that Francesco Maria was proferring accusations from envy and malice and to cover his own negligence. He ordered Francesco Maria placed under house arrest and stumped out of the apartment, leaning heavily on his cane. Francesco Maria flung off the officers who approached him and rushed wildly from the palace.

When Cardinal de' Medici warned Alidosi coldly that his accusations might recoil on him, Alidosi replied lightly: "I have spoken the truth. My shield is the Holy Father's belief in me."

"I pray God you have no greater need of your shield than you have had today," retorted Medici.

Alidosi smiled, saying that in whatever measure his need arose, the pope would provide it, for the pope's mantle was broad and his mercy endless.

Medici replied that he doubted the breadth of the pope's mantle. I agreed silently, for I believed what all the world, except the pope, believed — that Alidosi had sold Bologna, that all his intrigues tended toward one end — the winning of Imola for himself. The town and territory of Imola had always been the ancestral possession of the House of Alidosi. The cardinal had long demanded its return from the Holy See, and Pope Julius had as long refused. The French were willing to trade. It was as simple as that. I was of two minds about it. My own soldier's work had come all unraveled, the pope weakened and brought closer to the brink. In a sense I almost regretted that. On the other hand, Alidosi had helped save my neck five years before, not from goodness, certainly, but the result was the same whether he had acted from self-interest or disinterested humanity. Had you known Alidosi, you would have agreed that such a thought was absurd. Alidosi never performed a disinterested act in his life. He left us at this point, saying, "I am returning to my house at Rivo and shall await the pope's orders there."

Cardinal de' Medici and I left the palace. As we emerged into the street, we found Francesco Maria quarreling with Alidosi. We began to walk toward them, and at that instant Francesco Maria drew his sword and slashed down at Alidosi's shoulder. The cardinal slid from his mule with a high womanish scream. Before I could reach him, Francesco Maria sprang from his horse and stabbed Alidosi through the throat. When I seized Francesco Maria, he glared back at me, his eyes glazed. Then he regained control and said, "You and I know that he sold us to the French and yet I have no way of proving it. I could no longer stand by and see him cozening my senile uncle. Killing this carrion is the one useful thing I've done."

"Perhaps," I said. "In the meantime, if you wish to avoid a broken neck, start riding and put distance between yourself and the pope. If I know him, he'll drink your blood for this."

Francesco Maria tore loose from my grip, flung his stained sword at the dead Alidosi, and remounted his horse. Followed by his people, he galloped out of Ravenna.

Cardinal de' Medici took the murder badly. I led him back to the palace and he talked as though to himself, murmuring:

"Alidosi was an unworthy servant of the Church. Yet he was a legate and his person was inviolate. May God curse the criminal who struck down a Prince of the Church."

Cardinal de' Medici's reaction was a sighing breeze to that of the pope. The old man howled like a maddened wolf. He tore his beard, fell to the floor and beat his head on the pavement. When his attendants picked him up, he broke down into a storm of tears. He lowered his voice and said, "Of all the evils we have suffered, this is the blackest, that our nephew — may he burn in Hell, for we intend to send him there — should have murdered our minister. Let no one think that our wits wander. We shall chain him, rack him and tear off his flesh with red-hot pincers! We shall fling his bones in a quicklime pit to bubble there with vermin and robbers." Then he glared at me and said, "You, Baglioni, what part did you play in this?"

"His hands are clean," said Cardinal de' Medici wearily, and he related how I had rushed to prevent the tragedy.

"Perhaps," said the pope savagely, "but he is capable of such complicity. Brazen murder was always the way of the Baglioni." Then to me directly, he growled: "Count yourself fortunate that the cardinal speaks for you."

Five years of patient bile spilled over into my throat and I snarled back at him: "If you seek a sacrifice, you have come to the wrong sheepfold. Alidosi interceded for me in Orvieto and before. Would I have reason to slay him?"

My answer placated the pope instead of provoking him.

"We shall appoint a commission to investigate this murder," he said more calmly. "You, Medici, shall preside over it. Now go and leave us. We are quitting this damned city tonight and forever."

My servitude under Pope Julius was coming to an end.

22.

THE BATTLE OF RAVENNA

CARDINAL ALIDOSI was murdered on the twenty-fourth day of May in the year 1511, and I now still remember how Pope Julius' house of cards came tumbling down, as though that murder was a signal for all the misfortunes which followed. Bologna had been lost to the French, and Francesco Maria della Rovere was a fugitive. Thanks to Julius, the foreign grip on Italy's throat was tighter than ever. Venice had been an important buffer between Italy and the North. But Pope Julius, that sublime military genius, bemused by caprice, intuition and a ragtag of Divine guidance, had broken her back two years before at the Battle of Agnadello. The gates hung open and the French now swarmed through the north Italian plain, killing, burning and ravaging. Perhaps you will agree with me that this meddlesome pontiff wrought more hell and damnation in eight years than all the popes who had preceded him, not excepting Alexander Borgia.

Francesco Maria finally appeared in Rome to answer for the murder of Alidosi. An investigative commission had been formed under the authority of Cardinal de' Medici. It was before this commission that Francesco Maria was defended by an advocate as expensive as he was able. There were no real difficulties, however. The evidence against the late Alidosi was so

heavy that Cardinal de' Medici had no choice but to acquit the
accused. He did so with a bad grace and stored his hatred away
for use six years later, when he made it an excuse to invade the
Duchy of Urbino. But that will come when I tell you how I
fought against Francesco Maria in Medici's service — to my
own destruction.

The God of Battles at length became weary of the military
blunderings of His Vicar on Earth and struck him down with an
illness. Julius, sick, wrestled as cantankerously with the Angel
of Death as he had ever wrestled with men. Shemuel Sarfatti
joined the fray from the beginning and finally dragged his master back. I should not hold it against that learned Hebrew that
he saved della Rovere's life, if indeed he did so. We never know
when the physician has wrought the miracle, or Nature in spite
of the physician. I say this because another of Shemuel's tribe,
and a Spaniard at that, mended my Malatesta's broken skull
after the Battle of Ravenna and plucked him back from death.

Pope Julius summoned me to Rome. He was bowed, thinner,
grayer, and he spoke in a husky whisper. "Baglioni," he said,
"the Venetians have asked for you. They will give you the
governor-generalship if you press them, for their need is great.
We will interpose no objections and advise you to accept."
From under his bushy eyebrows he stared at me with a trace of
his old fire.

"You need not look so pleased," he snapped. "Their offer of
so exalted a military post is not because you deserve it. To such
straits have they been reduced that you are the only one qualified and available. You are the best of their meager choices."

"They have Your Holiness to thank for that," I replied, "and
so will I if this appointment materializes."

Pope Julius acknowledged my thrust with a grim nod, saying,
"There is malice in your words but we deserve the judgment,
since we brought the Venetians to ruin and thus admitted the

barbarians. Now must we make amends and aid Venice against the French. We must thrust them out, repair the gate and lock it." He gestured wearily. "You have our permission to return to Perugia to recruit fresh troops. Comport yourself well, Baglioni, and await the commissaries there. Try to be an honest man and perform some useful work. Perhaps that was why God persuaded us to spare you."

I accepted the Venetian offer with satisfaction. As employers, they have always been more reliable than most. As paymasters, they were preferable to the cautious nigglers of Florence. Despite the disaster at Agnadello, Venice was still wealthy. Unlike the Florentines, the Venetian oligarchs respected their contracts scrupulously and did not waste time seeking bargains where none were to be had. Like the Florentines, the Venetians were men of commerce; the Venetian aristocrat was a merchant first and a noble after. Yet the Venetians dealt with a broader hand. They did not weigh war and statecraft in florins, ducats and soldi as did the men of Florence.

The Venetian commissaries reached Perugia in September, and Malatesta, who had taken leave from his post in Padua, accompanied them on this journey. Amico Graziani and I examined the Venetian contract and did not bargain seriously; only to that degree which would not arouse Venetian awareness of my eagerness to accept, to prevent them from driving down the price and taking undue advantage. I had other thoughts in mind. In the service of the Most Serene Republic of Venice, I would be dealing with a stable engine of government, as opposed to the rickety erratic democracy of the Florentine Republic. Any condotta I concluded with them would be a desirable one. I was heartily sick of Pope Julius' service and yearned to put as much distance as possible between that demanding old man and myself. True, Venice was now the pope's ally, but in actual practice I would be able to operate with a relatively high degree of independence. Then there was the question of d'Alviano's captivity in the hands of the French. Who could tell? After entrenching myself in Venetian service, I hoped in some manner to effect the release of my brother-in-law or to engineer his escape. And, finally, in terms of my personal prestige, there would be a difference between my papal service and the offered Venetian condotta. As far as Pope Julius was concerned, I was little better than a reprieved felon on whom a signal favor had been bestowed. He had never lost an opportunity to remind me of my dependency through five and a half galling years. On all counts, a change was desirable and indicated.

We finally agreed that I was to receive the governor-generalship with a condotta of two hundred men-at-arms, five hundred light cavalry, a personal bodyguard of two hundred picked swordsmen and a salary of three thousand ducats per annum. The contract was to be good for the duration of hostilities with the French. Thereafter it could be abrogated after notice and the fulfillment of certain formalities at the pleasure of the contracting parties.

The contract was drawn up and signed in the presence of the Venetian commissaries and the principal dignitaries of Perugia. My induction into Venetian service had the immediate effect of strengthening my position within Perugia. The ward leaders came to renew their pledges of friendship and support. The lesser captains within the city came to seek audience with me. The wheels were beginning to turn and the world was brightening.

Malatesta and I plunged into the business of recruitment. Within two weeks after the departure of the Venetian commissaries, I had enrolled two thousand experienced soldiers, many of them veterans and survivors of the Battle of Agnadello. After marshaling and equipping these troops, I sent them on to Pesaro, where they boarded transports. On October 11, they disembarked at the Venetian naval arsenal of Chioggia.

With Malatesta and my principal captains, I left Perugia on September 20. Upon my arrival in Padua, the Venetian officials formally presented me with the baton of command amid all the pageantry and ceremonious splendor of which the Serenissima is uniquely capable. I was now Governor-General of the Venetian Army, subordinate only to the still vacant Captain-Generalcy. Once again, I faced the future with renewed hopes.

Malatesta, the fourth of that name in our family, was twenty-one years of age at this time. Like all the Baglioni, he was a tall athlete and a good soldier, if I myself say it. He resembled me even in the manner he managed his horse. I lacked somewhat this paternal feeling for the nineteen-year-old Orazio. My younger son has distinguished himself ably in the past four years, but I do not think he will ever qualify for a general's baton. It was during this sojourn in Perugia that I successfully concluded negotiations with the Monaldeschi of Orvieto for their daughter as Malatesta's future wife. I was confident we would come to terms and was satisfied with the match. The daughters as they bloom come to resemble the mothers. The Monaldeschi came to Perugia and I found the mother, Imperia dei Monaldeschi, to be a tall, well-hipped woman with clear straight eyes, an open countenance and a quick brain. Indeed, I took it for a good sign that she gave me the rough side of her tongue in our discussions. More important, I had the best of it in settling the dowry with Signor Francesco, her husband. Certain portions of the dowry are still to be delivered, but I do not doubt that Malatesta will be able to enforce successfully the marriage contract upon the Monaldeschi, for they are petty nobles who have been more honored by this marriage than ourselves — a good thing under the circumstances. Ideally, a man should marry his peer, but if he must go further afield, let him marry a little beneath his station rather than above it. If he marries a woman of a house greater than his own, he will seldom have peace, for women by nature will never let the husband forget the slightest disparity of lineage in the wife's favor. It will return forever at the heart of every argument. So it was between myself and Ippolita da Conti, who was never tired of reminding me that she derived from a House infinitely more ancient and illustrious than the Baglioni. Well, I will grant that the Conti are very great people, but it made for little harmony between Ippolita and myself and, among other factors, helped to destroy our union.

I favored Maddalena dei Monaldeschi, my daughter-in-law, from the beginning and am confident that Malatesta will ultimately succeed in reducing her to that state of amiable obedience which is so desirable in a wife and to which I was never able to reduce either Ippolita or Laura Crispolti. The fact that Maddalena was a small rebel from the onset disturbed none of us, for we were aware that Madonna Imperia was rearing the girl with the education more suitable for a son. Signor Francesco and I disapproved in vain, but Madonna Imperia had a mulish passion for learning and prevailed.

Malatesta served under me in the winter of 1512. In February of that year I failed to halt the French under Gaston de Foix at Isola delle Scale, a small place about eight leagues due south of Verona and some twenty leagues to the southeast of Brescia.

I was a small cog in Pope Julius' new alliance with the Spaniards and the Venetians to drive the French out of Italy. I came to be involved indirectly when a papal-Spanish army under Raimondo de Cardona, Pedro Navarro and Marcantonio Colonna besieged French-held Bologna. A Venetian force under Andrea Gritti simultaneously assaulted Brescia. Gaston de

Foix, King Louis' brilliant twenty-three-year-old nephew, sped from Bologna through Mantuan territory to relieve the French garrison there. I decided to intercept de Foix at Isola delle Scale and reached the town by forced marches. When he arrived on the following day, I was already in position with a mixed cavalry and infantry force of nineteen hundred men. De Foix attacked without hesitation and struck hard. The fighting was very heavy. My infantry, which comprised two-thirds of my force, broke before the murderous onslaught of the French heavy cavalry. We were forced to retreat across the river, losing our guns and some three hundred men who were killed or captured. It was an ominous failure on my part and it helps nothing to point out that the French cavalry was superior in numbers, weight and training. The sack of Brescia, in which eight thousand people (some say it was considerably more) perished, ensued from my inability to halt de Foix. His army drove onward toward Brescia, broke into the city and inexorably crushed the half-hearted defense of the citizens of Brescia and Gritti's Venetians. The French garrison issued from the citadel to join forces with de Foix and Brescia was given over to sack on February 19. The monasteries and the convents were stormed and pillaged. Houses, huts and palaces were looted; the women were raped. The men of Brescia were tortured and murdered for seven successive days.

Within a span of fifteen days, Gaston de Foix had quit the Bolognese, crossed Mantua, recaptured and sacked Brescia. It was a glorious feat of arms. Gaston de Foix, that illustrious and youthful Duke of Nemours, the kinsman of monarchs, was the new-risen star in the heavens. My prestige, dim enough before this French thunderbolt, flickered correspondingly lower. I bore a heavy responsibility and culpability for the ordeal which the Brescians endured. I fought and failed at Isola delle Scale. Yet let not the blood of Brescia be on my head alone. It is also on the head of Christ's Vicar, Giuliano della Rovere.

Great issues hang by small hinges. Perhaps if I had halted de Foix at Isola delle Scale, the Battle of Ravenna might have been prevented, delayed or never fought. With the remnant of my battered force extricated from the debacle at Isola, I joined the papal-Spanish army under Cardona and Navarro near Ravenna. Malatesta and I were assigned to the command of Fabrizio Colonna, who led all the papal cavalry. In all we had fifteen thousand cavalry under Colonna and thirteen thousand Spanish infantry under Pedro Navarro, and these combined forces were under the orders of Raimondo de Cardona. The Brescian river of blood aroused de Foix's appetite for more blood. He rushed southeastward from Brescia to meet us near Ravenna. De Foix had only fifteen hundred heavily armored knights, the peerless French gendarmerie. But he had nineteen thousand French and German infantry and a formidable artillery train which was commanded by Pope Julius' mortal enemy, Alfonso d'Este, the Duke of Ferrara.

Thus it was that on the day of the Resurrection of Our Saviour, the opposed armies maneuvered along the Ronco River until they collided on the plain of Ravenna. It is a brief but deadly tale. Go to the chroniclers for it and they will tell you why and how the kings, pope and generals came to grinning poisonous grips at Ravenna. All the great captains of Europe were present on that day and I was also there with Malatesta and the Cardinal de' Medici, who came as legate of our papal-Spanish army. The cardinal had established his headquarters at Sant' Apollinare about three miles from Ravenna. We came upon him astride his mule, conspicuous in his brilliant robe and tasseled hat. He was exhorting the soldiers to fight for God and the pope and shriving those who might die on the following day. I presented Malatesta and the cardinal gave him absolution. Medici's usually cheerful, moonlike face was sober and he squinted blearily toward the French across the Ronco stream, saying, "How unhappy I am in this place — there's a sultry brooding air here like the antechamber of death. See how the armies crouch like a pair of sullen wolves waiting to tear one another apart."

In the night before the battle, while Malatesta slept in the dreamless courage of youth, I dreamed of my uncle Guido, who appeared to me all naked with his wounds fresh and bloody as when the Corgna had inflicted them. While giving Holy Mother Church her due, Guido in his lifetime had always held with the Koran of the Turks that every man's fate is written on his forehead. Even as a child I had often heard him say that men died at a moment predestined at birth and never before.

"My favorite nephew," the vision of Guido seemed to say, "I will be with you in tomorrow's battle. Believe me that I saw the angel that wrote on your forehead when you were held at the baptismal font. Let your courage be absolute, for nothing can alter a man's fate."

I make nothing of dreams, holding them to be a fantasy and after-print of what we have done and said by day. As cats dream of mice and dogs of new-buried bones, so do men, having longer memories, dream of matters seen and heard in childhood. Yet, though my reason tells me that dreams are a vagrant wind, I woke refreshed and began to recall my uncle. Peace be with old Guido, wherever he abides! Peace to his body butchered in the Great Wedding Massacre! Peace to his raddled theology which made no quibble over Muslim angels presiding at a good Christian baptism! He had been no ordinary Christian. Many people intimated, when it was safe to do so, that Guido Baglioni was not a Christian at all. I have since come to savor the conflicting attitudes of various persons toward our family. Some, like the House of Tei, loved us like faithful hounds and were willing to die — and did die — for us. More, many more hated us root, trunk and branch, and swore that we were not Christians but infidels and worse. We were forever accused of things that grew in the telling until the poisonous butterflies of slander came to be fixed forever by some scribbler's idle pen.

I lay on my pallet and reflected in the dark. Guido's ideas concerning predestination seemed reasonable enough, nor was the fact that the doctrine was maintained by Turks a bar to its soundness. I am still of the same mind today and am in agreement with the common opinion of Italy that there is more equity among Turks than among the prelates of Rome. The closer one moves to the papal throne, the less Christianity one finds. The Holy Saviour Himself would have been confused in Julian Rome and would be in Leo's present Rome also.

I became aware of a weariness as the first slate-gray light of dawn stole in through the tent flap. I heard the faint rattle of the cooking pots in the distance as the cooks stirred themselves. An eager brazen trumpet note rose in the air and was suddenly still. Every man's fate was written upon his forehead and it would soon be time. It was the will of God or of whatever power played God. That was what the ghost of Guido had told me during the night.

The dawn strengthened in a rosy sky and the French guns, on the extreme right flank of the French line and against the Ronco, opened thunderously. We, the cavalry, on the far left flank of the papal-Spanish crescent, were the recipient of this murderous cannonade. Malatesta and I made a quick breakfast in a dugout under fire while the grooms watered our horses and gave them a final rubbing. Armor and lanceheads glittered and flashed in the swiftly rising sun. The banners floated free, and in the background the kettle drums boomed low and persistent. The troopers were in good spirits and made the usual jokes about which of them would die on this day. Our Spanish infantry on the right was protected by a ditch and well hidden by earthworks. The French had thrown a bridge across the Ronco during the night, and now their gendarmerie rumbled across the bridge, deployed, and charged the

Spanish foot. Our light horse met them in the plain between the two armies. They absorbed the shock, then broke before the French cavalry and were driven back. The shouts and curses of the combatants, the screams of the dying horses, the clash and grind of steel intermingled with the roar of the guns and all rose to a crescendo of sound. In the meantime, our cannon fired steadily into the mass of the French infantry. The French artillery directly opposite us responded, cutting a swathe into our cavalry detachments. We sat, waited and endured the hail of shot and fire falling among us.

Fabrizio Colonna, the cavalry commander, grew impatient and sent message after furious message to Raimondo de Cardona, the commander in chief, demanding permission to attack. Colonna and the Spaniards were on bad terms. Cardona, although in supreme command, deferred to Pedro Navarro's judgment. Navarro cared nothing about the cavalry and worried only for his infantry, insisting that they lie low behind their earthworks and safe from the French barrage. Hence, at Navarro's suggestion, the commander in chief returned orders that the cavalry hold their positions. So our waiting troopers continued to be blown to bits and mutilated until Colonna summoned me, saying, "That marraño Cardona cares nothing that my knights are being slaughtered like sheep. I am waiting no longer to sit here and be cut to pieces. Get ready to move out."

We rode out of our positions and into the field beyond our defensive ditches. The bugles pealed for a charge and we hurled ourselves against the lances of the French gendarmerie. The ordered ranks of my people dissolved into a melee of whirling swords, axes and maces as the horses reared and neighed. I saw a gigantic French knight aim a slash at Malatesta. My vision was blurred by sweat under my helmet, but I hacked my way toward Malatesta through the press of rearing horses and upward-stabbing pikemen in time to see the French knight crash his blade down on Malatesta's helmet. Malatesta fell from his horse and I was swept forward in a whirl of armored riders.

We, the cavalry, were fully committed and Navarro's infantry, stung by the French guns, finally tumbled out of their trenches and advanced to support us. They were steady and disciplined until the French gendarmerie struck them. No infantry could have withstood the concentrated weight of the French charge. The Spaniards buckled and enveloped the French horsemen in a swaying churning struggle. I hacked, parried and thrust among the knights with a feeling of impersonal detachment. I recall the French knights about me, Medusa-like in their metallic facelessness, who sat their horses and laid about them with an air of leisurely concentration. The wiry Spaniards dodged nimbly, avoiding the horse hooves, stabbing at the bellies and slashing at the fetlocks of the chargers. Some, with pikes and halberds, labored to drag riders out of their saddles. Any toppled knight was immediately dispatched by a dagger thrust in the nostrils. A bareheaded Gascon killed my horse under me with a pike thrust. I had time to stab him through and sprang clear of the horse as it collapsed. Filippo Cencio, who maintained his position behind me, pushed forward and cleared a momentary space about us. I clung to his stirrip and he worked himself into the open behind a small square of Spanish pikemen.

"I saw Malatesta dragged clear," said Cencio.

"Is he dead?" I asked.

He shrugged. "I know only that I saw him dragged away out of the crush."

By this time our cavalry was no longer an organized force and I ordered the buglers to sound the recall. The Perugians came drifting back. I gathered them along the Ronco causeway and we retreated in slow order with a body of Spanish arquebusiers and pikemen. I kept my people between the Spaniards and the still charging French knights, while the Ronco protected us on the far side. The struggle on the plain was slowly dissolving and the contending groups drifted apart like marionettes in a puppet show, revealing a field littered with dead and dying horses, knights and footmen. Further off, toward the northeast, many columns of wagons and guns, what had been our right flank, burned fiercely in the pale sun.

The French bugles pealed. The gendarmerie in the distance charged us once again. We watched them come on, their glittering armor and lanceheads reflecting the sun, and braced for the shock. They bore down in a confusion of tossing plumes, waving banners and a rippling rising wave of shouts: "Saint Denis!" "Foix!" "France!" "Navarre!"

Gaston de Foix was far out in front of his knights. I recognized him by his long blond hair flying behind him and his small fair beard. Not only did he ride without a helmet but his right arm, with which he brandished a sword, was bare. The sun sparkled on his silvery armor, and over his breastplate he wore a bright surcoat showing the blazon of the House of Navarre. When the French were sufficiently close the Spanish arquebusiers, very steady and composed, sent a heavy volley into the knights. De Foix, who was almost among them, shouted, fell from his horse and rolled down the bank of the causeway into the Ronco.

My Perugians charged the French flank and the fighting became general again. The Spaniards broke ranks and ran in among the French knights, slashing at the horses and killing any Frenchman my people brought down. The French had seen de Foix fall and a cry spread among them: "The duke is dead!" They wavered, fell back and wheeled away while we continued our steady retreat along the causeway. The gap between us and the French gendarmerie steadily widened. Everywhere on the plain, the fires near and distant began to burn lower.

There is nothing so lonely as a field on which a battle is ending. A brooding silence gradually succeeds the crash of guns, the scream of horses and the shouts of armed men. It is like a banquet hall from which the guests are dispersing. Everywhere over the plain along our right lay huddled writhing groups. Off on the horizon, baggage wagons were scattering in all directions. I saw soldiers raising themselves painfully to crawl aimlessly on all fours. The sun was beginning to set and I remembered the peasants who would emerge after dark to strip the dead and stab the still breathing. The peasant has no portion of the prize for which armies contend, and he snatches where he can. But most of all I was stirred by the sight of the dead and dying horses. Men, being noxious and prolific weeds, should not be discouraged from mutual destruction. But the beast is Nature's virtuous child and its death is the death of total innocence. As Nature is invigorated by the first, so is it enfeebled by the second.

Thus ended the Battle of Ravenna, which was fought on Easter Sunday in the year 1512. It burned down to sullen ashes with sixteen thousand corpses, with the death of Gaston de Foix and a bloody French victory which they could not afford and which persuaded them to depart from Italy. I saw none of our battle commanders, only the after-havoc of war on the monotonous plain of Ravenna. Then I made out Cardinal de' Medici at a distance, conspicuous in his scarlet robe, kneeling beside a group of fallen soldiers.

"Break off and go," said the cardinal when I rode up to him. "If I am taken prisoner, my office will keep me safe. Colonna, Cardona and Navarro are prisoners or dead for all I know. You will do us no good by letting yourself be taken."

"If you find my son among the wounded," I said, "watch over him."

Behind me, Cencio shouted for me to come away. More French patrols were approaching from the river side.

"Go with God," said the cardinal.

I spurred after Cencio and galloped away.

There are those who dismiss the Black Art as a lie. I agree — with one qualification. Men do have an erratic genius for raising demons. I saw them do so in that satisfying convulsion, the Battle of Ravenna, although I did not appreciate its magnitude at the time. This storm flung the necromancers in all directions and sent sixteen thousand pawns to their long sleep. It thrust Machiavelli down to prison and Cardinal de' Medici up to the tiara. And, finally, it consigned the High and Mighty Republic of Florence to the dunghill of oblivion. But witless soldiers often survive where wise magicians perish. Ravenna was, for me, no more than a fiery ordeal through which I passed unscathed.

BOOK IV

THE HOUSE OF MEDICI

1513-1520

23.

THE PRISONER

A GOVERNMENT, being the child of many fathers, is an impersonal monster concerned with power in terms of gold and human counters. The counters destroyed are ticked off the ledgers. The counters spared are mended and reassigned. Nor can it be otherwise, for a state suffers pain only through the flesh of its agents. It moves blindly and always toward survival. Following the blood-bath of Ravenna, therefore, the Venetian government ordered me back to garrison duty in Padua. Here I regrouped my decimated squadrons and spent the summer training replacements from Perugia, and Venetian levies also. I wrote to Laura, instructing her to sell our house in Bologna for whatever price she could obtain and to join me as quickly as possible. She obeyed and reached Padua in June.

Malatesta did not die. By virtue of a tough constitution, he survived his skull fracture received at Ravenna — but I think that it was more than luck and a strong body. He lived because it was his destiny to do so. The angelic scribe assigned to him at birth had another date in mind, allowing Malatesta to emerge from Ravenna like Daniel from the den of beasts. He spent the summer of 1512 recovering from his wounds in the Castle of Colazzone in Perugian territory. By the time his men reached Colazzone after an arduous journey over the mountains,

Malatesta seemed more in need of priests than physicians. They left him there never expecting to see him again on this earth, but three forces strove in Malatesta's behalf. Firstly, the citizens of Colazzone sent to Perugia for a Spanish Jew resident there, a man very cunning in the management of head wounds. Secondly, these people raised a votive shrine entreating Our Lady of Colazzone for Malatesta's life. And lastly, that aforementioned angelic secretary with whom lay the power reknotted Malatesta's thread instead of cutting it. It may be that the pious exerions of the citizens conjoined with the deft tinkering of the Spaniard persuaded the angel to forbear. But I do not think so — neither medicine nor prayers to Our Lady can avail when the hour strikes.

By August, Malatesta was sufficiently recovered to rejoin me in Padua and I assigned him to light duties. He told me of his illness and described the fresco above his shrine, saying, "It depicts me bandaged like the Grand Turk, with Our Lady and a squadron of cherubs flying overhead."

"I trust they included that Old Hebrew who patched your skull with a gold plate," I said.

"The artist did not omit him," smiled Malatesta. "He is somewhere in the background expounding Scripture to a pair of attentive cherubs."

Soon after Malatesta reached Padua, we began to receive garbled reports of the fate that had befallen the Florentine Republic. Pope Julius in Rome, far from disheartened by the Pyrrhic victory of the French at Ravenna, now began to prepare a heavy reckoning against Florence. His reasons were not mine. I will only say that Florence had a genius for irritating all manner of men, from saints (as some judge him) like Savonarola to princes like Cesare Borgia and soldiers like Vitellozzo Vitelli. But all men, and Pope Julius among them, were infuriated by Florentine inconstancy and effrontery, the talent for masking weakness with finespun guile. Suffice it, Pope Julius demanded that the republic dismiss the Gonfaloniere Soderini, pay heavy fines for what he deemed their treasonable dealings with the French, and allow the Medici to return to Florence. When Florence refused, the pope ordered a Spanish army under Cardona into Tuscany. To these seasoned regulars, Florence opposed citizen-soldiers, the creation of my friend Machiavelli. At the end of August, they collided at Prato some three leagues from Florence. The result was disastrous for the republic. Cardona's people compensated for their battering at Ravenna by ravaging Prato in a three-week sack. The buildings were left standing but every living thing was put to the sword. Few of Machiavelli's militiamen escaped, seven thousand Pratesi died and many of the women resolutely committed suicide to escape rape.

The real culprits were those selfsame gentlemen of the Signoria of whom I have spoken and of whom the urbane and indecisive Soderini was a prime example. Florence was given an opportunity to come to terms and should have done so. Having chosen to resist, these clever men sent raw citizen-levies — and few enough of those — to resist the best infantry in Europe. Yes, on that day the pope and the Spaniards crushed the rulers of Florence like veritable dung-beetles, and those like Soderini who survived were permitted to crawl away into ignominious exile. So the House of Medici returned to Florence in triumph, and as the republic crashed in ruin it dragged down with it a man I admired in despite — Niccolò Machiavelli, the War Secretary of the Republic, whose loving creation had failed to hold the line at Prato.

I can sum up this sack of Prato by saying that it was an action in which one of my enemies, the pope, mauled another of my enemies, the Florentine Republic. Cardona's men, the survivors of Ravenna, did the mauling and peeled back the

Signoria's quivering tendons, but Pope Julius was the author of the atrocity. Machiavelli understood the danger well enough and tried to give his countrymen warning. How does one explain the squandering of so much love and loyalty by so clever a man?

It was a pity that the Spaniards halted at Prato. They should have continued to Florence itself. But then, commanders, out of laziness, inertia or excessive conservatism, often halt at the half-way mark. Witness Cardona, that grave and indolent Spaniard! Gaston de Foix at Ravenna had been a different quantity. If that fire-eating boy had not insisted on committing suicide he could have taken Rome and put Pope Julius and his successors in a French cage, to the benefit of mankind. King Francis had a similar opportunity after the Battle of Marignano but he let the priests dissuade him. What a waste of time to speculate about alternatives!

Ten months after the Battle of Ravenna — in February, 1513 — Malatesta and I were still in Venetian service when word arrived in Padua of the death of Pope Julius II. It cannot be denied that he died repentantly, for he had the grace to admit on his deathbed that he had been a great sinner and that he malgoverned the Church. In this self-castigation he was justified, for he had painted Italy with three coats of blood. The people passed before his bier and beat their breasts. They kissed his cold feet and mourned him as the shield of the poor against their own tyrants and the barbarian scourge. But the people are children, light of heart and light of understanding. Potent lords like Alfonso d'Este wept with relief to learn of Julius' death, and small men too. When I, an obscure soldier in the hire of Venice and still an exile, heard of his passing, my heart leaped with new hope. I summoned Malatesta, placed him in acting command of the Padua garrison and made immediate arrangements to return to Perugia with Laura.

"With Julius dead," I told Malatesta, "it is our turn again in Perugia after seven years. It matters not who the Sacred College chooses, although Medici might help us most. But between now and the time they make themselves a new pope, I propose to settle accounts with all those whom Julius tried to resurrect. I will have Orazio to help me and you can be more useful here. You are well aware how della Rovere's memory is being revered. They will find out soon enough that he only fixed the yoke more firmly than ever across their necks. He was an amateur who, for the sake of snatching up a few strong places, has turned northern Italy into a ravaged pigsty. A few more such popes and the entire stable will collapse! No doubt God had His mysterious reasons for popes like Julius. If our Gentile had not bungled or betrayed me, I might have killed Julius seven years ago."

"What's done is done," said Malatesta. "There will be other occasions. In the meantime, there is talk that the rabble of Rome is boiling up again."

"It is the pattern," I said. "The Romans welcome these interregni for a bit of cozy looting and murder on their own account while the barons chivvy the College with their demands. There will be a reckoning some day with Rome. Rome, the snake pit, Cloaca Mundi, the sewer of the world! If it comes after my time, strike a blow for me and carry forward what I have left undone. Hit Rome and Florence also!"

"Is this a testament you are leaving me?" asked Malatesta.

"It may well be," I said, "so bear in mind all I have said. Remember what we are — condottieri, forever in the service of others. We get the leavings after the lions and the bears have gorged. But we are also strong. The walls of Perugia are high and thick and our people are the best soldiers in Italy. Were it not so, we would have been shredded and rolled flat long ago by the papacy. If another Cesare Borgia comes up after my death, join him. You will do no better for our House."

"Go with God," said Malatesta.

"Rather with a broom," I replied, "to sweep the vermin from Perugia."

With that parting, I mustered my veteran companies, gathered up Laura and took the highroad south.

It was while passing through Florence on our way to Perugia that I heard that Machiavelli was in disgrace and in prison. It appears that when the conspiracy of the republican zealots Boscoli and Capponi against the Medici came to light in January, 1513, Machiavelli was arrested in the Medicean dragnet on no other evidence than that his name appeared on their lists as a sympathizer. I decided to pay him a visit.

By the early spring of 1513, the new regime in Florence had already been in power some four months. The prison governor, a brisk and shiny Medicean appointee, escorted me with his guards along a corridor which was one level beneath the piazza. It was a gloomy, low-ceilinged place, spaced on either side with iron cell doors. It occurs to me here that the only political appointees who enjoy permanent tenure amid the rise and fall of regimes are the prison rats. I do not doubt that the new Medicean rats and the fallen republican rats lived side by side on terms of perfect amity. Wherefore I say to impatient politicians: "Go to the rat, Superb Ones, and learn philosophy."

When we reached a narrow stone staircase leading down to the next tier, the governor put himself nimbly at the head of our little procession and said, "The torches throw insufficient light; it is better that I go before."

My travel-stained appearance told him nothing. I might have been any captain returning from the wars. Nor was he interested in my business with his prisoner, for I had displayed a pass from Giuliano de' Medici.

The turnkeys unlocked the last cell, the dimmest in the tier. I stepped into the murky stench.

"Is it you, Machiavelli?" I said. I could barely make out a dim figure within.

The prisoner rose from a stool with a rattle of chains and came forward under a flickering oil lamp set in the wall by a bracket. He peered up at me for a long moment.

"Signor Baglioni? Yes, it's you." He gave a short laugh. "I'm honored, I suppose. You seem older and somewhat battered since last we met."

My eyes had adjusted to the light and I replied, "Time hasn't improved you either, Messer Secretary."

Machiavelli's face was dead white and emaciated, the skin stretched tighter than ever over his high cheekbones. He smiled and his black button eyes glowed with a feverish light. He adjusted the fetters around the torn sleeves at his wrists and said, "Take the stool. It's my one decent piece of furniture."

He settled himself on a pallet, adjusting the weight of his ankle chains to escape the chafing of the fetters. "When I last saw you in Perugia almost seven years ago," he finally said, "I was a rising man, the accredited envoy of the republic. Behold, how the world moves! And it will continue staggering along after we are gone. To tell the truth, since my introduction to chains and misfortune, I have expected no visitors except my inquisitors and the torturer who honored me yesterday with his attentions."

"You?" I said. "I would think torture a superfluity in your case. You could be persuaded without mechanical encouragements."

"Is that your professional opinion?" asked Machiavelli gibingly.

"I see you're still the jester," I said. "As a matter of fact, I have employed the Question sparingly in my practice. The last man I had racked, and that many years ago, was Metello Crispolti. He was stubborn and I, pressed for time."

"How temperate you are, for a tyrant," said Machiavelli. "Or are you now the ex-tyrant of Perugia?"

"Neither one nor the other," I said, "merely First Citizen, by consent of the people and my own abilities. I am now on my way home to reclaim my city."

"Indeed?" said Machiavelli with interest. "There's a new wind blowing then?"

"An irrepressible politician as well as a jester," I said. "It's the same old wind and has merely shifted to a new quarter. But you would not know of that, for I think you were clapped in prison before the event. Pope Julius is dead. The old warlock who sat on my shoulder for seven years has passed from this to another world."

"Ah," said Machiavelli, "this is of interest. Tell me about it."

"I shall," I replied. "Let me hear first what they have done with you."

"They gave me a taste of the corda," said Machiavelli, "two full hoists. They doubtless feel they let me off lightly." He grinned and rubbed his shoulders. "But it was painful."

"And did you tell them what they wished to know?" I asked.

"Not I," replied Machiavelli, "and for a simple reason. I had nothing to tell and they know it. Why do you ask? Have you come here to gloat over me?"

"Not at all," I said. "I have nothing against you. You know, Machiavelli, we have an affinity of a sort, although I would hardly call it friendship. When you're up, I'm down, and so it goes. Perhaps I seek you because your troubles give me a clue as to mine."

"I am always happy to oblige you," said Machiavelli, "as Fate's birddog or in any other capacity." He rattled his chains mockingly. "How may I serve you today?"

"What a clever man you are, despite your blind places," I

said. "I want to put you a serious question. I am free, I have a strong base in Perugia. My army, though small, is razor-edged. Your sharp wits could help me make it more than a dream."

"Make what more than a dream?" asked Machiavelli, his voice cautiously disinterested.

"Do you think I could continue what Cesare Borgia began?" I asked. "This trap we're in keeps me from eating and sleeping. If any man knows how we can break out of it, you do."

Machiavelli laughed and rattled his chains. "You! Never! The aim is too great for your abilities. Considering your performance when Pope Julius came calling on you seven years ago, you lack the character for such an enterprise." He reflected and shook his head. "Would you league with Francesco Maria della Rovere? He's little better than a hot-tempered arrogant bandit. With Alfonso d'Este? The Este wouldn't condescend to listen to a petty Umbrian robber baron. With your fellow princelings? You know them as well as I. Who else is there? Will you presume to match purses with the Vicar of God, the Holy Father of Christendom?" Machiavelli spat contemptuously against the wall. "As you say, Italy is a trap, but you are a very small rat, my friend, a very small one indeed."

"I'd serve any prince to bring this wormeaten house down," I said, savoring the naïveté of my own words. "The French, the Spanish, the Turk, the Devil himself. To burn this land clean, I'll even serve a better man's ambition. With money and soldiers anything is possible, and I have a beginning in both. Do you know of my ancestor, Braccio Fortebracci da Montone? He was a soldier of vision. He made a good beginning once; as good as Cesare Borgia's. I have no other thoughts," I added, "and I suppose it is addling my wits."

"It is indeed," said Machiavelli. "You are madder than myself. Would you help the foreigner put a collar around the Italian neck?"

"With pleasure," I replied. "What is Italy? You are clever, Machiavelli, and yet you are a fool. Your eyes are sharp but you can't see past your nose, and you have ink in your veins." I was aware of a deep and rising disappointment. "But why should I expect so much from you? You are only a prisoner of your petty Florentine beginnings, as fixed in your mold as all the rest of us. There must be a way out, but your shrewd squinting eyes will never spy it."

Machiavelli studied me sardonically. "A man will arise someday," he said. "You are not that man. You have neither the vision nor the power nor the greatness of soul."

Machiavelli spoke the truth. In that instant, I felt a deep self-hatred rise up within me. To have strangled Machiavelli at that moment would not have lightened or altered the judgment. I finally swallowed my bile and replied quietly: "Never mind, then. Now tell me what has been happening to you."

"The wheels of change began creaking right after the sack of Prato," said Machiavelli. "My chief of state, Soderini, had no belly for resisting and broke quickly when his colleagues deserted him." He laughed acidly. "A worthy fellow, Soderini! But hardly a hero. I stayed with him to the end. I can't tell you why. Perhaps I like to round off a mission properly."

"Always the conscientious bookkeeper," I said.

"I suppose you feel bitter," said Machiavelli, glancing at me, "but baiting me will not change the truth. As for me, the new government deprived me of my posts November last and sentenced me to a year in prison. In addition, I had to give surety for the execution of the judgment against me. They would not even permit me to fetch my books and papers from my office. They allowed me to do so later that I might show my successor, Michelozzi, how to continue."

"And what happens now?" I asked.

Machiavelli stared at me with a death's-head grin. "I am forty-three," he said, "and a pauper. After a lifetime of faithful service to the state, I sit in chains accused of conspiracy against the Medici." He spat again. "The abortions! The dog-mothered idiots! Is it likely that I, with my knowledge of conspiracies, would have puddled in the hot-headed treasons of the republicans while at the same time seeking employment from the Medici? Boscoli and Capponi have already been executed. Very well! I have no quarrel with the Medici on that score; if you plot and fail, you lose your head. I have never viewed myself as a partisan, simply as a permanent servant of the state, as ready to serve the Medici as I served the Gonfaloniere Soderini. Why should I be criticized for being able to reconcile my conscience with a change in the government?"

My back still smarted from his censure. "Why, indeed!" I said. "In your way, you are as much a mercenary as I am, though I do not hold it against you. I warned you eight years ago when you came to Perugia snooping for your Signoria. Do you remember? How loyal and righteous you were and how sure of your conclusions! Your noble purgatives are now being crammed down your own throat. The Medici cast you off like a dirty breechclout. They drape you in chains and swing you on the corda like a rag doll. Have you no pride? Do you not thirst for revenge?"

Machiavelli did not seem to hear me. His shoulders quivered and his lips worked convulsively. He sat hunched on the pallet and shook his bowed head.

"I suppose you know that they do not intend to kill you," I said. "Giuliano de' Medici tells me you are soon to be released."

"I'm deeply and humbly grateful," sneered Machiavelli. "Once I merely theorized about the blundering folly and ingratitude of men. Now I have a taste of its practice in my own joints. They've torn me from the place where I was able to do some good. Now they stroke their bellies and preen themselves on their magnanimity in kicking me out into the world like a stray cat. Who will feed my wife and children? No! That's no concern of theirs."

My bitterness had passed and I felt only frustration at being unable to reach him.

"If you were not such a clerk and recognized how little you have to lose," I said, "you would join me. I could glut you with satisfaction to the armpits. As I intend for myself, you could feed your enemies the hearts of their children."

Machiavelli shook his head.

I unhooked a leather purse from my belt and threw it on the pallet. "Here are three hundred ducats," I said, "all I have aside from my travel necessities. Let it tide you over when you are released."

Machiavelli weighed the purse and pushed it into his torn sleeve above the fetter. "Thank you," he said. "I'll repay it. You have made a point, Baglioni, but we could not work together. We live in two different worlds. I believe in law, order and in the people. And you do not. Even old Julius had principles and a policy of sorts, which you lack. Yes, there was a measure of love in the old man's heart, even though his policies aggravated the disease and spread it."

"At least we're in partial agreement about Julius," I said. "He lived like a ruffian and it is interesting that he died in the odor of sanctity. He is being adored today as a saint, the heroic savior of Italy. It is edifying to know that he died with more grace than he lived. It was Julius who stripped your breeches and brought your trumpery republic down around your ears."

"With the help of Soderini's bumbling," added Machiavelli.

"You had warning enough last summer of the shape of things to come," I said. "Did you apprise your masters that they could not afford the persistent neutrality they practiced in favor of the French?"

"I told them often enough," said Machiavelli moodily. "I smelled after Ravenna how naked we were to our enemies and Pope Julius' hatred. They would not listen; their minds ran only to florins, ducats and the price of wool."

"The sack of Prato is also your love-child," I said. "Your plowboys and clerks turned soldier hardly covered themselves with glory on that day, did they?"

"Let it be on my head," said Machiavelli. "I accept the responsibility. There is no point in philosophizing about the quality of courage. They were cowards. They broke and fled and that's all there is to say. But I am still right, despite what happened at Prato. A state can be defended by its citizens only, not by mercenaries like yourself. I have not changed my opinion of your profession and of the part your kind has played in the foul and sorry fortunes of Italy. You are a mercenary, and together with popes and princes a cause of Italy's evils. In the meantime, may God damn her, and Florence too, the pope, the priests, the people, and all of them together! May Florence come to a bad end, and I think she will. She and the Medici deserve one another like a dog and its vomit. May she end in blood and fire!"

"Amen to that," I said. "The Medici will bring it about, and the people, too. They have a genius to such an end. Courage, Messer Secretary! The curtain has not fallen yet for either of us."

With that farewell, I left Machiavelli and continued on my journey to Perugia.

24.

THE HOMECOMING

WE TRAVELED in a leisurely fashion from Florence, taking the southward road through Figline and Montevarchi toward Arezzo. From there the highway wound in a southeasterly direction until we came to the northern shore of Lake Trasimene and onward on the highroad toward Perugia. Laura, riding at my side, smiled at me with a rare radiance and said: "I would be even happier to be returning to my native land if your own face were brighter."

"I have been driven from Perugia three times in the past twelve years," I said. "If I am ever forced to run again, I shall leave the city toothless and pliant behind me."

"That has always been your first thought," said Laura. "This is our own country which you should be re-entering with joy. Instead, there is only vengeance in your heart."

"If the elimination of those troublers whom the late Julius restored will save the city further disorders," I said, "then let them call me an oppressor. The pain of a few will benefit the majority, and in any case there will always be those who curse me."

Laura sighed and said that my repeated insistence on the treachery in men was in itself a sign of fear. When I declared that men were constant only as long as they were not called upon to reinforce their good words with actions, that the bond of loyalty shriveled like dry kindling in the fire of performance, Laura broke forth hotly: "From what I have seen in the years that we have lived together, you have been served more than faithfully by the people whom you so affect to despise. Hatred is a treacherous mortar with which to build a city, a truth which the Baglioni never seem to learn. Be rash and brave for once! Trust, and I will like you better. Forbear with the exiles and let them live in peace."

I began to laugh at her anger, yet there was much truth in what she said. I replied that I would take her words into serious account.

"Do more than that," said Laura. "Your besetting vice is that you swallow your own false images too readily. You are at least as self-righteous as the prelates against whom you constantly rail."

"That was well said," I observed. "Machiavelli left some whole skin on my back and now you are stripping the rest of it. Very well, I shall be rash and take your advice."

And so we fell silent.

Five days after my prison-meeting with Machiavelli, Laura and I squinted through the gray haze for our first sight of the towers of Perugia. One hour later we rode in through the Porta Eburnea. The crowds clamored as we pushed on with our men toward the Great Piazza. The signal cannon above Eburnea discharged one salute after another, the smoke curling away lazily from the guns into the chill sky of early spring. A sharp wind whistled in from the hills. I have known it to snow there as late as the first of April, and this was only the first week of March. The bells in the communal campanile tolled merrily and the multitude bawled its welcome. All hail to the valiant captain come home! All hail to the magnificent Gianpaolo Baglioni!

"Listen to them," I said to Laura. "A crowd is the lungs of a Stentor, the heart of a girl and the memory of an ape, to be enjoyed in despite, as long as one does not mistake it for something else."

"That was well put," said Laura, "and it has only one defect — that of being untrue. A crowd is the sum of the people who compose it and they are all pouring out their hearts in the same impulse. Let us accept it for what it is without quibbling or seeking perfection."

So the people gave us welcome, and once again Laura brought me up short. Men came to take our bridles and to lead us through the packed streets. Doors and windows opened. The sun emerged timidly. The women draped bright tapestries over balcony railings. We entered the Great Piazza and the Priori delle Arti came forth from their palace to present me with a laurel wreath. With them appeared Amico Graziani, who pronounced a sonorous Latin oration comparing me to Scipio Africanus come home in triumph from the wars. At this, Laura could not prevent herself from laughing in an unseemly fashion and I placed the wreath on my head reflecting that I would have no choice but to forgive Amico Graziani his sense of humor. My troopers grinned and shouted mockingly: "All hail, noble general!" But their mockery was against themselves also. We had won neither glory nor profit. On the contrary, we had been macerated in the millstones of the potentates. We froze in the mountains of Romagna. The insects dined on us in the swampy plains of Venezia. The French beat our brains into our helmets at Isola delle Scale, at Ravenna and a dozen other places. Those who died, died miserably. Those who survived rode home with flat purses and fresh aching wounds. That was why my men laughed and shouted: "Olà for the life of a soldier!"

By the time the Baglioni palace was in sight, the multitude

was so great that I dismounted and walked the rest of the way on foot. It took a full hour to cover the short distance to the palace. I felt better for being back and surrounded by men I could trust. Implicitly? There was no such thing. I was about to voice that thought to Laura and forbore to do so. I finally contented myself with the reflection that I was pleased to be home.

The Feast of San Gregorio was being celebrated six days later when the courier of the communal treasurer came galloping wildly down the road toward the Palace of the Priori. He clutched an olive branch in his hand, waving it furiously and shouting: "Medici! Medici! Palle! Palle!" He dismounted, entered and gave us the news. The papal conclave had huffed and puffed for eight days and had elected Cardinal Giovanni de' Medici. He himself selected the fortunate and auspicious name of Leo. The world had a new pope and his name was Leo X.

"Now is the time to fulfill your promise and refrain from shedding new blood," said Laura. "Dispatch the petition which is traditionally sent to a new pontiff but do not take vengeance into your own hands."

"Madonna Laura is a wise minister," said Amico Graziani, who sat listening. "Violence only begets more violence and you could do worse than listen to her."

"These petitions to a new pope are only a mere show of submission," I said.

"Do not despise legality," said Amico. "Even the most arbitrary tyrant needs the forms of law and the respect of the people for those forms."

"Very well, Amico," I said, "I shall be guided by you and by Laura. The old ways are in abeyance. You shall go to Rome and petition him in my behalf as follows: those whom the late pontiff restored in Perugia shall be re-declared rebel, their goods confiscated and applied to the treasury of the Perugian Commune. Finally, such persons shall be permanently denied any hope of repatriation."

"Now that is a great improvement," smiled Amico. "Let harsh reprisal be clothed in the majesty of the Church and the dignity of the law. Let this fortunate new pope absorb the future onus of it."

"I am always willing to learn," I said.

"I believe you are," said Amico, nodding gravely. "But it was not always so."

Eighteen days later I left for Rome to attend the ceremonies of the new pontiff's installation. I took Laura and all my supporters with their wives, children and relatives. In addition, over two thousand picked cavalry, splendid in velvet, silvered armor and cloth of gold, escorted us as we wound down from the city toward Rome. The rear brought up a long train of wagons bearing the women and children followed by squires, pages and grooms.

Cardinal Giovanni de Medici was thirty-seven years of age at this time, five years younger than myself. His election made sense. The Sacred College had chosen in reaction to what they had had — a would-be warrior in the habit of a priest, an irascible hero who spoke of peace while stoking the cauldrons of war. The cardinals were tired of heroes and turned to the plump and sensible Medici. Everyone expected that Medici would make a good pope. He had had a taste of wandering, poverty and exile in his youth.

The ceremonial and pageantry surrounding the installation of a ruler have always left me with a sour taste. Perhaps it is the envy of failure and the frustration of unrealistic ambition which have curdled into a self-hatred. I attended Pope Leo's installation reluctantly. Now, writing in prison, I recall those scenes with the same reluctance. It is tedious and irksome for me to describe these matters. I am repelled by the gorgeously irrational edifice of which I am a part. The system is founded upon apathy, upon the miraculous passivity of the people and upon the sublime villainy of the rulers. The whole approaches a madness as grotesque as a nightmare. To accept it, one must abdicate one's powers of reason. If self-interest requires that a man participate in these intricate posturings, he must deposit his brains in the garden and remain a wooden doll for the duration of the play.

.The imminence of death is itself an awakening. I now suspect that men are mad and I have been mad with them. Would you except the priests from this censure? Observe their works and you must conclude that they, too, are mad, but ingenious also, seeing how they have been able to reconcile mundane evil and Divine Omnipotence by tortuous theology. It is a curious conceit that men should deem themselves the sole care of Providence, and God has labored to small purpose if His one concern is the conduct of such a magnum opus. Men hunger for the marvelous and their shepherds sway by lulling them into a belief of the manifestly impossible. Yet the people are blameless, being also helpless before the hammer of habit. The malleable infant blossoms into the besotted man. Once madness attains the dignity of revealed truth, all bow, fearful of opposing the weight of implicit belief. For the stubborn who resist armed revelation, there are simple modes of coercion. There is, at last, only a pasture, guarded by loving shepherds who have accepted their own wonders and call oppression righteousness. The sheep, having no other, follow the shepherd's example and the first of their delusions is that they are not sheep but men. But in truth they follow only the tuggings of belly and loin, and the structure of faith has been fashioned to content those same tuggings.

I became convinced at a relatively early age that the masses of the people are not human at all but mere puppets with the outward aspect of life. The common ruck of men, though they breathe and labor, are blindly immured, each in the warm wet sack of a private world. Their massive numbers are without meaning, nor can they affect the acts of that handful who knead and mold them at pleasure. From that moment forward, I dismissed the majority from my calculations and have concerned myself ever since with the minority. There are fewer inhabitants and more pieces of furniture in the House of Man than you may have supposed. For which reason I marvel all the more to find myself in this, my present predicament, in Castle Sant' Angelo and awaiting death. I have undoubtedly brought this situation about myself, as sleepwalkers tear down by night what they have built by day. I cannot explain it. I am unable to trace back the sequence of events wherein my position gradually weakened. The deterioration has been as gentle and cumulative as a succession of faulty moves on a chessboard. And then there is the factor of uncontrollable coincidence which can destroy us or elevate us without a significant pattern of meaning. This is the force which Machiavelli calls Fortuna. . . .

When we reached Rome, we joined an ever broadening river of guests flowing toward the Vatican to attend the installation of Pope Leo. I exchanged greetings with Francesco Maria della Rovere, who came in mourning dress for his uncle, the late Pope Julius. All the world had come to Rome in love and harmony. Alfonso d'Este, harried so long by Julius, rode splendidly in Pope Leo's train. The chiefs of the Colonna and the Orsini reconciled themselves for the occasion and rode hand in hand to demonstrate their amity in the forthcoming golden age. We moved slowly on this spring day along garden-bordered roads. Churches, half-seen through the foliage, were decorated with laurel. The streets were spanned by arches and inscribed banners. Before our Perugians marched two battalions of pikemen and companies of mounted stradiotti. Behind us followed the households of the prelates and the official standard-bearers of the City of Rome. Then came more prelates, bishops, abbots and, finally, the cardinals with their chamberlains and the Swiss guard. Last of all rode the new pontiff in his majesty.

For ten thousand other details, the appearance of the city, the ordering of the various parades and processions, go to the chroniclers. I have neither the time nor the desire to set them down. I have much to tell and must get on with it. I will say only that all the encrusted barnacled trivia of centuries was here to provide a feast for the eyes of the Roman rabble, of foreign observers and of the devout from every corner of Italy, so as to give the illusion of stability, of majestic continuity with an awesome past. The colors and variety of the spectacle were impressive. Those who arranged it had spared nothing. Arab chargers and mules from the papal stables, with golden trappings, were interspersed with marching camerieri in silk and ermine bearing the pontifical miters and crowns. All in all, it was a chaotic bedazzlement for the eyes. I saw Ippolita da Conti's father and brothers riding among the Roman barons but exchanged no word with them. The Florentines dominated the day brilliantly and I heard much grumbling that they had taken over Rome and clearly intended to make the most of their fellow countryman's election to the tiara.

It was dark by the time the great pageant of the installation ended. I had gone through the motions and performed my political duties. I was impatient to return to Perugia and settle my affairs there. From Perugia, I planned to leave for Padua, for I was still in Venetian service.

Passing through Florence on the road north, I inquired for Machiavelli. I was told that he had been released from prison and was living in the suburb of San Casciano.

Machiavelli did not apologize for his bleak, shabby little

villa, saying, "I am glad to be alive. Your ducats helped tide us over the worst and when I find employment, you will be repaid with interest. In the meantime, I make a living of sorts, selling the brushwood of my few acres. For company I have the local clowns by day and my few books by night. Books and bumpkins. Things you know little about, Baglioni." He put his hand on my bridle, adding, "Stay and dine with us. Tell me of the outside world. I'm withering, shriveling for a bit of news."

When I remember Machiavelli, I remember his courage and his sagacity, but it was the latter which impressed me. He was a cold little spinner of dreams, but he took his poverty with lack of pretense and stared Fortuna in the eye, unblinking. With a wife and four small children, he had little choice.

"I hear Venice has made peace with the French," said Machiavelli avidly. "I hear the French have returned to retake Milan with Venetian help."

He noted my lack of interest and laughed, saying, "You must pardon my gluttonous love of politics. One does not break the habits of a lifetime so easily. My mind is too active and I cannot sit idly by. If I did not busy myself with political speculation, I would go mad surely. As for my personal affairs, they stink to Heaven. The tax collectors hound me regularly. Sometimes I am tempted to go into the woods and hang myself."

"An extravagance," I said. "Out of any hundred men, ninety-nine may be safely spared for hanging. You are the hundredth who cannot. It is unfortunate that you had to serve the Florentine Republic. Otherwise you doubtless would have been a great man today."

"You are returning to Venetian service?" asked Machiavelli.

"I am returning to war," I said, "and it is a matter of indifference to me whether Venice fights with France or against France."

"And how did you leave Perugia?" he asked.

"Counting her teeth, yet surprised at my moderation," I replied. "I left her sober, repentant and amenable, though for how long, I don't know. The disease always returns. Sometimes I think Perugia will find peace only after she has been razed and leveled."

"Your city has a disease," said Machiavelli. "It is a political lunatic."

"I could use a physician of your cunning to heal her wits," I said. "You could make a new life for yourself in my country."

Machiavelli reflected and shook his head. "My wife is with child again. I cannot see myself removing to a foreign land with my brood and making another beginning. From what I know of your city, politicians there have a brief and violent mortality." He smiled slightly. "How long would I, a stranger, survive in your heady climate? In any event, the Medici will not permit me to leave the territory. I am still under administrative arrest. But I expect a position from them soon, if only to help me pay the tax collector."

"You'll have fair words and bare bones from the Medici," I said. "You are nobody and nothing to them — a scribbler and a discredited minor politician. Cast your fortunes with us and we'll mend them for you. Your skin will be at least as safe as it is here. Safer. Once these wars are over, I have plans to form a new league in Umbria against the papacy."

Machiavelli laughed. "You and your grand plans! Greater men than you are fashioning those same designs. They may succeed but you will surely abort. Baglioni, why don't you accept the fact that you are an upstart, a nonentity, and that your day is almost done?"

"As long as I take breath, I will never cease trying," I said.

"I think your courage has been broken for good."

"Perhaps," said Machiavelli, "but I am not your man. I've decided to remain neutral."

"Only the dead are neutral," I said. "You yourself once told me what happens to neutrals. Very well." I rose and placed a purse on the table. "Here is another hundred ducats to stop the tax collector's mouth. I take leave of you now. I suppose it is in the nature of things that thinkers should be small doers. Whatever people will say about me, I never failed to accept the hazard and act."

"You failed to act when Pope Julius out-bluffed you seven years ago," said Machiavelli.

"Admitted," I replied. "But the play has still to work itself out."

With those words I went on my way, and it was the last time that I ever saw Niccolò Machiavelli.

25.

THE SPIDER WEB

THE MASTERS of Venice are civilized men within their cautious limits. They understand the art of impressing people through symbols and enjoy a repertoire of sound experience. I came from Padua to Venice in May, 1513, when they welcomed Bartolemeo d'Alviano back from his four-year French imprisonment. France and Venice were now allies and d'Alviano's release was one of the terms of the peace treaty. Prison had not cooled my brother-in-law's imagination and he had vaunting plans. Venice agreed with his high opinion of his own worth and re-invested him with the supreme command. They led him through the various steps of the ceremony with workman-like solemnity and made it an effective bid for his loyalty and valor. The patriarch of Venice celebrated mass and blessed the battle standards in the presence of all the foreign ambassadors. Then the doge placed the banner of Saint Mark in d'Alviano's hands and said:

"Continuing in the paternal love which we have always borne you, and recognizing the singular ability, experience and faith which you have always kept inviolate, we have appointed you Captain-General of all our armed forces. In order that all may comprehend and recognize this rank and dignity which we have conferred upon you, we herewith consign to you this standard and this baton of command, both blessed symbols of the said dignity. We supplicate our Lord God, the intercession of the Blessed Virgin and of the glorious evangelist, Saint Mark, in whose protection and clemency we trust, to bestow upon you the ability and means of recovering and conserving our State to the greater glory of God's Divine Majesty and the aggrandizement of our faith."

It was an impeccable speech and one which I had often heard before. Politicians employ such phrases with the felicitous ease born of long practice, and their sonorous delivery never fails to impress the listeners, even those aware of the hollowness. Doubtless the doge spoke more fervently than a prelate celebrating God. The Venetians had much at stake. They were depending on d'Alviano to recoup their worldly losses; a matter somewhat more important than salvation. I enjoyed d'Alviano's pleasure in these grave and splendid pomps for his sake and hoped that he would be able to reverse the somber tide of Venetian fortune. He deserved some luck; he had been only partially responsible for the fiasco of Agnadello four years before.

D'Alviano accepted the symbols of Venetian command and made his vows. Bearing his baton proudly, he emerged from the cathedral and the parade began toward the Ponte della Paglia, preceded by standards, bands of music and brilliantly uniformed soldiers. Escorted by the doge, the patriarch and the senators, d'Alviano then returned to his palace, where a banquet was served to the guests.

When we made ready to rejoin the army, I said to him, "Venice has her share of the same disease which afflicts the whole of Italy. There is a rotten place under her gold and silk and an excessive readiness to give under a firm blow before the event justifies the action."

"True," he said. "It happened at Agnadello."

"And several times since," I said. "Venice did not have to lose that battle. The Venetians, like all of our people, tend to overestimate themselves and to take credit when things go their way. See that you avoid becoming their sacrificial goat should Fortune go against them."

"We will do our utmost," said d'Alviano. "Beyond that, let it be on Fortune's head."

Since there are none so tedious as old soldiers explaining away their failures, I will not go into the campaign which followed. The French and ourselves were now warring against Spain and the Holy Roman Empire, in that same weary battlefield, northern Italy. And why were the potentates fighting? For Italy, her whole body or pieces of her flesh. But Italy by now was a soldier's whore, exhausted, sickened and weary of her life. She lay supine and the armies trampled back and forth over her face. Our new French allies did well until they were crippled at the Battle of Novara. With the French defeat, d'Alviano and I were compelled to disgorge all the territory we had recovered in Venezia and Lombardy. The fighting raged all summer around Padua and on the Adige River. With d'Alviano, I held Padua while Raimondo de Cardona, the commander of the Spanish-Imperial coalition, battered it furiously and unsuccessfully. In revenge, he ravaged the countryside. The Spaniards and the lanzknechts slaughtered or drove off the cattle. The peasants were hanged in their own orchards. Farms were set aflame and the harvests were left to rot. Throughout Venezia a smoke-pall rose and blackened the mellow skies of autumn.

In October, 1513, four months after d'Alviano's appointment, Cardona crushed us near Vicenza and I was taken prisoner. When the news of my capture reached Perugia, Laura wrote to me, saying: "The Commune of Perugia is bestirring itself strongly in your behalf, from which you have another proof that men are not so fickle as you have always charged. We have spoken with Francesco Maria della Rovere, the Duke of Urbino. More than any other, he has exerted himself in your behalf and the Holy Father has also added his approval. Signor Francesco informs us that you are to be exchanged for a certain captain, one Señor Carvajal, whom the Spaniards are most anxious to have liberated. The Holy Father is agreeable to these negotiations provided that, when released, you quit Venetian service and accept a papal commission. I urge you to accept and I will hasten to meet you in Rome."

I should not have accepted the tempting offer, but I did. Sooner or later I would have been exchanged on some other terms which would have left me independent, as this release did not.

One month later in Rome I brought my new master a knot of law to unravel. "Holy Father," I said, "at the time the Spaniards exchanged me, they extracted my promise that I would return to captivity if the exchange did not prove satisfactory. It appears now that they made a bad bargain. As Your Holiness knows, this Carvajal died soon after the exchange was effected. Now my lord Cardona is calling upon me to honor my promise and to surrender myself."

"It is always a pleasure to cheat the Spaniards," said Pope Leo blandly, "even in a matter as light as this. We'll solve that riddle for you, Baglioni. Since you are now our servant and a stipendiary of the Apostolic See, we solemnly forbid you to depart from the States of the Church. We further declare that any pledge extracted from you by my lord Cardona under duress is wholly void." He chuckled. "We, the Pope, declare it and you may relay our words to Cardona with fitting gravity." He peered at me through his eye-glass with near-sighted benignity. "It seems you have had enough of war for a while. Spend the winter in Rome and join us in our hunting at the lodge of La Magliana. This is no invitation. We command it."

That was the beginning of my good and easy life under Pope Leo's favor. I let myself be sucked into his war against Francesco Maria della Rovere, the man who had befriended me. I should have kept clear of the whirlpool of compromise and Pope Leo's tortured politics. In failing to do so I committed treachery, and those who betray their friends and themselves come to a fitting reward.

Pope Leo had grown stouter since those days when he had served as cardinal-legate at the Battle of Ravenna. His broad moonlike face was constantly flushed. He was massively jowled, short of breath, and his eyes bulged. But his hands remained white, plump and shapely as ever. These, with his voice and his overly exquisite manners, were his assets. He had others; a keen mind and, while Fortune smiled on him, a sanguine temperament.

Our relationship was good, although not informal as in the old days. For all that the papacy is a deplorable institution, it has so sound a hold on its followers that the possessor of the papal office passes beyond the common touch no matter how much he struggles against it, and few can resist the corrupting distortions of power. I would set the boundary at the foot of the pontifical throne. Cardinals are men, but a pope becomes more than a man in the eyes of those who behold him, because of their need for a divinity. Pope Leo strove to remain a man, yet he was no longer Cardinal de' Medici but the Supreme Pontiff and God's Vicar on earth. He now sought to alleviate his new isolation by an increased benevolence toward all who came before him. He tripled his household, naturally with Florentines, and displayed an indiscriminate generosity, a long-slumbering talent for spending the treasure which Pope Julius had amassed. His hunting establishment gradually grew to several hundred people. But Pope Leo's hunting is a tale in itself. He gambled and lost at primiero each night, intentionally of course, as still another way of practicing liberality.

Many of the hills in Rome were still wooded with a scattering of isolated farmsteads. The ruins were being utilized as quarries for the new edifices which were being erected. I saw much building in the vicinity of the Vatican such as the palaces of the rising bankers and the more prosperous cardinals. But on the whole, Rome continued a noisome maze, far less attractive, in my opinion, than Perugia. Saint Peter's, for which Pope Julius had had such hopes, was a majestic façade without and a chaotic uncompleted clutter of masonry within. Where Julius had driven furiously, Leo preferred to amble comfortably. Julius Secundus Italiae Liberatori et Schismatis Extinctori had attempted too many things together, too soon. He had neither brought peace to Italy nor completed his temple. Now Leo dabbled and bathed like a Prodigal Son in the wealth and power stored up by stern Father Julius.

The pope was benevolent toward me and generous, as he was showing himself to be with everyone. He seemed impelled by a frantic need to compensate himself for his past indigence in exile. The papal court had become far more resplendent than that of Alexander Borgia. With all of the scholars and artists now in attendance, there were also a good many scribblers, daubers and poetasters cluttering up the halls of the Vatican. The general opinion was that these people were being indiscriminately and overgenerously rewarded. As I permitted myself to be drawn into the gaiety of the papal court, I began to wonder how long the treasure gathered by Pope Julius would last. Pope Leo was said to have squandered a full quarter of the treasury on the gorgeous pageant of his installation. He was forever surrounded by Florentines who had gathered in Rome

— like leeches, said the Romans with a grimace — to profit, if they might, from their countryman's possession of the supreme office of Christendom. Pope Leo's personal entourages overwhelmed the permanent working staffs of the Curia. It was said that he commanded a retinue of six hundred gentlemen, equerries and chamberlains. This took no account of the hundreds of clerks, attendants and servitors attached to the papal household. As for the pope's hunting people, they were a curious army apart, a throng of grooms, stablemen, huntsmen, falconers and trainers. A lordly and splendid existence, by God! There were times when I could not help admiring this royal aspect of the Medicean countenance. Here was a singular mode of beseeching God's mercy with whooping hallooing huntsman and packs of baying hounds. But God, being among other things a gentleman, must have understood.

The parade of social pleasures circled endlessly with the pope, suave and paternal, dominating the courtly carnival, scattering gifts, gold and good will. Laura and I attended banquets lasting seven hours, where the guests toyed with fifty courses. When we entered the banqueting hall, we were preceded by the master of ceremonies to the rhythms of the concealed musicians. Pope Leo had refurbished all the dining halls and decorated them with heavy golden candelabra. The feasts were illuminated by perfumed torches held aloft by richly costumed servants. We ate from silver dishes and the tables were burdened with golden platters bearing meats, fruits and confections sculptured into human figures and those of animals.

The febrile imagination of the papal master cooks cloyed my simple garrison tastes. Pope Leo's passion for sweetened dishes could not wait for the termination of a banquet — he had them served at the onset. The festivities invariably began with the serving of pastries of crushed pistachios, sugared walnuts and other nuts, on which were imposed layers of prunes cooked in honey, well mixed with whipped creams. Then followed pastries filled with larks, pigeons and doves, which in turn were stuffed with figs, dates and nuts, the whole layered over with honey and rose sugar. When we rested and repented our gluttony, the pope's fools cheered us on and raised our courage by bellowing jokes, banging on tambourines and blowing trumpets. These beginnings were followed by a joyous procession of capons, peacocks, swans, boar, deer, sturgeon and carp in a variety of wild-eyed disguises which rose to a crescendo of pensive suckling pigs riding in triumph on chariots of gilded bread and sugar. While we toyed pallidly with these monstrous dainties, the papal choir and orchestra regaled us with chants of thanksgiving. For post-desserts, pretty children tumbled from gigantic pies to recite eclogues and bucolics.

This pace was redoubled during the carnival season of 1514. Pope Leo was the scion of rich merchants and such a way of life has always been the *summum bonum* of those who weigh the world by gold alone.

After four months of such a regime, I begged Pope Leo's permission to depart from the papal court, pleading my personal business in Perugia. This was true enough, for I had been absent from my city for a full year. The pope gave his gracious consent, so Laura and I quit Rome with cloying tongues and impaired digestions and returned to Perugia.

Our life at home fell into a tranquil domestic pattern, punctuated by an occasional murder somewhere in the city, which only emphasized the serenity. We divided our time between Perugia and Castiglione del Lago. Guests joined us at Castiglione to fish in Lake Trasimene by day and to dance by night. The sporadic feud-killings throughout the contado fell into mannerly intervals consonant with the gentle pace of spring, altogether an improvement over the forthright fashion of the old days.

During the bleak first days of 1515, we received word that the fifty-two-year-old King Louis XII had finally killed himself trying to keep pace with the demands of a brisk new wife of sixteen. It would have been better if Louis had perished before he was crowned. After so much striving, treachery and bloody warfare in Italy, Louis died a failure and his twenty-year-old nephew of Angoulême assumed the throne of France as Francis I.

Malatesta took part in the great battle which was fought in September at Marignano, near Milan, between the French and the Venetians on one side and the Swiss on the other. "The battle lasted two days," Malatesta wrote me. "Thirty-five thousand people perished in it, of which twenty-two thousand were Switzers, six thousand Milanese and the rest French. Were it not for the generalship of my master Bartolomeo d'Alviano, the French king would never have gained this glorious victory and taken the city of Milan."

But in the following month of October, Malatesta wrote me of d'Alviano's death, saying: "I grieve to inform you of the death of our beloved and valiant kinsman, who departed this world five days ago, but whether of wounds or poison or merely a fever, none can say, and I do not believe it was poison. The Serenissima has accorded him a magnificent funeral and, since he died a poor man in her service, she has provided a princely annuity for your sister, Madonna Panthasilea, and her children."

This news reminded me once again that time was passing and that I had accomplished nothing. I almost envied my brother-in-law's demise at the height of success. If, in the future, Malatesta rises to be Italy's foremost general, it will have been more from d'Alviano's example than my own.

I left Castiglione del Lago and Laura at this time to resume active service in the Bolognese for Pope Leo. The pope had been shocked, and terrorized by the French victory at Marignano. He had been gambling frivolously at that time on a Swiss victory. Wiser men than myself have sought to comprehend the vagaries of Leo's foreign policy. He manipulated alliances with reckless speed, holding that a ruler should keep faith with treaties only as long as it served his interest. While blessing one side he simultaneously treated with the other, moving in a pattern of tortuous shifts, for the only goal he cherished was the aggrandizement of the House of Medici. Now since this pope aspired to become the arbiter of Europe, he should have had at heart not some unreasonably noble aim, but at least a consistent political creed. The truth is that Pope Leo, as a politician, was consistent only in his family pettiness. He was an incompetent dabbler — hence all of his mischievous strivings were foredoomed to failure.

I was in Bologna during the first week of December, 1515, when Pope Leo with fourteen cardinals came involuntarily and resentfully to meet the youthful King Francis and to minimize the French victory. They bargained and haggled for three days, and as an accidental aftermath my personal fortunes as well as those of Francesco Maria della Rovere were decided in those conversations.

The noose of my fate was braided from many fine threads into a cord of strength. It was fashioned by the greed and ineptitude of Pope Leo and the faithlessness of King Francis. Above all, it was fashioned by my own willing complicity. My judge in this present trial, Cardinal Armellini, has laid many crimes to my charge except the chief one, which is that I played pimp to the whoredoms of their princely politics. My head will pay the penalty, not for the sins with which they charge me, but because I was a compromised traitor to my friends and myself. The web in which I was entangled was spun at Bologna by Pope Leo and King Francis. The chief spider was the pope, since he was by far the subtler of the two. They did not spin for me alone. They did not even consider me. I was a very small fly and my entrapment was incidental.

If I may speculate further, perhaps my doom was struck when the Swiss failed to contain King Francis at Marignano. Still further — had King Louis not died childless, we might have been spared the French invasion of 1515, Leo's dark frivolities and the war against Francesco Maria which ended in the late spring of 1517. I am satisfied that my fate was set in the final mold at the hour I entered Pope Leo's service. Had I rejected that, it is possible that I might have lived at my ease and eventually died at Castiglione del Lago as snugly as a bishop. As I write here in Sant' Angelo, I find the vision of myself expiring peacefully, surrounded by wet-eyed — or dry-eyed — retainers, irresistibly droll. But there is no profit in threading the alternate labyrinths of the past. It is vain to follow up every clue; the variations of causes and effects are infinite and meaningless. Yet it is an engrossing game and one which I cannot resist. The fact is that I have been a pawn most of my life in the princely chess game of others. If I have survived thus far, I suspect that it has been due neither to my ability nor to my intelligence, but rather to a series of tangled accidents. It was finally in Bologna during that month of December that Pope Leo's plump hands began nudging me gently from square to square, so that I have finally arrived in this dead corner of Sant' Angelo from which there is no returning.

But what is the meaning of all this and how was I affected by the dealings between a pope and a king? Let me show you. Pope Leo was sincere and serious on one point alone — the establishment of a north Italian state for his kinsmen. This took precedence over God, Holy Mother Church and the welfare of Italy. The victorious King Francis' bargaining position was so strong at Bologna that Pope Leo was forced to disgorge all those cities on which he had designs for the House of Medici. To compensate the losses resulting from his faithlessness, Leo determined to seize Urbino from Francesco Maria della Rovere. He hated Francesco Maria for many reasons. A convenient one for his unjust war was Alidosi's murder, of which charge Francesco Maria had been acquitted. Where did I fit into this filthy coil? I was Leo's condottiero and executed his orders against the man I should have been aiding. But I did so reluctantly and so incurred first the pope's suspicion and ultimately his hatred. That is all there is to it.

Pope Leo commenced his aggression by reopening the case. He accused Francesco Maria in proper form of high treason and of Alidosi's death. It was to Francesco Maria's credit that he refused to appear in Rome to answer the charges. At this point I should have turned on the pope and gone to war as Francesco Maria's ally. Though honesty does not guarantee success, I think this would have been the safer course. But what is so clear in my cell today was not so apparent four years ago, when I sunned myself in the pope's favor and surrendered to my own rationalizations. I did not see because I did not wish to see. By the summer of 1516, when I was elbow-deep in Leo's operations against Urbino, I began to have misgivings. I was in a den of thieves, fighting those whom I should have been aiding. The pope was the master thief who escaped retribution because he was the pope. But that did not exculpate me.

With his interdicts and threats of assassination, Pope Leo finally goaded Francesco Maria into striking back. Francesco hired five thousand mercenaries on credit, crossed the Po River and carried the fight to Leo. I marched against Francesco in the winter months of 1517. It was a dreary merciless campaign in waist-deep snow and across mountain torrents. Meanwhile, Armellini, the Perugian speculator (then a monsignor, now a cardinal and my judge) exerted his imagination to squeeze out sufficient taxes for Leo's war and earn the red hat which Leo held forth as inducement. While straining for the hat, Armellini consoled himself by diverting a percentage of the tax-monies into his own pockets. His personal profit from victualling the papal army multiplied steadily. What monies Armellini could not raise, the Ridolfi, the Salviati, the Gaddi and other Florentine bankers were happy to lend the pope at up to 40 per cent interest.

The papal army was more interested in loot than in fighting. After some fortress was captured, the army seemed three times as numerous as before the attack. The soldiers disappeared during battle and crept out on pay day.

I hoped that as Pope Leo read my dispatches, he would groan over his leaking war chest and chew his nails at his hunting lodge of La Magliana.

I should have reproached myself. Instead, I reproached the pope.

26.

THE SIEGE OF PERUGIA

THE FIGHTING flamed higher. Francesco Maria della Rovere moved deeper into Umbria and raided the contado around Spoleto and Orvieto. I was openly at war with him, and Perugia was his legitimate objective. He now had ten thousand mutinous mercenaries in hand and no money with which to pay them. The pillage of Perugia offered a convenient means of bleeding these foreign wolves and lulling their restlessness with action. Unwilling to be trapped between the oncoming attackers and the walls, I finally withdrew into the city. The anxious Priori urged me to seek help in Rome, saying: "Perugia will also be the pope's loss. Surely, he will bestir himself in our behalf."

"I doubt Leo's concern for our predicament," I said, "but I'll make the effort, if only to convince you."

When I finally reached the Vatican, I found it impossible to approach Pope Leo. When I gained admittance to his presence, the swarm of petitioners about the golden papal honeycomb was too great. Pope Leo recognized me briefly, but only to invite me to remain for the evening's entertainment. Beyond that he declined to listen. I endured a five-hour banquet and the two-hour concert which followed. Paris de Grassis, the master of ceremonies, finally gave me some practical advice: "Winning the Holy

Father's ear is out of the question tonight and tomorrow it will be impossible. He leaves for La Magliana at noon and I suggest you follow him there. If he has a good day's hunting, he may be receptive and approachable, as you well know."

I bit my fingers with frustration and joined the train of assorted ecclesiastical and lay parasites who were bound for La Magliana. Pope Leo and his cardinals, garbed in boots and lay dress, led the procession. Many people were shocked by such uncanonical attire in a pope when they might have concerned themselves with more serious derelictions. Pope Leo's obsession with hunting was by now frank and open. With his purse full of holes, his prestige in the mud, and his anxiety over his nephew Lorenzo's fortunes, he went to hide at La Magliana as often as he could, and even when he could not, afford to do so. Leo's protracted absences at La Magliana often paralyzed the administrative business of the Curia in Rome. Lying near the seacoast on the right bank of the Tiber River, it was Leo's favorite hunting lodge. The Church of San Giovanni de Magliana had stood there in the old days and it was Pope Sixtus IV, the uncle of Pope Julius, who first raised the hunting lodge there; Pope Innocent VIII also added to it. Admittedly, princes are entitled to their little pleasures, but a prince who neglects state business for mere sport is a sloven and unfit to rule.

If you are curious concerning the pleasure-lodge of La Magliana and how the pope spent his time there, go and speak with Domenico Boccamazzo, the pontifical master huntsman. He will tell you what a vast and elaborate establishment it is for the indiscriminate slaughter of game. This effete and cultured Medici has a curious passion for killing animals, an unusual trait in a man who otherwise deplores bloodshed and violence with his mouth. On this obsession he spends huge sums of gold which flow into Rome from every quarter of Europe. But this will be for the pope to explain. I say no more.

Pope Leo consented to speak with me after he had dined, and his attitude was unpromising from the first. "We fail to appreciate your concern," he said curtly. "As a faithful servant of the Church, your first consideration should be our advantage. Although Perugia is our territory, why should we particularly favor you with aid? Our primary concern is for Lorenzo. Should della Rovere attack Perugia, it will relieve pressure on our nephew's forces, which is all to the good. You should be grateful for the opportunity to absorb a blow for him."

I felt profoundly unenthusiastic at that moment concerning the pope's arrogant diseased nephew and replied: "The Holy Father has not witnessed della Rovere's army. Should they break in, they will serve Perugia as Your Holiness permitted the Spaniards to serve Prato, where they still curse and shudder at your name. May we or may we not expect the Holy Father's assistance?"

The blood drained from Pope Leo's face, leaving it pasty and livid. His heart was armored in layers of grave benignant flesh, but my words must have struck home. If the truth must be told, Pope Leo was not directly responsible for the horrors which had been perpetrated in Prato by Cardona's soldiery. Yet the action had been undertaken in Leo's name and for the benefit of the House of Medici. Although Leo had tried to mitigate Spanish atrocities and at least to protect the women, the Pratesi still cursed Pope Leo as the author of their sorrows.

He controlled himself and replied in a still shaken voice: "You are unreasonable, Baglioni — and insolent. You are the pope's condottiero. You were engaged to assist and defend the Holy See, not the reverse."

"They outnumber us five to one," I persisted. "Our citizens are brave enough, but they are no match for Francesco Maria's ravening Spaniards, who are all veterans of the Venetian wars. As Your Holiness states — Perugia is your city. Do you propose to abandon it to those ravagers? Are you dissatisfied with my service?"

"We will answer your last question first," said Pope Leo. "We are displeased with your service. Our cousin, Cardinal Giulio, complains of your attitude, and we suspect that you are not as zealous in our war as you should be. Della Rovere's attack on Perugia may be beneficial after all. If you are holding back, Baglioni, be careful. Since your personal fortunes are directly involved, you may learn to fight better than you have fought thus far."

Perhaps my eyes revealed my hatred, for his voice turned colder. "And now, we shall answer your first question," he continued. "We are not abandoning Perugia. You are an experienced soldier and we feel that you can stand off della Rovere if you exert yourself." He stared at me with icy eyes. "We have been generous and forbearing to a fault. We have acceded to all your petitions. Show yourself now somewhat more forward and loyal in our service."

I would have said more, but he waved a jeweled and negligent hand.

I left for Rome the same night.

Here you have a simple example of how stranger pontiffs entangle the fortunes of an unwilling city in their ephemeral politics. If I could help it, I did not intend to see Perugia raped and dragged behind the Medicean chariot. In this struggle with Francesco Maria, Pope Leo was pursuing not the interest of the Church (which would have been equally odious to me), but the advantage of his own House.

Riding out of Rome on the following night, my escort and I were ambushed by Carlo Baglioni and a troop of horsemen. Carlo was serving during all of this time in the Pontifical Guard, so quietly that I had forgotten of his existence. He attacked me directly and his men assaulted my followers. Carlo and I were both thrown from our horses. We picked ourselves up, drew out our poignards and did our best to kill one another. For the first time in many years, I again saw his pale face and hate-filled eyes. Then a rush of horsemen drove us apart. One of Carlo's troopers bent over in the saddle as he trotted by, seized my cousin by the belt and carried him away. My men came away from this encounter with the best of it.

My first thought was that the pope was the author of this ambush. On further reflection, I dismissed the idea. Leo had enough troubles of his own. He had no need to buy what Carlo was willing to offer freely. What then? I decided it was no more than a continuation of Carlo's hunger to destroy me. See what a vital sturdy thing is the hatred of a Baglioni! There has seldom been a family such as ours.

When I reported to the Priori delle Arti their mouths opened and their jaws dropped in dismay. "Perhaps you are now satisfied of the pope's disinterest in us," I said. "Between his wars and his pleasures, the Romans say he is bankrupt. You will have to help yourselves; the pope won't do it for you. Let us make a beginning, I say, and proceed on the premise that we have no time left."

We immediately prepared the city for siege. It was none too soon, for the invaders were already butchering the inhabitants of the outlying farmhouses in the contado, cutting down orchards, burning houses and razing water mills. Our few advanced garrisons were massacred. My veterans maintained a taut discipline on the walls, and the citizens emulated them with a good will. Butchers, bakers, students, painters and their apprentices took up arms, and also those priests who were Perugians first and priests afterwards.

Francesco Maria's army finally appeared under the walls and hammered for admission on the Porta Sole. Here were no bandits, but seasoned professionals. There were among them those who had sacked Brescia and turned it into a torch of trouble. There were those who had stood and fought at Ravenna and sacked the city after. There were those who had turned Prato into a charnel house which long after gave off the stink of burning flesh. There were those here whose practice of villainy went back all the way to the sack and the violation of Capua seventeen years before. They were all before the walls, the arrogant French, the stolid lanzknechts, and the tough wiry peasants of Estramadura with their taste for girl children. Behind them rode the Albanian stradiotti squadrons who preferred to collect heads. We had done well in removing the greater part of the women and children to Orvieto and other nearby towns.

Despite the fact that so many citizens had fled from Perugia, the influx of wounded survivors of the outposts and refugee peasants from the contado created a pressure. The hospital of the Misericordia and the public palaces were filled with the sick and the wounded. Such medical supplies as we possessed finally had to be rationed out for the active defenders on the walls. The civilian refugees took care of themselves as best they could.

As the ring of the besiegers tightened, our food supplies dwindled steadily. I ordered that the active combatants were to have the first call on foods and medicines. The peasants were most vulnerable to the food shortage, and their younger children began to sicken. The livestock which they had been able to bring into the city were soon consumed. Although we maintained a sufficiently tight grip to prevent looting and lawlessness, there were sporadic cases of food profiteering. We established six district tribunals, one for each ward and the sixth in the Palace of the Podestà under Ottaviano Signorelli. We decreed that the buyer should be equally guilty with the seller. It is remarkable that in all we found only twenty-five cases of profiteering, twenty-four men and one woman.

Amadeo Armellini, that cardinal's brother whom Morgante and I had punished for usury sixteen years before, thought this a good time to bring out his hidden stores of wheat, olive oil, salt and wine, which he offered to certain favored buyers at royal prices. When called to account by Signorelli, Armellini declared: "If Messer Baglioni commands in this city, he does so as the pope's servant. My brother Francesco is, as you all well know, the Holy Father's chief minister. He has exempted me from your decrees. In touching me you risk the displeasure of my reverend brother and the Holy Father."

"Very well, Messer Armellini," said Signorelli, "we shall not touch you. Only be pleased to come with us."

They brought Armellini to the head of the Via della Gabbia, and Signorelli said to him: "Be good enough to enter our bird-cage, gently, and of your own accord."

This Amadeo Armellini did, after studying the pikes behind him. He was hoisted in the cage to the tower and was permitted to purchase his own supplies at a figure in excess of that which he had demanded of the public. Whether from grief or his weak heart, he expired within a period of eight days, long before his wealth was exhausted. His brother, the cardinal, took his demise with an ill grace.

As the siege wore on in those balmy days of late spring, the peasants began to die off in earnest. The carcass of a cat sold for a ducat and there were buyers. The rats of Perugia survived longer, being a proud and ancient breed. However, when the peasants took to hunting them, the rats revenged themselves perversely upon their hunters and took to dying of a self-induced disease. The first cases of siege-pest appeared. Those who sickened moaned with splitting skull-pains. The swellings in their armpits and groins grew and finally broke. They vomited and befouled themselves continuously until they expired in their own wastes. At this time, also, came the first processions through the streets in honor of Saint Ercolano and Saint Lorenzo. The rats continued to die in curious numbers.

Francesco Maria wrestled with the problem of holding his host in leash. He had a wild boar by the snout and was driven to make the first move. He offered a parley. In black armor and carrying a baton, he rode out of his lines resembling a small swarthy Moor on his huge charger. He was accompanied by a standard-bearer and a herald. Since all the gates had been sealed with masonry, the herald was hauled up to the battlements in a basket and brought before the Priori in the Great Hall of the Cambio. The herald had no authority to parley and delivered Francesco Maria's ultimatum in a grating voice:

"Thus says my master, the Duke of Urbino: The Priori of Perugia have lent themselves to the pope's robberies. They have repaid our kindness and friendship with treachery. All the world will justify our defense of our rights. Yet we are willing to forbear. Our terms are generous and we ask only that they restore Carlo Baglioni to the government of Perugia and that they expel Gianpaolo Baglioni and his sons. For ourself, we seek only reasonable stores of food and fodder for our troops and are ready to lift the siege. We have fifteen thousand people before the walls and a train of siege artillery. If you refuse our terms, we shall starve you out and destroy the city."

It was a good ultimatum and, on the face of it, a fairly reasonable one. Francesco Maria was, of course, exaggerating the size of his forces and was too bankrupt to afford cannon. My guilty conscience impelled me toward peace on any face-saving terms. Unfortunately, his demands concerning Carlo were an impossible obstacle. I finally said:

"If His Magnificence wants Perugia so badly, let him come and take it."

The Priori groaned and fidgeted. Many in the hall disagreed

with me bitterly. You shall presently know how bitterly, for Carlo Baglioni still had many friends within the city. We lowered the herald over the walls and prepared to fight.

At dawn, I shifted three infantry companies to the weakest positions on the walls. Eusebio Baglioni, one of our distant cousins, marched off with the first company and I fell in behind him. Following me came the other two companies, led by Cecco Carbone of the Spirito family and Giovan-taddeo Baglioni, another cousin. As we marched by the Church of San Domenico, we heard the booming explosion of a cannon. Eusebio turned his horse about and charged toward me, swinging his sword. I slipped the blow and his sword glanced off my helmet, biting lightly into my shoulder. The infantrymen came to a ragged halt and milled about in confusion. Now Cecco and Giovan-taddeo charged me, brandishing their swords. Giovan-taddeo rose in his stirrups as he passed, swinging a wild overhand stroke and shouting: "Son of a whoring bitch! The line of march ends here! There will be no war with Francesco Maria!"

As I parried and rode in under the blow, the soldiers broke from their trance, swarmed up to Giovan-taddeo and hamstrung his horse. He fell heavily to the ground, and the tumult of the fighting brought a mob running in from every alley behind San Domenico, shouting, "Murder! Treachery!"

I said to a mounted arbalaster beside me: "Take him from where you sit." The man took careful aim and sent a bolt whistling in solidly between Cecco's shoulder blades. Cecco halted, crumpled to his knees, relaxed face downward and rolled slowly down the steps of San Domenico. Nearby, the mob had dragged Eusebio from his horse and were raining blows on him. A few moments later, soldiers and citizens, now a howling mass among whom I rode swinging the flat of my sword, hacked off the heads of the three captains and impaled them on the spikes of Pisano's fountain. In the midst of all this tumult, the communal bells began tolling dolorously. I broke out of the mob, rode out to the battlements above Porta San Pietro and mounted the walls. Francesco Maria and his besieging army gave no sign of stirring. At this moment one of the officers climbed up to the battlements and told that Eusebio's steward, Panmolla, had been captured alive.

By the time we reached the Palace of the Podestà, the soldiers had already stripped Panmolla of his mail shirt and red doublet. He was a squat dark man whom I remembered vaguely. Since he was insufficiently frightened to speak of his own accord, the soldiers hoisted him and began dropping him from the strappado. His joints cracked audibly at the third drop and I urged him to speak, saying, "We have work to do and I promise you an easy death."

He croaked once, "Let me down," and fainted as the soldiers lowered him to the flagstones. One of them forced wine down his throat and another flung a bucket of water over him. Panmolla opened his eyes. The soldiers dragged him into a sitting position and shook him.

"Signor Eusebio sent me from the city three nights ago to deliver keys to the enemy," he said hoarsely.

"Where?" I asked. "What keys?"

"For the Porta San Pietro," he groaned. "They were counterfeit." Panmolla halted, mumbling to himself. I shook him and he continued:

"They planned to slay you first and then —"

"And in the confusion of my death —" I encouraged him.

"They planned to batter down the postern by the Church of the Angels and so admit the duke's people."

These final words exhausted Panmolla and the soldiers let him fall back on the floor.

It was a practical plan which, put to trial, might have succeeded very well. Panmolla was promptly hanged but without rancor.

With the Priori I issued proclamations to calm the milling

crowds, and the spontaneous penitential processions perceptibly increased in fervor. The priests bore the images of Saint Ercolano and Saint Lorenzo out of their cathedrals and the devout followed, carrying lighted tapers and chanting penitential hymns. And so the processions continued well into the night among bonfires and under flaring torches. They were viewed not only by the living, but also by the dead, for the severed heads of Eusebio Baglioni, of Cecco Carbone and of Giovantaddeo Baglioni glared down from their spikes with glum interest on the marching penitents.

Francesco Maria made no move to attack for two reasons — he feared the growing virulence of the pest, and he knew that my sons were marching to the relief of Perugia with a strong army. He hesitated to be pinned between our walls and the relief columns. On the following day, I received a letter from Pope Leo in which he wrote: "We know the dangers you face and have exerted ourself in your behalf. We have procured additional troops at great expense and they should arrive shortly. Our present fear is not that della Rovere will press the siege but that if he cannot be brought to terms, he will ravage Umbria as he retreats, to the hurt of the Holy See. We authorize you to make such disposition with him as will occasion us the lesser loss. Commence a parley, therefore, and keep us advised."

I could not agree that Perugia was Pope Leo's city or that Umbria was his province, but I was satisfied with the outcome. I wanted nothing better than to come to terms with Francesco Maria and notified everyone concerned of the pope's views — the Priori, the Ten of the Arbitrio, the papal legate and the troop commanders.

A minority of the citizens, rendered brave because the pope was now promising tangible aid, voted to continue resistance. I wanted to come to terms at almost any cost, for I personally stood only to lose by warring with Francesco Maria. The majority agreed with me, but for different reasons. On the whole they wanted peace, and the sooner the better.

After conferring with the Priori, I dispatched Amico Graziani to open negotiations. When Amico returned saying that Francesco Maria demanded ten thousand ducats indemnity, the Priori howled with disappointment. "He's sucking our blood," they cried. "Where will we find ten thousand ducats with this new army of idlers who are daily crowding into Perugia and eating us out of our houses?"

Their complaint had merit. Francesco Maria had relaxed his cordon while parleying, as though tacitly inviting a compromise settlement. This enabled reinforcements as well as new refugees to slip into the city. We now had at least fifteen thousand would-be saviors jammed tight in Perugia. Now that the danger was passing, the citizens resented the strangers and wanted only to be rid of them.

Despite the opposition of the Priori, I pushed the agreement through, paid out two thousand ducats on signing the truce and promised to deliver the remainder within fifteen days. This balance was to be collected from the citizens and each householder was to pay his share according to his ability. Now that we no longer needed so many defenders, they seemed to us voracious and wholly unwelcome. We turned to the task of getting rid of them tactfully.

The siege-pest was uninterested in politics. While we strove and haggled, its virulence worsened. The practical-minded sought to limit the pest by burning the clothing, houses and bodies of the dead. The religiously inclined marched barefoot in expiatory processions, scourging themselves, bleeding and crying: "Mercy! Mercy! We have sinned!"

We had still a sufficient store of aloes, agallochum, and dragon's blood, the medicinal red juices of trees from the Indies

which were deemed beneficial for fevers. These the physicians and the Brethren of Mercy administered to the sick. I
think many were saved by these remedies, although it is impossible to tell. I have no record to go by on this matter, but you
are perhaps aware of my sentiments concerning disease. I doubt
that it arises from Divine wrath. More likely it comes from the
filth which is spread by foul air, for I have often noted the raging
of these pests during and after sieges, battles and failures of the
harvest. It seems unreasonable to me that God would be concerned with such ailments of mankind. Yet there were few
enough who held with me. In the main, our scarecrow survivors
joined the processions in order that by their prayers and mortifications they might force Heaven's attention to their plight. It
seemed to me that the priests led the processions almost skepti-
cally, although it was they who gave permission for the images
of the saints to be borne out of the churches. It was rather the
people, in their faith, who led the priests. The people walked
devoutly, carrying censers to burn away the miasmic plague air.
Such precautions by no means prevented the priests from dying
together with the worshipers they led, and just as reluctantly.

For my part, I contented myself with impressing such of the
penitents as could work. They were needed for the labor of
pulling down many empty houses, the inhabitants of which had
perished, and collecting the corpses and burning them. I do not
know how much good was accomplished thereby, but surely it
let in the air and sunlight to many foul dark places of the city.
The burning of the pestilential dead was also beneficial, and
best of all it preoccupied the minds of those who labored and
plucked them from their fear and self-pity.

Some weeks before the pest burned itself out, it shot a Par-
thian arrow at Laura and killed her. On one day she complained
of the head pains. The swellings appeared under her arms and
she cried in her agony. Her maids feared to touch her and fled

from the chamber. I nursed her as well as I could. Between hours of fevered babbling, she would grow lucid. In one of these intervals, she said: "God is punishing me for my great sins."

"How has He punished you?" I asked.

"He took away my son and made me barren thereafter," she said stonily, "and now He is striking me down. But it is just that I should suffer."

"I do not think God took the child from us," I said. "It is but another form of pride to reason that God has singled you out among many."

She shook her head and spoke low. "You were always a scoffer and a skeptic, Gianpaolo. I am being punished for having lived in sin with an unbeliever and the enemy of my kinsmen, those whom I betrayed and abandoned." She stared at me with hollow black-circled eyes. "I could have loved you greatly had you permitted it."

"You have loved me in full measure," I said.

She smiled, shook her head and replied only, "You know not what love is, for which reason I have pitied you also, the only man I have ever known."

Her words filled me with a dull deep bitterness and a resentful need to end my life and go with her.

"I'll soon be rid of my burden and follow you," I said.

She closed her eyes, groped her hand to mine, and whispered: "Live. It will be over soon enough." Her hand was dry and hot. "Bring me a priest before it is too late."

I summoned the Brethren of Mercy, who came to her bed willingly and remained there willingly. They were strange men, bemused in a private madness, without doubt, but admirable and of a different faith than the prelates of Rome.

When I went in to Laura again, she was quieter and at peace.

"I have confessed and received absolution," she said.

She lasted two more nights and died before dawn on the third day. Laura had fled and I mourned her in numbness. What remained was a stranger piece of flesh, as blackened and distorted as any other victim of the pest. With the Brethren of Mercy, I washed and robed her and prepared her for burial. I ordered that her body should be interred in our crypt at San Domenico with the full and proper honors due a member of the House of Baglioni. There were some of the priests of San Domenico who demurred, but in the end they thought better of it and held their peace, which was well for their heads. Had they resisted I would have replaced the tears I could not shed with a holocaust.

What shall I say of Laura Crispolti? She had beauty, honesty, courage and intelligence, more than is given to many. She was my equal in all ways and my superior in common sense. Her counsel was always on the side of forbearance and moderation, and whenever I took it the matter turned out well. She had, as she once said, a bad bargain in me and she loved me with a love greater than my own. Had Fortune willed it otherwise, she would have been my wife and the mother of many captains. So peace be with her — she was the brightest page in my life.

I buried Laura Crispolti and returned to the world.

27.

THE SAFE-CONDUCT

As I EXPECTED it would, a certain clause in the truce gave Leo much distress. In legal phrases it prohibited my house from resuming hostilities with Francesco Maria in the pope's behalf.

"The Holy Father is enraged," wrote Amico Graziani from Rome. "There are rumors persistent here that you not only failed to contribute your share of the indemnity but that you split it by secret agreement with the Duke of Urbino. I have traced the story's source to our own native misfortune, Armellini. When the Pope dispatch created thirty-seven cardinals to meet the cost of the Urbino war, Armellini paid forty thousand ducats for his red hat and has much to profit from your destruction. Only by getting the Perugian tax revenues into his talons will he be able to regain his investment."

I wish to enter a categorial denial of Armellini's story. He spread it because of his personal hatred and because it was to his advantage to do so. This notorious speculator, the son of a thieving salt merchant, is now my judge and has risen to cardinal's estate by paying the price. In a few years he should retrieve his purchase price and more besides. There are men in Perugia more deserving of the honor, but Armellini possesses the prime qualification — gold, ill gotten or otherwise. He has much to gain from a change in the Perugian government. I know now that he has been dealing quietly with my cousin Gentile for the past three years, and after my death Gentile should make a tractable puppet governor for the pope.

Amico's next report made poor reading.

"The Pope is not only angered by your agreement with Francesco Maria, he is also in close correspondence with Gentile. I am distributing gold to discover in what regard and have some friends among the scriveners of the Curia. It is difficult to learn anything, because the Pope swears his underlings to secrecy under pain of purgatory and excommunication. This much is certain — he is sending money and good wishes not only to Gentile, but to Carlo Baglioni."

Amico sent a final report.

"By the time you receive this, I will be out of this God-accursed Roman latrine. The Pope has had Cardinal Alfonso Petrucci strangled in Sant' Angelo, despite a safe-conduct. The cardinals Riario and Sauli, who were accused as accomplices in Petrucci's alleged plot to poison the Pope, have been released upon payment of a heavy fine. The Pope needs gold to pay for his war and his pleasures. Riario has fled to Naples, poor as a mouse, who was once the richest man in Rome. Cardinal Petrucci's secretary, Nino, and the physician of Vercelli, who was to have introduced the poison, died hard on the bridge of Sant' Angelo. Their joints were broken on the rack, and after the flesh had been torn from their bodies with heated pincers, they were quartered. Now Armellini says openly that you were privy to Petrucci's plot."

Here again I can only say that I had nothing to do with this somewhat gaudy attempt to poison Pope Leo. We Baglioni never employ poison. Search the records, if you wish.

To everything there is a season, said the Preacher, and a time to every purpose under the heavens; a time to lose and a time to keep silent. That time had come for me. The sword with which I had served others had not served me. The state which Braccio had founded was as far distant as ever from completion. Perhaps it would never come to pass. Yet I did not regret the treaty with Francesco Maria. Leo's enmity was inevitable and would have broken forth elsewhere.

Laura's death contributed to my feeling of entrapment. Following Francesco Maria's departure, I went into seclusion at Castiglione del Lago, engulfed by a feeling of sterility and indifference. My followers, with a rat's sixth sense, felt the new mood and drew off within themselves. This is as it should be; one should eschew the declining and the unfortunate. They are accursed and no good can come of them.

Perugia raged with nightly murders and robberies. Pope Leo and Armellini distributed bribes throughout the city, and all crimes were attributed to me. As order collapsed, Armellini disseminated rumors that the Baglioni were indifferent and unable to bring to justice the slayers of respectable citizens.

"A brisk and merry life continues here," my partisans reported from Perugia. "Your cousin, Gentile, behaves as sole master of the city. He blossoms in the genial sun of the pope's favor and evinces a strange new garrulity. He bids for the support of the nobles at sumptuous banquets and bribes them with the pope's gold."

Each time I shrugged in response, another supporter deserted me. Even Carlo Baglioni's ignominious death in his bed at the close of 1518 failed to stir me. Carlo had become a mere husk of hatred for me. The memory of the Great Wedding Massacre was fading like a dessicated blood stain. There was a period of months when I noted my failure to distinguish between reality and fantasy. In some painful mysterious fashion, the stony winter world of Castiglione del Lago and the world of my chimeras blended, fused, and then tore apart again. I brooded on the past and the winter days dragged along, bleak and stubborn. During the nights I saw and spoke with the ghost of Pandolfo, and it seemed to me that I was once again with Laura in Pandolfo's great bed. I dreamed, too, of my father and Guido, of my brother Simonetto, and of Astorre. The nights were a reality filled with clashing alarms. The days were a paralyzed trance, a frozen nightmare. I sat alone by day until the pale orange sun sank down into the dark blue ice of Lake Trasimene. When dusk fell, the serving men stirred the burning logs on the hearths. The firelights rose, piercing the vaulted shadows of the hall, briefly illuminating the stone walls hung with halberds, axes, pikes, blazoned shields and all the old battle banners of the Baglioni. Thus I sat night after night, staring at the little fire demons as they played on the polished surfaces of the weapons, until one night the spell was broken.

Malatesta and Orazio arrived at Castiglione del Lago during a fresh snowfall. They galloped into the courtyard at the head of an armed troop, flung off their horses and tramped in.

"A plot is astir and we think our honored cousin Gentile is behind it," said Malatesta. "There is a rumor about Perugia that papal troops are about to attack us. Thanks to your long absence —" his voice held reproach — "Gentile's partisans dominate Perugia and we can expect little help from that direction."

I emerged slowly from my stupor.

"*If* all this is true," I said.

"It's true enough," said Malatesta. "I sought Gentile in the city and was told he had gone to stay at the Fortress of Mascione. More than that, I could not uncover."

I felt myself rising from the blackness of the past months, and the news which my sons brought cheered me. I told them we would go to Perugia first and then to Mascione.

We left immediately and rode toward the city in somber silence, each man occupied with his private thoughts. Once in Perugia, we called the Priori delle Arti into a session of emergency. They showed us a summons newly received from Pope Leo. It commanded me to appear in Rome within thirty days to aid an inquiry into my conduct of the government of Perugia. It was plain that if I did not honor the summons, the pope's troops would strike.

"Signori," I said to the Priori, "as good Perugians you all know that in bygone days the prelates thought twice before issuing their high and mighty parchments. Some distant day when the Baglioni are gone entirely, the Church will oppress here with briefs, lead seals and red ribbons. If the prelates ever truly get our city into their cold soft claws, the citizens of Perugia will know the true weight of ink and paper. None of you will be safe."

"We are caught between two fires," said the Priori, shrugging their shoulders. "We are powerless to aid you."

It was plain that there was nothing to be gained by further discussion. The Priori were paralyzed by indecision, and their necks were precious to them.

"There is still our visit to Gentile," I said to my sons. "Let us go."

Gentile had entrenched himself in the Fortress of Mascione as though for a siege. He received us in a room heavily guarded by retainers and bowed coldly.

I threw down the papal summons before him and asked. "What do you know of this? Are you with your own house or with the pope?"

"Why come to me?" said Gentile, spreading his hands. "I know no more about it than you. Am I in the pope's secret councils?"

"Sufficiently so," I said. "Pope Leo has become your dear and intimate friend, from what is reported to us. What does he plan in that woman's mind of his?"

"That is business entirely between you and the pope," said Gentile, his voice sullen. "Solve your difficulties without me. It is never my wish to interfere in matters that do not concern me."

"Papal encroachment on Perugia and the welfare of our house should indeed concern you," said Malatesta.

"There is nothing to be gained by talking here," I said finally. "It is evident that Gentile stands with the pope, and we must make preparations accordingly. It is time to leave."

"A final word, Gentile," said Orazio, "and mark it well. Some day I shall kill you."

"If you can," said Gentile, staring back.

"I shall feed you your wife and children," said Orazio.

"I shall wait patiently," sneered Gentile.

We left Mascione and rode toward Castiglione del Lago.

I instructed my sons to leave for Rome as soon as possible and attempt to sound out the pope's intentions. He was evincing or pretending a particular friendship for Malatesta at that time. It was doubtless a mask for his intrigues, but I hoped that they would be able to learn something of value.

Malatesta and Orazio left from Castiglione del Lago two days later and were absent in Rome for three weeks. "The pope was gracious enough," said Malatesta when they had returned, "yet he insisted the business he had in view could be disclosed to no one but you. However, he hinted that it was actually no more than a plan to reconstitute the rule of Perugia between Gentile and ourselves, to make an end of the quarrel between us. I have brought you a safe-conduct and a new brief."

Malatesta unrolled the brief and read aloud: "It has been brought to our notice by the vice-legate that the seeds of a new civil strife have been sown in Perugia, that the smoldering hatreds among those who contend for mastery have flared into open violence. We have considered most carefully the need to make a beginning in the affairs of the Commune of Perugia and to bring matters to a conclusion between Signor Gianpaolo and Signor Gentile. It is for this reason alone that we summon Signor Gianpaolo to repair to us in full freedom, secure in the knowledge that he may enter our city of Rome unhampered, where he will be received honorably by ourself."

Malatesta put down the brief. "And he repeats the assurance in this separate signed safe-conduct. Perhaps, for once, the pope speaks the truth. To be frank, I see nothing sinister and untoward in this brief. Can we not give the pope some credit for speaking the truth on occasion even though he is a Medici?"

"You are young and insufficently experienced," I replied. "I have had more years to learn the tortuous ways of the priestly mind. You will note that Leo says nothing about leaving Rome, only of entering the city. Notwithstanding, I have decided to take the risk and go. You and Orazio will accompany me."

I could see that my sons disapproved.

"We have no choice," I said, answering their unspoken question. "The pope has his troops in leash, but you will note they are in position to strike at us here immediately. Should I not honor his summons, he will use it as a justification to loose them at our throats. Add to that our Gentile's defection and we have never been so lacking in preparation. We would be in Francesco Maria's predicament, yet infinitely weaker." I paused and then added almost to myself. "I see now clearly that our place was beside Francesco Maria instead of against him."

We left for Rome three days later with a hundred-man escort. We traveled slowly and rode into the Vatican a week later. Paris de Grassis, the now aging Master of Ceremonies, received us, saying, "We have been awaiting you, Signor Gianpaolo. The Holy Father is taking his ease in the gardens of Castel Sant' Angelo. He commands that you wait on him there and he will grant you immediate audience."

But through his courteous words I sensed a looming danger.

"Return promptly to Perugia," I said to my sons as soon as we left the Vatican. "If Leo intends any treachery, let us not hand him the opportunity to take us all in his bird net. He has always been an ardent fowler."

"We can still retreat," said Malatesta.

"Nothing will be settled by retreat," I said. "It is too late. It may be safer to go forward. If I should not emerge from Sant' Angelo, you will know what action to take. Kill Gentile as soon as you are certain that I am dead."

Leading our escort, Orazio and Malatesta left me at the main gates of Sant' Angelo, and it was the last time I saw them. The pikemen at the gates saluted and Count Annibale Rangone, the commander of the Pontifical Guard, greeted me. I thought I detected a strange flicker, an expression, in Rangone's eyes.

"The Holy Father awaits you in the gardens," he said. "The grooms will take charge of your mount."

I followed him into the castle, mounted a flight of stairs and entered a long arms gallery illuminated on one side by a row of windows high above the floor. At this moment the double doors at the far end of the gallery were thrown open. A squad of Swiss pikemen entered, lowered their weapons and advanced, at readiness to thrust home.

"You are under arrest," said Rangone, staying me as I drew my sword. "It would be advisable not to resist. I have the Holy Father's signed orders."

"And I have his signed safe-conduct," I said. "That gives us something in common. Your family is an illustrious one, Signor Count. Do you not feel shame to have undertaken such a shabby charge for this merchant-pope?"

"Your weapons, if you please," said Rangone coldly.

I unbuckled my belt and flung sword and poignard clattering on the stone floor. The pikemen surrounded me on both sides, and six of them brought up the rear. We followed Rangone through several courts and passages which I did not recognize. The light of day was beginning to fail and I was weary after my long ride. As we came out into the open on the river side, a thin rain began to fall and the newly lit cressets of the guard flared and flickered in the gusty March winds. The wind suddenly chilled my bones. It was the first day of my imprisonment, a day I shall not lightly forget.

I was placed in a comfortable apartment in the castle's tower and allowed no outside communication for the first three days. The Swiss guards passed in food twice a day and that was all. When I tried to engage them in conversation, they shook their heads and did not reply.

On the morning of the fourth day, Cardinal Armellini came to see me with several other prelates whom I did not recognize. Since Armellini has the guiding hand in this business, I have no illusions on how it will come out. The Armellini were beneath our notice in Perugia and the hatred has been on their side, not on ours. They were never among our serious political opponents, like the Oddi. This Francesco Armellini's grandfather was a modest notary in the employ of the Priori, and the family moved in a world of quill-drivers with which we had no contact. Undoubtedly the cardinal has good and true grievances against me. If not, his fertile speculator's mind will fabricate a few. He is a tall man and a remarkably ugly one. When he came to visit me, he screwed up his little eyes, showed his blackened decaying teeth, stroked the while his scanty graying beard and smoothed his red robe in the awareness of which he takes a profound pleasure. He unrolled a parchment and said: "A commission is being appointed by the Holy Father to examine your case. In the meantime, you will remain here."

"What of my safe-conduct?" I asked.

"The pope gave you a safe-conduct, true," replied Armellini, "but only to come here, not necessarily to depart."

"These quibbles come naturally to priests," I said. "No doubt the wit to understand them is not expected of soldiers. But we will return to that. What are your charges against me?"

Armellini smiled and combed his beard with his right hand. "Of course," he said, "the charges. There are quite a number of them."

"I should not be surprised," I said. "The Curia has had long practice in such cookery."

"For instance," said Armellini, "you are accused of having tried to subvert the government of Orvieto."

What Armellini styled subversion was no more than a dispute concerning those Orvietan estates which comprised the Monaldeschi dowry promised to Malatesta.

"A moment," I began. "Let me be heard."

Armellini waved me silent, gathered himself and began to read.

"Item, you are charged with coining. Item, you are charged with having trafficked with the excommunicate rebel, della Rovere, at such time as you were the sworn condottiero of the pope, with having conspired with the said della Rovere to subvert the pope's possession of Urbino, to the hurt of the Apostolic See."

"Sonorously put," I said.

Armellini bowed. "I composed the indictment myself. To continue: Item, you are charged with having robbed the communal treasury of Perugia of certain monies which you allegedly paid over to the said della Rovere as indemnity for raising the siege. Item, you are charged with complicity in the late Cardinal Petrucci's plot to assassinate the pope."

"I have heard such rumors," I said. "They are all about. It was a loud squabble and, of course, I had no concern with it, but do not let that trouble you. When the wolf wishes to slay, a thousand justifications come to hand. Please proceed."

Armellini shuffled his parchments cheerfully and droned on.

"Item, you are charged with fratricide in having murdered your brother, Morgante Baglioni."

"My cousin," I said, "not my brother, and he died of a lung fever eighteen years ago at Lake Trasimene, as all the world will attest. Your bill of particulars is slovenly."

The other prelates stood by wearing their expressions of pious horror as Armellini made his charges. He read on in a momentum of dark satisfaction. "Item, you are charged with parricide in murdering your father, Ridolfo Baglioni."

"It is well known," I said, "that my father died in 1501 of the mal francese, as you will shortly, by your appearance. Is this all?"

"If it seems insufficient," smiled Armellini, "we will be pleased to charge you with heresy and atheism, which we should have no trouble in proving."

He rolled up his parchments and continued: "Reflect on your sins and consider the welfare of your soul, my noble countryman. You shall soon have an opportunity to defend yourself." He knocked loudly on the door and the guards flung it open. Armellini and his prelates rustled out and I was left alone with my thoughts.

This, then, is how I have come to be in Sant' Angelo. Having escaped the wrath of the Borgia, the anger of Pope Julius II, from great battles and a thousand ambuscades, it is an unpleasant irony that I have now fallen into the trap of this plump amiable dilettante, Giovanni de' Medici.

I whiled away the hours reading the "Orlando Furioso." When weary of reading, I asked for writing materials and they were given to me. Having commenced to write, I resolved to record my past life and the vicissitudes of the House of Baglioni in order that posterity's version might not depend wholly on hostile history. Since no family can rise to eminence without incurring hatred and envy, there will be an abundance of such reports.

28.

THE TRIAL

I HAVE been considering the stars which glow and pulse over the sleeping city of Rome. If they are insensate bodies of light, without beginning and without end, where is the answer? I only know that it is neither in the Church nor in those who lead her. In the past, when my judgment was dulled by superstition, by mundane preoccupation, and by an indifferent tolerance born of sentiment, habit and convenience, I thrust such questions into the stagnant marshes of my mind. But circumstances alter one's perspective. The scarlet-clad politicians of the Curia are one-eyed shepherds, themselves half-puppet, leading blind sheep. Who would trust such guides on the shaky bridge between Heaven and Earth? Only the childish and the gullible, for there is no bridge.

My judges have decided not to hang a charge of heresy about my neck. Armellini sought to do so but Pope Leo, from considerations of logic and the Medicean sense of humor, restrained the vulgarian. Who is a heretic? One who holds and disseminates error in willful defiance of official dogma. But these priests cannot successfully maintain that I have ever thrust my soldier's nose into the recondite mysteries of their establishment. My quarrel has been with their political meddlings and with that bland towering arrogance whereby they have rendered unto themselves that which is God's, that which is Caesar's and that which is every other man's.

The sheep will survive by sheer massive fecundity until they pass into new hands. But what of the shepherds? The future fortunes of Rome interest me. I think they will be harvested with a dull scythe. But prediction is vain, and in voicing a hope I must guard against the blandishments of hope. Perhaps a day will come when new priests, bearing new mysteries and new myths, will seduce the sheep from the moribund tenacity of Rome. But for the moment all is well. Pope Leo disposes the plums of office and the world's treasure with a schoolboy's delight. Who can say whether he will ever be corrected in his lifetime? With Giovanni de' Medici the man I have no quarrel. He has some tinker's feeling for the arts as long as they do not interfere with his ease, and he has covered the sores of Rome with bad paintings. The Florentine rats flock to his pontifical granaries and the Roman rats grumble at having been elbowed from the feast. Pope Leo fears only tedium and demands nothing from the faithful but gold. He pants after pleasure and has gold for all things but a policy to save his pleasant world from destruction. But, since such folly is desirable, why should I complain of this Medici by whom I have allowed myself to be captured? My discontent must be against myself, arising from no better cause than the knowledge that I will soon be moldering in a crypt with my severed head between my legs.

This does not denote that I have surrendered the world and resigned myself. To pine in the dark is vanity and squandered time. I have attempted escape, although my most recent effort has come to nothing. Malatesta was successful in bribing the castellan of Sant' Angelo with a thousand ducats and the promise of four thousand more, if he would connive at my flight. This man once served us in the time of Borgia and della Rovere

and was willing to do so again. Besides, the sum was a great
one, and the castellan, a man of consummate avarice, was ready
to risk his thick red neck for gold. His mistress, a Ferrarese
woman living in Rome, was used to visit his quarters twice a
week. It was planned to disguise me in her skirts and shawls
and so smuggle me out of the castle and beyond the walls of
Rome, where Orazio would be waiting with horses and armed
men. The guards were also bribed, but the plan failed. We
neglected to take into account those guards who were in Gentile's pay and who gave the alarm before our plan could be put
into effect. Pope Leo had the castellan and his mistress strangled and four archers of the guard were hanged from the walls.
So the plan came to nothing, save that Pope Leo came puffing
back from La Magliana vowing that God, in a dream, had
shown him the manner of my attempted evasion. This, he said
with a sour smile (for his self-induced misfortunes have embit-
tered his former amiability), was a Divine Manifestation, be-
stowing Heaven's approval on the spurious safe-conduct which
lured me to Rome. I interpret the matter somewhat differently,
but there is no arguing with clerics who juggle God as a gypsy's
bear juggles leather balls. Now Pope Leo has appointed a new
jailer to watch over me, a zealous palleschi who guards me as an
anxious mother, fearing God and the pope's displeasure.

In other respects Pope Leo has not grown more harsh, for he
was never given to purposeful cruelty. It is his nature to be so
and I am fortunate in that degree. I have walked into this
absurd trap almost of my own volition, and the pope wishes to
remove me from this world for his reason of the moment which
he calls policy. There is nothing more to be read into it. In
the meantime, my chamber is both spacious and light. It is a
lenient captivity but, decidedly, nothing awaits me at the end
of it.

*   *   *

I often re-examine my reasons for the composition of this memoir. My outward concern is indeed to anticipate and correct posterity's verdict. But it is also true that men write to relieve tedium, to express conceits and to convince themselves that they are still alive. There was once a slave in Roman Sicily who carved on the walls of his prison barrack: "Marcus, the slave, wrote this." My scribblings are carved in the same spirit, saying: "Gianpaolo Baglioni, the Perugian, wrote this."

A talented chronicler might illumine matters on which I have barely touched. I have failed to examine many things to their depths: my complicity with the faulty princes of Italy, my failure to lay a strong foundation in Perugia, and my unworthy relationship with that most unworthy of all states — Florence. Even as Machiavelli has predicted, Florence will come to a bad end. She is too mean-spirited a city to survive and is celebrated only for the shabbiness with which she has treated her best men. But in some respects I think Machiavelli is wrong. She will limp in the ignominious half-life of a slave. The barbarians will make pimps of the Florentines and they will eat the leavings of the foreigner's dogs. Whether this is the punishment of God or the handiwork of men, I cannot say. I know only that one error has led to and compounded another. Perhaps our most unfortunate error has been our tendency to involve God in our human puddlings. It is possible, although not probable, that He may some day become aware of the faint persistent itch and crack the lice of Adam's progeny once and for all between His thumb and forefinger.

I have not been at my writing for more than two weeks. I have been unable to hold a pen. Count Rangone came at that time with a detachment of halberdiers and read me a parchment, saying:

"You are summoned to appear before a court approved by

the Holy Father and constituted under the authority of Cardinal Armellini to answer such questions as the court may put you. It is my duty to conduct you there."

Rangone led the way, with myself between the halberdiers. Behind us followed six monks, their faces masked by visored hoods. They may have been of that same order of the Brethren of Mercy who did such good work during the time of the pest in Perugia and who attended Laura's last hours. On the other hand, they may have been merely familiars of the court with their faces and purposes conveniently masked. I found their presence less than cheering. Since such human apparitions invariably appear at the end of some human play to hearten the condemned, they ought to afford a welcome sight. Yet such a grim show must frighten the prisoner from any sentiments of pious resignation. I looked back at my six ill-omened ravens padding silently behind us and said to Rangone: "Who are they?"

"The Brethren of Saint John," he replied and added, "I doubt if the time of the harvesting has come. I think Armellini has sent them along only to intimidate you by their presence."

"I thank you for your good will," I said. "And how is it with you? Does your gorge still accept the service of these heavenly hounds without rising?"

Rangone shrugged his shoulders and said nothing.

We marched along a broad corridor and down many staircases and ever-narrowing passages where the air grew chill and musty and the massive stonework was beaded with moisture. The steps of the halberdiers rang sharply in the dead stale silence. At last, they brought me into a large low-ceilinged hall which was lit by many waxen candles in wall brackets.

Behind a long writing table sat Cardinal Armellini. Flanking him sat others — notaries, assessors and scriveners of the Curia, each man in full regalia and exuding that degree of infallibility proper to his station. To face one's judges, knowing they are political enemies and churchmen, is to taste glowing sulphur.

"Be seated, Signor Count," said Armellini. "The prisoner is to occupy this bench before us."

The halberdiers took positions against the walls. More guards entered and took posts behind me. The doors of the judgment hall were slowly closed.

His face illuminated by the tapers before him, Armellini seemed a brazen Moloch squatting over an open hearth. The underground chamber was cold and the judges wore fur mantles and caps. Armellini's eyes, shadowed by the fur cap on his head, were inscrutable. "It is the Holy Father's desire that this tribunal make as rapid a disposition of your case as is possible, consonant with justice and mercy," he said impassively. "You have already heard the toll of the charges brought against you. Do you wish our scrivener to repeat them?"

I replied that it would not be necessary, but Armellini insisted that the court must be at pains to accord me a meticulous hearing even in the finest detail. He ordered that the indictment be read again, and a faceless one in a black gown rose and droned out the text. I was accused in sonorous legal form of being a parricide, a coiner, a subverter of the public weal, a poisoner, an idolator and so many other good things that the least of them sufficed to grind me to fine powder.

Armellini, scrupulous to maintain a show of fair dealing, often halted the reading and asked if I had any comment. I made no reply, and when the reading was ended, he asked me if I acceded to the form in which the charges were drawn. When I replied that I did not recognize the jurisdiction of the court nor its right to try me, Armellini observed blandly that the pope was my liege lord with unquestioned right to sit in judgment on his subjects.

I retorted that the pope was never my liege, adding: "Assuredly, I am no jurist, but our archives in Perugia hold three hundred years of precedent to condemn these proceedings as wholly illegal. Though a renegade Perugian, you know enough of law to be aware of this fact."

Armellini replied that the archives of Perugia were beside the point in the Castle of Sant' Angelo. I continued to protest that I did not recognize the court or the pope's right to try me and Armellini finally observed, "Never shall it be said that we have not been patient, that we have not given you ample opportunity to re-enter into the grace of the Apostolic See which you have so deeply offended by your damnable crimes." He continued in a more unctuous voice: "I have no doubt as to your guilt. It is only by the profound and all-embracing compassion of the Holy Father that you are being accorded a trial at all. Is there any statement you wish to make?"

"I would be grateful if you dispensed with ecclesiastical jargon," I said. "You are not wrestling to bring an errant sinner back to the path of grace. This is a political trial and you are the pope's legal bravo. Since you are here to murder me with briefs and perjured witnesses, let us get on with it. You only offend the believers in the court by enlisting Holy Writ in your assassin's work."

Armellini's face darkened and he shouted: "Silence, blasphemer! Silence, minion of the Devil, or I will have you gagged."

Here I attempted to address the other members of the court, saying that Cardinal Armellini should disqualify himself since he was tainted with self-interest. I stood before the court by a false safe-conduct and was guiltless of any offense against the Church's canons.

Armellini gestured impatiently at my words to his fellow judges and insisted that I plead to the charges. When I demanded that he produce witnesses, he replied, "We shall depend on you for such intelligence as we need. The law does not require us to bring forth those who have testified against you. But have no fear. Before we are done here, you will admit your guilt amply. Your crimes are the common knowledge of the world. Heaven itself accuses you!"

"It must be convenient to be on such excellent terms with Heaven," I said. "But since I have already been pre-judged and condemned, I have no more to say."

Armellini declared that my body had been condemned and that he was concerned at this juncture with that which was infinitely more precious than the flesh.

"By which an Armellini can only mean gold," I said.

"Your soul, insolent mocker," said Armellini. "Although the House of Baglioni has always been one with Apollyon and Ashtaroth, with Pagiel and Belial, it is the Holy Father's desire that you should not depart this life with your sins heavy upon you. This tribunal urges you to purge yourself by a full confession before you are given over to the justiciaries."

I maintained that the court was illegal, for which reason my constrained confession could have no value. It was a demonstrable fact that I was a political prisoner, the captive of the pope on his most profane and secular business rather than an offender against the Church. It was plain that he was serving his own vengeance in this trial. When I produced Pope Leo's letter ordering me to conclude peace with Francesco Maria, Armellini said, "Your treasonable dealings with the so-called Duke of Urbino are but one of many counts against you."

At this point a tall gaunt Dominican observer for the Holy Office rose and said: "Since those days many centuries ago when that pontiff of blessed memory, Gregory IX, entrusted the Holy Office to us, we have zealously striven to root out heresy. We have labored that the goodly edifice of our faith might not fall into the damnable confusion of a Tower of Babel. Concerning the evidence compiled to support this indictment, we cannot agree that this is a matter for the Holy Office and shall so recommend. Whatever else, this prisoner has not offended against faith and is, hence, beyond our jurisdiction."

Cardinal Armellini looked dark with disappointment at his words and declared the court adjourned.

Back in my chamber, I found matter for grisly humor in the support of the Holy Office. The Dominicans may have been using me to register disapproval of the pope's worldly ways. More probably, they were dismissing me from their jurisdiction on legal grounds. Though I was not to be cast out of the fold, my back would be broken just as thoroughly for all that. In the fold or out of it, I shall have to go to God in my own fashion. I have a sufficiently high opinion of the Almighty to feel that He has other avenues of communication with men than through such dubious vessels as these popes and their prelates. Wherever I find myself after death, it should not be intolerable, for I shall not lack good company such as the great men of antiquity who lived out their lives without benefit of the Curia's rancid balm.

On the following day, Cardinal Armellini sat composed and ready to resume the battle. He regarded me with an air of patient compassion. "Customarily," he began, "the mercy of the Holy Father would have afforded you an additional week for prayer and reflection, in the hope that you might thereby be moved from your hardened impenitence. However, the affairs of Holy Mother Church will admit of no further delay at this critical juncture. This court urges you to confess and avoid the unnecessary suffering which your own obduracy will bring upon you."

We had arrived at the moment of truth. I tried to delay the

clock by reflecting on who I was and on the brevity of time lengthened by the illusion of physical pain. My flesh turned cool in anticipation. For the first time, I knew truly that I was a prisoner.

Armellini whispered to his fellow judges. They nodded in affirmation, rose and came forth from behind the table. My guards and I followed them into the Hall of the Question.

"Behold," said Cardinal Armellini, indicating with a gesture the papal machinery of persuasion. "We are nothing if not charitable. The logic of our minds has failed to move you to repentance." He pointed to the corda, the boot and the forge in which pincers were heating. "Perhaps the logic of these instruments may prompt you to reconsider."

"I respect your instruments," I said, "yet am tempted to observe that they are a confession of ineptitude."

"On the contrary," said Armellini benignly, "here is an excellent way of softening a sinner's heart, as long as it is applied skillfully. Where the torturers are overzealous, the sinner is apt to take leave for other realms before he comes to appreciate our benevolent intent. Rest assured, Prisoner, you will not escape us by death. Our tormentor is a most careful master."

I had already recognized the tall man with the bald skull as the muslim Orlando, Persuader-in-Chief to the Apostolic See, whose trained hands had closed Cardinal Petrucci's account in 1517. He was a slit-eyed Tartar, perhaps seven feet tall, and his shaven head was surmounted by a topknot. He was clothed in tight black hose which revealed the massive musculature of his limbs. Three of his black-masked assistants, garbed in bright red, now seized and stripped me. They did so with an insolent skill which is as much a mark of their trade as their virtuosity in inflicting pain. When the history of these times comes to be written and the earnest student asks: "What manner of age was it?" he will be answered: "It was an age wherein one man stripped another preparatory to torturing him. Soldiers stripped peasants, lords stripped subjects, condottieri stripped lords and the pope stripped them all. It was an age with a passion for nakedness which strove not only to strip the clothing from a man's back, but the flesh from his bones, the heart from its tissues and the soul from the body."

Orlando's familiars swiftly bound my wrists behind my back.

"It is my duty," said Cardinal Armellini, "to show you this hoist on which you will be tormented, and to exhort you once again to make a full and true confession of all the crimes with which you are charged."

"You have done your duty," I replied. "I have nothing more to say."

With deft movements, the familiars attached to my wrists a rope running upward to a block and riven through it. They bore down on the other end of the rope and quickly hoisted me high above the floor. A deep grinding pain spread across my back, shoulders and neck as my arms were forced upward and forward. Armellini and his fellow judges stood in a semicircle staring upward at me. I felt almost disembodied as I looked down at them and thought — this is how a treed cat feels surrounded by hounds. Armellini gestured and I plunged down to a jerking halt, just clear of the floor. I heard a sharp cracking sound, there was a roaring in my ears and Armellini's face, glaring into mine, filmed over and receded. So untrustworthy is the human body and its parts that the eyes dim behind a veil of pain. Then Armellini's face swam into view again and his lips mouthed words I could not hear. When I awakened, I was lying in my chamber.

Count Rangone came to visit me. "Cardinal Armellini ordered the torturers to attach weights to your feet," he said. "They were about to hoist you again when an emissary from the

Holy Father came in and thrust a written order under the cardinal's nose. You are most fortunate, Signor Baglioni. His Holiness ordered them to desist and you will be subjected to the Question no more."

"Did I speak?" I asked him.

"No," said Rangone, "but then you were not really put to the test. Moreover, the corda is so clumsy a device that it often puts a man out of his senses and renders him unconscious before he has been fully persuaded to speak. There are other methods more burdensome from which the prisoner cannot escape by a faint."

"Then do not hold it against me that I did," I said.

"You have acquitted yourself well," said Rangone. "But they that take the sword shall perish by the sword."

"That is a risk of my profession," I said. "If I have survived this test with some credit, I am also glad that I need not meet it again."

"The Holy Father has been more merciful to you than you merit," said Rangone severely.

"Let us simply say that he has been indiscriminately merciful," I replied.

Armellini came thereafter with a black-gowned, white-bearded physician who treated me and said: "I have set the bones and have given him opiates. He should begin to mend swiftly from this hour."

"It is beyond my comprehension to understand why the Holy Father wastes consideration on him," said Armellini. "See to it that he recovers, or the pope's anger will fall on both of us."

"Be easy, Reverend Cardinal," said the physician, "your prisoner is a man of strength and blessed with a sound constitution. You will have him back within several days."

This physician came to see me again and gave me medicines which, he said, were soporifics to help me sleep. They seem to have had the contrary effect, for I dream now every night, dreams so vivid that I remember them in each detail and have decided to write them down. I see the horsemen of many confused battles galloping through my mind. I see the Baglioni charging in a brave line across an open plain. Sometimes they ride stealthily in a secret night action. Sometimes they skirmish in small parties with the scouts of the Oddi. Often I see myself afoot with Astorre and Simonetto, marching and countermarching through the mountain snows. The siege guns are mired down in the mud of spring and the drovers crack their whips, shout and coax the serene white Umbrian oxen to strain forward and drag the guns out of the mire. I see myself emerging from my tent on a slate-gray winter morning with the rain pelting down in straight arrows. The troopers are rolling out of their shelters, sullen and bearish. No fires are lit under the cooking pots. The weary columns of horses, the baggage mules and the cursing muleteers trudge away into the mists, crawling ever closer to assignation with the enemy. In my dreams, I hear the bold brazen peal of the trumpets and they quicken in my blood. I feel the deep incessant rolling of the kettledrums and the steadily rising rumble and thunder of the French gendarmerie as they draw closer until the knights finally burst into view over the last rise in the plain in sun-flashing armor and tossing plumes, the great whipping silken banners borne on the right.

Last night I dreamed that I sat with my uncle Guido and my father on the steps of the Communal Palace. A solemn procession of the Priori delle Arti went by in their crimson gowns and golden chains on their way to pardon prisoners for the love of God. Then the prisoners, who had lain weary months in the cages below the pavement level of the Via della Gabbia, came forth. They fell on their knees and wept and praised God before departing from Perugia into banishment. Then I had a vision of Perugia as a locked and jealous grave, circled with a spiral of stubborn walls. The walls were malignant old men with stones in their eyes and the ice of indifference in their hearts, walls mossed over with hate and suspicion. These were the walls that listened and smiled on the night the boulder crashed from Guido's balcony to signal the Great Wedding Massacre. I saw Simonetto sinking to his knees with Fioravanti's sword in his chest. I heard the crashing glass as Astorre's mutilated body was hurled from his bridal chamber to the cobblestones below. And in the shadows was Machiavelli's face wreathed in hateful smiles and saying: "Your city is a lunatic, Baglioni; it will never recover."

I awakened from my dream sweating in terror, and I think the city has come here to haunt me. Perugia is filled with vengeful ghosts, other than the Baglioni, ghosts gathered through the centuries, sitting on the walls in their ranks like brooding ravens.

29.

THE SOLUTION

I HAVE heard myself formally sentenced to death by decapitation.

The journey from my chamber to the tribunal hall was a tedious and painful one. I will give only the gist of Cardinal Armellini's pronouncement, omitting the flourishes:

"This court condemns you to have your head cut off by the executioner's sword upon the battlements of Sant' Angelo one hour before dawn on the twelfth day of June in this year of Our Lord, 1520."

He was evil-humored in pronouncing sentence and added: "You are a most fortunate man, Prisoner. The Holy Father in his mercy has shown you consideration which you ill deserve."

"Pray for your own account," I said. "Death sits on your own face but nothing can save you."

I am now rid of Cardinal Armellini forever. I have been fortunate to the last and will not press my luck further.

As I write, I feel myself no different than before. After a lifetime of habit, shock cannot render my wits more brilliant or more original, and I am hard put to bring forth profound and inclusive observations suitable to the occasion. I can only retreat to the shallow reflection that it is easier to deal out death than to await one's own. Yet I am no longer plagued by sleeplessness.

Last night I dreamed of Guido once again. "Patience," he said, "iron patience. It will soon be over and we shall meet you." And Laura Crispolti, too, has appeared in a dream riding beside me on the road to Perugia and saying with her slow smile: "You have been a fearful man all your life, Gianpaolo, but the time of troubling is over."

The hope of seeing her once again tempts me to accept the Church's charts and lanterns for the journey. Yet I know that I shall not surrender. Fear and love at the heart of human imperfection prevent us from accepting the void of reality. It is too vast and cold and we prefer to hug a fire which gives an illusion of warmth. Men fear and believe because the alternative is incomprehensible. Despite myself, I think only in terms of life.

My thoughts, moving in a slow circle, return again and again to the beginning of all things. My head will soon be parted from my neck with a sharp sword. I have played the judge many times and this is my first role on the wrong side of the bar. It is plain that former experiences have not prepared me for the present. Judges, when stripped of their robes, are as other men, mere naked worms. I once saw at Vicenza a military surgeon tremble when it was his turn to endure the knife. But this is a poor example, for none know better than surgeons what bungling assassins are their colleagues. When the enemy has honestly wounded a man and he falls into the hands of the leeches, he is doomed. They have a passion to complete with their ministrations what the enemy has well begun. I have seen a soldier recover when left to Nature. Not so, when the physicians lay their learned paws on him.

My thoughts revolve about the headsman's block like a moth in the taper light. It is tedious to think in circles, yet understandable, for it is a vast and absorbing prospect. I never credited myself with such an excess of imagination. Death grins at me through the barred window. Death twitters on the frescoed ceiling like a drunken bat and rustles slyly behind the tapestries. Surely, if one does not die in battle, the headsman is an honorable compromise. It is absurd that I should be thinking of Honor in the French fashion, even while my reason rejects the thought. The French are men of honor — boasters and braggarts, gay, gallant and murderous in battle, and, with all of that, still men of honor. What is it they call Honor? It is a quality to make men fight hard, a quality our Italians could study with profit. Barbarians or not, the French have acquitted well on all occasions, not their common sort, but their knights such as that Pierre du Terrail, whom men call Bayard and who had nothing else in his head but tales of chivalry. Come, let us reason together. There is no honor in decapitation. It is merely the lugubrious vocational hazard of war and politics and there is no more to be said about it.

All of my life I have been called the Favorite of Heaven and of Fortune. On balance, my life has been a good one and this ending is not hard — save that I have not mastered the uncertainty which besets me. I do not know to what degree Fortune rules our actions and I think we are more responsible for our predicaments than we are willing to admit. There is no outer force that rules our lives, no matter what men call it — God, the stars, Fate or Fortune. We rule ourselves in large measure. Beyond that, it is a matter of senseless random coincidence. I am burdened by a conviction of failure, but that also is an illusion. Were I a believer, I might have said that my present lenient imprisonment is a compensation for mercies which I showed my own captives on past occasions. Perhaps if I had been a man of faith, I might have made a better soldier. But what is faith? A fanatical zeal capped by a name, another illusion which I would have used to fire soldiers before leading them into action. Perhaps faith is another form of love which I have never known.

Woe unto those that have no faith, say the priests, for they shall lose both battles and their souls. But I do not expect to be moved by priests at this late hour. I have lost battles and I have won them also. War has been a game for me, to be played for profit and for the glory of the House of Baglioni. The priests have still to convince me. There is neither good nor evil, and if it is difficult to walk out into the night on such an uncertain note, I am nevertheless incapable of reconciling myself with these ecclesiastical actors whom I know too well behind their sacerdotal disguises. They are as incapable of comprehending my way as I am of comprehending theirs. I maintain communication with them, for it is good to strive to understand everything even when one is the butterfly skewered on a pin; but it is evident that they lack a logical argument.

Count Rangone came to visit me this night and said formally: "Signor Baglioni, your writing is finished. They will come for you in the fourth hour of the morning. Prepare yourself to make a good ending."

"I will do my best," I said. "If I spoke bitterly when I came here, I ask your pardon. I have had only honorable treatment from you."

"I have come to esteem you," said Rangone. "My prayers will go with you."

"I consign these writings to your safekeeping," I told him. "Will you see them delivered to my son, Malatesta, with this letter?"

Rangone drew out his sword, kissed the cross hilt and said: "By God and my faith, I promise."

Then he left me.

In less than two hours, the breaking dawn will thrust back the darkness far off in the western heavens. How swiftly time gallops — like a warhorse. Once again, I am charging the

French line at Ravenna. It is only right that I should look for the last time in the direction of Perugia and pay my respects to the mad, angry, ancient city of my birth. I leave behind me in the world two good sons of whom the popes will have reason to be mindful. But there is no longer time to think such thoughts. I am done with the world and they will soon be here. The bells are already beginning to toll.

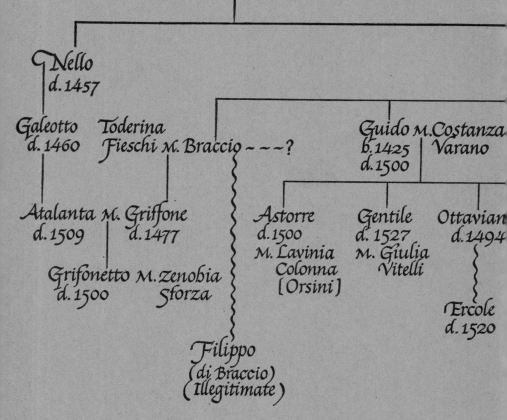

Genealogical Table showing the Relationship between the more Important Members of the House of Baglioni during the Fifteenth and the Early Part of the Sixteenth Centuries ~ ~ ~ ~ ~

Pandolfo
d. 1393

Nello
d. 1457

Galeotto
d. 1460

Toderina
Fieschi M. Braccio ~ ~ ~?

Guido M. Costanza
b. 1425
d. 1500

Varano

Atalanta M. Griffone
d. 1509   d. 1477

Astorre
d. 1500
M. Lavinia
Colonna
[Orsini]

Gentile
d. 1527
M. Giulia
Vitelli

Ottavian
d. 1494

Grifonetto M. Zenobia
d. 1500   Sforza

Ercole
d. 1520

Filippo
(di Braccio)
(Illegitimate)

Sam H. Bryant